PRAISE FOR

THE WITCH HUNTER

"*The Witch Hunter*, translated with icy precision by Kristian London, is written in short, sharp present-tense chapters, a technique which adds to its relentless tension."
—*The Wall Street Journal*

"*The Witch Hunter*, Finnish novelist Max Seeck's pulse-quickening English-language debut, is a genre twofer: It gives crime-novel enthusiasts a satisfying puzzle to logic out, and it offers fans of supernatural tales a look at the world of, as one character puts it, 'amulets, rabbit feet, you name it' . . . a police procedural with paranormal activity at its black heart."
—Shelf Awareness

"Seeck's debut is dark and intricate—the moments of revelation are as vividly cinematic and impactful every time . . . a vivid, robust thriller."
—*Booklist* (starred review)

"One twist follows another, baffling the police and readers alike. Seeck imbues this riveting procedural with a deliciously creepy undertone."
—*Publishers Weekly* (starred review)

"*The Witch Hunter* is everything I wish for in a thriller: exceptional story, exceptional characters, exceptional writing, and shocking twists—exceptional everything. I loved this book, and you will too."
—Chris Mooney, author of *Blood World*

"One of the best books I have read. Ever. Absolutely thrilling, well-written, and oh-so-hard to put down."
—Emelie Schepp, author of *Slowly We Die*

"The heroine's personal problems provide a fascinating counterpoint to a disturbing tale of murder and madness." —*Kirkus Reviews*

"With its hint of the occult and a powerful story line, *The Witch Hunter* is a thoroughly chilling thriller making a solid entry as a first novel in a new series." —New York Journal of Books

"*The Witch Hunter* is a cinematic spin on Nordic noir: it's perfectly paced for a binge read, brimming with unpredictable plot developments, and its elements of witchcraft and the occult give it an extra-chilling and unique edge. Compelling characters, an intricate plot, and a clever premise make *The Witch Hunter* a propulsive, up-all-night Nordic thriller." —Crime by the Book

THE ICE COVEN

MAX SEECK

TRANSLATION BY
Kristian London

BERKLEY
New York

BERKLEY
An imprint of Penguin Random House LLC
penguinrandomhouse.com

Originally published in Finnish as *Pahan verkko* by Tammi Publishers, 2020

Library of Congress Cataloging-in-Publication Data

Names: Seeck, Max, 1985- author. | London, Kristian, translator.
Title: The ice coven / Max Seeck ; [translated by Kristian London].
Other titles: Pahan verkko. English.
Description: First U.S. edition. | [New York] : Berkley, 2021. | Series:
Jessica Niemi | "Originally published in Finnish as Pahan verkko by
Tammi Publishers, 2020"
Identifiers: LCCN 2021013688 (print) | LCCN 2021013689 (ebook) |
ISBN 9780593199695 (trade paperback) | ISBN 9780593199701 (ebook)
Subjects: GSAFD: Mystery fiction. | Occult fiction.
Classification: LCC PH356.S44 P3413 2021 (print) | LCC PH356.S44 (ebook)
| DDC 894/.54134--dc23
LC record available at https://lccn.loc.gov/2021013688
LC ebook record available at https://lccn.loc.gov/2021013689

First U.S. Edition: September 2021

Printed in the United States of America
1st Printing

Book design by Katy Riegel

To Otto and Frans

THE ICE COVEN

Prologue

THE PLASTIC MASK is getting sweaty, and Akifumi adjusts it before opening the drawer of the kitchen island where the flatware—genuine silver—is divided into compartments. Little knives, big knives, appetizer forks, forks for the main course. Steak knives separate. Dessert spoons. Four pairs of metal chopsticks. A few mesh tea balls, clipped chains dangling from the ends. Classy. Elegant.

"Are you still hungry, Asuna?" Akifumi asks, bringing a fork to eye level. The precious metal at its neck is blemished by a dark blotch. An irritating flaw in the otherwise perfect milieu—a matter that easily could have been corrected by scouring the handle with a bit of fluoride toothpaste.

"No," the girl says, crossing her legs. At Akifumi's orders, she sat on the bed without wiping her mouth. *Goddamn, the little whore looks young.*

Akifumi pulls a plate from a drawer, fills it from the platters laid out on the island: roast beef with green peppercorns, lox, garlic scalloped potatoes, salad, bread. The sort of fare served at mediocre wedding buffets and arena VIP boxes, but the details, like the presentation, the superior flatware, and the dazzlingly white unscratched china, lend the whole meal a sense of luxury. Akifumi lowers the plate to the table, pops open a bottle of champagne, fills a glass. The just-downed double-strength malt whisky is still burning in Akifumi's throat, along with the temporary invincibility it imparted.

"You can't have this," Akifumi says, tapping the flute with a fingernail. "Schoolgirls aren't allowed to drink alcohol. It's against the law."

As the words echo in the room, Akifumi grows even more aroused.

Asuna is no schoolgirl. Of course not. But young enough to look like one. Akifumi's hand clenches into a fist.

Fucking whore.

No, Akifumi's not hungry after all. The glass of champagne disappears in a single swig.

"What school do you go to, Asuna?"

The girl hesitates, and just as she's on the verge of answering, Akifumi raises a finger. *Shh.*

"You know what? Never mind. . . . I'm done hearing you talk," Akifumi whispers. A hooked forefinger calls the girl over. "Come here. Come here now."

The girl straightens out her miniskirt and teeters over in her high heels.

Akifumi inhales, drawing in the bracing scent of oranges, evoking memories of travels to the Far East, of searing sun and sunscreen. Then Akifumi grabs the girl by her braids and pushes her to the floor.

"Do it again, Asuna. Do it again, bitch, but this time do it like you want to."

And then I'll bash your skull against that concrete wall.

SATURDAY, NOVEMBER 23

1

LISA YAMAMOTO WAITS for the chrome doors to close, then releases the air trapped in her chest in a single prolonged breath. She slides her black Prada sunglasses off and eyes herself in the mirror on the rear wall. The concealer hides the stress and exhaustion, but it cannot summon joy to her eyes. There's not a hint of the over-the-top exuberance an invitation to a drop party for Finland's hottest rap artist—or any artist, for that matter—would have sparked a year or two ago. Now the predominant emotion is one of unpleasant suspense, and she regrets not having done something before leaving the house to boost her confidence—something stronger than champagne. But no doubt one of her fellow invitees will make sure her needs are attended to. Shoot the right person the right look, and she'd be strolling into the ladies' with a bump that would guarantee a nice pick-me-up.

Lisa scans her body, sheathed in a beige Hervé Léger bandage dress: fit and just the right amount of curvy. At least her look is on point. Not that things aren't fine or that she doesn't have it all under control. The sole item on tonight's agenda is getting a couple of good selfies with the man of the moment and maybe shooting a few video stories with other celebs. Considering whose release party it is, Helsinki's most famous faces are sure to be out in force.

Lisa hears her phone vibrate in the side pocket of her purse. Probably Jason again. He's already tried three times. *Get a life.* She shifts her gaze from the mirror to the digital number panel above. A red four. Five. Six.

A short melody plays, and a moment later the doors open. The elevator is flooded with pounding bass and loud chatter, accentuated by shouts and sporadic bursts of laughter.

Lisa looks down the red carpet toward the coat check, which is mobbed by guests bearing bouquets and bottles. *Nobodies, nevers. Lucky I don't have to introduce myself to them.*

The bouncer, a guy named Sahib whom Lisa has known for years, gives her a discreet nod as she steps out of the elevator.

Lisa passes the floor-to-ceiling windows giving onto a panoramic view. Helsinki's rooftops are slick from days of rainfall. The strikingly lit Torni Hotel rises in the distance, a miniature Empire State Building that dominates the city's low-slung silhouette. The light from the streetlamps and windows sets the dark scene glistening. The city has yet to be brightened by a first snow.

"Hey, Lisa, nice to see you," the black-blazered, white-T-shirted Sahib says as he helps her out of her dripping overcoat—artificial leather trimmed in fake fur. The couple in front of Lisa has stopped a few feet away to whisper, by all signs about her. There was a time she got off on the looks, the attention of complete strangers. Now they just make her uncomfortable. *What the hell are they staring at?*

"How's it going?" Lisa asks the bald, muscle-bound Sahib as she lowers her purse and shoe bag to the counter. She steadies herself with one hand as she deftly slips off her black, white-striped Superstars with the other and slides her toes into a pair of patent beige heels that came equipped with an extra four inches.

"Party's already bumping," Sahib replies smoothly, carries Lisa's coat and bagged sneakers over to the rack, and hands her a numbered tag creased by the sweaty fists of thousands of partyers.

Lisa feels her phone vibrate again along with the thump of the bass. Maybe it's been ringing this whole time. She pulls it from her purse, glances at the screen, and silences the device. *Shit.*

"Thanks," she says, flashing Sahib a quick smile.

"Be careful out there—a lot of bad boys on the loose tonight," Sahib says with a wink. And although she can't stand the bouncer's patronizing flirtation, Lisa smiles and winks back.

The highway created by the red carpet cuts through the dark drapes and into the glare of the photographers' flashes. The air is permeated by that distinctive nightclub odor—stale cologne, spilled alcohol, and cigarette smoke absorbed by the floor and curtains over the years—a reek even a series of remodels hasn't managed to eradicate. A female bouncer Lisa doesn't recognize cracks the curtains, and Lisa steps into the club proper, a tall space packed with partyers showing off the latest trends. Hair dyed in flaming tints, off-the-wall makeup, plumped lips, custom-made suits and sport coats accentuating trained bodies, ironic hipster mustaches, trimmed beards. Lisa pauses to take in the photo wall, the size of a soccer goal, and the guests being brusquely manhandled toward it as if it were a medieval gallows.

"Yamamoto!" a female voice squeals. Lisa's eyes strike on an overweight reporter with glasses whose name she can't remember, despite having been interviewed by the other woman at some point.

Lisa gives the reporter a practiced smile that shows her white teeth. "Hi!"

"We'd love to do a little piece on you. . . ."

Lisa glances at the photographer standing behind the reporter; he has a tabloid press card hanging around his neck. Probably legit, and good advertising for her blog.

"Let me go over and take my picture first."

"Sure. We'll be right here."

"OK, great," Lisa says as she leans in to hug a young English-speaking man she doesn't remember ever meeting. *Hi! Good to see you. Sure, talk to you soon!*

After extricating herself from the stranger's excessively eager and overpowering aftershave-drenched embrace, Lisa drifts to the photo wall, joins the short queue snaking up to it.

She scans the room bathed in low lighting, the sea of bodies surging there. Some faces are familiar, others aren't; the majority are some-where in between. Faded memories, distant flashes of Helsinki night-life. *CDKF. Chat, dance, kiss, fuck.* Typically in that order, although Lisa remembers a few nights she skipped directly from the chatting to the fucking. And maybe one or two when she arrived at the same out-come without so much as a chat.

Over at the back, Lisa spies a knot of revelers corralled off from the main herd, camera flashes, men and women taking turns rubbing shoulders for the paparazzi. And at the eye of this storm, the top-hatted, sequin-tuxedoed guest of honor himself, Kex Maces, aka Tim Taussi, the twenty-six-year-old rap artist whose pop-influenced hip-hop album made Spotify history last year: it rose to the top of the streaming lists not only in Finland, but in the other Nordic countries, and Germany too.

"You're up, Lisa," calls the woman with the telephoto lens. Purse in hand, Lisa steps up to the backdrop: an album cover illustrated with a huge spider. *Kex Maces' Spider's Web.* The flashes click briefly, annoy-ingly so. The photographers haven't always let Lisa off the hook so easily. Just last year, she would see camera flashes in her sleep. *Thanks!* She is free to go. *Great seeing you, Lisa! Have fun tonight!* The smiles feel almost genuine, the words almost sincere, but the underlying chill does not go unnoticed by Lisa. She has an eye for social cues that has been honed by dozens of such events. No one is really interested in who you are, only what you look like and what you represent. Some people are interested solely in whether you'll be available for an after-party blow job at five a.m., once the bottles have been emptied and the Ziploc bags vacuumed of every last gram.

The next item on the agenda is a glass of champagne; a server in a black shirt and yellow bow tie is conveniently carrying a tray of them in his gloved hand.

A promo girl in a tastelessly short skirt and a breast-baring top hands Lisa a program, winks, and says: "Don't get tangled in the web."

Don't get tangled in the web. So damned pretentious and overproduced. Lisa has been inside for only a few minutes, but she already has the urge to spin right back around and get the hell out of here. She's more desperate for a shot of courage than she realized. *Snow White. Marching powder.* Her gaze seeks out anyone who could offer relief. Teme, Sakke, Taleeb . . . Her usual guys are presumably present but obscured by the hundreds of faces.

And then Lisa feels her heart skip a beat. There he is again: standing, hands in his pockets, at the windows overlooking the city. His gaze, vaguely accusatory and penetrating, is exactly the same as last time. Lisa turns on her heels and heads for the bar.

But she knows the man won't let her out of his sight.

WEDNESDAY, NOVEMBER 27

2

THE SONG BLASTING through the earbuds—En Vogue's "Free Your Mind"—pauses as the running app provides its audio feedback. Despite being friendly and female, the voice exudes the stark soullessness of any recorded announcement: *Distance five kilometers, average speed ten point two kilometers an hour.* The music returns, and Jessica Niemi inhales the fresh air through her nostrils. It smells of morning after the first freeze of the year: of the frost on the leaves being swept away by the sun's early rays; of melting puddles, their film of ice giving under the flexible soles of sneakers.

Jessica feels like she's flying; her step is light. A few months ago, she started running to work again after a prolonged hiatus. It's a form of exercise she has dropped more than once due to agonized protests from her broken body. Aching joints, nerve pain boring into her knees, shooting down her legs to her toes, and all of it immune to normal pain medications. But now her legs are moving, and the pain hasn't returned. It will, of course; it always does. But until then, Jessica means to relish every footfall, every spurt that ends in a flood of endorphins. In retrospect, her taking up running again on a whim feels miraculous. After the funeral of her former boss Erne Mikson, Jessica spent weeks in a daze, sat at home brooding over everything that had happened. Until one day she pulled on her running shoes and lunged out into the mild spring air. *Like Forrest Gump,* her colleague Yusuf later joked.

The distance from her Töölönkatu flat to police headquarters in Pasila is about three and a half kilometers. The route hugs the bay, skirts the Winter Garden, then continues past the Stadium hill to Helsinki's Central Park. In order to double the distance, Jessica frequently turns west—

as she did today—at the Laakso equestrian center and crisscrosses the park's rocky, spruce-sheltered paths all the way to the allotment gardens at Ruskeasuo.

Jessica passes the riding school and Helsinki's mounted police just to the northeast. The sandy path is poorly lit along this stretch of track. The lampposts among the tall trees are few and far between, and the bright lights of the arena plunge instantly into forested gloom. A large bird prowls the treetops.

Hey! Did you hear me?

Jessica glances backward, but the path is deserted. It's hard to say whether she truly heard the shout over the music blasting in her earbuds. Sometimes she hears things when she's running: random words and cries. The voices have followed her for so long she doesn't always pay attention to them.

Stop!

This time the voice is too real. Jessica pulls the earbud from one ear and glances over her shoulder just in time to catch a glimpse of a male figure with outsized hands scrabbling at her windbreaker. The assailant throws his full weight against her, knocks her to the ground. Jessica can feel his mass on her back as her cheek digs into icy mud and damp leaves.

"Listen . . . ," the voice says.

Jessica reels from the stench of boozy breath. Thighs wrap around her glutes, the attacker planted on her lower back. Bare fingers reach around her neck as the mouth growls in her ears. The breath smells of salt-licorice schnapps. Then Jessica's attacker flips her over, and she sees his face: a stranger's. Alcohol-flushed, angular cheeks, heavy mustache. An unkempt, ethanol-rotted forty-year-old. Jessica remembers passing a bench at the side of the sawdust path a few minutes back; a creepy guy in a leather jacket sat there, swigging rotgut from a plastic bottle.

"Christmas Eve." The voice isn't much more than a whisper. "Christmas Eve."

Jessica stares at him, bewildered. The guy is clearly out of it; Christmas Eve is a month away. The fingers of one hand squeeze her jaw as his other hand holds her left wrist down.

Jessica exerts every ounce of strength she can muster and knees him in the crotch, but her legs are locked under the asshole's weight, and he must be too drunk to feel his balls.

Jessica hears her pulse pounding in her ears. She takes a deep breath. Rough gravel scrapes her cheek; she sees icy sand and decomposing leaves in her peripheral vision. She could scream for help, but she doesn't remember seeing anyone else nearby. In the distance, someone calls after a barking dog.

"Christmas Eve." Now the man is foaming at the mouth, teeth bared. "Christmas Eve."

Jessica's fingertips graze the tiny canister at the bottom of her pocket. It's classified as a firearm under Finnish law, and these days she always carries it with her. A second later, the man takes a long squirt of pepper spray to the eyes. An instant of disbelief, and then his drunken ranting turns into screams of anguish. With her free hand, Jessica slams her attacker in the face over and over. The upper teeth break; blood spurts from the mouth to the sallow skin. He loses his grip. And then, with surprising agility, he hauls himself off Jessica and bolts into the woods.

Jessica gasps for breath and lurches laboriously to her feet.

The knuckles on her right hand are bleeding.

Jessica hears branches snapping in the underbrush, but there's no sign of the man anymore.

She doesn't lower her hand; she brandishes the pepper spray, vigilant against a repeat attack. She waits and listens to the noises carrying from the woods. But the man doesn't return.

Jessica grabs her phone and dials the station switchboard. After giving a description of the attacker, she starts jogging in the direction she came from, this time on high alert.

Distance six kilometers, average speed nine point one kilometers an hour.

3

JESSICA STEPS ACROSS the threshold and leans her hip against the doorjamb. The after-sweat brought on by the hot shower she took in the locker room has glued her dark blue dress shirt to her back, and she discreetly tugs it out from under her belt. Her right hand, the one she used to whale on her attacker's jaw, hurts like hell; she should probably let occupational health x-ray it.

"Shut the door, Niemi," Superintendent Helena Lappi says, tapping her wireless mouse with her forefinger. Uttering Jessica's surname seems to leave a bad taste in her mouth. Jessica closes the door behind her, making the room seem even smaller. The perfume wafting around the office smells like an expensive, overpowering bar of soap.

Helena Lappi, more familiarly Hellu among her colleagues, continues staring at her computer screen, affording Jessica a chance to observe her surroundings. The office is much as it was in Erne's day: a spare minimalist cubbyhole, with white walls downright begging for an injection of shapes and colors to break the bleakness. The venetian blinds sag at the windows' upper edges; the electrical outlets clump in groups of four, even in spots where power is unneeded. When it comes to institutional drabness and dreariness, the office is in a class of its own. But it's only now, without Erne, that it feels oppressive and lifeless: the presence that brightened the entire unit with his big heart is gone.

"We haven't had a chance to have a proper talk yet," Hellu says, indicating for Jessica to take a seat.

Jessica obeys, folding her hands in her lap. She looks into the eyes of the forty-plus woman across the desk; their brown is somehow incongruous with the cropped bleached hair.

The directorship of the Violent Crimes Unit has seen some turbulence since Erne's departure last March. The first candidate, a beer-bellied old-timer approaching retirement, did the job for only a few months before railroading himself into the shelter of a post in administration. The second left with little fanfare after a similar amount of time in the position: a credible source asserts malt whisky was his downfall. His enduring friendship with the bottle had deepened into a fatal attraction during divorce proceedings. Classic.

Hellu, on the other hand, doesn't appear to be going anywhere. She exudes enthusiasm for the position and the self-assurance endowed by her new status, which unfortunately makes her an infuriatingly pedantic boss. Jessica has worked under Hellu for only a couple of weeks, but it's already plain her new director loves punctuality, protocol, paramilitary discipline, and principled bureaucracy. There has been friction between the two of them since day one, and Jessica isn't sure what the cause is. In any case, the corridors at police HQ have grown narrower and narrower by the day—it's as if Hellu and Jessica weren't meant to walk them together.

"Congratulations on Kalasatama," Hellu says drily. She's referring to the preliminary investigation of a homicide Jessica has wrapped up with surprising speed. The crime wasn't exactly a major mystery: a man with a record of violence beat an old friend to death with a baseball bat in an alcohol-fueled frenzy, then carried the body out to a dumpster wrapped in a Persian rug—or, more accurately, a Chinese copy of one.

Jessica tries to reply with a neutral smile—the most diplomatic variety, but also the hardest to maintain. "Thanks."

Hellu fingers the papers in front of her and glances at Jessica from under her brow. Jessica crosses one leg over the other. Her knee hits the corner of the desk, setting the pens rattling in their stand.

"I just spoke with the prosecutors. They were pleased. They'll have an easy time taking it from here," Hellu says.

"It would be pretty hard to screw up, seeing as how we gave them a weapon, a motive, DNA linking the—"

"As I said, congratulations." Hellu releases the mouse. There's something calculated about the way she does it. The gesture, trivial in and of itself, signals the end of the prelude. Of the foreplay. Of the small talk. *You got your praise, Niemi. Now I'm going to wring your neck.*

The superintendent leans back in her chair and clicks her tongue ominously. "I've tried to meet with everybody. Get to know the team. You and I haven't had a chance to chat yet, since you've been busy with Kalasatama, but now . . ." Hellu clenches and unclenches the fingers of her left hand. The ring finger is adorned by a band of steel or white gold, its stark simplicity clearly intentional. The wrist sports a massive smartwatch, presumably part of Hellu's scheme to biohack herself eternal life. Or something like that.

"I've gathered you were particularly close to Superintendent Mikson. That you and he worked together for . . . how many years?"

Jessica hears Erne's name and can't help seeing the pockmarked face. The gray stubble, the kind eyes. Hearing the vaguely comical accent. Smelling the pungent whiff of cigarettes that lingered after he left the room.

She answers a moment later, as if having dedicated the entirety of the intervening seconds to counting the years she and Erne shared as colleagues. "Eight."

"I also heard you knew him before you joined the force. That you were friends."

"We were. Yes."

Hellu looks probingly at Jessica, as if studying Jessica's face would enable her to divine further information about her subordinate's relationship with the former boss. Then the stare relents slightly.

"Yes, it was unfortunate. My belated condolences. None of us can have too many good friends."

"Thank you."

"Cancer . . . cancer. It's a real bitch."

"Agreed."

"The reason I'm mentioning Mikson now and opening wounds I assume may not have properly scarred over yet is I believe you and I will be working closely with each other. Compared to the other detectives in the unit."

Jessica licks her dry lips and waits for the superintendent to continue. She doesn't.

"Working closely?"

Hellu looks vaguely disappointed, as if she expected Jessica to be able to read her mind.

"Listen," she says, and inhales sharply. "I know you're a good police officer, Niemi. I've heard it so many times I have no cause to doubt it. I've also heard that, during Erne's era, you had certain tendencies to . . . go rogue. Ignore instructions and orders from time to time."

Jessica struggles to remain calm. She can feel her mangled hand throbbing beneath the desk; she needs pain pills, and fast. "OK."

"This information did not come from your fellow detectives, but from higher up."

"You would have to say that, I guess."

"My question for you, Niemi, is whether this pattern was because you and Mikson had a long, close working relationship or in spite of that fact? There's a big difference, you see." Hellu flashes a nearly imperceptible smile before continuing. "Naturally the latter possibility is, from my perspective, more challenging. It means I need to be prepared to fight fire with fire. I do not allow grandstanding. Period. I am not Erne Mikson."

You could never touch Erne, you pompous sow.

Jessica looks at the woman, whose gleaming eyes are boring directly into her own. At moments like this, Jessica burns with the desire to give authority the finger: tell the unit to fuck itself, then quit. The Violent Crimes Unit needs her more than she needs it. It's always been that way.

The windows creak annoyingly at the seams, and it's not even windy outside.

"Erne and I had a specific way of working together," Jessica says. "Occasionally things may have looked more dramatic to outsiders than they actually were. Whoever your source is, they probably didn't quite grasp the dynamic between Erne and me."

"So you're saying you'll have no trouble doing things my way?"

"It's hard to say, because I don't know what your way is yet," Jessica says, despite guessing the reply will send Hellu over the edge. And indeed, the superintendent slams her hand down on the desk—not furiously, but hard enough to make Jessica jump—and her mouth produces an annoying sound much like the buzzer that accompanies the big red X on a quiz show display board.

"Wrong answer, Niemi."

"All I'm saying is that if, as new director, you jump into a complete overhaul, of course that's going to spark negative feelings and resistance to change. And not just from me, but probably from everyone. We always generated excellent results under Erne's leadership. Why fix something if it isn't—"

"Niemi," Hellu says calmly, "right now you're saying everything I *don't* want to hear."

"OK—"

"And as a matter of fact, this conversation reinforces the image I've already formed of you."

"I don't want to be—"

"You and I will discuss this again, sooner or later. Hopefully for the sole reason that I'm acknowledging your capacity to adapt to new circumstances."

"Let's hope so," Jessica says tiredly. She stands.

"Niemi."

Call me by my last name one more time and I'll drag you by that stupid bottle blond crew cut.

"Yes?"

"We're not finished."

Jessica sits back down and silently counts to ten.

"I also have a police matter for you." Hellu moistens a fingertip with her tongue. "You recognize these faces?"

Hellu pulls a printout from a stack: a screenshot of a tabloid cover. Jessica picks up the sheet of paper and studies the pictures of the young woman and young man. Both are beautiful and fashionable in their own way, and the photographs exude an undeniable vitality and a lust for life. Tastemakers, trendsetters. Over the past forty-eight hours, Jessica has seen the photos multiple times.

"The bloggers."

"Exactly."

Lisa Yamamoto and Jason Nervander. Finland's most-followed social media celebrities and lifestyle bloggers. For the past couple of days, concerned calls have been raining down on the police: apparently neither arrived home after attending a major Finnish rapper's record launch Saturday night.

Jessica lowers the printout to the desk. "Is the case coming to us?"

The possibility of the case ending up on their desks had already occurred to her. Maybe she had even secretly hoped for it. Missing persons are generally more interesting than normal murder investigations. They're like opera performances in which you have to find the body before intermission—if the missing individuals are found alive, there is no second act. But sometimes they're never found at all.

"Just yesterday, there didn't appear to be any doubt it was a stunt of some sort. They know each other, and both got a hell of a lot more followers as a result of the disappearance. But this morning something happened that made us suspect a crime."

"What?"

"A new photo appeared on Lisa Yamamoto's Instagram." Hellu sets a second printout down in front of Jessica. It's a screenshot of an Instagram post: a photograph of a tall lighthouse built of yellowish stone.

"What is this?"

"Söderskär lighthouse. The Porvoo archipelago. Read the caption."

Jessica drops her eyes beneath the symbol indicating thousands of likes. For a split second she imagines the dampness she feels on her lower back isn't sweat, but a fine rime drawn to the surface of the maple leaves by the freeze. A keen cold pierces her.

Deepest sea, darkest grave
A princess sleeps beneath the waves
Soon sea will freeze, snowfall cover
And none shall her tomb discover

4

JESSICA HEARS A gunshot. And another. And a moment later, another eight, at an ever-accelerating rate. Every shot follows faster than the one before until the ten-shell magazine is empty and the slide remains in the rear position. The heavy smell of gunpowder rolls over her.

Jessica removes her ear protectors. "Too fast. You're never going to be in a situation where you'll have to fire ten that fast."

Yusuf removes the magazine and sets his gun down on the counter. His fingers clench and unclench. "They were all hits," he says unenthusiastically as he heads toward the target.

The shooting range at police headquarters is deserted aside from them. Unlike the setup familiar from American television series, it does not have targets that slide out at the press of a button. What it does have are moving, rotating targets that can be adjusted to the desired configuration.

Jessica ties her hair back and follows Yusuf, taking a moment to eye her colleague's muscular back. Yusuf has always been athletic, but he's been spending more time at the gym in recent months. The impulse for his more active training schedule was presumably the sick leave that lasted from late February to May, during which his long-term relationship came to an impasse.

Since returning to work, Yusuf has been aloof and distant. Maybe because of the breakup. Or what happened in Kulosaari in February: when he was drugged and nearly killed by a murderous cult. Most likely the sum of the two, plus whatever else.

"Look," Yusuf says. He takes a small roll of brown stickers from his pocket and begins patching the bullet holes. "Head, head, chest, head, chest, head . . ."

The casualness with which Yusuf lists the hits to the piece of cardboard modeled after a human torso makes Jessica shudder. She knows Yusuf isn't himself, isn't doing well. Sure, he's able to perform his duties and shoot accurately enough. But this isn't the same old Yusuf who strolled the corridors of police HQ, infecting the whole open-plan office with his irresistible laugh. Jessica feels a fleeting wistfulness about how much things have changed over the past year. And yet many things remain the same. Only Erne and Mikael are gone. They're both dead. The angel and the demon.

Jessica and Yusuf slowly return to the firing line. Yusuf slips off his protective goggles and ear protectors and squats to pick up the nine-millimeter shells strewn across the concrete floor. The fluorescent tubes at the ceiling radiate the only color they know: hospital white.

"How are things, Jessie?"

Jessica shakes her head. "Weird morning. Some drunk attacked me in the park while I was running to work."

A worried look falls over Yusuf's face. "Jesus Christ, Jessie. Are you OK?"

Jessica raises her right hand; the knuckles look like she's socked a brick wall. "*I'm* fine. But a missing front tooth should make that psycho pretty easy to identify."

"Holy shit," Yusuf says. But he doesn't drop his gaze.

"I'm fine," Jessica insists. "It won't take long to find him."

"You come down here to shoot?"

"Nope." A heavy door closes in a nearby corridor. Jessica sweeps a strand of hair back from her brow. "I just had a chat with Hellu."

Yusuf grunts. "Superintendent Lappi. Erne *had* cancer. That woman *is* cancer," he mutters.

"Yeah. I'm getting the sense she doesn't like me too much."

"I don't think she likes anyone."

Jessica tilts her head and smiles. "That's not what I heard."

"What did you hear?"

"That she checks out your ass every time you walk past. And every time you get up from your chair. And that you've been known to stand up for that very reason."

"Am I missing something? She has a wife."

"An ass is an ass."

"So let her look. I try my hardest." Yusuf wipes sweat from his temples. The biceps thrusting from his T-shirt snake with recently surfaced veins, a result of his new training program and diet. Jessica hopes Yusuf doesn't go overboard with the gym-rat routine. A light pump and a limber build look better on Yusuf than a broad back and stiff, swollen biceps.

"You're available, aren't you?" Jessica asks.

"Available?"

"I mean, you don't have any ongoing investigations."

"I was thinking you had a lady in mind for me. But no . . . I don't have any ongoing investigations. I've been helping Nina pick apart this one construction-site thing, attempted manslaughter."

Jessica looks at the gun resting on the table and wonders whether Yusuf means to empty another magazine into the targets.

"What's that you have there?" Apparently Yusuf is only now noticing the folder under Jessica's arm. A shell slips from his fist to the floor and rolls away. Yusuf eyes the bit of turned brass like a shepherd whose charge has broken from the flock.

"The bloggers," Jessica says.

Yusuf's face brightens, and his eyes rotate toward Jessica. "You're shitting me."

"You know the case?"

"Of course. Everyone thinks it's a publicity stunt."

"I heard that too." Jessica hands Yusuf her phone. Her Instagram app is open to the profile of the twenty-five-year-old Lisa Yamamoto.

Jessica points at the photograph of the lighthouse. "Check out the latest post."

Yusuf taps on the image. Jessica studies his reactions, expects to catch the familiar spark in his eyes. But the surprise spreading across his face isn't as intense as Jessica hoped. She wants to believe Yusuf hasn't grown indifferent; he must be suffering from chronic exhaustion. Either way, it's like some colors are missing from his palette of facial expressions. The clearest, purest ones.

"'. . . *sea will freeze, snowfall cover / And none shall her tomb discover.*' What the hell?" Yusuf hands the phone back.

"On its own, it could have been an off-the-wall prank, part of some attention-seeking PR stunt, just like you said. But that's not everything; this is even crazier." Jessica brings up Lisa's profile, showing all her posts. Jessica points at the profile description. "Check this out."

```
Lisa Yamamoto
Public figure
Blogger/influencer
RIP
1994–2019
```

5

THE CONFERENCE ROOM is dim; the ceiling lights are off. Not to make the image projected on the screen brighter, but because no one has had the energy to get up and turn them on.

"Yamamoto?" Rasmus Susikoski says, and coughs into his fist. Then his hands return to the table in the prayerful aspect that for him is a default state of sorts—the starting position from which all Rasmusian gestures and movements, including nose scratching and thumbnail gnawing, spring.

If there were a category for sitting muscles, Rasmus would be the Violent Crimes Unit's undisputed champion. As a thirty-four-year-old law school graduate who still lives in his parents' attic, Rasmus is not particularly socially gifted, but he has been blessed since birth with good instincts and a mammoth hard disk inside his skull. Rasmus' ID reads SPECIAL CONSULTANT; he works at HQ in a civilian role. Jessica has often wondered how Rasmus ended up working for the police, and in Violent Crimes to boot. Maybe it's a calling of sorts: a bullied schoolboy's attempt at breaking the cycle of evil. Or something like that.

"She's half Japanese," Jessica says, bringing up a new picture.

Yusuf, who is sitting at the head of the table, cracks his knuckles and frowns at the photo.

"And some sort of celebrity?" Rasmus asks.

"Social media celebrity."

"Never heard of her."

"You have Instagram?" Jessica continues clicking on the thumbnail images, which open up on the screen one at a time.

"Me?" The look that flits across Rasmus' face telegraphs the sheer absurdity of the question. "No. But I do have a Facebook—"

"Even if you did, you probably still wouldn't know her," Jessica says. "Eighty percent of Yamamoto's followers are young women. Another ten are young men, and I guess the rest are perverts or fake accounts."

Yusuf laughs. "So Rasse would fit in perfectly with that last ten percent. And I don't mean the fake accounts."

"I'm not active—"

Yusuf shoots his colleague a look. "Rasse, I'd bet a hundred euros you have some stalker account you use to check out girls, Fasmus Nusikoski or something."

At first Rasmus appears to blush, but then a tiny approving smirk spreads across his face. Although introverted, Rasmus seems to enjoy his established status as the target of the unit's crass humor. Besides, Yusuf knows how to tease his colleagues without being malicious, poke witty, funny jabs without going so far that they feel uncomfortable. Just the opposite: the butt of the joke always laughs along. Yusuf is a master at picking his way through minefields, even if the interactions might appear to match the hallmarks of bullying to outsiders. "Huh, Rasse?" he continues. "Butts, right? Or tits?"

Jessica sighs, but she can't hold back a grin. "All right, Yusuf."

"Or feet? You a feet guy? You like to jerk off to—"

Rasmus replies tentatively: "If I had to choose, I guess—"

"Hey, come on, guys. Focus."

Yusuf and Rasmus exchange quick smiles, then turn their attention to the large screen on the back wall. Images march past as Jessica browses through hundreds of posts. In most, Yamamoto is posing for the camera alone. The pictures are high quality, and the subject is dressed in on-trend designer wear or, alternatively, the images successfully evoke a superficially casual ambience. Some shots were clearly taken abroad, and many make room for a passel of friends in the shade of palm trees or in Central European squares. The profile and Yamamoto's personal brand are masterfully crafted: despite the changing outfits, hairstyles, settings, and groups of friends, the photos communicate a unified mood and style. If you click Follow, you know exactly what you're signing up for.

Jessica releases the mouse. "Lisa Yamamoto was reported missing by her roommate, who wasn't able to provide any theories as to where Lisa might be or who she might be with."

"What about the other one . . . the guy, Jason Nervander?" Yusuf asks.

"His parents live in Lapland, and he doesn't appear to be very close to them. He was reported missing by a close friend, a pastor from Kallio parish."

"And this pastor said what?"

"Just that he hasn't seen Jason for a couple of days," Jessica says.

"So in other words there's no unambiguous, probable explanation for the disappearance of either one?"

"We're starting from scratch."

Yusuf leans his elbows on the table. "Well, goddamn."

"Who's on the team?" Rasmus asks.

Jessica's answer comes quickly: "The three of us."

"Huh? Not even Nina or—" Yusuf swallows the rest of the sentence.

"Hellu stressed that even if we suspect homicide, there isn't enough evidence yet. The three of us are going to kick things off, and we can expect assistance as soon as it's confirmed that at least one of the two is dead." Jessica rubs her eyes. "But we'll be getting some extra hands from tech right away to help filter through the data."

"What happened to your hand?" Rasmus suddenly asks. He's staring at the appendage in question, which is now resting on the table.

Jessica doesn't immediately respond. She glances at the swollen back of her hand and bruised knuckles, shrugs. "Workplace injury." Then she leans back and crosses her arms, hiding her fingers deep in her armpit.

Jessica gazes at the image projected on the screen: Lisa Yamamoto standing in turquoise water up to her knees, back to the camera, face toward the waterfall roaring in the background. Dripping black hair skims a sun-bronzed neck and shoulders. Jessica can almost hear the thousands of gallons of water trapped in the image shudder into motion. Beyond the cascade's powerful reach, the pool's unbroken surface glitters in the sun.

"Jessica?" Yusuf says, rousing her from her thoughts.

"What?"

"Assignments?"

A few seconds pass before Jessica begins delegating tasks. "Rasse, I want you and tech to go through both Instagram accounts. Keep an eye out for anything suspicious."

"You mean, the comments?"

"Primarily. And suspicious followers—"

Rasmus finishes Jessica's sentence: "Among the four hundred thousand the two of them have between them."

Jessica glances at Rasmus. The remark may have sounded like a protest, but there isn't the slightest hint of defiance on Rasmus' face. It's an enormous undertaking regardless, more or less literally on the scale of looking for a needle in a haystack.

"Start with the comments. If this is what it looks like—meaning, if some lunatic killed Lisa and Jason and hijacked Lisa's social media account—I'm sure something will turn up there." Jessica shuts her computer. "Yusuf and I will go talk to Lisa's roommate."

"What about that damned lighthouse?" Yusuf asks.

"Söderskär. The local police have been called in to help. Hellu said a couple of detectives from Porvoo are headed out by boat to have a look. They might find something."

"Bodies?"

"I doubt they'll have any frogmen."

"Shouldn't they though?" Yusuf flips through the papers strewn in front of him. "*A princess sleeps beneath the waves / Soon sea will freeze, snowfall cover . . .*' They ought to take some diving gear if they want to find anything."

"I assume they know what they're doing. They have the same facts we do." Jessica stands and pulls on her coat. "Get to it, Rasse. Yusuf, let's you and I go check out Lisa's place."

6

THE LIGHTS TURN green, and Yusuf turns the car from Veturitie onto Nordenskiöldinkatu. Jessica looks at her wrist to check the time; a ladies' Cartier Panthère Vendôme gleams there. There's no question the eighteen-carat-gold watch Jessica inherited from her mother stands out in flashy contrast to her otherwise reserved style, but it isn't actually much of an extravagance. Jessica checked online once: if she decided to sell, she could get maybe a couple of grand for it, mostly due to its vintage pedigree. Probably more, if Jessica revealed who the previous owner was. The names of famous ex-owners pump plenty of air into the prices of watches: a couple of years earlier, the legendary Paul Newman's Rolex Daytona brought in almost eighteen million dollars at auction. Jessica's mother wasn't as famous as Paul Newman. But to date, she remains the only Finnish actor successfully launched into the highest reaches of the Hollywood firmament.

Starring Theresa von Hellens.

Jessica catches a whiff of Yusuf's leather coat; it smells new.

An old-school Chevy Camaro with museum plates races past, motor thundering.

"Uh-oh, speeding, and probably without snow tires too." Yusuf jams a pillow of snuff under his lip. "If only we had a radar and some extra time."

"I bet he was doing one thirty-seven," Jessica says.

"What?"

Jessica frowns at Yusuf; does he really not know what she's talking about? "Don't you remember one hundred thirty-seven? When the measured speed on every other traffic ticket written up was one hundred thirty-seven kilometers an hour? And for some reason, it was always raining?"

Yusuf shakes his head.

Jessica smiles. "The new radars were grabbing the speed from the windshield wipers. Always one hundred thirty-seven kilometers an hour. Those wipers were the cause of major travesties of highway justice."

Yusuf bursts out in rollicking laughter. "Jesus."

They pull up to a crosswalk, and Jessica twists the crown of her watch. The kindergartners in fluorescent vests toddle past in a row, like ducklings.

"I'm glad we'll be working together on this," Yusuf says.

"As long as it's not a repeat of last time."

Jessica contemplates the children stepping onto the island between the two crosswalks, where the teachers pack them in carefully. Those little Kewpies whose trust in adults and the fairness of life is unshakable— it will be years before the anguish of the world's insanity worms its way under those floppy-eared hats. Their little bubbles of safety would burst if they knew the park ladies and their teachers, their mothers and fathers . . . none of them know squat about the meaning of life.

As the light turns green, Yusuf asks: "You OK?"

"Are you?"

"I have to admit . . . last spring put me through the wringer big-time."

Jessica doesn't reply; she just turns to look out the passenger window. Talking about things felt difficult last spring, almost unreal in the summer, and they feel somehow pointless now. The clan of murderous witches succeeded in accomplishing something it never should have: it slithered into the core of the investigation like a venomous serpent and sank its fangs into all of them. And then to top it all off, managed to escape.

Jessica's phone rings. It's Rasmus.

"Hi. Are you guys already at Lisa's?"

Jessica sighs. "We just left the station, Rasse."

Yusuf wraps his fingers more tightly around the steering wheel. "He miss us already?"

Jessica puts her phone on speaker.

"I just wanted to call right away, because I spotted something interesting on Instagram." Rasmus is speaking at the faster-than-normal rate that for him usually signals enthusiasm.

"Already?"

"Yes, we haven't had time to even get started yet really, but—"

"Spit it out."

"It's about Lisa Yamamoto's most recent and final post—"

"The lighthouse?"

"Exactly. It's received a lot more comments than her other posts, almost a thousand. Mostly shocked and incredulous. I guess her followers have read the little poem in the caption and the RIP message on the profile. They're expressing horror and their condolences and—"

"What is it you found, Rasse?" Jessica says, and Yusuf shoots her an intrigued look as he pulls up at another red light.

"This one comment caught my eye when I was browsing through the reactions to the lighthouse picture. It's the only one that isn't in Finnish or English. It's in Japanese, in kanji characters—"

"What does it say?"

"I copied the characters into Google Translate. *Masayoshi.* It means 'justice.'"

"Justice?"

"Yes."

"Might the person who posted the comment mean that whatever happened to Lisa was justice? That she got what she deserved?"

Rasmus coughs away from the microphone. "That's what I was thinking."

"Who posted the comment?"

"The handle is Akifumi2511946. It's a private profile, but the profile picture looks like a young Japanese man."

"Send me a link."

"OK."

Rasmus ends the call a second later. The car jerks into motion again, and Jessica impatiently stares at the screen of her phone.

Yusuf turns on the wipers. "Look, sleet."

Jessica lifts her head and sees fat snowflakes turn to water as they strike the windshield. Despite the awful weather, some sort of flea market is taking place outside the Ice Hall. The stands are swarmed by a large crowd, many of whom are pulling their hoods up over their heads. The display board announces HIFK has a home match that evening against the Tampere-based Ilves. Jessica thinks back to the nineties, when the Jokerit still played their home matches here at the old arena and her foster parents took her regularly to watch the two Helsinki hockey teams battle it out. Jessica understood long ago that those were her only normal childhood years. Before that, there was early childhood, with its huge homes and chauffeurs, Bel Air and palm trees, the dry wind blowing from the inland deserts. And all that reentered her life after the wonderful years spent with the Niemis. Adulthood. The enormous fortune she inherited from her birth mother when she was of age. Her foster parents' deaths. As if the money were the cause of all the pain, as if a curse had been placed on the fortune deposited into her accounts.

She turns to her colleague. "Yusuf?"

"Yeah?"

"You ever thought about having kids?"

Yusuf exhales in bemusement. "Huh? Anna and I just broke up. . . . I figure it's going to take a minute."

"Yeah, I know. Sorry."

"Why do you ask?"

"I don't know. Right now it feels like it wouldn't be fair to anyone, most of all the child. The world is such a sick place."

And at that moment, the text message from Rasmus pings up on her phone.

7

THERE ARE A few spots available in front of Lisa Yamamoto's building, and Yusuf parks as close to the front door as he can. As she climbs from the car, Jessica pulls up her zipper to keep the drifting wet flakes from making contact with her bare neck. The six-story corner building is painted a light green that reminds Jessica of a veggie smoothie that's been left sitting out. There's a modest patch of grass outside the front door, adorned by a lone leafless tree. Beyond it rushes busy Topeliuksenkatu, now a cramped, backed-up, road-rage-inspiring battlefield, thanks to seemingly endless roadwork.

Yusuf slams the door. "I used to live over there."

Jessica turns to see Yusuf pointing back at the intersection they just passed. "Where?"

"Corner of Minna Canthin katu and Messeniuksenkatu."

"Really? When?"

"Ten years ago. When Anna and I moved from the sticks to the city."

Yusuf shoves his hands into the pockets of his hoodie; he left his brand-new leather jacket in the car, presumably because he doesn't want it to get wet. He shakes his head and gazes into his past with evident longing. Jessica isn't sure if he's trying to start a conversation on the topic, about himself and Anna and their failed relationship. She decides not to probe.

"What was the code?" she asks.

But as she speaks, there's movement on the other side of the door glass. An elderly man steps out and holds the door for Jessica and Yusuf. His voice is vigorous for his age: "Didn't maintenance fix it yet?"

"What?" Yusuf asks.

Apparently unfazed by the wet weather, the old man pauses and waves dismissively. "The buzzer. About damn time."

As the two detectives step in, the old man points at the IDs hanging around their necks. "Wait. Police?"

Jessica nods.

Tiny needles of drizzle are penetrating the shoulders of the old man's coat. "You here because of the noise?"

"The noise?" Jessica asks.

"Yes. Someone was really pounding on the walls again."

"Again?"

"Same damn noise Saturday night."

ROOM-FRESHENER-SWEETENED air wafts heavily through the flat, and Jessica has the urge to open a window. Water is rushing through the pipes in the building's belly, and a distractingly loud spin cycle is drumming in the apartment's bathroom. During interviews like this, prolonged silences are a given: they have to be allowed to come and go; they have to be respected. And during them, any surrounding noises are particularly conspicuous.

Jessica leans against the windowsill, arms folded across her chest. "Tell me the whole story from the beginning, in your own words."

The young woman on the couch is brushing her blond hair nonstop, clearly a distraction intended to channel a sense of helplessness into something useful. As she waits for the response, Jessica eyes the pleasant living room and the spacious, practical-looking kitchenette. The stylish flat, heavy on Scandinavian design, looks exactly the way one would expect a home for two young urban women to look. There are two bedrooms, one for each tenant.

"Lisa went to a party on Saturday. Around six o'clock," Essi says softly.

"Whose party was it?" Jessica asks, despite having read the missing-persons report twice. Yusuf takes a seat on the couch at a respectful distance from Essi.

"Tim's record drop."

"Tim?"

"Tim. Taussi. He's a rapper. Kex Maces."

Jessica shoots Yusuf a look. Kex Maces' name is familiar to anyone in Finland who hasn't been living under a rock. It's mostly young women who are attracted to his overproduced beats and over-the-top lyrics glorifying American culture. Guys too, of course, for instance Fubu, whom Jessica was still seeing up until recently. Fubu's taste in music wasn't what prompted their decision to stop hanging out, but it didn't do much to improve their evenings together.

"You know him?" Yusuf asks.

Essi raises her glazed eyes and looks at Yusuf as if the answer is obvious. "Tim? Yeah."

"Why didn't you go?"

"I didn't feel like it." Essi lowers the hairbrush to the table. "I was getting over a cold."

"OK," Jessica says, studying the twentysomething woman. Essi is a beautiful blond with bobbed hair, a pert nose, and big brown melancholy eyes.

"I was in the shower around nine or ten, when I heard the front door. I thought it was Lisa coming home from the party, but there wasn't anyone there. So then I thought I was making things up. But everything's so weird right now. . . ." Essi's lips pinch into a firm line.

"Is it possible someone had entered the apartment? Did you notice anything missing?" Yusuf asks.

Essi shakes her head. "When I woke up the next morning . . . it was around eight or so. I went into the kitchen and noticed the door to Lisa's room was open. She always closes it at night. Always. So I peeked in and noticed she wasn't passed out on her bed in her clothes, like I thought. The bedspread hadn't been touched. . . . That was when I realized she never came home. Because I would have definitely woken up if she had gone out that morning."

"Does that happen often? Lisa spending the night somewhere else?"

"Not often. Sometimes. But she usually texts me when she does. So I won't worry. She's pretty good about that."

"*Pretty* good?"

"Well, sometimes things get out of hand or her phone dies or, you know. . . . But somehow this time I just knew something was wrong."

"And you called her?"

"First I sent her a message. When I saw an hour had passed and my WhatsApp message hadn't been received, I called her. Her phone was off. Or at least my call didn't go through."

"So at four thirty on Sunday afternoon you called the police and reported her missing?" Yusuf asks.

"I had already called every single one of our friends. No one knew what time she left the party or where she went. She didn't go to the after-party—or at least to Tim's after-party in Ullanlinna. I know that for a fact."

"Do you know Jason Nervander?" Jessica asks.

"Of course." Essi lets out a tremulous sigh. "This is so fucking sick. . . ."

Jessica waits for Essi to blow her nose and glance at her phone before continuing: "Do you know if Jason was at the party?"

"I don't know. I doubt it. Jason doesn't really hang out with that crowd."

Jessica slowly circles the couch toward the kitchenette. "Do you think it's possible Lisa and Jason disappeared together?"

The living room's white walls are hung with framed manga drawings. The enormous eyes and minimalistic noses call to mind the animated works of Hayao Miyazaki, or Silver Fang or Pokémon.

Essi blows her nose again, this time harder. It sounds like the trumpeting of a baby elephant. "You mean, like, they would be hiding some-where on purpose?"

"Yes."

Jessica stops in front of one of the drawings: a girl with big eyes raising a sword that shoots blue lightning into the sky.

"I guess it's theoretically possible. But then that post appeared on her Instagram today." Essi shifts her restless gaze out the window. "Lisa wouldn't post a pic like that, even as an April Fools' joke. . . ."

"Why don't we come back to Jason? How well did he and Lisa know each other?" Jessica says calmly.

"They had a thing at one point."

This visibly catches Yusuf's attention. "A thing? You mean, a rela-tionship?"

Essi nods. "Maybe a year ago. But they never went public with it. Jason spent a lot of time here back then."

"Are they still involved?"

"I don't think so. The breakup was pretty ugly."

Jessica moves on from the sword girl to the next drawing. "Ugly in what way?"

"Jason cheated on Lisa. And lied to her when she asked him about it. Then got caught. Lisa would have told me if they were hanging out again."

"Even so, people who know both of them assume they disappeared together," Yusuf says.

"People don't know shit," Essi mumbles weepily. "People think they know . . . Not very many people know Lisa. People see a few pictures on social media and think they know everything about her."

"I know what you mean," Jessica says so softly she's not sure the others hear.

She has stopped at a manga-style felt-pen drawing of a smiling girl with blue eyes. A wreath of red roses encircles her white hair, and she's wearing what looks like a Japanese school uniform: knee socks, a short navy blue skirt, and a white sailor top with a red tie. Despite its comic-book associations, there's nothing happy-go-lucky about the drawing. It lacks a sense of playfulness, of irony.

For an instant, the big eyes immortalized in the image trap Jessica's gaze, and she's overwhelmed by a strange sensation that they conceal something ghastly behind them. Jessica has felt this before. She stares at the face in the drawing too long and it starts to lose its shape, like a word repeated to the point of meaninglessness. Meanwhile, the girl's brown skin pales, her white hair runs through a full spectrum of colors before eventually turning black. The bones of her face grow brittle, like wax paper left in the oven too long and falls apart at the slightest touch. Dark red fluid begins streaming from the crown of the head to the brow, from the nose to the mouth, from behind the ears to the cheeks. The sclera of the eyes and the row of perfect teeth form islands of white amid the scarlet skin. And throughout this transformation, Jessica hears a hateful scratching, as if thousands of spider eggs laid in her ear all hatch at once, and the little arachnids are scuttling toward her brain.

Jessica shuts her eyes, and when she opens them, the girl's big eyes are twinkling and her hair is white again. Jessica's fingertips are prickling. Essi must have said something, but Jessica hasn't registered a word. "Sorry—"

She shifts her gaze downward to avoid eye contact with the girl in the drawing and notices something she almost missed: at the bottom edge, it reads *L.Y. 2018* in stick characters.

"Signed L. Y., as in Lisa Yamamoto?"

Essi nods and coughs to open her throat. "Lisa did all of those." Essi points out a few works of art. "There are a ton more in her room. The walls are plastered with them. Most are framed; some aren't finished yet."

After a moment of silence, Yusuf asks: "Does Lisa understand Japanese?"

"Yeah. I've heard her speak it before."

"With whom?"

"Her dad. And actually some Japanese person came by not very long ago. A guy. Ordered a painting from her or something . . ."

Jessica and Yusuf exchange glances. Jessica pulls her phone out of her pocket and walks over to Essi. She taps at the device until a zoomed-in view of the photograph Rasmus just sent her appears on the screen: a young Japanese man standing in front of a pale background. *Akifumi*. Maybe the photo is genuine; maybe it was lifted from someone else's profile or a photo bank and doesn't have anything to do with the person who posted the comment. Maybe the comment itself doesn't have anything to do with anything. But right now it's the only clue they have.

Jessica hands the phone to Essi. "Is it possible this is the guy?"

Essi looks at the screen for a second and shakes her head. "I don't know. . . . I didn't see him. I just heard them. I was in my room when he came, and my door was closed."

"But you could hear enough to tell they were speaking Japanese?"

"Well, it sounded kind of weird at first, so I went over and listened at the door. Out of curiosity, I guess."

"Did he sound young?"

"I don't know. Maybe. I thought he was young because he used strong aftershave or something. . . . Our living room still smelled like it after he left."

"What sort of aftershave? Can you describe it?"

Essi looks reflective. "No. Maybe kind of saccharine. Really strong."

Jessica writes down *saccharine* in her notebook.

Yusuf breaks in: "Was it a calm conversation?"

"They didn't seem upset or anything, if that's what you mean."

"OK. When was this?" Jessica asks.

"Maybe a week ago."

"Can you pinpoint as precise a time as possible for us? Maybe you were texting or emailing someone while he was here. Is there any reference point you could use to check the date and time?" Yusuf says.

"Sure. But why? Do you think he—"

"We don't think anything. But we'd like to talk to him." Jessica slips her phone back into her jeans pocket. "And they were speaking Japanese, so you didn't understand what they were talking about?"

"Right."

"So how did you know it was about Lisa's art?"

"Lisa told me after he left."

"That he bought a piece?"

"Yeah. Commissioned."

"Did Lisa finish the piece?"

"Beats me."

"Was this a common occurrence? I mean, did Lisa sell a lot of art?"

"Yeah, she advertised it on social media, and now and again someone would buy something."

The wall between Lisa's room and the living room is surfaced in decorative brick. There's a roll of brown protective paper on the floor, as well as a bag of plaster and a trowel for spreading it. A can of white paint and a paint roller stand next to them. The leftover bricks are stacked tidily on the floor.

"You guys have been remodeling lately?"

Essi nods. "Lisa was. She's good at all that sort of stuff." Essi points to where the living room meets the kitchenette. "There used to be a wall there. Lisa took down part of it so it would be more open in here. All by herself."

Jessica eyes the sledgehammer standing in the corner. The wooden handle comes up to her knees. "That's quite a job."

"That's the great thing about Lisa. Her Instagram might give the impression everything's really amazing and luxurious. But in reality she's not afraid to get her hands dirty. She wouldn't need to call in a builder to do stuff like that." Then the smile on Essi's face dies and fades to grimness. Reality must have crept into her consciousness again.

"OK if we take a look around Lisa's room?" Jessica says.

Essi turns her glassy eyes toward Jessica. Eventually she nods, raises her café au lait to her lips, and says: "I'm gonna go have a smoke."

"Oh, yes, Essi. I doubt this has anything to do with Lisa, but . . . an old man downstairs just said he heard a loud noise in the stairwell Saturday night and again this morning. Pounding. Did you hear it?"

Essi pulls on her coat. A cigarette has appeared between her index and middle fingers. "Yeah. Now that you mention it. But I have no idea where it came from, and it only lasted a second."

8

THE WALLS OF Lisa's room are covered in framed drawings, oil paintings, and graphics. Dozens of manga-style dolls and figures stand on the dresser.

Yusuf whistles softly. "Manga heaven."

He and Jessica hear the front door close and the subsequent hollow clunk of the old elevator gate sliding shut.

"Pseudo-manga," Jessica says.

Yusuf shoots her a questioning look.

"It looks like manga, but it's not from Japan. Pseudo-manga."

"Is it really that deep?"

"I can't claim to be an expert."

Jessica turns up the lights with the dimmer switch next to the door. A pair of fluffy white slippers have been kicked off under the tidily made bed. There's a yellow volume on the nightstand; the spine reads *Paul Auster* in fine print. Next to the book stands a framed photograph of Lisa posing with a couple who must be her parents: the man is presumably Japanese, the woman Finnish. Both appear to be about sixty.

It would have been good to question the parents as quickly as possible. But the police tracked them down vacationing in Brazil, and they won't be back until tomorrow morning.

"You stopped and stared at that girl."

Jessica is roused from her thoughts. "What?"

Yusuf fingers a doll with enormous eyes peering out from under electric blue bangs. "The girl in the drawing. You stared at her for a long time."

Jessica turns to him. "I was looking at the initials."

Both of them take a moment to look around the room. A desk stands between the bed and a dresser. At one end, a mountain of makeup, powders, and eye shadows rises next to a round vanity mirror.

"Holy hell," Yusuf says softly.

"Huh?"

"Do you ever feel—what am I trying to say?—that it's disconcerting or creepy being in a room where a missing person just was? Sitting, putting on her makeup, breathing. Doing everyday things, totally clueless the entire world will be looking for her before long."

"I know what you mean." Jessica pulls the white wooden chair up to the desk. As she sits, she catches a glimpse of her eyes in the mirror. She turns it aside.

A wooden easel is propped up next to the desk. There's no canvas. At the rear of the desk, there's a stack of oversized drawing paper, sketchbooks, a candy-box sampler of oil colors, and dozens of felt pens in different colors. Turpentine and linseed oil. Behind them, half a dozen glass jars containing vividly colored powders stand against the wall.

"What are those?" Yusuf asks.

"Pigments." Jessica points at the bottle of oil. "You mix them with linseed oil to make your own paint."

Yusuf walks over to the window. "Look at you, Ms. Walking Wikipedia."

A few brushes are jammed into a glass jar. A splash of what's presumably turpentine is pooled at the bottom, drawing the paint out of the brush hairs. The liquid is dark gray. The dried paint on the palette is also various tones of gray.

"That's weird," Jessica says.

"What?"

"All of Lisa's drawings and paintings are really colorful. . . . The only things that're black are the outlines and the hair of some of the figures."

"And?"

"The last thing Lisa painted was something gray."

Jessica takes the stack of drawing paper, browses through the sheets one at a time. Manga drawings, every single one. Each work is unfinished in its own way. Some are no more than sketches scribbled out in pencil; others are refined, nearly completed pieces skillfully rendered in felt marker. The works in the stack represent every phase of the creative process and demonstrate Lisa's meticulousness and professionalism as an artist. Their invariable depictions of cheerful girls or women in childish, garish clothing toy with stereotypes of innocence.

"You find it?" Yusuf asks.

"No."

"So it must be the piece that was commissioned?"

"I was thinking that too," Jessica says thoughtfully. She sets the stack back down on the desk. "The girl definitely knows how to draw."

Yusuf grunts and pulls up the blinds. "So we'd better hope the guy ordered a picture of himself from Lisa." The grayness of the sky is so life sucking it's almost absurd.

"Now, that would be like winning the lottery."

"You clearly have the sense the Japanese guy is somehow related to this."

"I don't know. It seems weird how he just happened to commission a piece from her recently."

"Sure. But then again . . . maybe someone just wanted a painting from her. Maybe some perv ordered a picture of a girl in her school uniform, something he can jerk off to while he rubs his nipples with sandpaper."

"Ah, so that's how you spent your Saturday night?"

"My whole weekend."

Jessica shakes her head, takes a red spiral notebook from the desk, and opens it. "My first thought was Lisa's Japanese visitor is the same guy Rasse spotted on Instagram." The notebook's pages are full of writing, thoughts on video blog topics, and what are presumably notes on sponsor meetings.

Yusuf holds up a slim laptop from the windowsill. "We should probably take this?"

Jessica doesn't react. She flips to the middle of the notebook, the last page that has any marks on it, and her senses instantly electrify. It's as if a high-voltage current has shot through her.

"Yusuf . . . ," she says softly.

"Yeah?"

Jessica turns the notebook so Yusuf can see it. "Look at this."

Yusuf approaches warily, as if the notebook is a skittish animal he has to catch without scaring it off. "Goddamn," he whispers.

It's not a finished drawing, but a pencil sketch lacking the felt-pen contours and the punch brought by color. The surface of the page is littered with crumbs of pink rubber, flecked with erased graphite.

Jessica brings the drawing closer to her eyes and stares at it. A solemn girl in a school uniform is standing on rocky terrain—and behind her, a lighthouse towers against the brooding sky.

9

DETECTIVE SERGEANT JAMI Harjula turns up the fur collar of his winter coat and gazes out to sea. For a moment he imagines it's summer, that the sand under the soles of his shoes isn't rock-hard and gray but soft and golden yellow. That the air is pleasant and warm, that the sun is shining, just hot enough, behind a veil of clouds. That his eight- and ten-year-old daughters are squealing and scampering into the water from the oversized towel Sini has spread out on the sand. The smell of sunscreen, the sounds of screaming seagulls, the images of satisfied smiles. The sensation of sun-warmed skin on sun-warmed skin, the radiating heat that in so many ways is like falling in love, those days when a lover's touch is still new, exciting.

But this November day could not be more different. An icy drizzle falls from the gray sky, and the waves of the frigid-looking water pound the shore threateningly. The hard wind has given the sea goose bumps.

"Harjula!" The voice belongs to the technical investigator who just finished combing the area. Apparently spirit departed flesh elsewhere, abandoning the latter to the powerful waves and currents until it eventually washed up here. "Wagon!"

The tech investigator is referring to the ambulance that has come to collect the body. It has crept down the promenade to the summertime site of the ice cream stand. The responding medics are long gone, off to another location—one where saving patients' lives remains a possibility.

Harjula nods absentmindedly. "OK."

He turns around and scans the vicinity, sees the gawkers gathered at either end of the promenade. The patrol officers are valiantly trying to keep them as far as possible from the corpse on the shore.

You can always count on them, the gawkers. There's something so compelling about tragedy that people have to witness it with their own eyes. Get up close. So close they can record it in photos and videos. Even selfies. The way people consume accidents and death through their phone screens makes Harjula sick to his stomach. It's a phenomenon he runs into with unfortunate frequency in this line of work: the backs of smartphones at vehicle windows passing an accident scene, the apartment-balcony flashes that deepen the color of the blood spilled on the asphalt to the unnatural red of old movies. When it comes down to it, humans are scavengers, scanning for tragedies that will break the monotony of everyday existence.

Not that Harjula isn't guilty of the same—for purely professional motives, of course. Even so, he often wonders why, year in, year out, he keeps deciding to work with death. Sometimes in the morning when he leaves for work, he feels like he is choosing the dead over the living. That death takes priority over all else. At this very moment, Sini is with the kids on a school field trip at the Heureka science center. It's where he should be too. Today was supposed to be his day off, but Helena Lappi decided otherwise when the report about a dead woman reached the station a little over an hour ago.

Harjula pulls his leather gloves more tightly over his hands and slowly walks toward the lifeless figure on the beach, dragged from the water by a passing jogger. He eyes the woman lying on the frozen sand. She's so lightly dressed, she must have ended up in the water directly from an indoor space, if that's even possible. Perhaps she fell from the deck of a boat. Or else she was killed indoors and her body was tossed into the water from, say, a bridge. But there isn't a single bridge between Kallahdenniemi and Uutela, which nips that theory in the bud.

Harjula pulls off his lightweight cotton beanie and rubs his psoriasis-irritated brow.

The death seems suspicious, but there is no immediate indication the woman was harmed. There are no external signs of violence: no choke marks or other visible trauma, no bullet holes or puncture wounds. Not even a shark bite—now that would be something. Harjula grunts at the thought and immediately feels guilty.

"See you soon," the tech investigator calls out.

Harjula raises a hand in response and slips his beanie back on without turning around.

He takes off his right glove, raises his phone, and snaps a few more shots of the victim, each from a slightly different angle. He doesn't see anything on the body he hasn't already noticed during his half hour at the scene. Even so, the corpse is crying out for him to pick up on something. Harjula knows perfectly well that the more likely cause of death here is accident as opposed to homicide, that the majority of drownings do not involve a crime. But there's something odd about this corpse. Maybe it's the clothing: the schoolgirl uniform on a grown woman is cliché sexy and somehow perverse. It's also unusual that twenty-two-year-old Olga Belousova, per her ID a citizen of Ukraine, never officially arrived in Finland. Confirmation just came in from the Border Guard.

Harjula sighs and slides his phone into his coat pocket. Time to get back to the station. The cause of death will come out during the medical examiner's analysis.

Wait a sec.

Harjula's gaze pauses on something on the white arm: a round black mark barely visible under the white sleeve.

A tattoo?

Harjula squats down by the body, takes a twig from the sand, and raises the white sleeve enough to view the mark in its entirety. He sees another one, several more. Together they form a nearly perfect circle in the crook of the woman's elbow. Up close, the black spots look like burn marks; judging by their size, they could have been made with cigarettes. But they're too symmetrical, too flawless. They must have been made with something blunt and solid: perhaps heated metal.

Harjula pulls his phone from his pocket and takes one last photo, as he hears footfalls approaching behind him. They belong to the men who have come for the body.

She was branded.

Harjula looks back out to sea. Something in the crashing waves puts him in mind of his family, makes him wonder whether the science center still has the dinosaurs. They're the whole reason he wanted to go there when he was a kid.

10

RASMUS SUSIKOSKI GLANCES at the door. When he doesn't hear anything from the corridor, he pulls a golf ball from his bag and sets it down carefully on the floor. Then he slips off his shoes and places his foot on the ball. The rolling motion hurts, but the physiotherapist says it's good for him. In recent years, Rasmus, who has spent a lifetime hunched over a monitor, has begun to suffer from stiff muscles, poor posture, and the gradual development of *pervasive blocks throughout the body* due to perpetual stress. That's what the all-knowing witch doctor said, that he couldn't remember the last time he came across such tense muscles, which is doubly unusual, considering Rasmus gets almost no exercise. How a golf ball placed under the sole of his foot is going to release tension from his entire body is a mystery to Rasmus. Nevertheless, the exercise is so simple and easy to do that ignoring the physiotherapist's instructions would be, if nothing else, an insult to his mother, who encouraged him to go in and paid for the treatment. *Three minutes per foot twice a day.*

"In the conference room," a voice says in the distance. Rasmus jumps and grabs the ball from the floor, quickly slips on his shoes. He's enough of an odd duck without his coworkers seeing him massage himself with athletic supplies. Besides, his feet smell foul. Even to him.

"Here you are," Hellu says as she steps into the conference room a moment later.

Rasmus nods, moves his laptop a hair toward the center of the table, and uses a remote to turn on the video projector hanging from the ceiling. "Are we having a meeting?" he asks uncertainly.

"Yes. A quick briefing." Hellu runs a hand over her cropped hair as she seats herself across from Rasmus. Despite behaving much more officiously and formally than Erne in most ways, Hellu relies less on symbolic authority. Unlike Erne, Hellu never sits at the head of the table in the conference room, let alone the canteen, preferring to position herself at random among her subordinates. Now, this could be a lack of ceremony or a conscious signal of solidarity. But the more likely explanation is it's Hellu's calculating way of ensuring she's not the subject of the slightest mutinous thought or glance, targeted by discreet eye rolls or whispered jokes. Maybe in her former life she was a teacher driven to the brink of insanity by note-passing students. If that's the case, Erne may have simply been braver and more at home in his role than his successor.

"Who's coming?" Rasmus asks after avoiding his superior's gaze with poor success.

"Nina."

"Nina?"

Hellu frowns. "Is that a problem?"

Rasmus lowers his eyes. Nina hasn't been herself since the events of the previous February. Maybe there's something that permanently changes in a police officer when she nearly loses her life in the line of duty. A premature violent death is one of the risks of police work, but only a close call can drive home how real that risk is. Not that Rasmus questions Nina's ability to perform her duties in an exemplary fashion. He's more perplexed by what happened between Jessica and Micke. By how, amid all the chaos, Nina had to hear her coworker was screwing her boyfriend. A coworker who was also a friend. *What on earth was Jessica thinking?*

"Of course not," Rasmus says, surprising himself by not stuttering. And at that moment, Nina enters the room and shuts the door.

"Have a seat," Hellu says, opening her laptop.

Rasmus can't help glancing at the trained arms and powerful neck emerging from Nina's black T-shirt. She has always emanated both inner and outer strength, but for some reason, many don't see it. Unintentionally or not, Jessica has attained the status of alpha female and most desirable woman at police HQ, thanks to her humor-cloaked cynicism, petite figure, and no-nonsense attitude. But for Rasmus the woman and colleague of his dreams has always been Nina. Fit, lethal Nina. With her black belt in judo, she could knock Rasmus to the floor and smother him with a pillow in ten seconds flat. The thought is both terrifying and titillating.

"Rasmus?" Hellu snaps her fingers. "Are you awake?"

"Of course."

"I have a meeting starting upstairs soon, so let's get this done." Hellu taps her password into her laptop, and the familiar Windows melody sounds. "Nothing for days and now we're swamped. The body of a young woman was found in the water at Vuosaari."

"A young woman?"

Hellu instantly knows what Rasmus is driving at. "Yes, but it's not Lisa Yamamoto. It's some Ukrainian. Her ID was in her backpack." Hellu stares absentmindedly at her computer screen and appears to belch silently into her fist before abruptly continuing: "OK, back to the first one. Jessica and Yusuf suspect the individual who commented on Lisa Yamamoto's Instagram post in Japanese visited her about a week ago."

"Did anyone see who it was?"

"Only Lisa Yamamoto herself." Hellu scratches her upper lip. "But her roommate heard the voice. A man. Not very old. It could well be . . . Show me again." Hellu snaps her fingers demandingly. Rasmus projects the profile for Akifumi2511946 onto the wall from his laptop. The round profile picture shows an Asian man in a black turtleneck. There's something odd about the face, as if it was edited into the photo.

"But we don't know if the guy in the photo has anything to do with the case. He could be a troll," Rasmus says, looking to Nina for a nod of approval.

"Or whether anything very dramatic has even happened," Hellu notes laconically, as if doubting the necessity of the just-initiated investigation.

"I guess."

"What's that in the background there?" Hellu asks, pushing up her glasses with the back of her hand.

"Art. Paintings?"

"White walls. The photo could have been taken in an art gallery."

"True." Rasmus squints at the image. The edges of two paintings are visible behind the man. Oil paintings, perhaps. Fat brushstrokes and bright colors. Pretty universal and difficult to identify.

"Do we have any way of accessing the profile's data?" Hellu asks.

"Probably. Theoretically we can get a name, credit card information, email addresses, and the IP addresses of recent log-ons and logouts without a subpoena. But even for them, we need court documents translated into English. And some sort of memo confirming the existence of a preliminary investigation—"

"For Christ's sakes," Hellu says softly, and shakes her head. "OK, I'll get all that for you. How long will it take you to send the request off?"

"Hard to say. I'll submit the request through the online form; the reply could come pretty quickly if we title it a murder investigation."

"I'll see what I can do." Hellu rises from her chair. "Brief Nina on the project. Let's all meet here at four unless something else crazy happens before."

11

JESSICA SLIPS HER hands into her coat pockets and gazes at the wet asphalt under her feet. The drizzle has stopped, and for a moment the air smells fresh—until Yusuf lights a cigarette, and the smoke tramples all else underfoot.

"Last Wednesday between five and six." Yusuf blows smoke from the corner of his mouth. This is what Essi just told them: a simultaneous Skype call with her mother has pinpointed the time frame of the visit by the man who bought the piece from Lisa.

Jessica doesn't answer. She gazes down Messeniuksenkatu and imagines the receding back of the man who bought the piece, the slightly stooped figure and turned-up collar, like a secret agent's from some old spy movie. The man who disappeared back to wherever he came from. In reality, they know nothing about him. Other than that he spoke Japanese with Lisa and had strong aftershave. That's it.

"We could ask him to get in touch with the police," Yusuf says.

"If he has anything to do with Lisa's disappearance, he's not going to react to a public request like that," Jessica says quietly.

She thinks back to the encounter with the white-haired schoolgirl in the piece Lisa painted, how quickly the work came to life, only to die again before her eyes.

"The eternal dilemma," Yusuf says.

"Those gray colors . . . Lisa used them to paint the lighthouse." Jessica studies the picture she took of the lighthouse sketch. It's nearly identical to the image posted on Instagram, the only difference being that in the former a solemn girl is standing in front of the lighthouse. The perspective and distance to the lighthouse are basically the same.

Yusuf flicks his cigarette butt into the gutter. "Lisa may have based the painting on a photograph. The person who commissioned the piece sent her this picture and asked her to paint it exactly the same way, but just add the girl."

"Which means the picture posted on Instagram is at least a week old."

"It could be straight from Google. Image-bank stuff."

"But what the hell does it have to do with Lisa?"

"Maybe nothing."

"I don't believe that for a second. There's a reason that man specifically wanted Lisa, who isn't even a professional artist, to paint that lighthouse. And then the Instagram post. The little poem. The RIP."

"Shit," Yusuf says, unable to think of anything better to say.

He and Jessica walk toward the car. Yusuf continues: "Lisa probably finished it. And the man either picked it up . . ."

"When Essi wasn't at home . . ."

". . . or Lisa hand delivered it to him."

"Not necessarily. Maybe she used a messenger or a delivery service." An incoming text message interrupts Jessica.

"True. That's information we can dig up." Yusuf opens the driver's door. "We can reach out to the bigger companies right away."

Jessica stares at her phone, sighs deeply, then shoves it back in her pocket.

"What is it?" Yusuf asks as he and Jessica climb in and pull their doors shut.

"The body of a young woman was found at Aurinkolahti. Twenty years old or so. Bobbing in the water at the beach."

"Could it be—"

"No. She had ID in her backpack. Ukrainian."

Yusuf starts up the car and lets his head fall back against the headrest. Jessica sighs again.

"This is so goddamn grim," she says.

"It sure is. Who knows? Maybe we'll get to investigate her too."

"Or only her, unless we come up with something more concrete on these bloggers. A body is always a body, but a missing person is nothing more than a missing person."

As Yusuf backs the car out of the white rectangle painted on the street, Jessica turns to him. But then her eyes look past him, to the front door of Lisa's building. "Wait."

Yusuf stops the car. "What?"

Jessica points at the columns of names and numbers next to the door. "Didn't that older gentleman say the buzzer had just been fixed?"

"Yup."

"Do you think it might have been broken last Wednesday?"

"Maybe. So what?"

"The Japanese man would have had to call Lisa to get in."

12

Yusuf pulls up to the red light and turns the music up a notch.

The deliciously lazy beat of SMC Hoodrats' "Lahden Sininen" kicks in, but Jessica doesn't start bopping her head. On rare occasions, one of Yusuf's songs gets her going, but his playlists are usually too deep for her taste. Yusuf's Spotify mixes are chock-full of music that hasn't been played to death on commercial-radio hit lists. And it's not all Finnish rap either; there's plenty of room for punk and progressive gems. When the song gets to the chorus, she says: "Put on something poppier."

"Do it yourself."

"Your car."

Yusuf grunts. "Exactly."

The light turns green, and they join the long lines of cars crawling down the four-lane street past Sibelius Park. Yusuf glances over at the monument to the famous composer, the tourists mobbing it. The buses that chauffeured them here are presumably parked over on Merikannontie and will be continuing on to Temppeliaukio Church. A homeless man sits on a park bench closer to the road, the leafless branches dancing overhead in time with the gusts of wind.

Yusuf looks at Jessica, who has also turned toward the monument. The truth is, she's gazing blankly out the window, indifferent to what she sees. It's what she always does during investigations: locks her reflective gaze on the world passing by, looks through the window into what is perhaps another reality until she catches hold of some fresh idea. Jessica reads the world by observing it attentively and at length. Yusuf thinks it's the most attractive thing about her.

But Jessica isn't saying much today; she just turns to the windshield and sighs deeply.

"You doing OK?" Yusuf asks.

Jessica frowns. "How do you mean?"

Yusuf doesn't have an answer at the ready. He feverishly tries to think of something to say that won't sound condescending. That's one thing Jessica cannot stand: the patronizing is-everything-OK? quiz.

At that moment, Yusuf's phone rings through the car's speakers. The little screen on the dash reads *Nina Ruska*. Yusuf shoots Jessica a questioning look and, when there's no change in her expression, answers.

"Hey, Nina."

"Hey, did I catch you in a bad spot?" Nina's voice is calm but joyless, a perfect reflection of the prevailing mood in the unit these days.

"Nah. We're in the car."

"Am I on speakerphone?"

Yusuf gulps and shoots another glance at Jessica. Relations between the two women haven't been exactly collegial since it came out that Jessica had a short affair, or more like a couple nights' stand, with Mikael—a colleague who also happened to be Nina's boyfriend at the time. The fact that Mikael eventually turned out to be part of the murderous cult didn't make any difference—it was a betrayal all the same.

"Yup," he says, pinching his lips together.

No further greetings appear to be in store until Jessica eventually folds her arms across her chest and closes her eyes: "I'm here too."

But her body language clearly says Yusuf can handle the rest of the conversation.

After a moment's silence, Nina says through the speaker: "Hellu assigned me to the case."

"The Instagram case?"

"Yup."

"But . . . wasn't a body found at Aurinkolahti today?"

"So what? Are you saying you guys don't need me?"

"Of course not." Yusuf downshifts so violently the gearbox lets out a nasty crunch. It's an ingrained habit Jessica frequently remarks on. "I just assumed Hellu would throw everyone available at it."

"Well, I'm on this case, at least for now," Nina says.

Jessica and Yusuf can hear fingers tapping at a keyboard and indistinct hacking in the background, the latter presumably emanating from Rasmus' dry throat. It's incredible how the chronically cold-ridden, prepubescent thirty-four-year-old still catches every day-care bug on the planet.

"Good." Yusuf coughs into his fist. "That's great."

He feels like an intermediary stepping in to break up a catfight. Why should he have to put up with this? He didn't screw anyone's boyfriend. As a matter of fact, it's been months since he screwed anyone.

"Anyway, I just got preliminary tele data and payment methods for both missing persons," Nina continues.

"Let's have it."

"First off: according to the base station data, Nervander dropped by the Phoenix. He also tried to call Yamamoto a bunch of times between six oh one and seven thirty-two p.m. And then both phones were powered off between around two and three thirty Sunday morning. Network-based positioning puts Yamamoto's phone in Kamppi, at the Phoenix, at that time."

"What about Nervander's?"

"The last signal from Jason Nervander's phone was picked up at two oh four a.m. in Vuosaari. Now all we have to figure out is what he was doing on the other side of town."

"After that?"

"Nothing. Yamamoto's card was run the last time at one twenty-three a.m. at the Phoenix. Nervander swiped his card at the grocery store on the ground level of his building at twelve sixteen p.m."

"OK. Thanks, Nina. We're just on our way to the Phoenix to take a look at the CCTV footage. The GM said at least one bouncer remembers seeing Lisa and Jason that night." Yusuf shoots Jessica another glance. Two fire engines race through the intersection, sirens and horns blaring. "Do you have a complete list there of the calls they made or received that evening?"

"Not yet. Rasse will get it to me soon."

"Will you please pass it on the second you get it? There might be something interesting there."

"As soon as I get to my computer."

By the time Jessica utters a quiet thanks, Nina has already ended the call.

A moment passes without either Jessica or Yusuf speaking. The wet asphalt ignites the arsenal of orange roadwork lights in the next lane, and they storm the car. Behind the construction vehicles, a massive drill attached at the tip of a huge hydraulic arm chews through the street as if it's crusty bread. Most of the workmen are standing around the machines in apparent idleness. *Come on, guys—at least finish one stretch of road before you take your smoke break.*

"One works; the rest supervise." Several cars are nudging their way in from the lane blocked by the roadwork. When Yusuf's comment doesn't immediately land, he says: "Jessica?"

"What?"

"It'll be fine. Nina just needs a little—"

Jessica looks at Yusuf and unexpectedly blurts: "Why did you and Anna break up?"

"What does that have to do with this?"

"You never told me."

"I'm not sure I want to talk about it. At least not right now."

Jessica turns back to the orange lights. "So let's forget about Nina and Anna and focus on the case."

Yusuf pulls up in front of the Tavastia nightclub on Urho Kekkosen katu. Jessica opens the door before the car has even stopped moving.

"In a rush?" Yusuf asks, yanking up the hand brake.

"Clock's ticking."

Yusuf steps out of the car, wallet in hand. "You go ahead; I'll catch up with you. I'm going to pop into the store to buy some smokes."

"Don't be long."

Yusuf takes off in the opposite direction at a lazy jog.

Jessica shoves her hands deep into her coat pockets and crosses the street to stand in front of the doors of the shopping center at the corner. She opens the glass doors and enters the warm vestibule to wait for Yusuf.

A bus emits a powerful hydraulic hiss as it approaches the nearby stop.

And then she notices it—the slumped, vaguely eerie figure at the bus stop, like a scarecrow plunked down in a field. Jessica's heart skips a beat. For a split second, she imagines she sees something she has seen too many times before: as the figure raises its gaze from the wet asphalt, long, curving horns seem to sprout from its head. Then the stopping bus blocks her view, and when it pulls away again a moment later, the figure is gone.

Jessica scans the bus as it passes, but she doesn't see a single passenger inside.

13

Helena Lappi opens up the app on her phone that packages the data gathered by her activity tracker in a digestible format. She has been biohacking her body for six months now and seen improvement in many areas requiring attention: her sleeping rhythm is more sensible, and the recovery level that appears every morning has gradually climbed the scale from yellow to green. But her damned HRV remains unusually low, and it's driving her crazy.

"Good morning, Helena." Deputy Police Chief Jens Oranen steps into his office and strides briskly to his desk. The creaking office chair and adjustable electric desk are no different from Hellu's. Oranen's office is larger, and hers is two stories lower, but it's not as if this oversized closet has a view of Central Park either—the New York one, that is. Nor does a cart stocked with premium tawny distillations and crystal stand in the corner. Of course not. Jens Oranen of the dark hair and strong jaw simply happens to resemble Don Draper from *Mad Men*. And yet there's an atrophied, gray quality to the deputy chief, not to his hair but his skin, that somehow lends the impression his best days are behind him. Maybe it's due to the grimness and grief a superintendent working in serious crimes subjects himself to over the years. Without his snazzy blue uniform—and particularly now, in his slouchy beige sweater and black jeans—Oranen is the picture of a father waiting for the evening hockey match to begin, a remote in one fist and a beer in the other.

He speaks without looking up from his phone: "How's it going?"

"We began our investigation of the Yamamoto case today."

Oranen tears his eyes away from his phone. He shoots Hellu a frown and shakes his head. "The papers. Every single one."

"I know."

The deputy chief nods, leans back, and lets the phone slide casually to the desk. "I'm glad your gang is working the case now."

"We just have to hope we can turn something up quickly."

"Exactly."

"Until then, use of the homicide team's resources is a little questionable," Hellu says, unsure why she is pulling the rug out from under her own feet.

"But you don't have many open investigations, do you?"

"No. Except of course the Aurinkolahti woman now."

"Right," Oranen says distractedly, retrieving his phone again. He stares at the device for an agonizing stretch without saying a word.

Hellu shifts in her seat and glances at her watch. "What can I—"

Oranen lowers his phone back to the desk. "Jessica Niemi."

Hellu's heart skips a beat. "What about her?"

Oranen leans back again and casts a long pensive look at Hellu. He's like a surgeon unsure how to inform his patient he left a pair of scissors in her stomach, which he has since sewn up. Finally he asks: "How do you and Niemi get along?"

"Perfectly well. Of course."

Hellu gulps. The truth is, she can't stand Niemi's nasty attitude and is scared to death she won't be able to rein her subordinate in—which is why Hellu has to lie through her teeth now. Her predecessor Erne Mikson knew Jessica through and through, managed her impulses and brought out the best in her. If Hellu doesn't do the same, she will compare poorly to Mikson in everyone's eyes, and the Estonian bull downed by substance abuse will laugh in his grave every time the impertinent Ms. Niemi questions the authority Hellu has worked her butt off to earn.

Oranen continues probing: "Of course?"

Hellu clarifies as confidently as possible: "I just mean . . . I don't have a problem with Niemi. Why?"

Oranen grunts as if he knows full well Hellu is dissembling.

"Listen. I don't know her well. . . . She's an exceptionally good police officer. Really damn good at investigating homicides. A complicated character, I've heard. But the best are often a bit eccentric. She shows initiative, is smart, and on top of everything else is a team player. Her colleagues seem to have a lot of respect for her."

Hellu settles for a tentative nod. Jessica Niemi feels like a movie the critics adore but Hellu herself can't stand.

Excruciating seconds pass; Oranen appears to be carefully framing what he is about to say.

Suddenly Hellu is overwhelmed by curiosity. "What is this about?"

The deputy chief looks at her intently; the answer loiters at his full lips. "I've been considering for a long time whether or not to share this with you, at least so soon. But because you're the new boss . . . because you haven't had a chance to make friends with anyone yet, I assume you won't leak this to anyone on your team."

"Of course not."

"A hell of a lot has happened this year. In your unit specifically. And how should I put this? Through an unbelievable series of twists and turns, I have been made privy to rather sensitive information. While the NBI was trying to get a handle on the occult murders of last spring, the whole witch thing, Mikael Kaariniemi's employment, and why Jessica Niemi was at the center of it all—"

"What information?" Hellu interjects. Why is the deputy police chief forcing her to beg and whine like a six-year-old at a candy store?

And then Oranen blurts it out in a single rapid exhalation: "Due to her medical history, it's unclear whether Jessica Niemi should be a police officer."

Hellu feels her pulse accelerate—and her HRV decrease. "Unclear whether . . . What do you mean?"

"This material is, of course, classified. The documents are presumably authentic, even though the information they contain has never been entered into the database. I doubt there's any trace in Niemi's medical records."

Hellu's brow furrows and her lips draw into a firm line. "What exactly are we talking about here?"

"Listen, Hellu. I want to stress that this is all absolutely confidential. We need to advance delicately, and if and when we decide to take action, we need to develop a sound strategy. Otherwise the whole thing will blow up in our faces. And we don't want that, do we?"

"Of course not, but—"

"You know the Security Police conduct a basic investigation of all applicants to the Police College."

"Sure."

"Well, for a couple of weeks now, I've been looking into this discreetly. I requested a second investigation on Niemi, and it turns out that quite a bit of material was either unintentionally or intentionally omitted from the Security Police report delivered in 2007. Material that wouldn't have necessarily prevented Niemi from applying, but that wouldn't have looked very good on paper. And Erne Mikson played a sizable role in this. At the time, he had one foot in the Security Police, and he wanted to clear the path for Niemi."

"Did Mikson cover up old crimes?" Hellu asks, sounding more hopeful than she'd like.

Oranen shakes his head. "No crimes; something else. You're about to have a chance to familiarize yourself with everything." He pushes a file across the desk. "The cherry on top, the strangest thing . . ." The deputy chief looks uneasy and annoyed. "Years ago, Jessica Niemi was evaluated for a psychiatric condition."

Hellu is simultaneously shocked and jubilant. Finally! A weapon she can use against Niemi. "A psychiatric . . . What condition?"

"Some sort of schizophrenia."

14

NINA RUSKA HEARS the sirens wailing over the line as she lowers the phone from her ear. She touches the red receiver icon and Yusuf's name vanishes from the screen. She glances across her desk at Rasmus, who is hard at work—and hacking into his fist as if a hair ball is caught in his throat. Now that she thinks about it, Rasmus, who on the cusp of middle age still lives with his parents, has mentioned cats—how all three of them have their different personalities and preferences.

"You have a cold?" Nina asks, twisting the cap of her water bottle.

"No. Why?" Rasmus says quietly.

Maybe Rasmus really did sleep with a cat's tail in his mouth. Nina eyes him, then shakes her head. "Never mind."

"Was that Yusuf?"

"Yup. They were headed over to check out the CCTV footage at the Phoenix."

"OK," Rasmus says, before slumping behind his computer screen once again.

Nina shuts her eyes, leans forward, and lets her fingertips sink into her neck muscles. She can still feel Saturday night's shenanigans in her body. Last week was extremely abnormal in that Nina didn't go to the gym a single time. Instead, she dropped by the pub after work—on three nights, no less. In a way, it was a distorted mirror image of her usual routine, the difference being that her athletic exertions were once a daily event. Nor did she go overboard every night: a couple pints on Wednesday, a few on Thursday. Saturday's half dozen beers chased with a few shots of mint liquor had given her the courage to climb into a cab with a good-looking doctor who ultimately lost his nerve, shamefacedly shoving a wedding band on his left ring finger at Nina's front door. *I can't do this to Minna.*

Super. Great. I'm thrilled you figured it out at my doorstep. Take your bad conscience and get the fuck out of here.

"Nina?" She's roused from her thoughts by Rasmus' soft voice. The hacking has stopped.

"What?" As she answers, the big swig she just took from the bottle goes down her windpipe, and now it's her turn to have a coughing fit.

Rasmus adjusts his glasses. "I'm reading Jami Harjula's description of the area where the body was found. It says here the woman wasn't wearing any outerwear. There are no obvious signs of violence, and she had been in the water at most a few days."

"What does that have to do with—," Nina says, hacking into her fist. The water in her windpipe makes Nina think about drowning. The desperation you must feel when you can't cough up the water, when it forces its way into your lungs and pushes the oxygen out. Presumably that's what happened to the woman from Aurinkolahti. What an awful way to die.

"Rasse, I thought you were supposed to focus on *this* case?" Nina's eyes narrow as her compulsive hawking eases. "Let the Boy Scout handle her."

"But I can't help thinking about the backpack—"

"The backpack?"

"The woman's ID was in her backpack. She had it on when she was found."

"So?"

"Well, she wasn't wearing a coat. But she had a backpack on. Don't you find that curious, considering the temperature is hovering around freezing?"

Nina wipes her teary eyes with the heel of her thumb. "Curious? Yes. Our problem? No."

"Why would someone end up in the sea in November with a backpack on, but no coat?"

"Maybe she fell from the deck of a cruise ship."

"I already checked the passenger lists of the major carriers . . . and with the Border Guard—"

"Rasse . . ." Nina is pleading now; she doesn't have the energy to go back and forth with him. There's more than enough to chew in the Yamamoto and Nervander disappearances.

But Rasmus clearly has no intention of giving up. "Her name doesn't appear anywhere. Furthermore, the disappearance of a passenger—from any vessel, small or large—would have been reported to the police. And if we look at the routes of passenger ships off the coast of Helsinki, we can eliminate that possibility. The body was in good condition when it was found and—"

Nina shoots Rasmus the icy look she uses to silence men who aren't particularly self-assured or smooth, men like Rasmus. "Come on, Rasse, I thought your hands were full with Akifumi's Instagram."

"They are, but—"

"But what?"

"It says here she was wearing knee socks, a lavender miniskirt, a dress shirt, and a tie."

"So what?"

But now Nina realizes the perpetual uncertainty on Rasmus' face has given way to determination. He's looking at her as if she's missing something incredibly elementary. "What are you trying to tell me, Rasse?"

"Knee socks, a white dress shirt, a short lavender skirt, and a tie. And a pink backpack." Rasmus shifts his computer to the side, and now Nina has a clearer view of him. The dandruff that has accumulated on the shoulders of his sweater is surprisingly visible from a distance of a couple of meters.

Then Nina finally grasps what he's driving at. "Goddamn it, Rasse. Are you saying—"

"It's like she's straight out of a manga comic."

15

JESSICA HEARS CLINKING behind her and steps aside. A tattooed woman passes, pushing a hand truck stacked with crates of booze. It's only lunchtime, but preparations for the upcoming night are well under way. The employees' chatter echoes in the empty nightclub; the bottles create a wall of sound as they clank from the crates to the refrigerators humming hungrily beneath the bar.

"This way," the black-haired man in jeans and a sweater says in English, opening a door marked STAFF ONLY. The nightclub's middle-aged general manager—based on the accent, an American—introduced himself a moment earlier with a self-deprecating James Bond shtick: *Dominis. Frank Dominis.*

"You guys know how to use these?" he asks, sweeping long curls back from his forehead.

Jessica casts a quick glance around the room: it's overflowing with receipts and folders; the sole desk is home to a computer and several monitors. Pushed up against the wall is a cheap black leather sofa that, under a black light, would probably be as spotted as a leopard. Staff quarters are notorious for having seen and suffered much: dozens of clubbers have doubtless spread their legs in this room in exchange for VIP entry.

Yusuf steps past Jessica and seats himself at the desk. "I'm pretty sure we can handle it."

"You set the time frame here and choose the camera here. We have two at the front door, one in the elevator, one at the coat check, one at the bar—"

Yusuf gives Dominis a get-lost smile. "Thanks, Frank. I think I'll manage."

"Absolutely, Detectives."

Dominis folds his arms across his chest and smiles enigmatically at Jessica. His eyes are intense and probing, and he doesn't let his pupils wander from Jessica's face. He's too experienced a Casanova to devour a woman's body with his eyes, to reveal his agenda too soon. Dominis is clearly a man whose superficial finesse is carefully calculated—and, for that reason, disarmingly straightforward. "You look really familiar," he says. "Do you ever come here?"

Jessica feels an air current stirred by the ceiling fan's blades ruffle her hair. She replies coldly: "No."

But the truth is, she doesn't mind the banter. Dominis has a little Hank Moody from *Californication* in him: the years spent at the heart of late-night action have endowed him with a certain man-of-the-world charisma. Despite the serious nature of the meeting, he seems harmless, fun.

"I could swear I've seen you here," Dominis insists.

"Maybe you did. Ten years ago," Jessica says neutrally as Yusuf starts opening the video files.

"Or why not next weekend?" Dominis chuckles, revealing straight, not perfectly white teeth. "Or ten years from now? Things change."

Then Jessica sees it: in some ways, he's like a dandified, extroverted version of Erne. "I understood we'd be able to talk to the bouncer."

"Sahib," Dominis says softly, nodding toward the open door, where a big guy in an oversized hoodie and sweats has appeared, as if by magic.

"Sahib Alem," the bouncer says, extending a hand to Jessica.

As she shakes it, Jessica takes in Alem's paradoxical appearance: a shaved head, a boxer's cauliflower ears, and tender, intellectual eyes. His massive paw takes her hand gingerly, as if he's afraid of hurting her.

"Detective Niemi," she says before releasing the hand.

"Frank asked me to come in."

Jessica glances at the GM and Yusuf, who is concentrating on the computer screen. The room is getting a little cramped for all four of them.

"I appreciate it." Jessica nods toward the floor-to-ceiling windows and the glazed terrace beyond. "Why don't we go out there?"

Dominis tells them to let him know if they need anything and heads across the nightclub. As she strolls toward the windows, Jessica casts a final glance over her shoulder at the club's manager as he dives behind the bar with the rest of the staff.

ALEM PULLS A metal case from his pocket and lights up a cigarette. Jessica catches a whiff of butane before the lighter snaps shut and disappears into a pocket of the loose sweats. The sequence of movements has been honed by perhaps thousands of repetitions, a smoker's simple but elegant choreography.

"You know Lisa Yamamoto," Jessica says.

"I wouldn't say I know her. But I know who she is. From working here."

"Does she come here often?"

Alem takes a drag from his cigarette. "I've worked the door here for almost five years. Every weekend. How would I put it? Lisa used to come more often. A little less recently. If at all. I guess everything gets old after a while." He exhales smoke toward the infrared heaters at the ceiling, where it dissipates in a reddish-tinted haze.

"But you saw her Saturday?" Jessica says.

"Yup."

"Tell me in your own words."

"About Lisa?"

"Kex Maces' party. About that night. Did you see or hear anything out of the ordinary that could be related to the fact that Lisa hasn't been seen since?"

As Alem takes another long drag of his cigarette, Jessica notices the tattoos on his hand and knuckles. The tobacco smoke wafting through the air and the citrus aftershave carry her back through the years to a time long ago. Tattoos. She remembers seeing them at close proximity, lying facedown on the bed as she experienced an earth-shattering orgasm. And later, soul-rending anguish. But the hand that brought her glorious pleasure followed by unthinkable pain didn't belong to a bouncer named Sahib Alem; it belonged to someone totally different, in a different life. To someone who met his end in the back room of a concert venue in Venice. Jessica shuts her eyes for a moment, and the memory evaporates as quickly as it formed.

"Did I see anything out of the ordinary . . . ? Not really." Alem trains his gaze above the rooftops. "Lisa came to the party alone and left at last call."

"Did she leave alone?"

"Hard to say; I probably had a line of a hundred people waiting for their coats. I vaguely remember her claiming her stuff, but I couldn't tell you who she was with."

"Were you at the coat check all night?"

"Pretty much. I made a couple rounds of the dance floor. At the end of the night, I woke up a guy who passed out on the couch over there."

"So you have no memory of who she might have been hanging out with that night?"

Alem grunts and slips his thumbs into the pockets of his sweats, the cigarette still smoking in his fingers. *"Impossible."* He pronounces the word the French way. "But I'm sure you'll see something on the camera footage. At least whether she left alone or with someone else."

Jessica fingers the notepad in her coat pocket. So far Alem hasn't told her anything worth writing down.

"Do you know Jason Nervander?" Jessica asks.

Alem grunts again. "Same as with Lisa. Don't know him. But I know who he is."

"And he was here at the party on Saturday?"

"No."

Jessica shoots the bouncer a quizzical look. "He wasn't? I understood from your GM that you'd seen him here."

"I did," Alem says. He puts out his cigarette by rolling it in a waist-high ashtray, then rubs his hands together as if that will get rid of the ingrained smell. "Jason wasn't at the party because I wouldn't let him in. At the beginning of the shift, I was given a list of names where I marked down everyone who showed up. I asked anyone I didn't recognize their name. The instructions from Kex's record company were clear: they only get in if their name is on the list. No exceptions made. Not even for the president, not even for Fintelligens."

"So Jason Nervander wasn't on the list?"

Alem shakes his head. "No, he wasn't on the list."

"But he tried to get in?"

Alem sighs and turns to Jessica, arms folded across his chest. "He stood right over there, whining about how he knows Kex and Frank and Greta Thunberg. I told him, tough luck. The list is the list."

"Did Jason think his name was on the list?" Jessica takes hold of the railing with one hand. Rain has begun pattering on the terrace's glass roof.

Alem shrugs. "I guess. But I don't know why he did."

"What do you mean?"

"Social media celebrity, sure. But he's in a totally different genre from Kex's crew. Those guys have zero respect for Jason. So it would have been pretty weird if he'd been invited to the drop, even for PR. And he knew it. Definitely."

"What time did Jason try to get in?"

Alem shoves his hands back into his pockets and raises his chin almost imperceptibly. It's as if he is showing Jessica his most street-credible pose. "It'll be on the coat check cam. I'd say an hour, hour and a half after the party started. Maybe seven thirty?"

"And he left without a fuss when you told him he wasn't getting in?"

"He bitched for a minute, tried to call someone a couple of times, yelled, told me, Kex, and Frank to fuck off. Then he got in the elevator, and I haven't seen him since." Alem glances at the watch poking out from under his sleeve. It's stainless steel, massive, and tacky.

"Did Jason mention Lisa or ask anything about her?"

Alem shakes his head and coughs into his fist.

The rain starts coming down harder, and the wind wails against the glass. Jessica's eyes follow a bird flying past the terrace until it disappears from view. Off the radar. Just like Lisa and Jason, who were both here only a few days ago and are now God knows where. Jason probably called Lisa from the coat check. He was desperate to talk to her, maybe to ask her to get his name on the list. But Lisa didn't want to pick up. And now they're both missing.

"You know, you might be the last one who saw Jason Nervander before he went missing," Jessica says.

Alem shrugs, hands buried in the pockets of his sweats. "Yeah. That's deep," he says. "But the list is the list. Grown man, he should be able to take care of himself. I'm not planning on losing any sleep over him."

Jessica is roused from her thoughts by a drumming on the window. It's Yusuf, gesturing for her to come in. And the look on his face is one she hasn't seen for a long time: he is eager. Excited.

"WHAT IS IT?" Jessica says. Alem holds the terrace door for her as if he is on the clock and Jessica is a guest entering the club.

"Come take a look." Yusuf strides determinedly toward the GM's office with Jessica in tow. Dance music is playing from the speakers now, but at nowhere near the deafening volume of when the club is open. Yusuf hustles up to the desk and grabs the mouse. Jessica leans in behind him. A window opens up, showing black-and-white footage shot from overhead.

"This footage is from the main room, toward the front of the dance floor."

"OK."

Yusuf points at a man standing at the windows. "You see this guy? He was one of the first to arrive. The bouncer took his name and crossed it off the list. He's the only guest who didn't step up to the Spider's Web wall to be photographed, even when he was ushered over."

"OK, so he may be Asian. But he's a lot older than Akifumi."

Yusuf zooms in on the grainy image. "I never said I thought it was Akifumi."

"Who, then?" Jessica asks, biting at a hangnail. "The guy who bought the painting from Lisa?"

"Exactly. Check this out," Yusuf says excitedly. He fast-forwards through the video, and the minutes at the bottom of the screen race past like seconds.

"You see that? Almost forty-five minutes have passed, and he hasn't budged. The bar is filling up; people are mingling and moving around.

But this guy is parked at the window, literally like a statue, except for maybe glancing at his phone a few times. He clearly doesn't know anybody. No one approaches him to say hello."

"He's waiting," Jessica says.

"Exactly. And then . . . look." The man in the black-and-white footage pulls his phone from his pocket, taps at it, and raises it to his ear. The clock at the bottom of the screen reads 18:41:12. "He's calling someone, but his mouth stays shut."

"Because whoever it is doesn't answer."

"Right. He waits for a second, ends the call, and puts the phone back in his pocket. And here—" Yusuf smoothly brings up the footage from the coat check cam. "Lisa is dropping off her stuff at the coat check. And glances at her phone."

"And the time is—"

"18:41:18. I don't think there's any doubt. He tried to call Lisa."

"And she didn't answer."

"Maybe she didn't know he was waiting for her inside. That she would run into him in a second anyway. Whether or not she wanted to."

Once more, Yusuf brings up the footage of the poker-faced man standing at the window. Despite the less-than-ideal resolution, his face is surprisingly easy to make out. It looks as if it has been snipped from a painting and pasted into one with a totally different sensibility.

"Fast-forward to when Lisa enters the room," Jessica says.

Yusuf clicks fast-forward, and the time at the bottom of the screen sprints off again. A moment later, he and Jessica see Lisa appear in a stunning dress. Yusuf dials it back to normal play. In the footage, Lisa briefly chats to a middle-aged woman with a photographer standing behind her. A reporter. Then she pauses to hug someone. Eventually she steps up to the photo wall alone. Flashes blaze as she poses for the photographers.

Yusuf points at the man, who is still standing in the same spot, a dozen or so meters from the photo wall. "See how he stares at her?"

"Like some damn zombie," Jessica whispers. "Or phantom."

"A phantom," Yusuf repeats softly. "You said it."

Lisa gets her hands on some champagne and scans the room.

"Now watch this."

The camera doesn't show Lisa's eyes, but as she turns to the window, her body language reveals that she has spotted and recognized the man.

"His patience has been rewarded," Yusuf says quietly.

For a second, Lisa and the man just look at each other. Then a gaggle of young women swarms Lisa, forming a wall between her and the window. One of them grabs Lisa by the wrist, and it looks like she's being dragged into the sea of clubgoers. Lisa shoots the man one last look before disappearing from the screen. And then the man steps out of view too.

"OK. They recognized each other," Jessica says.

"Clearly."

"So? What happened afterward?"

"I need to watch the tapes for the whole night. Maybe they talk to each other at some point."

Jessica pats Yusuf on the shoulder. "Start from the end. The coat check. See who Lisa leaves with. And whether our phantom leaves at the same time—or maybe even with her."

"This is gonna take a sec."

"Then it takes a sec. I'll call Rasse and ask him for Lisa's call data. I'm especially interested in the number that placed a call to Lisa's phone at twenty to seven that night."

"Let's hope it's not a burner he dumped in the nearest trash." Yusuf stretches his arms before continuing: "And then we need a copy of the guest list."

Jessica steps over to the door of the GM's office and watches the bouncer with the wide stance light another cigarette on the terrace.

"I'm sure that won't be a problem," she murmurs, then catches herself smiling. "The list is the list."

18

ALEM SETS A stapled sheaf of paper down on the counter. The names, several hundred in all, are listed in two columns. Frank Dominis has come by once to ask how things are going and stress the need for absolute confidentiality when it comes to the guest list.

"You guys want something to drink?" Alem says, circling around behind the bar. Jessica glances at the hallway leading to the coat check and the curtains, where Dominis is talking to a young woman tattooed from head to toe. Her face appears to suffer from chronic Botox-induced duck face. The way Dominis' fingers graze her shoulder says more than a thousand words.

"Some water, please," Jessica says, and Yusuf doubles the order with a nod.

"So you remember the guy, but you don't remember his name?" Yusuf says. He and Jessica have shown Alem the CCTV recordings from the club and the coat check. He studies the shots of the man intently, as if giving them a second chance.

Jessica feels her phone vibrate. She pulls it out and reads the text message—twice, to make sure she understood correctly. *What the hell?* She has to have a word with Yusuf.

"I remember he was one of the first people to arrive. And it wasn't a Finnish name . . . ," Alem says, grabbing two pint glasses from under the bar and splashing water into them from a long hose.

Jessica shoves the phone back into her pocket. "Did he speak Finnish?"

"Shit, I don't remember. I guess he just said his name. Like almost all the other ones whose names I didn't recognize."

"Aside from Yamamoto, there aren't any Japanese names on the list as far as I can tell," Jessica says a moment later. She sighs deeply, then starts going through the list again from the top.

Yusuf bursts out in an incredulous guffaw. "Wow. That's pretty narrow-minded. He could have a Finnish name."

"Sure. But if he's a second- or third-generation Finn, why didn't he and Lisa speak Finnish at her place," Jessica says after Alem disappears behind the bar, "when he went to commission the painting?"

Yusuf shrugs and takes a swig of water.

"I'm assuming you didn't ask anyone for their ID?" he asks the bouncer, when the latter reappears with a crate of beer.

"Some of them. If I didn't know them and they looked young. But your guy is probably forty."

Jessica frowns. "So you don't remember at all?"

Alem shakes his head and gives her a crooked smile. "It was pretty crowded from the jump. There wasn't much time to think. The routine's pretty simple: say hello, ask for the name, cross it off the list. Take their coat, give them their number. The guests are listed alphabetically by last name." Alem opens himself a can of Coca-Cola Zero. "I guess his name must have been an English one, then."

"There are quite a few of those here," Jessica says, turning back to the stapled sheets of paper. "Take one more look through the entire list and try to remember. We need this guy's name. Cross out the names of any men you know personally. After you're finished, we'll have Dominis do it too. Then we'll see who's left." Jessica turns the list toward Alem and pulls a ballpoint pen from her pocket.

Alem takes a lazy swig of his cola. "OK."

Jessica gently tugs Yusuf by the sleeve of his sweater and steers him toward the terrace doors.

Once they're out of earshot, Yusuf asks: "What's up?"

"Rasmus texted."

"About the call data?"

Jessica glances over Yusuf's shoulder to make sure they're still alone. "No. Listen. He and Nina have found a possible connection between this case and the woman found at Aurinkolahti."

"What?"

"It looks like the Aurinkolahti victim, a twenty-two-year-old Ukrainian woman, was dressed—maybe someone dressed her—in a schoolgirl's uniform."

"Schoolgirl's?"

"Apparently like something straight out of a manga comic."

"What the fuck?"

"Tell me about it. I think the manga woman from Aurinkolahti turns this whole thing into a clear homicide. And that's not all. The location where the body was found is right about where Jason Nervander's phone transmitted its last signal."

Yusuf rubs the crown of his head. "I need a smoke."

Jessica nods toward the terrace. "Go have one."

Jessica gathers her thoughts as she watches Yusuf trudge out to the patio. Then she turns back to the open curtains and the coat check beyond. She sees Dominis standing there staring at her, phone to his ear. Then he ends the call, perhaps a little hastily, smiles at Jessica, and vanishes behind the curtains.

19

HELENA LAPPI PRESSES the round button and the doors close, leaving her alone with her wildly hammering heart. The documents delivered into her care by the deputy chief are clutched to her breast, and she can feel the power within them transfer to her body. If this information is accurate, if Jessica Niemi truly has a personal history of even the mildest psychiatric problems, things are suddenly much simpler. It turns out spoiled, rebellious Sergeant Niemi is psychologically unstable, which explains her unpredictable behavior and offers a superb reason for getting rid of her. Jens Oranen stressed the need for thorough review behind closed doors, and then, if the outcome so dictates, Niemi must be discreetly released from service, without the media catching the slightest whiff that a mental patient carried a pistol and a badge for over a decade. Easier said than done, of course. But from Hellu's perspective, there are no negative outcomes to the scenario: the first possibility is that Niemi is allowed to stay but, because she's afraid of being exposed, she dances along meekly to whatever tune Hellu chooses to play. The second possibility is that Hellu quietly gets rid of Niemi once and for all. And the last possibility, the one the brass fears: a very public termination that gets a lot of press, which would show the somber police headquarters in an unfavorable light but make Hellu look like a welcome whistleblower and demonstrate that the era of Erne Mikson has finally come to an end. Whereas the old windbag swept problems under the rug, Superintendent Lappi blew in like a brisk wind: came, saw, and took action.

The elevator doors part on the third floor, and Hellu strides purposefully toward her office. En route, she hears a low male voice, deepened by a generous dollop of whisky bass, call out behind her, "Excuse me, Helena. . . ."

It's Jami Harjula, the junior detective Hellu sent out to inspect the body of the young woman found at the beach. Of Hellu's new subordinates in Violent Crimes, the tall, gangly Harjula is clearly the most receptive and easiest to manage: he respects authority and, on top of that, is the only one of the investigators on her floor who seems to be turned off by Jessica Niemi. And for that reason alone, Hellu wants to keep him close.

"Harjula." Hellu stops and waits for Harjula to catch up. *Harjula.* Everyone else at work goes by their first name or a nickname, but Jami Harjula goes by his last name alone. Just like in the army, where Hellu was Corporal Lappi to one and all.

"The woman from Aurinkolahti is with S.S." Harjula is referring to the infamous medical examiner Sissi Sarvilinna, who seems almost always to be on duty when the police deliver a body to pathology. The joke on the force is that Sissi Sarvilinna marks murders on her calendar a month in advance so as not to miss a single opportunity to conduct an autopsy.

"OK." Hellu darts a discreet eye at the folder in her arms. The plastic sheath carries within treasure beyond measure, invaluable intelligence. "Anything I should know?"

"Maybe." Harjula brings up something on his phone and hands it to Hellu. "She has a pretty fresh burn tattoo in the crook of her right arm. Dots forming a circle."

"What does it mean?"

"No clue."

Hellu glances at Harjula, then browses through the photos he took at the beach. She pauses on an image in which the entire body is visible. A beautiful young woman lies on the sand, her blond hair braided. The skin isn't bluish, more like pure white. Her schoolgirl uniform consists of a dress shirt, a tie, and a miniskirt. The knee socks cover a bit of the thigh left exposed by the short skirt. Strips of pink fabric loop at either side of the chest, presumably the straps of a backpack. Hellu feels a pang in her breast. Sure, collegial joking about crimes and their victims happens, but seeing photographs of a corpse is always a shock.

"Burn tattoo?" she eventually says. "Could it be some sort of symbol?"

"That's exactly what I was thinking."

"Did you show this to Rasmus Susikoski?" Hellu asks, gauging the subordinate towering above her, hands on his waist. Under the bright fluorescent lights, he literally casts a shadow over her.

"Susikoski? No. Why?"

"The clothes." Hellu hands the phone back. "That missing blogger Niemi's team is tracking down. Lisa Yamamoto. She's a manga artist."

"I'll be damned," Harjula says.

Hellu watches his long, slender fingers hook around the phone. "Right? Inform Niemi you just joined her team."

Harjula looks skeptical, which makes Hellu feel indescribably good. Jami Harjula is clearly an ally. Hellu bestows an almost imperceptible smile on him.

"Let's have Jessica lead the investigation this time, even though you were the first detective on the scene at Aurinkolahti." She glances at her watch. "Don't worry. I'll make sure you have everything you need. And if you run into any trouble, I want you to report to me personally."

20

JESSICA SITS DOWN at the computer and crosses her ankle over her knee. Yusuf is out having a smoke, but the monitor in the GM's office is still on. Jessica takes the mouse and zooms in on the face of the man standing at the windows. She pulls out her phone and, despite the less-than-optimal resolution, snaps a shot of the computer screen. She checks the photo on her phone; hopefully Yusuf can find another angle, one showing the man's face at closer proximity and in greater detail.

Rasmus' name suddenly replaces the face on her phone screen.

"Hey, Rasse."

"Hi. I have all the call data now. The number . . . It starts +81, so it's a Japanese number. It placed calls to and received calls from Yamamoto's number numerous times over a period of a few days."

"What about now? Is the phone on?"

"No. The last time it was on was yesterday. Base station data indicates the most recent signal was at three ten p.m. in Töölö, only three hundred meters from Lisa's apartment."

"Damn it." Jessica grabs a pen from the desk and snatches a sheet of paper from the printer. "When were the calls to Lisa's number placed and vice versa?"

"In addition to the time you gave me . . . at five fifteen and five fifty-six p.m. that same day, Saturday. Lisa didn't answer any of those three calls. But the previous day, Lisa called the number at nine thirty a.m., and the day before that at eight twelve a.m. The last call—or the first, chronologically speaking—was placed to Lisa on November twentieth at five twelve p.m."

"The twentieth . . . That was Wednesday," Jessica mutters, glancing at the calendar hanging on the wall. "Lisa's roommate told us a man who spoke Japanese came to the apartment on Wednesday between five and six p.m."

"The call only lasted five seconds."

"Makes sense. The building's buzzer was broken, so he called Lisa from downstairs. Which makes it likely he's the same guy who appears on the CCTV footage from the nightclub."

"Fantastic," Rasmus says. "I did find out the number is unlisted in Japan. I'm just typing out a request to the authorities in Tokyo. If all goes well, we'll know more about the owner of the subscription and the phone before long."

"Any text messages?"

"Not from this number."

"OK. Ask the mobile service providers for a map of the phone's movements. And send me that call data right away." Jessica is about to hang up, but then she quickly raises the phone back to her ear. "And, hey, Rasse."

"Yes?"

"Good work. Thanks."

Jessica can almost hear Rasmus blushing. "No big deal. Thank Nina too. She—"

Jessica ends the call. *We're not quite there yet.*

She studies the dates and times she jotted down on the sheet of paper. Lisa and the Phantom met on Wednesday. Then Lisa called him on Thursday and Friday. On Saturday, the Phantom tried to reach Lisa, but she didn't take his calls. The fact that the Phantom didn't try to call a single time after Saturday night indicates he knew she wouldn't answer.

Jessica lowers the pen to the desk.

There's a knock at the door, and Jessica looks up to see Sahib Alem standing in the doorway, the stack of papers in his hand.

"There are still a few names neither Frank nor I recognized." He hands the papers to Jessica with one thumb still in the pocket of his sweats. Now Jessica notices the black band on his forefinger, presumably one of those sensor-equipped smart rings that are all the rage. "You should probably call Kex or the people at his record company. You'd think they would know all the guests, or at least recognize their names."

Jessica eyes the papers on her lap. The majority of the guests' names are crossed out. "OK." Her gaze is lowered, but she can feel the bouncer's eyes are still on her. She looks up and answers his stare confidently. "Did you need something else?"

Alem smiles. "Did you?" he growls. "You're the one who wanted me to come in."

"Two people are missing. I'm not sure *wanted* is the best way to put it."

Alem glances at his enormous watch. "Probably not."

Jessica takes in his wrinkle-free tracksuit and spotless white sneakers. He's stylish in his own way, or at least perfectly at home in this casual habitus.

"Keep your phone on," she says.

"Yes, ma'am." Alem drums his fingers against the jamb, then vanishes from the doorway.

A moment later, Yusuf steps up to it, filling the void Alem left behind. The smell of stale cigarettes is replaced by the odor of freshly smoked ones.

"You let him leave?" Yusuf asks, arms folded across his chest.

"There are about ten men on this list we need to check. I'll talk to Maces and, if necessary, his record company."

"*You'll* talk?"

"You stay here and finish watching the tapes. I'll have someone from the station come down and make copies so you can continue at the station if you don't finish up here."

Yusuf shakes his head. But it's not a protest; it's more of a reflex meant to question his choice of profession, not Jessica's authority.

"How's the list looking?" Yusuf asks. Jessica hands him a sheaf of papers, and he curses as he flips through them. "He's not any of these, goddamn it."

"Rasmus just called. The phone number is Japanese."

"Great. Am I wrong in assuming the Japanese authorities haven't gotten around to digging up the owner of the subscription yet?"

"No. But the fact that one of the parties is half Japanese may help expedite the process."

"When can we expect more info?"

Jessica shrugs. As she stands, she steadies herself on the table and is suddenly overtaken by a strange sensation of déjà vu, as if she has been in this office before.

"Are you guys leaving?"

Dominis has appeared in the doorway at Yusuf's side.

"I am; Yusuf isn't," Jessica says, pulling on her coat.

Dominis brushes nonexistent lint from his chest. "That's a shame."

"How so?"

"I was hoping it would be the other way around." Then Dominis winks and hurries back to the tattooed woman. Jessica wearily watches him go.

Goddamn. What a player.

21

THE TALL, LEAFLESS trees in Kapteeninpuistikko Park dip their branches to the beat of the wind. A woman on a wooden bench leans over, chiding three little dogs. Their leashes seem to have gotten tangled, and she is anything but pleased.

Jessica opens the door to the restaurant abutting the park and comes face-to-face with a doorman in a dark suit.

Even at lunchtime, leaving your coat at the coat check is mandatory at the Sea Horse, which makes it an unusual restaurant in Helsinki. The spot is exotic in other ways as well: the surrounding neighborhood has grown younger and trendier over the decade, but the restaurant's decor doesn't seem to have changed since the place opened its doors in 1934. As Yusuf once put it, *The Sea Horse is so out that it's in.*

Jessica discreetly flashes her police ID, then passes the doorman without shedding her coat.

Lunch service is at its briskest, and the restaurant is packed. The aroma of the meat loaf laid out at the buffet wafts enticingly into Jessica's nostrils. At the bar, a trayful of Moscow mules is being mixed in copper cups, presumably en route to the group of gentlemen sitting in the first booth.

Jessica makes her way to the rear of the restaurant. There's an open door there; a sign reads BLACK HORSE. The way to the private dining room is guarded by a muscular, tattooed young man sitting at a small table. *Maces' bodyguard.*

He looks up from his newspaper and glances at the ID hanging from Jessica's neck, then gives a patronizing nod, as if Jessica needs his permission to pass.

She stalks by him and into the private dining room.

At the back there's a long table, where a young man in a black hoodie and white jeans sits tapping at his smartphone. When he sees Jessica, he gives her a casual "Hey," sets the phone down on the white tablecloth, and rises to shake her hand. The rapper known as Kex Maces has gotten so much media attention in recent years that his face is recognizable to every Finn. Even so, his voice is different from what Jessica remembers; it's not the one he uses to spit lyrics, or even the one he uses when speaking on radio or television.

Jessica introduces herself and cracks her wallet and her ID for the artist's perusal.

"Tim Taussi," he says, which is a polite gesture. Jessica has always found celebrities who don't bother giving their real name irritating.

"That doorman is a beast when it comes to confiscating coats." Taussi is smiling; his voice is low and charismatic. "Only a cop could make it this far wearing one."

Jessica takes a seat across from the rapper, who seats himself too.

"Now the whole world knows I'm hanging with Lady Law," he says playfully.

Jessica looks briefly into Taussi's eyes. Despite their superficial cool, there's a restlessness, an exhaustion, there. The black hoodie bears an Oakland Raiders logo; his neck is draped in a thick rope of white gold.

Jessica nods toward the door. "You giving your security guard a coffee break?"

Taussi bursts out laughing. "My homey. I asked him to step out so we could talk in private."

"Nice to have homeys." The sarcasm in Jessica's tone scrubs away Taussi's glibness.

Jessica eyes the rapper. Angular face, strong jaw. Bright blue eyes that look treacherously trustworthy. He's both guy next door and man of the world. Kex Maces is unusual among Finnish celebrities in that he has consciously elevated himself above his fellow mortals. His image has been cribbed from international stardom from the start: the drivers, the bodyguards, the helicopters. According to the tabloids, he flew his friends to Stockholm on a private jet last year to see Eminem in concert. And yet, up close, he doesn't radiate the star power of a pop icon. He seems like a pretty average guy, one who's presumably hungover after days of partying.

"Thanks for meeting me on such short notice," Jessica says, crossing her ankle over her knee.

"I'd like to ask you a couple of questions about Lisa Yamamoto," she says.

When Taussi hears the name, he instantly drops the playfulness. "Man, I have no idea where she is. Fucking wack."

Someone starts pouring glass bottles and jars into the recycling bin outside the large window, and the noise is deafening. It lasts only a minute, but the sound of breaking glass continues ringing in Jessica's ears.

"Tell me about Saturday night, your record launch. Did you talk to Lisa?"

Taussi frowns and looks out the window. "Yeah. We must have. We're buds. But if you're asking if she said anything that would explain . . ." He shakes his head. "Nah, I don't remember anything like that."

"You guys had an after-party here. Upstairs, at your place."

"Yeah, we came here straight from the Phoenix."

"Was Lisa there?"

Tim's gaze sails from the window to the ceiling, then to Jessica, and eventually to his knuckles, which he is stroking with the fingers of his other hand. A gold Day-Date glitters on his hairless wrist.

"Man, to be honest, I'm not sure."

"You're not sure?"

"I was hella lit. There were maybe twenty of us. . . . Nah, I don't think she was with us. 'Cause I thought about it when I read she was missing. And I talked to some friends about who was at my spot. No one remembered seeing her."

"Would you do me a favor and get me a list of everyone who attended your after-party? I need to be sure whether or not Lisa continued her night at this address."

"Aight. But I'm ninety-five percent sure she wasn't here. At least not for long."

Jessica taps at her phone to open a magnified screenshot from the CCTV footage, then turns her phone so Taussi can see it. "Do you know who this is?"

Taussi gazes intently at the Phantom's image. Animated cries carry through the wall; apparently the Moscow mules arrived safely at their destination.

"Nah," he finally says.

"Do you remember seeing him?"

"Where? At the drop party? Nah . . ."

Taussi's bafflement seems genuine. The Phantom was one of the first people to arrive, but he refused to take a photo with Kex Maces. The artist himself spent the first forty-five minutes at the photo wall, and the nightclub filled up with guests over that time. It's more than plausible Kex and the Phantom didn't exchange so much as a glance.

"OK." Jessica unzips her coat a little, pulls out a slim sheaf of papers from her breast pocket, and sets it down on the table. "I'd like you to take a look at the names that haven't been crossed out."

Taussi quickly shuffles through the papers. His silenced phone is bombarded by a steady barrage of texts. Jessica can't help reflecting that being the center of the universe could easily turn someone into an asshole.

"Aight," Taussi says, looking up at Jessica. "What about them?"

"You know all of them?"

"Yeah. Every one."

Jessica grunts in surprise. How the hell can that be possible? Yusuf said the security cam footage clearly shows Alem marking the Phantom's arrival on the guest list. And yet his is not one of the names on the list. Someone has to be lying.

"And none of them are this guy?" Jessica presses her finger to the phone screen. She has to ask the question multiple times; more often than not, investigative police work consists of reminding people, nudging them toward trivial details that are easy to miss unless someone forces them to look.

"Like I said, I have no idea who that dude is. He's most definitely none of those names." Taussi glances at his watch.

"OK." Jessica does her best to conceal her frustration. She flips through the three sheets of the guest list to make sure Taussi didn't miss anything. But everything is disappointingly unambiguous; his statement doesn't seem to leave any room for interpretation. Jessica shoves the list back into her pocket.

"What about Jason Nervander?"

Taussi's face darkens. "What about him?"

"Do you have any idea about his movements before he went missing?"

"Man, I haven't seen his punk ass in a long time."

Jessica folds her hands on the table. She remembers Alem's words. *Those guys have zero respect for Jason.* Judging by Taussi's reaction, the assessment appears accurate.

Jessica tilts her head quizzically. "You have something against him?"

Taussi glances at the door, as if to make sure he and Jessica are still alone in the private room. And also to make sure his homey-cum-bodyguard is still at the door.

"Fuck yeah, I do. He treated Lisa like shit."

"In what way?"

Taussi sighs heavily.

Jessica knows talking to the police can be tough, especially when it's about other people's business. Tough and sometimes even dangerous. For some, it's against their principles. But Kex Maces and his music don't represent that socially conscious school of hip-hop that disdains authority and the systems that sustain it. For someone like Kex, who has raked in millions, the police aren't the enemy.

"They used to hang. Maybe a year back. But that little bitch Jason . . ."

Taussi falls silent. Jessica remembers Essi said Jason cheated on Lisa. But in view of Taussi's reputation, the rapper's sitting in judgment on anyone else's moral flexibility strikes Jessica as hypocritical and totally corny.

"He beat her," Taussi says a moment later.

Jessica instantly snaps to attention. Essi didn't say a word about this. "Jason beat up Lisa?"

"Hey, I'm not exactly a saint, aight?" Tim flashes a melancholy smile. "But when Jason got caught cheating and Lisa confronted him about it, he lost it and knocked her around. I guess it happened a few times before they finally split. He burned all his bridges on the scene." Taussi suddenly sounds more like his public rapper persona than himself. Maybe Kex Maces is more than just an artistic name: maybe it's a brazen alter ego that occasionally breaks through the surface, one with strong feelings and a loud voice.

"Did Lisa report him to the police?" Jessica asks, even though she knows she would have already come across any reported abuse or subsequent charges.

Taussi shrugs lazily and shakes his head.

"One last thing." Jessica brings up another image on her phone. It's a screen grab from Facebook: a sunny shot of Olga Belousova, the woman who is lying on an autopsy table as they speak. In the photograph, Olga stands on the deck of a small motorboat wearing a captain's cap. The location stamp indicates the city in the background is Odessa, Ukraine.

"Have you ever seen this woman?" Jessica keeps her eyes nailed to Taussi's face, the way she always does when trying to detect the tiniest hint the person she's questioning isn't giving her everything they know.

This time the negative response comes a hair too quickly, as if Taussi is in a rush to spit out the answer he's settled on in advance.

"Nah," he says, handing the phone back. "Who is she?"

Jessica looks probingly at the rapper, then stands.

"Call if you remember anything. Anything at all. And get me that list, please."

Taussi nods and folds his arms across his chest. Not defiantly; jadedly, perhaps. Jessica steps out of the private dining room to a long, disparaging glare from Kex's homey.

"Good dog," she says, and catches the stupefied reaction out of the corner of her eye.

As she walks past the seated diners toward the front door, Jessica is suddenly convinced Finland's top-selling artist just lied straight to her face.

22

JESSICA WALKS DOWN Kapteeninkatu toward the taxi stand by the park. She often takes taxis when she's in the field alone, or sometimes in the morning to make it to work on time. But she never pulls up in one at the station; doing so would arouse needless suspicion among her colleagues. She already dips into her own funds on occasion to offer sources generous motivation; a few extra fifties in your pocket never hurts when dealing with snitches.

There are times Jessica suffers from a bad conscience for taking advantage of it: her substantial fortune.

Hiding her affluence from her coworkers is damned stressful and a lot of work. Jessica doesn't have a single colleague who knows that her grubby studio apartment in Töölö is merely a facade, that her real home is right next door: a two-story spread ten times the size and jam-packed with antiques and invaluable works of art. That the value of the investments she inherited from her deceased parents once equaled tens of millions of markkas. The figure is even larger now, despite the currency's turning into euros somewhere along the way.

On the rare occasions Jessica has invited her fellow detectives to her apartment for a drink before a night out on the town, she has conscientiously checked to make sure her studio is furnished with all the necessities. She hasn't always succeeded. Yusuf mentioned the stench rising from the bathroom drain one time when the shower hadn't been used in over a month. Since then, Jessica has tried to spend a few hours in the tiny apartment before her guests arrive to ensure it feels lived in to some degree. At times she wonders if there's any point to the charade. Would her colleagues really think differently of her if she revealed she was a millionaire? Would Yusuf break off their friendship if he knew?

Erne was the only one privy to Jessica's background, her family's tragic fate, and her substantial fortune. Erne also knew she was broken. But those secrets were buried with him last April.

Jessica's phone rings.

"Hi," Jessica answers.

It's Yusuf: "Hey, where are you?"

"I just left the Sea Horse. The artist is pretty sure the girl wasn't at his after-party. He also knew all the names left on the list, so the Phantom must have gotten in without being on it."

"Weird. Because the footage specifically shows Alem checking him off the list—"

"I know. You get anything else from the cameras?"

"Lisa and the Phantom chat briefly around eight thirty. A few minutes in the corner of the club, alone. Then he takes off."

"Like, leaves the venue?"

"Yup."

"What about Lisa? Who does she leave with?"

"At last call with the rest of the core crew. It's hard to tell, but the good thing is Narinkkatori Square and Kamppi are like Monaco when it comes to security cameras: not many blind spots. We'll be able to follow her pretty far, at least until—or if—she grabs a cab."

"Call Rasmus and have him request the relevant tapes from the city."

"Sure."

Jessica glances at her watch.

"Yusuf, it's already one o'clock. Let's go pay Olga a visit. Can you be at the lab in fifteen?"

"It'll take me half an hour to get there."

"See you in a bit," Jessica says, and hangs up.

She's about to cross the road, staring at her phone, when someone bumps into her and nearly knocks her over.

"What the . . . ?" Jessica mumbles, and turns toward the person, who keeps on walking like nothing has happened. Now Jessica sees that it's an old lady. She turns her head, enabling Jessica to see the other half of her face. She looks all too familiar, just like . . .

"It cannot be. . . ."

Jessica feels dizzy—she closes her eyes for a moment, and when she opens them again, the old lady has vanished.

23

Sissi Sarvilinna opens the wooden box, fishes out a small transparent packet of honey, and pinches the contents into a mug of steaming water. Then her long fingers dip back into the box, another packet opens, and its contents dissolve in the water too.

Sarvilinna presses the trash bin open with the toe of her wooden clog and drops the empty plastic in with the rest of the waste.

"You get used to everything. Your tolerance increases," Sarvilinna says, stirring her beverage with a teaspoon.

Jessica and Yusuf exchange uncertain glances.

"Honey," Sarvilinna continues in her impassive voice. "One packet used to be plenty. Now I need two. Before long, I'll be craving three."

Jessica nods and smiles tentatively: after her run-in with the old woman, the conversation is a balm to her frazzled nerves. The mundane operation they just witnessed is fully consistent with the medical examiner's gruff, pragmatic brand. Someone else might scoop honey straight from the jar, but that would make it harder to gauge the amount. By filling the wooden box with little packets that probably can't be found at a normal supermarket, Sissi Sarvilinna has once again satisfied her need for absolute control. Maybe she stole them from a serving cart on an airplane or the breakfast buffet at a hotel.

"Do you use honey?" Sarvilinna asks, raising the mug to her lips. Jessica is on the verge of replying, but the medical examiner does it for her: "I always have. Always, ever since I was a child."

It boggles the mind how Sarvilinna can sip, let alone swallow, liquid that was boiling in the electric kettle barely a minute ago.

"But then again, I've always taken it for granted. Honey, I mean—

its perpetual supply. I read not long ago that one bee produces a twelfth of a teaspoon of honey over the course of its lifetime. Can you imagine?" Sarvilinna continues without batting an eye. "So one teaspoon of honey requires a lifetime of effort from twelve bees."

"Pretty wild," Yusuf says.

"Pretty wild?" Sarvilinna says disdainfully before she takes another sip. "One of those packets contains twenty-five grams of honey. I drink hot honey water twice a day and dissolve two packets into each mug, which means I consume a hundred grams of honey per day. Am I right?"

"Math's not my forte, but sounds about right." Jessica slides her hands into her coat pockets. She doesn't recall Sarvilinna ever being this talkative. Nor would she have ever guessed the topic of their first non-work-related conversation would be bees and honey.

"My daily consumption requires two hundred thousand blossom visits, eight thousand kilometers of flying, and the entire lifework of seventy-five honeybees."

"How long do bees—"

"So, should we get down to business?" Sarvilinna says brusquely, as if Jessica and Yusuf were the ones who wanted to talk about bees in the first place. "We don't want to be frittering away the taxpayers' money."

Sarvilinna lowers her mug to her desk, then steps between Yusuf and Jessica and over to the metal table where the body lies under a plastic sheet.

For a moment, no one speaks. Jessica listens to the air-conditioning hum at the ceiling; it keeps the headache-inducing smell of formaldehyde from growing intolerable.

"What do we know?"

"I'm going to have to disappoint you at this stage."

Sarvilinna picks at her teeth with a fingernail, and Jessica frowns.

"Cause of death . . . ," Sarvilinna continues, pulling on her gloves. "In this instance, its determination hasn't been unproblematic. However, diatom analysis indicates she did not die by drowning."

Sarvilinna glances at Jessica, as if to verify whether the investigative lead knows what she's referring to. Jessica does, of course. Developed in Finland, diatom analysis is a surprisingly reliable way of discovering whether a victim drowned or was submerged after death. The basic idea is that if a person dies by drowning, they inhale diatoms—or microalgae—from the water, which then make their way from the respiratory system into the circulatory system. The circulatory system spreads the diatoms throughout the body at lightning speed. During the analysis proper, blood samples are taken from the brain, the lungs, the heart, the liver, and the kidneys. The presence of diatoms in these organs supports a determination of death by drowning. Furthermore, because there are millions of types of diatoms, the analysis also makes it possible to tell whether the victim drowned where they were found.

"So the lungs didn't fill with water until after death?" Jessica says, and Sarvilinna nods.

After a brief pause, the medical examiner continues: "The sole signs of external injury appear at the breastbone and ribs. Little fractures."

"From resuscitation?" Yusuf says.

Sarvilinna flashes an unenthusiastic smile. "Impressive."

She pulls back the plastic sheet. Dark splotches are visible on either side of Olga Belousova's sawn-open and sewn-shut chest. "As you can see, a vigorous attempt at resuscitation was made—not this morning, of course, but before she was submerged."

"Using the correct procedure?" Jessica says.

Sarvilinna shrugs. "Such injuries often occur when extreme pressure is applied to the chest. Even by trained, seasoned professionals. It's impossible to say whether this is the handiwork of an experienced lifesaver or an amateur. One can, of course, assume the resuscitation didn't achieve the desired outcome." Sarvilinna grunts. "Otherwise our friend here would not have shown up at my lab."

Sarvilinna takes her time circling the table, lets her fingers slide across the sheet covering Olga's lower extremities. Jessica has long been of the mind that medical examiners have an unusual relationship to the dead—and it's not characterized by indifference or dispassion, as many seem to believe. Just the opposite: they treat bodies like comrades. As if death doesn't separate us. After all, we're all basically dead anyway; the only thing dividing us is the timing of the end. *We're right behind you, Olga.*

Eventually Sarvilinna continues: "One thing, however, is worth noting: she suffered significant dehydration." She glances at the watch visible at the sleeve of her lab coat. "Not the sort where one has gone without consuming liquids for an extended period, but rapid-onset dehydration. She vomited profusely prior to her death, which is supported by findings in the mouth and esophagus. Initial blood tests show elevated hemoglobin and red cell volumes, which indicates dehydration."

"Vomited profusely . . . So the cause of death is related to something she ate or drank?" Jessica asks softly. The words seem to twist Olga's face into a retch.

"It's likely, because I didn't find any signs of puncture wounds. The stomach contents have been sent to toxicology. As has the blood sample."

"How long—"

A sharp look from Sarvilinna cuts Yusuf's question short. "The results will come when they come." She seems to be trying to establish eye contact with someone at the rear of the room. And then suddenly, as if catching hold of a distant memory, she blurts: "Your name is Yusuf, isn't it?"

Yusuf nods, hands on hips. "Yusuf Pepple."

"Listen, Yusuf Pepple, could you please fetch me my hot honey water? The mug containing it, I mean."

Yusuf shoots Sarvilinna an incredulous look, then hooks a questioning thumb in the direction from which the three of them approached the deceased.

"If you would be so kind. I don't like fumbling around with these gloves on."

Yusuf turns to fetch the mug.

Jessica nods at the crook of the deceased's arm. "What about those?"

"First-degree burns. There's no doubt. Surely a painful procedure if she was conscious. I took biopsies of the burned tissue; they may tell us something. Perhaps contain traces of the material used to produce the burn marks."

Yusuf returns, mug in hand, and passes the honey water to Sarvilinna, who smiles in gratitude. "Thank you, Yusuf Pepple. Now have a look at this." Sarvilinna touches the uneven skin around the burns with her gloved fingertips. "Something happened to the skin the burns alone do not account for. An inflammatory response, I presume."

"What might have caused it?"

"A substance that made its way into the wounds, for instance."

"Introduced into them?" Jessica asks.

Sarvilinna takes a sip, swirls the sweet water around her mouth, and shrugs. "Patience, Niemi. We'll learn more from toxicology."

"Is there anything else?"

Sarvilinna tenderly lifts the white fingers of the dead woman. "There's some discoloration on the fingers. Bits of black gunk—presumably the same substance—were extracted from under the nails and sent to the lab. It might tell us something. Or it might not."

"What about time of death?"

"I'd say she's been dead for three to four days."

Jessica counts silently. Olga died late Saturday night or early Sunday morning. Jason Nervander was apparently in the vicinity at the time of death.

"Do you have any idea when we might be able to expect results?" Yusuf says.

Sarvilinna's face brightens in an unexpected, impenetrable smile. "I have a two-week vacation starting Friday." She drains her mug. "Bali. They say it's gorgeous. In any case, I'd like to get these results before I leave, so I'll put some pressure on the lab to hurry things along. For some reason, this case intrigues me. Not least of all due to her clothing and those burn marks. Ugh, such a mystery."

"Great." Jessica glances at her watch. She has a hard time imagining the concrete gray medical examiner anywhere sunny. Sissi Sarvilinna is the type who would bring rain clouds to the Sahara.

Sarvilinna removes her gloves and walks over to the chrome washbasin. She tosses her gloves in the trash, looks around, and shakes her head before adjusting the green hood protecting her bun.

Sissi Sarvilinna is tall and slim, beautiful in a classic if slightly intimidating way, but her sharply drawn white features don't give off the slightest hint of sexual energy. "I don't remember the last time I took a two-week vacation," she says, rubbing her hands together. "What you smell here in this room, death . . . I grew numb to it long ago. But two weeks away from this place, and I'm afraid I'll contract the occupational disease of medical examiners: *desire cadaveris*."

"What's that?"

Sarvilinna once more reveals her teeth, which are firmly planted in enormous lavender-tinged gums. "Longing for the dead."

24

RASMUS SUSIKOSKI TAKES off his glasses and looks at his blurry reflection in the men's room mirror. He rubs the sides of his nose with his thumb tips, feels the uneven edge of the nasal bone, which was deformed during a one-sided scuffle that took place in grade school long ago. Scuffle, dustup, scrap: innocent-sounding attacks that the law treats differently from assault due to the youth of the perpetrators. Rasmus remembers looking up at a fist so many times during his school years he couldn't tell you now who punched him, when, or why, and probably couldn't have at the time. But one thing is certain: Rasmus was generally the cause of his classmates' violent outbursts. They inevitably followed something he said or left unsaid. He offered his opinion when no one asked for it or froze when clarification was sought on some comment he had made. *What did you say, faggot? Give me one good reason why I shouldn't punch your fucking face in right now.*

Rasmus slides his glasses back on and sighs. It's not the crooked nose that makes him ugly. Or to be more exact: it's not the crooked nose *alone* that makes him ugly. His being an ugly and repugnant creature is an incontrovertible fact. Why else would he be living upstairs at his parents' place, in a room where his mother vacuums and strips the sheets every Tuesday?

Every now and then, Rasmus feels like all he would need to strike out on his own is a little poke, a nudge in the back: some sign of support from his father and mother, no matter how imperceptible. But Rasmus' parents don't appear to believe in his potential. It's as if they've always known their son's wings are no good, that the second he ventured from the nest he would plummet to the rocks and break his neck. *It's a hard world, Rasse. Really hard. What's wrong with living here?*

Intermittently, and usually at night, Rasmus wakes up to reality: he wants to cry, scream into the pillow, take his lightsaber and sweep all the stupid plastic crap from the shelves to the floor. Then, after cleaning up the mess, vacuuming the floor and mopping it squeaky clean, he would pack his bags and move as far away as possible. The other side of Helsinki at least.

But that's not who Rasmus Susikoski is. He has always done what his mommy and daddy have told him to, gritted his teeth, and stifled his rage. It's been impressed on him that few things in life go the way you want, that complaining won't get you much of anywhere. *Just let them hit you, Rasse. Let them laugh. Deep down they're jealous, and as long as you know that, you'll be fine.*

Jealous of what, exactly?

The bathroom door opens, and Rasmus almost jumps out of his skin. A tall, thin, and altogether odd-looking man steps in. Narrow fingers dangle from plate-sized hands that could envelop a basketball.

Rasmus nods. Jami Harjula heads for a stall, then abruptly turns back. "Hey, Susikoski." He steps up to Rasmus, hands on his waist. "What's your take on this manga case?"

Rasmus raises his chin, then lowers it again as the tall man's intense gaze grows too oppressive. "I don't really like—"

Harjula interrupts him with a gentle laugh. "I mean, do you think the cases are related?"

Rasmus grabs a few paper towels from the dispenser and dries his fingers meticulously. The pipes inside the wall thunder as a toilet flushes in the ladies' room. He gulps and says: "Yes. I don't think there's any question."

Harjula studies Rasmus for a second and nods. Not critically. Not skeptically. He's intrigued, perhaps. Harjula is one of the few male investigators in the unit who don't use their physical presence to take up all the space in the station's corridors. Harjula's ego, such as it is, is probably more evident at home, off the clock. Even so, Rasmus feels like a puny bug in the taller man's presence.

"Is there anything that supports your conclusion, other than what Olga Belousova was wearing when she was found?" Harjula asks.

"You'll find out in the meeting." Rasmus tosses the crumpled toweling in the trash. "Fifteen minutes from now."

He grabs the door handle, but Harjula steps sideways, blocking his way.

"OK, all right. I'm not saying I don't believe it. Or, how would I know . . . ?" Harjula must notice his incursion was unnecessary, because he takes a step backward. "But I was really going to ask you about something totally different. About someone you know a lot better than I do."

"Who?"

"Niemi."

Rasmus feels his pulse accelerate. "Jessica?"

"Yeah. Jessica. I've never really worked with her before—"

"Under her." The second he mumbles the words, Rasmus regrets it. He sees himself in the schoolyard, outside the portables, blurting stupid things in earshot of classmates a head taller than him.

But Jami Harjula doesn't hit Rasmus, of course; he simply grunts good-naturedly. "Exactly, under her. This time." Harjula scratches his chin. "And apparently you've worked *under* her on more than one case."

"Yes . . ."

"I was just thinking—"

Rasmus shoots a questioning look at Harjula. *Whatever scheme you're coming up with to get rid of Jessica, you can count me out.*

Harjula draws his mouth into a firm line and glances at the stall doors to make sure the two of them are alone. He opens his lips to ask another question, but can't bring himself to. In the end, he laughs and shakes his head.

"Forget it, Susikoski. My bad. I'm just jabbering. See you in the meeting."

25

JESSICA CLIMBS THE stairs two at a time, the way she did when she was a kid, and feels the lactic acid in her thighs as she approaches the fourth-floor landing. Thirty-four isn't old, but it isn't young either. She should probably take a break from running; it's been getting a little manic lately. Especially when there's a chance of coming across Christmas Eve–obsessed freaks in the woods who want to strangle her between shots of salt-licorice schnapps.

Jessica bounds up the last few stairs and opens the door to the Violent Crimes Unit with her key card.

She passes workstations where officers sit, badges around their necks. Someone's phone is ringing nonstop. Dozens of fingers flit across keyboards. Usually there's a cluster of people gathered behind someone's back to ponder some work-related matter or maybe laugh at a funny cat video. But there isn't a single watercooler meeting in the open-plan office today; everyone is parked at their own computers, raising their chins in acknowledgment as Jessica passes. Jessica has only recently become conscious of the fact that almost everyone notices and greets her. She's always known she attracts attention, despite her best efforts to melt into the drab mass. But the unusual interest shown her by male colleagues isn't due to some striking feature of her appearance. It's her way of carrying herself that's unintentionally arresting. *Broish but cute.* What the dummies don't realize is she knows exactly what they say when the locker room door shuts.

But for some reason, she doesn't inspire negative emotions among female colleagues the way the recipients of collective male attention might at some workplaces. OK, so it's becoming apparent Hellu hates her, and as for Nina—well, Nina has a superb reason to dislike Jessica.

Speak of the devils.

Hellu taps at her smartwatch as Jessica walks up. "It's ten past." Nina, who has been standing at Hellu's side, slips into the conference room without saying a word.

"We came straight—"

"Where's Yusuf?"

"Parking in the garage. He'll be here in just a sec."

Hellu waves Jessica in. "We're starting without him."

The conference room is as depressing as ever, but if Jessica had entered with her eyes shut, she might have mistaken it for a small-town bakery: coffee and sweet rolls are always served at an investigation kickoff, and today is no exception. But no bell tinkles as she arrives; no warm voice welcomes her in. There's no turning Helena Lappi into a sweet little lady standing behind a glass case with a paper bag in her hand.

Jessica doesn't direct her greeting at anyone in particular: "Hey."

Rasmus, Nina, and Harjula are already at the table. Hellu seats herself between the latter two and reaches for a cardamom roll.

What a team. It's like stepping into the lion's den.

"Hi," Rasmus replies in his typical manner, which reminds Jessica of a mole that crawled underground to escape a nuclear blast. But at the moment Rasmus' presence is more precious than gold. Of the quartet sitting across the table, he's the only one who likes Jessica. Or tries hard to amid all the turbulence.

As far as Jami Harjula goes, Jessica figures he's fine as a police officer and human being, a family man with a good head on his shoulders. For whatever reason, their personal chemistries have just never gelled. She sometimes gets the sense Harjula sees through her, rightly guesses something's off about her. Erne warned her years ago: *Watch your step with Harjula, Jessica. He's like a smart, well-trained dog. He's not bad, but he's only loyal to one master: the system.*

And Nina Ruska is the warm, lovely person whose trust Jessica shattered last spring by screwing her boyfriend, Mikael. Twice. His turning out to be a cold-blooded criminal, a real rotten apple on the force, doesn't change the fact Nina loved him.

Jessica can't quite wrap her head around it herself: how could she have forgotten Nina's kind, smiling face? The bottles of homemade limoncello Nina gave everyone last Christmas, the painstakingly crafted cards of native winter scenes worked in Nina's meticulous hand? Jessica has saved both but can't bring herself to look at either. She would love to taste the lemon liquor waiting in the icebox, but she knows she doesn't deserve it.

And yet. She was never close to Nina, and no one was supposed to find out. Things were supposed to go on the way they always had. For Jessica it was just meaningless sex, the sort of impulsive lust that steamrolls all rational thought and is often followed by regret, especially when others' feelings end up in the firing line. Of course the whole thing was wrong and she shouldn't have done it; there's no arguing that. But it's too late to do anything about it now.

Jessica folds her arms across her chest, hears the rustle of the paper bag, and watches the cardamom rolls disappear into greedy gobs.

And then of course there's Helena Lappi: the wicked stepmother from a Disney film, Annie Wilkes and Cersei Lannister rolled into one. A woman who seems as protective and jealous of her status as if it were a new relationship and she didn't realize her blended family included a stepdaughter until it was too late. That's where the real problem lies: Erne's ghost is everywhere. The respect and longing for Erne are so palpable at HQ that the boots that need filling must feel enormous. The Estonian legend permeates everything: the framed photograph in the unit's place of honor, next to the drinking fountain; the clever quips that live on; the jokes and memories team members still associate with them. The tears shed now and again. They are all reminders of Erne, an example of a leader who, on the force of his charisma and humanity, rises above the rest and achieves an almost saintlike status at the workplace.

The team wants to remember; Hellu wants them to forget. And there's one particularly goading reminder of Erne that Hellu cannot escape: Jessica Niemi. As long as the daughter is still living in the mansion, the wicked stepmother will never have what she wants: the unit's undivided attention and respect.

"Sorry I'm late," Yusuf says behind Jessica's back.

The door closes, and Jessica feels her anxiety dissipate. Luckily she has Yusuf. Her last real ally in the unit and truest friend.

26

HELLU LEANS BACK and eyes the room as if it is a bank vault whose robbery she has been planning for ages. Jessica generally feels she has a pretty good read on her boss. But then there are the moments Hellu just stares ahead with that inscrutable look on her face. There has been more than one such moment today.

"All right. Everyone's here." Hellu presses her smartwatch. Could she actually be measuring her pulse during their meeting?

Hellu rubs the sugar from her fingertips onto a small paper plate and leans forward in her chair. Her jaws munch languidly on cardamom roll, then suddenly stop. "Take a look around. This is the investigative team. We'll bring in extra hands as needed."

Jami Harjula is the only one who actually glances at the others because Hellu told them to. *OK, add another item to the characterization, right after "good head on his shoulders": unapologetic brownnoser.*

Hellu shoots Jessica a pointed look. "Jessica is investigative lead."

Jessica nods. A few minutes ago, in Yusuf's car, the possibility crossed her mind that Hellu would choose to assign investigative responsibility to Harjula instead. After all, he'd been pegged to investigate the Aurinkolahti woman, the only body caught up in this whole web. But now that Jessica thinks about it, it's obvious: Hellu has tapped her as a lightning rod. As investigative lead, Jessica has a higher chance of failing. Of making a mistake, of looking stupid, even if the case is solved. And Hellu wants it solved, of course; it's only the second homicide during her tenure as superintendent. But who knows? Maybe the plan is to sacrifice Jessica on the side. So the case isn't solved *thanks to* Jessica, but *in spite of* her.

"As you all know by now, we're dealing with an unusual investigation here in that it ties together three separate cases, only one of which we know for a fact involves a death. That death doesn't necessarily involve a crime either. Of the three, two—the disappearances of Lisa Yamamoto and Jason Nervander—are presumably related, but for now the connection to Olga Belousova, the woman found at Aurinkolahti, is circumstantial, based solely on the clothing the deceased was wearing at the time of discovery. Nevertheless, I decided to combine these two investigations because as a principle I don't believe in coincidence."

Hellu opens her laptop. The projector starts humming, and a moment later a square of light appears on the white wall.

"Base station data indicates that Jason Nervander was at Aurinkolahti at the estimated time of Belousova's death. In addition, tech found a piece of manga art at Lisa Yamamoto's home depicting a figure whose getup is an exact match with the clothes the Ukrainian woman was wearing."

Hellu clicks up a slide showing the two images side by side: Lisa's manga drawing, and Olga Belousova lying on her back on the frozen sand. The outfits in both images are identical, down to the backpacks.

"Oh my," Rasmus exclaims.

"Whether Lisa Yamamoto drew Olga Belousova or Belousova's clothing inspired Lisa's drawing remains unclear at this point. Which came first, the chicken or the egg?"

"But the girl in the drawing isn't Olga Belousova," Yusuf says.

Everyone toggles their eyes between the images, as if to remind themselves the women look different.

"No. But I doubt that changes anything." Hellu slides the cardamom rolls across the table toward Harjula.

Polly, have a cracker and say something to make your boss look good.

Jessica feels a glare boring into her forehead and glances at Nina, who quickly turns to the pictures projected on the wall. The conference room is like a keg of gunpowder that would blow to smithereens at the scratch of a match.

"All right, Jessica. The floor is yours," Hellu says, before fiddling with her smartwatch again.

Jessica sits up straighter in her chair and folds her hands on the table. "First of all, Rasse, I'd like to ask you to report on whether the CCTV footage shows where Lisa headed after leaving the Phoenix."

"She left on foot, in the direction of the Kamppi metro station. The cameras show her getting into the taxi queue for a while. But she got tired of waiting and started walking down Runeberginkatu, in the direction of Töölö."

"Toward home? Is she visible on other cameras along the way?"

"That gets a little tricky. There aren't many cameras in Etu-Töölö," Rasmus says.

"Keep looking. OK?"

Jessica now addresses the group: "When it comes to suspects: at this point, we have clear evidence that this"—Jessica slides a printout to the center of the table—"man of Asian descent, approximately forty-five years old, average height and build, uses strong aftershave, is mixed up in the disappearance of Lisa Yamamoto, if not more."

Hellu seems amused. "Strong aftershave? Where did this information come from?"

"From Essi, Lisa's roommate. He visited Lisa at the apartment, and Essi said the smell lingered after he left."

Harjula chuckles. "So now all we need is a trained Labrador retriever."

"We don't have any reference scents," Jessica replies drily.

Harjula's tone is defensive: "It was a joke."

Jessica doesn't so much as glance his way. "This man, who for the time being we are calling the Phantom, commissioned a painting of a lighthouse from Lisa, which she presumably delivered before she disappeared. Based on a sketch found in Lisa's room, the image is almost identical to the photograph posted on Instagram this morning. The sole difference is there's also a girl in Lisa's painting, whereas in the photograph there's only a lighthouse."

"Who's the girl in the painting?" Hellu asks.

"We don't know."

For a moment, the only sounds in the room are coffee slurping and pastry munching. Jessica continues: "When it comes to Olga Belousova, Yusuf and I just came from seeing Sarvilinna." She pulls a folded printout from her pocket. "The only thing we know at this point is that Belousova did not die by drowning. Sarvilinna said she died either late Saturday night or early Sunday morning."

"Cause of death?"

"Indeterminate, as of preliminary postmortem. Some internal injuries were discovered, but not severe enough to cause death. Two broken ribs and a fractured sternum."

"Had she been beaten?" Hellu asks.

"Sarvilinna didn't think so. The trauma appears more congruent with classic resuscitation injuries. Apparently an attempt was made to save Olga's life by applying significant pressure to her chest, and the procedure presumably caused the fractures."

"Someone who didn't know what they were doing," Harjula says.

Jessica shakes her head. "Resuscitation injuries are extremely common. Similar injuries appear in two out of three cadavers on which resuscitation was attempted. Not only in instances when the first aid was administered by amateurs, but by nonemergency hospital personnel as well. I suppose emergency room staff has a lot more experience, which is why injuries are rarer there."

"So her heart stopped and she died?" Harjula says.

Yusuf smiles. "Don't we all die when our heart stops?"

"For God's sake," Harjula says, but he doesn't lose his tranquil bovine-Buddha cool. "I mean, the victim showed no visible signs of violence. She just suddenly stopped breathing."

"Yup." Jessica bites her lip. "That's what the attempted resuscitation would indicate. But Sarvilinna wasn't able to tell us *why* her heart stopped yet."

"Overdose. Then someone panicked and dumped the body in the sea," Harjula pronounces serenely, tearing into his cardamom roll.

"That's theoretically possible, of course. But if that's the case, the drug was ingested. Olga didn't shoot up; her veins are intact. No traces of cocaine or other snorted substances were found in the mucous membranes of the nose or mouth. If there are any toxins in her stomach, that will come out during the toxicological analysis. She had vomited though. A lot. Sarvilinna is looking into that as well."

"When?" Hellu asks.

"When what?"

"When can we expect the toxicological analysis?"

"*As ASAP as possible,*" Jessica says.

Yusuf chuckles discreetly, but no one else laughs. The phrase is from the repertoire of tension lighteners Yusuf has developed for use in the field. *Very important VIP. RIP in peace.* And so on.

Hellu clicks up the next slide: a close-up of the black dots in the crook of Belousova's arm.

"Now, this is interesting," Jessica says.

"What am I looking at?" Hellu asks.

"At first glance, it looked like a tattoo. But the marks were created by burning the skin, not injecting ink."

Harjula looks pleased with himself; evidently he feels some sort of pride at having been the first to notice the burn marks.

"Some symbol? A gang emblem?" Hellu asks.

"It's not out of the question. In any event, the marks have been positioned with care; the little circles form a symmetrical ring. In that sense, it's like a carefully designed and executed tattoo. There's nothing random about the pattern. Burning the skin with a cigarette, for instance, wouldn't leave such clean marks. Sarvilinna suspects they were created with some sort of solid substance, perhaps heated metal."

"Did the medical examiner say anything about when the burn marks were made?" Harjula asks.

Jessica nods. "They're pretty fresh. Presumably made the day of her death."

"So they have to be somehow related to why she died," Hellu says.

"That's likely."

"Harjula," Hellu says, turning to the man at her side, "everything supports your theory."

Harjula beams.

"Theory? Care to share it with the rest of us?" Jessica says, pinching a hangnail from her thumb.

Harjula smiles a mild but vaguely smug smile and shrugs. "Well, this is just a guess. . . . It came to me the second I saw the body on the beach. What if Belousova is a human-trafficking victim who was smuggled into the country? Maybe she was drugged and branded."

"That would explain the overdose," Hellu says.

"As of yet, there is no indication she overdosed. Just the opposite." Jessica's quiet reminder to the room calls down a murderous look from her boss.

"What if she was transported by boat to one of the marinas near Aurinkolahti or somewhere else in eastern Helsinki . . . ? If the boat was a little bigger, it could have come all the way from Estonia." Harjula takes a swig of coffee. "The sea was rough on Saturday night, but not impossible. I checked."

"Go on," Hellu says encouragingly.

"The burn marks are fresh, so she was probably branded or otherwise tortured on the boat. Then something went wrong and they dumped the body overboard."

"The burns are tidy," Jessica says. "I don't think it would be possible to do that to anyone who's conscious and struggling. Even if she were being held down by four big men."

A momentary silence falls over the room.

"So she was unconscious. Like I said, she was drugged—"

Jessica's tone is intended as a challenge to Harjula: "And then she just died out of the blue?"

"What if some asshole living in a big house on the water ordered a woman who wasn't just dressed in a sexy outfit but was also unconscious?" Yusuf says.

Nina looks up, eyes focused. "The sleeping-princess syndrome." All eyes turn to her; this is the first peep out of her this meeting. "It's a real thing. Somnophilia."

"Wanting to bang someone who's already unconscious?" Yusuf discreetly eyes Hellu to see how she reacts to the coarse language. Erne would have reprimanded him with a shake of the head.

But Hellu appears unfazed by the language and fully engaged with Nina's explanation. "Like screwing a doll?" For some reason, the words sound truly filthy coming from her mouth, as if your grandmother or Mary Poppins said a dirty word.

Nina shakes her head. "No, doll diddlers are different. Many somnophiliacs get off on having sex with a living being—against their will of course. But to my understanding, the turn-on is the other party being out of it and unable to resist."

"So basically a rapist who wants to make things easy on himself," Yusuf says.

"Technically speaking, yes." Jessica feels like Nina is directing her words to everyone in the room but her. "And as you can probably guess, somnophilia can take on new forms and easily evolve into necrophilia, which I presume is a more familiar concept to everyone."

A silence follows, which Rasmus breaks by pumping coffee from the thermos.

Harjula looks at Jessica. "Did Olga suffer any sexual violence?"

Jessica holds up the printout. "No. I probably would have mentioned that already." Her lazy cadence elicits a grunt from Harjula.

"All right, this is clearly a fruitful direction to explore," Hellu says. But Jessica shakes her head.

Hellu glares at Jessica as if she means to ignore the silent protest and end the meeting, then folds her hands on the table and clicks her tongue several times. "Apparently Niemi disagrees."

"There are holes in the theory." Jessica discreetly glances at her hand. The hangnail is bleeding.

Despite the frustration in his tone, Harjula doesn't raise his voice: "What do you mean?"

"Don't get me wrong; I think most of that scenario works. A beautiful young woman smuggled from Eastern Europe to Finland dressed like a schoolgirl. She's drugged on the boat, so it's easy for the client to rape her either at the client's home, to which the victim is carried straight from the dock, or else the rape takes place on the boat. But they screw up the dosage and the woman stops breathing. The traffickers choke, then panic, administer first aid on the boat, and, when she doesn't recover, dump her body into the sea under cover of darkness. The body floats for a bit, then drifts toward the nearest beach, propelled by the strong wind." Jessica takes a deep breath.

"Makes sense," Hellu says. She looks at Harjula, who looks pleased with himself.

"But?" Yusuf says without raising his head. He knows Jessica better than anyone else at the table.

"But," Jessica continues, "in the first place, we don't have any proof the woman was ever on a boat. There were no boats moored at the nearby marina. Secondly, I don't think the bad guys would take a woman they'd branded earlier that night and dump her overboard. They might as well have written a phone number on her forehead the police could call."

"Come on, that's a bit of an exaggeration," Harjula says. "The mark or symbol or brand, whatever it is, is completely unfamiliar to the police and wouldn't automatically lead us to the perpetrators. We still don't have any idea what it means."

"Fine." Jessica clasps her hands behind her neck. "Thirdly, explain to me why Belousova had her passport in her backpack. Aren't victims of human trafficking always stripped of their passports so they can't escape?"

Silence falls over the room again. The projector screwed into the ceiling is new, and its soft purr doesn't dominate the room's acoustics the way the loud thrumming of the old model did. Jessica turns to Hellu, and judging by the look on her boss' face, the low growl setting the tone in the room could just as easily be coming out of her ears.

27

JESSICA HOLDS THE bleeding hangnail under ice-cold water until the flow is wholly stanched. She fills her bottle at the tap, pops a painkiller, and washes it down with a swig of water. The static in the conference room has set her temples throbbing, and she hopes the ibuprofen pressed into white pill form will bring relief.

Jessica studies her reflection: the black hair pulled back in a ponytail, the practically makeup-free face. The budding pimple that has surfaced above her right cheekbone and the scratch running beneath it, presumably a memento of that morning's wrestling match on the jogging path. To top it all off, pain is shooting through the knuckles that laid into that creep's jaw. She really ought to go show her hand to Occupational Health.

The door behind her opens.

"Niemi."

Jessica shuts her eyes and longs for the days she could get away from her boss by going to the bathroom. With Helena Lappi's assumption of her post, this privilege has shifted to the men. Unless Hellu, blinded by power, decides to make the bathrooms on the floor gender-neutral. Then no one will be safe.

"Yeah?" Jessica starts rinsing her hands under warm water.

Hellu is standing behind her, hands on her hips. "What the hell was that?"

"What?"

"Why do you have to be so fucking rude to Harjula?"

Jessica dries her hands on a paper towel and turns around. Hellu is unpleasantly close, maybe even too close, considering Finnish notions of personal space and social distance.

"Rude? I just said what I thought."

"In other words, you were rude, damn it." There's something hilarious about the way Hellu says "fuck" and "damn it." *Was I fucking rude, damn it?*

"Was I? It wasn't intentional."

"I expect you, as investigative lead, to demonstrate a more receptive attitude. From now on I want you to listen to the views of all team members without immediately shooting them down." Hellu's tone is calm but emphatic. "At least Harjula is trying to form an overall picture of things. The same cannot be said of your old team. Apparently some sort of yes-man culture has developed here. Mikson talks. Niemi talks. Occasionally Rasmus mumbles something and Yusuf cracks a stupid joke."

For the second time in under twenty-four hours, Jessica is burning with the desire to show Helena Lappi the true meaning of "rude." Hellu hasn't seen *rude* yet.

But she nods and settles for: "Understood. I'll do better next time. Should we go back and continue?" She tosses the crumpled paper towel in the trash and steps past Hellu toward the door.

"Niemi."

Jessica takes a deep breath and turns to look at her boss.

"I could have made Harjula investigative lead."

So why didn't you, goddamn it?

"I'm aware," Jessica replies.

The two women are standing so close to each other that, for the first time, Jessica spies Hellu's black roots desperately thrusting through the peroxide, as if screaming for attention.

"Don't make me regret that I didn't," Hellu says as she stalks past Jessica and opens the door.

28

JESSICA STEPS INTO the conference room. Hellu is already seated, and Rasmus, Nina, and Harjula are fiddling with their smartphones. Yusuf is at the window, holding the cord for the blinds. It's already growing dark, and the lights from Tripla Mall and the high-rises sprouting around it blaze brightly against the gray sky.

"Sorry about the interruption," Jessica says. The others look up from their devices; Yusuf remains at the window, arms folded across his chest. "I think things will start to clear up when we get more information about the cause of Olga Belousova's death. Until then let's try to find a connection between Olga and Lisa."

"What do you suggest?" Hellu asks. Her tone is pure job interview; Jessica has never felt so alone at work.

She focuses on Rasmus, who is staring at the ceiling, and clears her throat. "Rasse?"

"Yes?"

"You've been looking at Instagram and the photos posted there. Do you have anything to share?"

Rasmus shifts and hides his hands under the table. "Well," he says, then pauses a few seconds for dramatic effect. "I began by looking at the metadata of the lighthouse photo uploaded to Yamamoto's account—"

"In Finnish, please," Yusuf says from his post at the window.

"You want me to explain what *metadata* is?" Rasmus says quietly; he'd probably roll his eyes if he dared. Jessica has never heard anyone snap in such an apologetic tone.

Yusuf nods. "Yes."

"Metadata is descriptive information about a file. For every file uploaded to the Internet or other digital platform, whether image, video, or text, there's a large amount of information available. For photos there's usually all sorts of data, including some less relevant in terms of an investigation: shape, size, resolution, color specifications, copyright. But there's also incredibly useful information, like the exact time the photograph was taken and even the brand and model of device it was taken with."

Rasmus opens the laptop resting on the table before him, taps at it intently in silence, and a moment later the image on the wall changes.

"I understood it was no longer possible to save photographs posted to social media for meta-analysis," Hellu says, demonstrating how well-informed she is. "Instagram, Facebook, and Twitter have blocked the saving of uploaded images for privacy reasons."

Rasmus looks at the superintendent as if this is the most preposterous claim in the world. "*Hampered,* sure. But all you need to do to get around the block is to copy the image's link into a developer tool." Rasmus continues tapping. A moment later, the rear wall of the conference room turns black, and dozens of rows of green text appear there. The sight recalls the MS-DOS operating system Microsoft computers ran on back in the day. Now we're deep in Rasmus' world.

Jessica takes a seat. "So can you see what type of device was used to take the photo of the lighthouse?"

"Yes. Fortunately it's an original photo, not a screenshot." Rasmus points at the digital universe projected on the wall. "Look. '*Device Manufacturer: Apple*' and '*Device Model: iPhone 8.*'"

"Jesus Christ, why didn't you tell us earlier?"

"Because this is as detailed as the information gets," Rasmus says. "Tens of millions of iPhone 8s have been sold around the world. All we know is that the picture was taken with one of them."

"So what fucking good is the information then?" Yusuf says. Rasmus looks deflated, and Yusuf notices. "I'm not trying to be harsh, Rasse. But if we can't pinpoint the specific device—"

"So we can't fish out the MAC code or any other data that would tell us whose device it is?" Jessica says.

"No. But when we get the information from Japan on the Phantom's subscription, we'll also learn his phone model. And if it's an iPhone 8, we can be relatively sure that—"

"The same guy took the photograph," Jessica interjects. "OK. And we can also see up there when the photo was taken."

"Yup. When and where. The time stamp is twenty-eleven-nineteen—in other words, last Wednesday. At eleven twelve a.m., which I find rather interesting."

"How so?" Hellu says.

Rasmus magnifies a row of numerals on the screen.

60° 06′ 34″ N, 25° 24′ 36″ E

"These are the coordinates where the photograph was taken. The Söderskär lighthouse. This indicates the photograph is new, taken specifically for this scheme. At first I was sure it was a photo-bank image or a screenshot. But no. Based on the metadata, the guy who's mixed up in the bloggers' disappearances took this photograph at the lighthouse himself."

A moment of silence falls before Jessica speaks.

"So the picture was taken at eleven twelve a.m. And we know that five hours later, the Phantom marched up to Lisa's door and commissioned a painting based on this photograph."

"Has anyone been in touch with anyone at the lighthouse? They might be able to tell us who visited there last Wednesday," Yusuf says.

A concerned look falls over Rasmus' face. "That's what's so strange. Söderskär is located approximately twenty-eight kilometers east of Helsinki. It would take an hour or so to get there in your average boat. There isn't any scheduled traffic to the island this late in the year."

"So the photographer must have gone to the island in his own boat?"

"And the seas were pretty rough all week," Harjula says.

"We need to figure out whether some boat rental or fishing vessel took someone out there in exchange for payment."

Yusuf's suggestion is met with nods of approval.

"The local police in Itä-Uusimaa can look into that. I'll get in touch with them," Hellu says.

"Wait." Yusuf focuses his eyes on Jessica, then continues, now more keenly: "Is the phone model visible in the CCTV footage from the Phoenix?"

"The image is pretty blurry when I zoom in, but it might give us some indication," Jessica says. "What else from Instagram?"

Rasmus looks her in the eye, which he usually does everything in his power to avoid.

"I found Akifumi."

Jessica pushes her chair back from the table. "What? Why didn't you say so right away?"

"I mean . . . I didn't find him, but I know who the person in the picture is."

"Well?"

"We were wondering why the face looks so weird. Somehow out of proportion with and distinct from the rest of the photo," Rasmus says. "It's because it's a mask. It's a mask of a Social Democratic politician from Japan. I Googled an article that said tens of thousands of masks were made of the party's chair, Akifumi Sato, for a student protest."

"Goddamn it," Yusuf says.

"It's not as if we were counting on getting much out of that picture anyway," Jessica says.

"So that means we're back to thinking the Phantom from the club and possibly Lisa's apartment and the Akifumi who posted the comment to Instagram could easily be one and the same person?" Yusuf asks.

"Yup," Jessica says.

"Great. Let's continue!" Hellu glances at her watch impatiently. "What happens next, Niemi?"

Jessica's thoughts stall for a moment; once again she feels like she was just posed an unexpected question during a job interview. She coughs into her fist to buy some time and looks through her notes.

"We need to talk to Lisa's roommate again. See if she knows anything about Olga. Or if the burn marks on Olga's arm mean anything to her."

Hellu nods approvingly and makes a note of something.

"Yusuf and I already talked to her once, so it would be natural for the two of us to go back," Jessica says to a nod from Yusuf. "Rasmus, you keep working Instagram and the photos. Hopefully Hellu can get you some more hands and eyes if that will make things go faster."

Rasmus nods, takes off his glasses, and rubs the lenses with a black cloth that on inspection proves to be a strip of chamois torn from somewhere.

Jessica's gaze shifts clockwise, skips over Hellu, who is staring intently back at her, and comes to rest on Harjula. "Harjula, you take the reins on Olga's death. I'll ask Sarvilinna to contact you when they know more."

Harjula glances at the superintendent out of the corner of his eye, then nods his agreement. His face has remained calm and composed throughout the meeting. Like a male Mona Lisa who knows something no one else does. *This guy's going to be trouble.*

"Nina," Jessica says. She has reached the trickiest part of the meeting. She and Nina haven't spoken since they both returned from sick leave in April. "We know the least about Jason Nervander's movements. You look into them. And try to find out if Jason was generally violent or just with Lisa."

Nina replies without looking at Jessica: "OK." Her mouth draws into a taut line.

The friction between the two women appears to please Hellu. And no doubt it does.

It's a quarter past two and lunchtime is drawing to a close, but the joint known for its take-out pizza is packed. The decor may be slapdash and heavy on plastic, but the ambience is authentic and hectic, loud exclamations in Turkish carry from the kitchen, and the buffet is replenished with meats hissing like snakes in fry grease. The persistent aromas of garlic, coriander, and sweet tomato permeate the air.

Rasmus and Jessica take seats at a four-person booth at the rear and order kebabs with side salads.

Fifteen minutes before, Jessica spontaneously extended a lunch invitation to Rasmus, who accepted with surprised delight.

"How are things, Rasse?" Jessica says, filling both of their glasses from the water pitcher.

Rasmus seems ill at ease. He eyes the Persian rug on the wall before finally opening his mouth. "Fine."

Jessica grunts sympathetically. "That's good. Things at the unit have been a little abnormal lately."

Rasmus folds his hands on the table. "Yes. They have."

"I hope you feel like . . . like you can do your work in peace. Without anyone breathing down your neck. And I hope you know you're an extremely critical link in the team."

Rasmus looks at Jessica as if they are speaking different languages.

Suddenly Jessica understands how clumsy it is of her to probe Rasmus as if he is a child. Sometimes his reclusion and introversion give the impression that he's incapable of reading situations and emotions. The truth is anything but: you'd be hard-pressed to find a more astute observer at HQ. Which is why he's an irreplaceable member of the team.

"What about you, Jessica? Are you OK?" Rasmus asks in concern, to a weary chuckle from Jessica. "Because if you're worried that"—and now Rasmus lets his gaze wander to the wall so he won't have to meet Jessica's eyes—"that I won't be loyal to you . . ." Rasmus falls silent and shakes his head. "You don't have to worry about that, Jessica."

Jessica lowers her head, ashamed of seeking solace from Rasmus in her insecurity: from a man who knows he occupies a certain neutral position on the team. The lunch's true agenda has just been made embarrassingly plain to Rasmus.

"Besides, Jessica," Rasmus continues, "since when have you cared what they think about you upstairs?"

The server brings bread and tzatziki to the table. Jessica looks at Rasmus and nods almost imperceptibly. She feels like the world has turned on its head: the most self-conscious bachelor in greater Helsinki has just prodded her toward the light, encouraged her to keep her chin up.

She is abashed. "Thanks, Rasse," she says, and sits up straighter.

"Plus," Rasmus continues, and Jessica struggles to recall another instance of him showing such initiative in a social situation, "Jami Harjula. People think he's a good guy. But I think he's a total dick."

Jessica's jaw drops in shock. "Rasmus Susikoski! Did you just call Harjula a dick?"

Rasmus raises a finger to his lips and giggles surreptitiously into his fist. "A total dick."

Jessica wipes the smile from her face and looks around. Three women in business suits and a man in a tie are sitting at the next table. Behind them, four construction workers are chowing down, eyes glued to their smartphones. Neon safety coats are slung over the backs of some of the chairs.

An enormous street sweeper rumbles past the window, and the Middle Eastern music playing from the speakers is momentarily drowned out.

"Do you think we're going to get anything from Akifumi's profile, or that it has anything to do with the case?"

"I don't know, Jessica. But there is one thing I was thinking of mentioning during the meeting . . . an incomplete thought I'm wrestling with."

"What?"

Rasmus tears off a hunk of soft bread and crams it into his mouth. "*Masayoshi*. Justice. What Akifumi wrote on Lisa's picture. I conducted some searches; I wanted to see if it referred to anything in particular. . . . It was basically shooting in the dark, but—"

"You found something?"

"I found a website, masayoshi.fi. It's also some sort of blog."

"Dot fi? A Finnish blog?"

"That's what the domain indicates, of course, but that's not all—the blog is administered by Lisa Yamamoto."

Jessica can feel her fingertips prickle with suspense. "What? Lisa already has a blog linked to her Instagram account."

"But this one is different," Rasmus says, then continues more circumspectly. "There was nothing on the site: no images, no text. Just the usual search function at the side. So it's a blog where nothing has ever been posted. Either that, or . . ."

"Or what?"

"The contents have been deleted."

"Why didn't you say anything about this during the meeting?"

"Because there's something there I don't quite get yet," Rasmus says sheepishly. "Lisa did a surprisingly careful job covering any tracks that would indicate she's the administrator for masayoshi.fi. She hid her IP address, presumably with a Tor network, which in and of itself demands a little deeper initiation into the arcana of computer science."

Jessica leans back in her chair when the server brings their meals to the table. Her long years as an investigator guarantee she understands what Rasmus is telling her. The Tor network is free software that hides its users with layered encryption, or *onion routing,* which is the source of the name: *The Onion Router.* For many, the Tor network evokes hardened criminals—pedophiles or drug or weapons dealers—but in reality there's nothing illegal about downloading or using the software to hide an IP address. Even so, Jessica knows a slew of cases in which Tor provided anonymity for criminal filth.

"Hold up, Rasse," Jessica says as Rasmus reaches for his fork. "So, Lisa has been site administrator and went to a lot of trouble to hide the fact. She erased her tracks."

"Correct."

"So how the hell did you figure out Lisa is behind the site?"

Rasmus flashes a shy smile as he lowers his fork back to the table. An annoying ringtone, a loop of a barking dog, has been playing incessantly behind the counter for over a minute now.

"I'll give you some background. Are you familiar with the activist hacker collective Anonymous?"

Jessica takes a piece of lettuce in her fingers and drops it into her mouth. "Of course."

"In 2011, two Anonymous hackers created an anonymous website in Nuevo Laredo, Mexico, and posted a threat to reveal sensitive information about the local drug cartel. Not long after, they were found dead, hanging from an overpass. And these guys were skilled hackers who had carefully covered their tracks. The cartel would have never been able to fish out information about their identity if they had only . . ."

"If they had only what?"

"If they had only avoided a critical mistake. They wanted to use Google Analytics to monitor traffic to the site. In order to do that, you need an Analytics ID. Now, an Analytics ID can be used to monitor the traffic on multiple sites. Anyway, the cartel dug into the source code of the site where the threat was posted and found the Analytics ID, which one of the hackers had also used on his personal blog. Once you have the ID, you can conduct a reverse search with any reverse search engine and link two apparently unrelated sites to the same source."

"So the cartel had no trouble figuring out the guy's name and what he looked like?"

"And made an example of him and his friends."

"And that's how you found Lisa? Using an Analytics ID?"

Rasmus nods, and his eyes beam with professional pride. "Lisa wanted to monitor the number of visitors to both sites—understandable enough, when you consider that the commodity bloggers sell brands is visibility. But if she wanted to keep the other site a secret, using the same Analytics ID was a mistake. The public website exposed the private one."

Jessica looks at Rasmus and bites into her kebab. Surprisingly peppery. "Do you think this is similar to what happened in Mexico?"

"That someone was looking for the administrator of masayoshi.fi, found Lisa, and did something to her?" Rasmus shrugs. "It's possible. It's the reason I suspect contents were deleted from the site."

"Before Lisa disappeared or after?" Jessica glances up at the chrome lamp shade hanging above the table. The sticker and bar code reveal it to be a mixing bowl from IKEA. Simple, surprisingly functional decor.

"I'm not sure. That's why I decided not to say anything until I had a better idea what it all meant."

Jessica chews on this information in silence. "OK. Thanks, Rasse. You'd better tuck into that kebab now."

30

NINA RUSKA SLIPS her police ID back under her top. She patiently waits for the super to pick out the skeleton key from the rest of the keys on the ring and open the door to Jason Nervander's apartment. When she called the maintenance company, they said they would send the super over, and Nina was expecting to find a heavyset middle-aged man with a mustache, thick-soled safety shoes, and a faded flannel shirt standing in the stairwell. Instead, the door is being opened by a fit female, clearly younger than Nina, with a bunch of keys and the odd tool dangling from the belt looped through her tight jeans. The super's delicate but determined fingers are stained with oil.

"There you go," she says, and her dark eyes smile as she holds the door for Nina, then shuts it behind her.

Nina stands alone in Jason Nervander's entryway and hears the super walk down to the ground floor. A patrol was already sent out this morning, so Nina knows there's nothing dramatic in store: no starvation-enraged Dobermans, brain-splattered walls, or rotting corpses. Nervander presumably hasn't been home since Saturday. Even so, Nina's footsteps are wary as she wanders the empty flat, as if someone might lunge out at any moment. The one-bedroom unit, located on the second floor of a corner building in Kallio, strikes her as cold, ghostly. Curtains have been drawn across the windows, and the yellow light filtering down from the spots is startlingly weak. The home's asceticism is extreme: the white walls are naked, as is the stained hardwood floor. There's a black leather sofa and a TV stand in the living room, along with a big bookcase containing a smattering of hardback books. Stacked boxes of shoes and clothes, presumably sent by partner companies, line the walls. Nina has spent the entire day studying Nervander's social media updates. She has to say, the contrast between Nervander's manicured posts and this grim bachelor pad couldn't be more dramatic. Real reality versus social media reality.

Nina walks up to the bookshelf and scans the covers. Richard Dawkins: *The God Delusion* and *Outgrowing God.* Sam Harris: *Letter to a Christian Nation.* Christopher Hitchens: *God Is Not Great: How Religion Poisons Everything.*

Nina is familiar enough with the works to know they are critiques of religion authored by prominent atheists. As a matter of fact, Nina read one of the Dawkins books—albeit in Finnish—and appreciated the author's logical, pragmatic approach to the subject. In any event, considering how lean Nervander's book collection is, it seems a bit odd that the friend who reported Jason missing is a middle-aged parish pastor. Then again, Nina has friends who don't believe in the police as an institution.

Nina moves on from the books and passes through the kitchen on her way to the bedroom. The bedroom suffers as acutely from cheerlessness as the rest of the apartment. Jason has not nailed up a single painting, and the only things to break the starkness are the colorful boxes piled on the floor and the dark red bedspread covering the tidy bed. Neat rows of right-out-of-the-box skin care and shaving products stand on the desk. It's not that the apartment is messy: the surfaces have been dusted, the boxes neatly stacked. It's just incredibly uncomfortable.

There's a narrow wooden door in the back wall, next to the bed, that must lead to the closet. Nina crosses the room and tests the handle. Locked.

As she releases her grip, her imagination gallops off with her. Did the patrol not check the entire apartment? She holds her breath. The horrific events of last spring well up in her head: being held captive by the cult and almost losing her life. She survived, recovered, and solemnly swore to herself she would never put herself in danger's way like that again. She would never go alone on any assignment that felt even remotely risky. Yet here she is. Alone in a creepy, dark apartment, standing at a locked closet door. With God knows what on the other side.

Nina takes a few steps backward and considers whether she ought to have the super with the tight tush come back. Or call in a patrol. *Fuck.* She peers through the keyhole, then turns around, rummages through the desk, and finds an old-fashioned brass key in one of the drawers. *Too easy.*

She returns to the narrow door, fits the key into the lock, twists, and, after hearing a light click, presses down the handle and pushes. The door creaks ominously. Nina instinctively jumps back and chokes down a scream when she sees the human figure hanging from the ceiling.

"Dear God," she whimpers, believer or not.

31

Yusuf parks in the same spot he parked in earlier in the day. Over the course of the dreary afternoon, the temperature has dipped below freezing, and tiny snowflakes are drifting down now.

"Looks like this spot is reserved for us," Yusuf says. He opens his door, and this time he pulls on his leather jacket.

Jessica steps out of the car and sees Essi, lugging plastic grocery bags, headed their way.

Yusuf lights up a cigarette. "Perfect timing."

"What the hell is taking the telecommunications companies so long to get us that location info?" Jessica says, as she waves at Essi.

"So the Phantom's phone is off now?"

"It was turned off in Taka-Töölö yesterday at three ten p.m."

The smoke spilling from Yusuf's nostrils mingles with the wind and instantly dissipates. "Should we ask the roommate about the other blog?"

"I'm not sure. Somehow I think we need to be really mindful about how we use that information. If we use it at all."

Essi crosses at the crosswalk, and Yusuf approaches her. "Hey, I can take one of those bags for you."

Essi grunts and accepts the offer. She looks more tired, more shocked than she did earlier. Maybe the severity of the situation has gradually grown more concrete.

The three of them walk up to the building. As Essi opens the door, Jessica glances at the new buzzer that has been the topic of so much conversation today.

A moment later, the tiny, almost awkwardly cramped elevator arrives at the third floor, and Essi opens the old-fashioned gate. Yusuf decided to climb the stairs, and the three of them meet at the door to the apartment.

"Everyone is telling me I need to remember to eat. I have, like, zero appetite." Essi slides the key into the dead bolt. Jessica watches her fuss with the sturdy key: evidently Essi hasn't been in the habit of using the dead bolt much, if at all. But circumstances have changed fundamentally since her roommate's mysterious disappearance.

Essi moves on to the regular lock, but the door won't open. "Come on . . . ," she pleads.

Jessica and Yusuf exchange discreet glances.

"I never used to . . ." Essi starts fumbling with the dead bolt again. "I keep this locked all the time now. . . ."

A moment passes as Essi gives the dead bolt another shot. Jessica can't help thinking it was unlocked the whole time, that Essi is so distraught that she left the door unbolted after all.

At long last, the door opens. Essi steps in and lowers her shopping to the floor. "You can leave your shoes on," she says, continuing into the living room.

Jessica and Yusuf leave their coats on and follow Essi. They look around. The pictures have disappeared from the walls, and the living room looks ravaged, stripped.

"They came and took all of Lisa's drawings," Essi says.

Jessica nods. Helena Lappi's order to confiscate all manga art as evidence seems like the action of a totalitarian dictatorship.

"It's only now . . . ," Essi says, hands on her hips, then wipes her eyes. "It's only now that the walls are bare that it feels like Lisa's really gone."

"They'll return the art," Yusuf says in a soft voice. He knows it's cold comfort; the blank walls aren't the cause of Essi's grief.

"I could give a shit about the art." Essi sobs, takes a tissue from the box, and blows her nose. Then she sits down on the sofa and turns her teary eyes toward the detectives.

For a moment, it appears Essi will be able to pull herself together pretty quickly. Then something in her expression shifts. Her sorrow turns to bewilderment and, an instant later, panic. Jessica has seen this before: a young woman's face struck by explosive, overwhelming terror. Essi has just had a horrific insight.

"Oh my God . . . ," she says, lifting her hand to her mouth.

Jessica shoots a glance at Yusuf, who looks both confused and alert. She takes a step toward the couch. "What, Essi? What is it?"

Lisa's roommate is hyperventilating. "He's here . . . ," she whispers.

"Who?" Jessica's fingers instinctively reach for the gun strapped under her arm.

And then she notices it: the saccharine smell that wasn't in the apartment earlier in the day. Aftershave. The Phantom.

In that instant, the door to Lisa's room bursts open, and before anyone can react, a large figure barrels into Yusuf, sending him flying onto the coffee table. The wooden legs give, and the glass tabletop shatters under his weight. The room is filled with the tinkle of breaking glass and Essi's desperate shrieks.

"Stop!" Jessica shouts as the figure dashes through the hall and out the door.

"Catch him, Jessie!" Yusuf yells, heaving himself up from the glass shards and splintered wood. Blood is pulsing from his hand.

Jessica pulls out her gun and lunges into the corridor. She hears footsteps echoing below and flies after them.

"Stop! Stop!" she yells, bounding down the stairs. Through the steel grilles framing the elevator shaft, she catches glimpses of a man in a black coat and brimmed hat advancing with surprising speed toward the ground floor and the main door. Jessica hears him run across the lobby. Hears the downstairs door open. A big dog is barking in one of the second-floor apartments.

Jessica reaches the ground floor, sprints out the door. An old couple is standing there; the man is pushing a walker. They both eye the gun in Jessica's hand fearfully.

"Which way did he go?"

The old woman points toward the corner, and Jessica dashes off in pursuit. She passes the patch of grass and the lone tree and starts running down the flight of granite stairs leading to Topeliuksenkatu. They're slippery, and Jessica's left hand grabs hold of the steel railing bolted to the wall.

I have to catch him. He was looking for—

A sudden blow to the diaphragm knocks the wind out of her. She crumples and slumps to the ground.

She sees a man-sized recess in the wall of granite blocks; the metal door it shelters is scrawled with graffiti. Clever little hiding place. Jessica waits for the kick to the face, the muzzle flash from the gun barrel—whatever it is that's going to put the finishing touch on her farcical pursuit. But neither comes. The dark figure steps over her and vanishes around the corner. Jessica gasps for breath and holds in the vomit, her cheek against the wet asphalt. *Motherfuck me. . . . Two beatdowns in one day.* Then the throbbing pain in her stomach grows overpowering, and bile spews from her esophagus. As she spits out the taste of stomach acid, she hears Yusuf's approaching footsteps.

32

"BDSM," NINA RUSKA says as she parks on Itäinen Papinkatu, just to the west of Kallio Church. "Black rubber. Zipper across the mouth. The works."

"In Nervander's closet?"

Nina thinks she catches an amused note in her boss' voice.

"Yup. On a doll that was handcuffed to the ceiling."

Now Nina hears Hellu actually laugh. "I'm sorry, Nina. But this isn't something you come across every day."

Nina kills the engine. "He had boxes of sadomasochist paraphernalia in there. Magazines, books. It would appear Jason Nervander is a true adept."

"But no sign of anything illegal? Or manga?"

"No. Most of it looked like pretty typical SM stuff. Kinky, but that's about it."

"OK. I'm assuming you haven't told Jessica about this yet?"

"No—"

"I thought not." Hellu continues to sound curiously chipper, as if she was in a splendid mood even before Nina phoned. "It's probably best not to call right away. Jessica and Yusuf are licking their wounds in Töölö at the moment. They took a little beating."

Nina climbs out of the car. "From whom?"

"The Phantom. Don't worry. He got away," Hellu says sarcastically. "Talk to you soon."

Nina frowns to herself. She gazes at the granite edifice designed in the National Romantic style by Lars Sonck and, if memory serves her, built in the early years of the previous century. The towering church is an imposing sight: it stands on the crown of a hill, making it the tallest point in central Helsinki. Nina has lived in the city her entire life, but it's only in recent years that she has started appreciating the beauty of its architecture. Like everywhere else in the world, Helsinki's inhabitants often pass off local splendors with a shrug.

Nina climbs the stone stairs to a landing that wraps around the building, and continues along the curving walk that hugs the facade. The parish offices are located at the end.

She barely has time to glance at the buzzer before the door is opened by a smiling bearded man with a clerical collar visible under his dark red sweater.

"Nikolas Ponsi?"

"Yes. Please come in," he replies, extending a hand. Nina takes it.

Ponsi is trim and rather short, but his handshake is powerful. As a lifelong practitioner of martial arts, Nina has learned to recognize strength hidden inside a deceptively slight shell, and that's exactly what Nikolas Ponsi exudes.

Nina steps inside and follows Ponsi past a few rooms; Nina catches glimpses of parish employees through the open doors. They reach Ponsi's office and he welcomes her in.

"Care for some coffee?" Ponsi asks, gesturing for Nina to take a seat. She shakes her head politely and conducts a quick analysis of the little office. It's tidy and smells of church: old sawdust and empty tar barrels. The odor evokes the musty tomes of libraries and a hymnal comprising a thousand finer-than-fine pages. A wooden sculpture hangs behind Ponsi's desk: Christ on the cross. Although not a believer, Nina has never had anything against attending church. Like many other things, it's a deeply rooted custom. Besides, why would she be opposed to anything that offers hope to people, especially those whose lives have been filled with tribulation?

"Thanks for taking the time to meet with me, Pastor—"

Ponsi raises a finger accompanied by an unctuous smile. "Chaplain."

"Excuse me?"

Ponsi smiles awkwardly. "No, excuse me. I'm splitting hairs, of course, but I'm one of this parish's dedicated pastors, or chaplains. The position requires the completion of an additional pastoral degree." Ponsi laughs incredulously, as if amused by the pettiness and ridiculousness of his boasting. "There I go again, being vain. Just call me Niko, and we should get along just fine."

"Great, Niko," Nina says, sitting on a wooden chair.

Ponsi takes a seat on an ergonomic-looking office chair on the other side of the desk. Nina studies the vicar's round face. The complexion could best be described as being like dirty snow, and the heavy beard covers only some of the pockmarks. The expressive eyes are unusually blue and bright and seem to curve up into a smile with the friendly mouth. As she looks around, her gaze falls on a framed photograph on the wall: a group of people posing with a large LGBTQ sign.

Ponsi coughs into his fist. "That's from last year's Pride. I've been involved in the church's queer advocacy activities for almost ten years now. As a matter of fact, I'm also a trained sexologist, but . . . well, that has nothing to do with this. Excuse me for babbling about myself." Ponsi smiles and sighs, but then his expression darkens. "As you can tell, I'm nervous, although I'm trying to stay positive. Jason might be fine." He folds his hands on the desk as if he is about to pray.

"Positivity is good," Nina says, pulling a notepad from her pocket. "It's absolutely possible Jason will turn up safe and sound."

But the smile doesn't return to Ponsi's face. "Possible but not probable, is that it?" He reaches for a pen resting in its stand as if it's a safety blanket.

Nina looks Ponsi in the eye and waits for the question to dissipate, along with the need to answer it.

"Who is that?" She nods at a black-and-white photo on the wall, primarily because she wants the questioning to start from a blank slate. It's a picture of a handsome young blond man with a medal pinned to the breast of his uniform.

"That," Ponsi begins vigorously, pressing his fingertips together, "is Witold Pilecki. He fought against the Nazi regime as a member of the Secret Polish Army. As far as I know, he was the only person to voluntarily arrange to be imprisoned at Auschwitz as part of a plan to help the resistance take down the Germans. Against all odds, he managed to survive for over two years in that godless place, even building a radio and transmitting intelligence to his fellows outside the camp. Think about it: millions were hauled off against their will to concentration camps to die . . . and Pilecki purposely had himself imprisoned in one to help others."

Nina finds herself surprisingly intrigued; there has clearly been a Pilecki-sized gap in her education. "What happened to him?"

"While at Auschwitz, Pilecki formed a group that was supposed to take over the camp and free the prisoners. But when the moment approached, the Secret Polish Army wasn't able to provide the expected support from outside the gates and the plan went awry. Pilecki had sacrificed his freedom and suffered in vain."

"Did he die at the camp?"

Ponsi chuckles. "This is the incredible part! Pilecki pulled a rabbit out of the hat and escaped from Auschwitz. It was supposed to be impossible but he pulled it off. The story doesn't have a happy ending, however. After the war, the Communists decided Pilecki had been a spy for the Western powers and executed him in the summer of 1948. The epitome of a miscarriage of justice."

"Fascinating story."

"Isn't it though? Now, the reason that photograph is here . . . The picture of some other brave individual could be hanging there just as well; history is full of worthy people who put the common good before their own interests. But for me, Pilecki represents the values and virtues extolled in the Bible. And I can't help but see certain similarities—"

Ponsi smiles enigmatically. For a fleeting moment, the weak light falling through the window puts some color in his pale skin.

"With Jesus?" Nina says.

Ponsi casts a lingering glance at the photograph. "Let's just say the world could use more people like Pilecki."

Nina shifts her gaze to her notes. Time to get down to business. After their little warm-up, Ponsi seems more disposed to answering questions.

"You and Jason are friends?"

Ponsi nods, fingering the pen. "He's originally from Rovaniemi, and when he moved here to Helsinki . . . When would that have been, four years ago?"

Nina checks her notes. "Autumn 2014."

"Right . . . Jason has been active in our youth activities here in the parish. That's how we got to know each other, and we've spent a lot of time together since."

"So you two are close?"

"Very. We see or talk to each other just about every day."

"Do you have any idea where Jason might be?"

Ponsi shakes his head, then sighs listlessly and looks out the window shaded by a large maple.

Nina moves on: "Does anyone come to mind who might wish Jason harm?"

"I've tried to think about that. But no."

"When was the last time you saw Jason?" Nina knows from experience it's best to ask many questions as quickly as possible, without being overbearing.

"Friday."

"Did you notice anything unusual then? Did Jason say anything about his plans for the weekend?"

A cryptic look falls over Ponsi's face. "Jason was a little off that day.

More anxious than usual. He said someone was saying malicious things about him."

"What kinds of malicious things?"

"Someone was lying, spreading rumors about him. But I didn't get the impression it was a particularly serious tiff. What I mean is, judging by that conversation, I don't think it had anything to do with the fact that Jason is missing now. He just felt bad that someone was making things up about him, that's all. He said he would clear it up over the weekend."

"But you never found out what he was talking about, or who he had to clear things up with?"

Ponsi shakes his head. Eventually he says: "Jason mentioned he'd been trying to get in touch with Lisa. But she hadn't answered his calls."

"Did Jason say why he wanted to talk to Lisa?"

The look that flashes across Ponsi's face telegraphs possible regret at having neglected his duties. "I didn't ask."

Nina swallows a few times; her throat feels rough. Hopefully she isn't getting sick. She was supposed to start working out again tonight, after a week of slacking.

She returns her gaze to the crucifix on the wall and remembers the books she spotted in Nervander's apartment. "Is Jason religious?"

Ponsi appears to rouse himself from some sort of reverie. The look on his face says it's not a simple question to answer. "Jason is open to different interpretations of life. Of everything. That's what makes him such interesting company," Ponsi says gravely. "Jason and I have had numerous conversations, deep ones, about all these topics: existence, the meaning of life."

"Did Jason turn to the parish for comfort? Was he experiencing problems?"

Ponsi squints as if he is looking straight into the sun. "I shouldn't discuss Jason's spiritual life," he blurts, massaging his forehead.

"This could be a matter of life and death. And as a matter of fact, it probably is, despite the fact we're hoping for the best. You need to tell me everything that could help us find Jason."

"I understand, but—"

"What sort of relationship did Jason have with Lisa Yamamoto?"

"With Lisa? They were together for a while."

"Why did they break up?"

Ponsi shoots Nina an injured look, as if bitter the police are putting him in the position of having to make an unpleasant decision. Then he seems to seek courage from Pilecki's photograph. *Things could be worse, Nikolas.*

"Jason wasn't faithful to Lisa," he eventually says, stroking his beard. He pushes his chair back a little, then leans under the desk. A moment later, Nina catches the faint odor of foot sweat wafting up. The pastor, or oracle or chaplain or whatever, just made himself more comfortable by taking off his shoes.

"Who was the third party?"

"He didn't say. He just told me he had cheated on Lisa."

"Was Jason ever violent?"

Ponsi looks up in surprise from the pen in his hands. He then returns it to its stand. "Why would you ask that?"

Nina keeps her eyes nailed to the chaplain and doesn't answer.

Ponsi stares back for perhaps a second too long. "No."

"No? Are you sure?"

"Jason wouldn't hurt a fly. He has his problems: he drinks too much, and sometimes that causes issues with self-control. But it doesn't manifest as violence—perhaps at most in the sort of moral failings that end up causing these problems in his relationships." Ponsi restores the sad smile to his face.

Nina can't help but think of the latex-sheathed doll hanging in Jason's closet. "And by moral failings, you mean . . ."

"Sexual relationships. His partying has always been marked by a certain lack of inhibition."

"So you've never heard that Jason hit Lisa?"

Ponsi folds his arms across his chest and pinches his lips. "No. Never. I don't believe anything of the sort ever happened."

"OK, thank you." Nina rises from her chair. "Oh, yes, one more thing. Do you have any idea why Jason would have been in Aurinko-lahti last Saturday night?"

Ponsi stands. For some reason, he looks shorter behind his desk than he did before. "I have no idea. I'm sorry."

33

LISA AND ESSI's living room clock chimes, signaling the hour. Yusuf and Jessica are sitting on the couch, staring solemnly ahead.

Helena Lappi has arrived on the scene with a patrol because, as she says, she takes violence against police officers—particularly those in her unit—seriously. But Jessica knows perfectly well her boss is taking secret satisfaction in her and Yusuf's humiliation. She has come to personally twist the knife before returning to skulk around HQ with a parrot named Jami Harjula on her shoulder.

"Gone, baby, gone. Evaporated like a fart in the Sahara." Hellu takes a seat in the armchair and eyes the shattered coffee table, the blood staining the rug, the white gauze wrapped around Yusuf's right hand. Sitting there, relaxed, hands resting on the chair's arms, Hellu looks somehow dangerous, like an unpredictable, impulsive queen who at any moment might order the head of someone present to be liberated from its neck.

The door to Essi's bedroom opens, and the young man Hellu has brought in to provide crisis counseling steps out.

"What's the situation?" Hellu asks him calmly.

"Better. Knowing the maintenance company is changing the locks today . . . ," he replies, pulling on his coat. "But there's quite a lot there for a young person to process."

Hellu nods, then turns to Jessica and Yusuf as the crisis counselor exits through the front door. The back of a police uniform flashes past in the stairwell. An officer will be posted at the apartment for the remainder of the day if not longer, no matter how minute the chance the Phantom will return anytime soon.

"You said Essi smelled him?" Hellu eventually asks.

Jessica looks up from the floor. "Yeah. The whole place smelled like it."

"The same aftershave as . . ."

"Last Wednesday."

"Damned Phantom." Hellu sighs. "What about his face? Did you see it?"

Jessica and Yusuf shake their heads.

Hellu sighs again, then stands and steps over to the window with her hands clasped dramatically behind her. The back of her blazer is flecked with long white hairs. The flared legs of her loose-fitting jeans date to the previous millennium.

"Did it occur to anyone the Phantom might return to the apartment? That if he has Lisa, he probably also has Lisa's keys?" she says, gazing out the window.

Jessica glances at Yusuf, who looks anguished. So much has happened over the course of the day that even the simplest things are easy to forget.

"I guess this sounds dumb now," Jessica says with a sigh, "but it doesn't seem likely a kidnapper would return to the home of the person they abducted when the police are trudging in and out all day. I mean, he almost got caught this time—"

"But he didn't, damn it." Hellu raps the window frame with her fingers, then walks to the middle of the room, hands again clasped behind her back. "What was he looking for?"

"I don't know. All the manga art and Lisa's laptop are at the station," Jessica says.

"Might he have thought they were still here?"

"I doubt it. My guess is, he was looking for something he knew Lisa had hidden."

"Did it look like he had anything with him when he ran off?"

Jessica shakes her head.

Hellu chuckles to herself, and her disappointed gaze skims the ceiling. "Tech will come fingerprint the place again. Let's hope there are some new ones. Other than yours, that is. Yusuf, is that hand of yours going to be all right?"

"This is nothing," Yusuf says as convincingly as possible. As usual, he's putting on a brave face. Jessica caught a glimpse of the long shard lodged in the heel of his thumb before the medic yanked it out of the muscle and stitched up the wound.

Hellu nods and glances at her smartwatch. "Imagine. One lucky break could have solved this case. But it was only you two against one."

She walks to the door.

"Oh, yes. Nina called. She found a stockpile of sadomasochistic gear in Jason Nervander's closet." Hellu smiles to herself as Jessica and Yusuf turn their stunned faces toward her. "Whatever floats your boat, I suppose."

34

JESSICA KNOCKS ON Essi's door and hears a soft voice tell her to come in.

She sees Lisa's roommate lying in bed on her side, her eyes red from crying.

Jessica pulls up a chair. "You're totally safe here at home now. The locks are being changed any minute, and a police officer will be watching the building."

Essi sits up in bed and blows her nose.

Jessica looks around. The room is wholly unlike her manga-obsessed roommate's. The walls are painted dark blue and hung with large prints of iconic photographs and World War II propaganda posters. *Keep calm and carry on*—that sort of thing.

"It was him," Essi says.

Jessica nods. "Do you have any idea what he was looking for?"

Essi shakes her head.

"OK. The reason we originally came back is, I wanted to ask you about this woman." Jessica hands her phone to Essi.

"Ask what?" Essi says quietly.

"Do you know her?"

Essi shrugs. "No. Who is she?"

"Her name is Olga Belousova. She's Ukrainian. Does the name mean anything to you?"

Essi appears to concentrate. She zooms in with her fingertips. "Beautiful," she says, handing the phone back to Jessica.

"But you don't recognize her? Even the name?"

"No."

"OK." Jessica stands. "There's one more thing. . . . It has to do with Jason."

"OK."

Jessica pauses to consider how best to raise the matter, then settles on a direct approach: "Was Jason violent with Lisa?"

Essi scrunches the tissue in her hand but doesn't say anything.

"Was he, Essi? Did Jason hit Lisa?"

Essi's head bobs quickly; it's a series of clipped nods.

"I think so, yes. Right at the end," Essi whispers. "Lisa had these bruises on her face and . . . she said she fell after she got drunk at some party, but . . . no one falls that way. I was positive Jason hit her."

"Why didn't you tell us before?"

"Well, because . . . Lisa's a strong personality and she wouldn't want people to know. Besides, it couldn't have anything to do with this, right? I mean, Jason disappeared too . . . and this was, like, a year ago."

Jessica reaches for the handle and cracks the door.

"If you remember anything, Essi. An hour from now, tonight, tomorrow. Or if you notice something's missing. Or that something you've never seen before has appeared. You need to call me right away, OK? Any piece of information would be really valuable now."

Essi nods. "OK."

"Try to get some rest," Jessica says, then exits and closes the door.

35

JESSICA CLIMBS INTO the car, pulls the door closed, and clicks in her seat belt. Yusuf is standing outside, a half-smoked cigarette in his fingers, studying the white gauze wrapped around his hand. As if by stealth, darkness has fallen over the city, and the wind-borne snowflakes are like yellow fireflies in the streetlamps' glow. The wet asphalt of the deserted sidewalks mirrors the sky.

A moment later, Yusuf steps into the car and starts up the engine. A sense of déjà vu washes over Jessica, but the moment has repeated itself dozens upon dozens of times in reality too. The car door opens, the smells of just-smoked cigarette and Yusuf's aftershave wafts in, and the Golf's small but spunky engine snorts into action. The music fills the car like a massive swarm of wasps.

"We should have guessed he'd come back," Yusuf says.

Jessica sighs. "Hindsight is always twenty-twenty."

"Do you think the Phantom poisoned Olga Belousova?"

Jessica turns to Yusuf. "You've decided she was poisoned now?"

"If she didn't drown."

"Hard to say."

"Think about it: the manga art, the clothes, the burn marks. Maybe we're dealing with some weird cult here. Maybe Olga dressed up in that getup of her own free will and took some designer drug the Phantom smuggled in from Japan." Yusuf buckles his seat belt. "Maybe we'll get lucky and Sarvilinna will find some new drug in Olga's blood we can trace."

"Like Jiminy Cricket?"

"Yup," Yusuf says.

Jessica shrugs. Jiminy Cricket was the in-house nickname for a Romanian gang that brought a new synthetic drug to Finland a couple years back; the police were able to trace it after a young man overdosed. A big role in the case was played by a technical development in toxicology: presumptive analysis of molecular structures.

Traditionally, pathology has to have a reference—a sample of the drug in question—on hand for comparison with the sample taken from the deceased. Customs or the police typically provided the forensics laboratory with the samples.

But over the past few years, toxicologists have managed to develop a method that can be used to predict the molecular structure of any substance based on its molecular mass. This makes it possible to identify, say, a substance possessing the basic structure of an amphetamine to which a manufacturer has added something. This simplifies the search for both the substance and its source, even if the specific substance itself is unknown to the authorities.

As he backs out of the parking space, Yusuf sighs. "I guess they didn't find anything at Söderskär."

"Nope, nothing. And they had divers comb the coastline."

"Damn it. Dead ends in every direction. Rasmus texted that none of the delivery companies picked up any packages from Lisa's address over the last month. Dozens were delivered, though."

"I can imagine. All the products for Lisa to push, the freebies influencers get . . ." Jessica remembers the mountains of empty boxes lining Lisa's bedroom walls.

"Plus Nervander's taste for stronger stuff. Do you think it's related to the manga?"

Jessica shakes her head. "Apples and oranges. If manga gave Nervander a hard-on, Nina would have found manga in his closet, not black latex."

"I guess. What now?"

"I have to close my eyes for a second and think. Drop me at home?"

Yusuf grunts gruffly. "Always a pleasure."

Somewhere behind the blanketing grayness, the sun is dropping below the horizon, staining the low-hanging clouds with a wash of yellow. It's perhaps the most beautiful moment of the day. A glimpse of life, of fresh starts, before the relentless eighteen-hour darkness sets in.

36

Jessica turns the key in the lock, opens the door, and steps into her studio apartment.

Two letters and the free local paper lie on the floor.

Jessica listens to the sounds carrying from the stairwell: someone climbs to the second or third floor, rings a doorbell. A moment later, a door opens and the stairwell fills with children's shrieks of delight. Then the door slams shut, and the voices fade to faint mumbles.

Jessica shuts her front door and takes off her coat. She retrieves the mail from the floor and crosses over to the window overlooking the courtyard. The view is typical for the neighborhood: bike racks, dumpsters, a rug-beating rack welded together from steel pipes. Plaster walls exposed as beige by the yard lights, dozens of illuminated homes. Black and metallic sheet-metal roofs that glisten, lethally slick, in the freezing precipitation. Massive metal-clad chimneys, some puffing gray smoke into the sky.

Jessica props herself against the windowsill and turns toward her tiny studio. Its sole function is to serve as a facade for outsiders: odds are high there's something molding in the fridge, and the bed hasn't been slept in for ages. As a matter of fact, the last time the bed was used, it wasn't for sleeping: Jessica and Fubu came to the mutual conclusion five weeks ago that there was no future for them and sealed the split with breakup sex. It wasn't better, worse, or more dramatic than usual; with Fubu, sex was always reliably relaxed. Even when they knew it was the last time.

In retrospect, it seems absurd that Fubu visited the apartment so many times without knowing the truth. Lying in bed after Fubu left, Jessica reflected that once you get to know someone through half-truths, revealing the whole truth becomes almost impossible. Even if you come to trust them enough to tell them the truth, there's no way of knowing if they will stick around after hearing it. That's what encourages continued secrecy.

Jessica's phone rings in the pocket of her jeans.

Blocked number.

She hesitates. She has made plenty of new acquaintances today, including the scumbag from the jogging path. Saw someone or something at the bus stop in Kamppi, bumped into a frighteningly familiar old lady who just kept walking. Or did she just imagine it all? What if she took the call and heard his voice uttering the words again: "Christmas Eve"? But as investigative lead, she can't really afford to pick and choose her phone calls right now: any piece of information could be significant.

Jessica presses the green icon and lifts the phone to her ear. She hears music in the background. Then she hears a man's voice. Speaking in English to someone else.

"Hello?" Jessica says.

"Sorry! Hi, Detective," the voice continues in English, and it takes Jessica only a second to realize the person at the other end of the line is the GM from the Phoenix. The guy who looked at her in such a memorable way earlier that day: lustfully perhaps, but at the same time affectionately, like an old friend. "It's Frank Dominis." The voice is charismatic, warm. "Sorry. The number at the club is private. I have your card here on my desk."

Jessica walks back over to the window, phone at her ear. Across the courtyard and a couple of stories down, a man and a woman are doing yoga in their living room while a nature documentary plays on their television. Jessica sits on the windowsill and exhales the air from her lungs. She could, she supposes, lower her guard for a moment and be something other than a frigid lady cop who's afraid of giving in to life.

"How can I help you, Frank?"

37

IT'S ONLY A couple of hundred yards from Jessica's front door to Manala, but the cold wind still finds a way to snuggle up against Jessica as she briskly crosses the street.

With evening's approach, the temperature has dropped to a few degrees below freezing, and the rain that fell all day has given the asphalt a skim of black ice. Jessica narrows her eyes at the little snowflakes tumbling in the gusts.

A few taxis loiter at the stand. The drivers don't let the wind deter them: they have stepped out of their vehicles for a chat and a smoke. A dozen people are clustered around Jaska's Grill, some already munching on their street food, the others still queuing for theirs.

Despite—or perhaps because of—the surrounding darkness, there's something heartwarming about the little clutches of humanity; they demonstrate that the city's inhabitants can generate a homey atmosphere during even the darkest and most depressing times of the year. Cries, laughter, and alcohol-fueled insights carry over the frigid wind. Heavy winter coats with dress trousers or skirt hems, tights, and high heels underneath. *Upgraded after work.* The electricity of early winter in the air, as well as flirtation, excitement, anticipation, and the hope that summer will come again someday.

Jessica opens the heavy door and steps into the bar. A cavalcade of strong odors, primarily of cheese and garlic, marches from the kitchen.

She sees Frank Dominis where she expected: in the corner facing the door with a glass and a bottle of cola on the table in front of him.

"I haven't been here in ages." Dominis politely rises to his feet as Jessica approaches. "It must have been before they remodeled."

"I live nearby." Jessica takes off her coat and hangs it on the back of her chair. The two of them sit. The intro to Eppu Normaali's "When You're Gone" is playing from the restaurant's speakers.

"So you're a regular," Dominis says, bringing his glass to his lips.

"I wouldn't go that far."

"What are you drinking?" Dominis raises a finger to get the server's attention. "I'm buying."

Jessica glances at the empty bottle on the table, the ice-filled glass with a drop of brown liquid at the bottom. Dominis notices her looking.

"Ignore that. Order whatever you want." He smiles broadly, revealing his teeth. Then the smile fades a little, and he reveals what Jessica guessed seconds earlier: "Eight years, five months, and two days."

"Since your last sip?"

"Sip, line, hit, anything."

Jessica looks at her tablemate, impressed. There's some cliché or romantic notion, what have you, that a hero has to hit rock bottom before he can reach his potential. People celebrate artists and athletes who have conquered alcoholism and drug addiction while those who never let things get out of hand are left on the sidelines. The same strange appeal lurks in reformed criminals: just knock out an autobiography and the lines will be out the door. *It's so cool how you gave up a life of crime and substance abuse. Respect! Let me grab a selfie.*

Jessica orders a glass of white wine from the server. The notion of a dark past fascinates her; it would be hypocritical to pretend otherwise.

"Did it change? Life?" Jessica asks.

Dominis stares out the window, where the unpredictable movements of the snowflakes somersaulting under the streetlamps provide the most stunning performance: the sort that might end at any moment and, for that reason, must be enjoyed right now.

"No," Dominis eventually says, turning his gaze to his glass and then Jessica. "Nothing changes. Not counting the group you drank with, everything stays the same: life, the people around you. Celebrations, pleasures, sorrows, dramas, crises, wars, deceptions, betrayals, love . . . The only thing that changes is the way you look at the world." He rolls up his sleeves.

Jessica crosses her ankle over her knee and lowers her hands to her lap. She knows plenty of alcoholics and addicts for whom quitting would no doubt be the solution to most of their problems. Then again, many who struggle to liberate themselves from substance abuse are daunted when they realize quitting, in and of itself, isn't enough: you have to be prepared to face the world without the security of intoxication, to clean up the messes you've made.

After a momentary silence, Dominis drains his glass and asks: "You know where Anchorage is?"

Jessica shakes her head.

"Anchorage is the biggest city in Alaska." He points his fingers at the floor, as if the city is on the exact opposite side of the globe. "That's where I'm from."

The server lowers Jessica's glass of wine to the table and Dominis orders another cola.

"You moved to Finland and got sober? Or the other way around?"

"I got sober on the flight. I was drunk when I boarded. I was running from alcohol, from myself, from Anchorage. I could have moved anywhere."

"So why Helsinki?"

"If you're giving up everything you know, you might as well hold on to one thing that's familiar."

"The climate?"

"The climate." Dominis leans back, arms folded across his chest, and continues more cryptically: "And the darkness."

Jessica tastes her wine. Her lips are still cold from her short, brisk walk, and the cool glass feels almost warm against her mouth.

"Anchorage and Helsinki are really different," Dominis continues, "but the climates are almost identical. Nice, light-filled, relatively warm summers and long, cold, hellishly dark winters."

"You feel at home in the darkness?"

"Let's say I feel at home *indoors*. In which case it might as well be dark outside. Know what I mean, Detective?"

"Jessica."

"Whatever you say, Detective." Dominis thanks the server and refills his glass. "Folks in Alaska drink a lot. People usually think it's bored soldiers. Ex-military. It's true that there are a hell of a lot of soldiers in Alaska, but the people there drink for the same reasons people drink here: they want to escape the darkness, celebrate the glorious summer. No one knows shit about either at lower latitudes. Summer and light are taken for granted there, and absolute darkness is such an absurd concept they can't even imagine it unless they've read Frank Miller's graphic novels or seen the movie adaptions."

"Were you in the military, Frank?"

Dominis bursts out laughing. "Do I look like a soldier?"

"You look like you could have been just about anything before you gave up drinking and moved to Helsinki."

"I'll take that as a compliment."

"Maybe you shouldn't. I was talking about something you might have been a long time ago."

Dominis smiles again. "Indeed you were."

A group of partyers streams into the restaurant, clomping their shoes on the mat.

Jessica glances at her watch. She's both on and off the clock, and she has to keep work in mind. "You have something to tell me. Something that relates to Yamamoto and Nervander," she says, trying to look uninterested.

The truth is, she is anything but. She can't lie to herself; she knows herself too well. But Frank Dominis doesn't need to know what she's thinking. There's something extraordinarily genuine about the guy:

the way he disarms himself during conversation is incredibly attractive. Even though they've just met, he's giving a lot of himself. Jessica has seen enough men, made enough mistakes, and fallen for enough smooth talk to tell when vulnerability is authentic and when it's faked. Of course that doesn't tell the whole truth about a person; vulnerability can conceal murky motives and bad intentions too. But that's a totally different matter.

"I'm all ears," she says.

Dominis looks momentarily caught off guard, perhaps a little disappointed.

"Right." His thick hair is stippled with gray at the temples; he rakes it back and smiles. "I was thinking I'd keep my cards close to my chest until you've finished your wine."

"Why? What good would that do?"

"You might order another."

"I'll go ahead and drink this first one while you talk, if you don't mind."

"What I have to say won't take long."

"But it's still important enough you asked to meet in person." Now Jessica takes a bigger gulp. The stem of the glass is wet; maybe she splashed her wine without noticing.

"There are worse crimes, I assume."

Jessica doesn't answer. She lowers her glass to the coaster and dries her hand on her napkin.

A burst of laughter splits the room. The party that stepped in has settled at the bar, only a few yards away from Jessica and Frank.

Dominis has stripped his voice of the nonchalance that captured Jessica's attention earlier in the day: "What I'm about to tell you . . . I don't want it to be used against me. OK?"

Jessica nods. She could say something reassuring about how she always does her utmost to protect her sources, how behaving any other way would be a violation of her professional ethics. But right now that would feel phony. By the time he called, Dominis had already decided to tell her what he's about to tell her.

"Lisa's a nice girl. Smart and somehow above all that superficial bullshit. She plays along, took to the scene like a fish to water. But she's only doing it to survive. She doesn't actually enjoy it, and she doesn't crave approval the way other people in that crowd do. That's why I've always liked her."

Jessica's tone leaves no room for interpretation: "How close are you and Lisa?"

Dominis grunts, takes a drink, then chews on an ice cube that found its way into his mouth. "I know you see through me, Detective. But Lisa's one out of ten. I've screwed the other nine."

Jessica falls silent and takes another sip. Her indirect query is of questionable relevance to the case. She'll be skating on thin ice if she starts probing into the details of Frank Dominis' sex life.

"But Lisa has told me certain things." The clamor at the neighboring table is loud enough to drown out conversation at a normal volume, but even so, Dominis lowers his voice. "The sort of stuff you wouldn't share with anyone under normal circumstances—"

"The circumstances are anything but normal, Frank." Jessica leans in to create more favorable conditions for a confidential exchange.

Dominis swirls the ice cubes in his half-empty glass. He looks like he's about to cross the line, step out of the comfort zone where friends' secrets are typically honored. "Lisa told me her dad has a shady past. That's why he packed his bags and left Japan. Moved somewhere no one would think to look for him."

"Finland."

"Exactly. He brought Lisa, who was only a few years old at the time—"

Jessica frowns. "Wait a sec. I thought Lisa was born in Finland."

Dominis shakes his head. "Lisa's dad married a Finnish woman after he got here. Apparently Lisa's biological mother died in Japan. Complications from Lisa's birth."

Jessica thinks back to the photograph she saw in Lisa's room. She realizes now that she had simply assumed Lisa's mother was Finnish. Lisa isn't half Finnish; she's a full-blooded Finn whose parents happen to be Japanese. And the conversation at hand is a textbook example of how the police can give sources an unprofessional image of themselves.

"OK. So Lisa's father had reason to hide where no one could find him. But from whom? The police?"

"I don't know. Lisa didn't know either. And this was all just a guess on Lisa's part. Evidently her father refuses to talk about his past. About why they had to leave Japan."

"And all this happened . . . in the late nineties? And you think it has something to do with Lisa's disappearance."

"I don't think . . . I mean, I don't know if it does. But I do know Lisa was afraid of her dad."

"How so?"

"Apparently everything began when Lisa's popularity started to skyrocket on Instagram. Over the course of a few years, she attracted hundreds of thousands of followers in Finland and abroad. Lisa's dad wasn't happy about it. It soured their relationship."

Jessica watches Dominis' lips form the words. Now she understands why he thought this was relevant. "Was the disagreement over her social media presence in general? Or over the things Lisa was posting on Instagram?"

"I don't know. Her dad just told her to stop posting. Said that if she didn't, it could be the end of her."

"By which he meant . . ."

Frank Dominis shrugs and empties his glass. "Being threatened by your own father that way. For no good reason."

"And now Lisa has gone missing," Jessica says softly. She pictures the Phantom waiting for Lisa at the Phoenix. Could the Phantom know Lisa's father? Is that ultimately what this is all about?

"I figured you might want to know." Dominis lowers his hands to the table. Now that he's gotten the matter off his chest, he seems like his relaxed self again.

"Absolutely. Thanks for getting in touch with me. When did this happen? I mean, when did Lisa tell you this?"

"The last time I saw her alone. At the club, after closing. A couple of months ago."

"I see." Jessica tosses back the rest of her wine.

"You want another?"

Jessica takes a twenty from her coat pocket, slips it under her glass, and stands. "You go ahead. A third Coke."

Dominis looks disappointed. "I came all the way from Lauttasaari."

"And I appreciate it, Frank." Jessica pulls on her coat. "Maybe you can call one of the nine."

Frank chuckles mournfully and swirls the ice in his empty glass. Jessica turns to leave.

"Hey, Detective."

"Yeah?"

"You think Lisa's father has something to do with her disappearance?"

Jessica gazes at Dominis for a moment; the wan yellow light lends his face an almost painterly aspect.

She gives him a serene smile. "Have a good night, Frank."

"You too, Detective."

Jessica tosses her scarf around her neck as she steps out into the icy wind. She strides into the crosswalk and pulls out her phone.

Her head is roiling with conflicting thoughts. It's unlikely Lisa's father, who's due to return from Brazil tomorrow, is responsible for her disappearance. But he must have caught wind of some approaching threat, whatever it was.

Yusuf answers surprisingly quickly.

"Hey. Find out what time Lisa's parents' plane is due to land tomorrow morning. We'll go meet them at the airport. And have Rasse or someone else look into Lisa's dad's background."

"You have something new?" Yusuf says.

"Yeah, maybe. I'll tell you tomorrow."

"Where are you?"

"Just heading home."

"Alone? Are you sure?"

Jessica sighs audibly. "Good night!"

Yusuf's rollicking laugh echoes down the line. "I'm just saying, be careful, Jessie. That Dominis is a beast. Those old-school players—"

"Go fuck yourself, Yusuf," Jessica says, and hangs up.

38

YUSUF STARES AT his phone; Jessica's name and face have just disappeared from the screen. He slides the device into his breast pocket, zips up his leather jacket, and breathes in the cool, fresh forest air. Fifteen minutes ago, he was on his way to the parking garage. But then he changed his mind, decided to take a little walk. From HQ he headed south along Pasilanraitio, continued on to Winqvistinkatu, then Fanninpenger, and finally to the jogging path in the woods. At first: lights, car horns, the rumble of engines, the clank of tram tracks. And then: nothing. The way urban Helsinki cuts to a natural environment that kills the city's cacophony is mind-blowing. Especially in the darkness, it's like another world: the pitch-black enchanted forest from "Hansel and Gretel," a gingerbread house hidden deep within.

The narrow dirt track running among the spruces is like a labyrinth: in many places, the trees stand so close their lowest branches have withered. They're sentenced to die without sunlight that doesn't reach them. On this November night, the dead branches are covered by a thin layer of snow. For a brief time, they get to adorn themselves in veils of white, like the living.

Yusuf has never been afraid of nocturnal rambles in the woods. Just the opposite: he grew up surrounded by trees in the bedroom community of Söderkulla. Hunting frogs, hitting a wolf in the rump with a slingshot, spending the night in a lean-to he built himself, roasting hundreds of sausages so black their crisp skins tasted of nothing but charcoal. Damming streams and building a tree house so high on a pair of oak boughs that his city cousins didn't dare climb up to it. Yusuf is a country boy who has tapped into the city's pulse for one fleeting phase of his life. There are days he reflects on whether it's too soon to leave behind the bustle of Helsinki and the draining work of being a detective. Whether it's time to go back to his roots and try something new.

Yusuf shuts his eyes. He inhales the earthy smell of standing bog, hears the melodious call of cranes, and suddenly he's eight years old again. He's pedaling down the dirt road with Basse, Sebu, and Jepe, wondering out loud what the monster that rises from the muck every night looks like. Whether it's green or brown. Whether its torso sprouts alligator legs with long claws or tentacles like an octopus.

It all comes rushing back: the Sipoonjoki River cleaving Söderkulla like a sword, the smell of the lush bankside greenery carrying to the rowboat, the fragrance of wood-burning saunas trapped in the mists hovering tenaciously over the water.

Springtime: blossoms and pollen. The conditioner his mother used. Red roses. And the girl. Both of them are wearing graduation caps, and the world exists for the two of them alone.

Anna's family lives only a few blocks from Yusuf's house. They've known each other since childhood, but didn't start dating until the end of high school. Aren't such stories meant to end happily? Two people know each other, confide in each other, find each other. Or are they doomed because everything is too perfect too soon?

Yusuf stops and draws the scent of the woods into his nostrils as if it's the last time. Which it is, for tonight.

His lighter clicks in the darkness, and the smell of tobacco dominates all other scents. Maybe it's his way of killing the nostalgia, clipping the wings of something that's trying to be more than a memory.

Maybe he and Anna really will move back someday, build the white house on the banks of the river or maybe nearby, as the budget allows. Have children and watch them enjoy the same things he and Anna enjoyed in their youth, make the same silly mistakes they made when they were kids, and come through with nothing but bruises to show for it, like their parents. Drive a big car to the big supermarket and grill in the yard shaded by supple birches, with a sauna in one corner and a trampoline for the kids in another. Maybe. Why not?

But they'll never do these things together. They'll do them separately, with other people. With people they haven't even met yet. And that hurts more than the memories ever will.

39

JAMI HARJULA CLOSES the garage door and turns to survey the overcrowded space. The walls are heaped with stuff: tools, blue IKEA bags, battery-powered devices. On the surface, it all seems organized, but the pointlessness of the accumulation lends the scene a chaotic aspect. Over the years, Harjula has collected an appalling number of tools in his little workshop—not because he ever thought he'd need them, but because owning them is mandatory for the middle-class dream.

Harjula opens the door in the side of the garage.

Once inside the house, he slips off his shoes and hangs up his coat. The hum of the extractor hood and the aromas of sautéed onions and fresh herbs carry from the kitchen.

"Hey," Harjula says from the kitchen doorway. Sini glances over her shoulder as she drains water from a pot. The quick look and distracted smile are supposed to be enough. Apparently hugs and kisses are a thing of the past. They planted them on each other when the girls were little. Before the girls. Back then hugs and kisses were given because he and Sini wanted to give them, not because they were expected. Nowadays there's not even the expectation.

"Dinner's almost ready," Sini says, flipping the roast in the pan.

"Great." Harjula walks into the living room, hands on his hips.

He knows he could wrap his arms around Sini and give her a peck on the cheek, tell her he loves her. But some mystical force prevents him from doing so. Maybe resuscitating the body that went rigid long ago seems pointless, although he might feel less like a quitter if he tried.

The television is advertising consumer goods to an empty couch. The girls are in their own rooms, doing homework or fiddling with their smartphones. He and Sini have likely provided overly effective modeling of the latter.

Harjula sits down and turns off the television. He hears the grease sizzle in the pan and the cupboard door slam shut. And then he is struck by a curious and contradictory insight: the house is full of life, all the members of the family at home, but even so, it feels deserted. In a moment, the meal Sini has prepared will be laid out; the girls will bound hungrily into the kitchen, greeting their dad. The four of them will sit down at the same table, each on their own side, and share a peaceful meal.

Harjula twirls the remote in his hand and stares at the television's void screen. *A self-perpetuating cycle.* Maybe his uncompromising ambition is what Sini originally fell for. And then she lost interest when she realized her husband would never rise through the police hierarchy. He will never be more than he is right now. Hellu's lapdog. *Damn it.* It's not exactly a novel insight, but it has never taken such clear shape: Sini thinks he has lost his edge. Now he's sitting on the couch waiting for his dinner like some domesticated milksop, even though his doggedness, unshakable work ethic, and nighttime responsibilities were what kept the relationship fresh. When did he stop trying? He needs to do more. He needs to excel above Jessica.

"Where are you going?" Sini asks indifferently when Harjula stalks across the kitchen and reappears a moment later with his coat and beanie on.

"For a drive," he says, opening the door to the garage. "I love you."

40

JESSICA GLANCES AT her watch; it's five to nine. She shuts her eyes and listens to the old elevator clatter and clank as it climbs the shaft toward the sixth floor. The building is dark. Jessica didn't turn on the stairwell lights when she entered, and the landings flashing by are illuminated solely by the wan yellow light of the rising car.

The century-old apartment building that has seen two world wars is a repository of troves of information, experiences, sensations, savored tastes and smelled scents, lived lives, loves, divorces, childbirths, and, inevitably, deaths.

Death has been present in Jessica's apartment. Erne drew his last breath in Jessica's guest room as she stroked his gaunt knuckles. Half a year has passed since then, but to Jessica it seems as if Erne was here just yesterday. And yet it somehow also feels as if an entire lifetime has passed between Erne's departure and the present moment.

Sometimes the timeline against which life is measured blurs, and Jessica feels as if it all just happened: she imagines she remembers what it smelled like in the car the morning her mother steered it into an oncoming truck. How Toffe's soft fingers felt wrapped around her own, how Dad roared like a beast when Mom wrenched the wheel, sealing her small family's fate with this one act.

And how Jessica still managed to tell Toffe—she wants to believe, wants to remember she said it, although she can't be sure she did—that everything would be fine. That her little brother would never have to worry. All he needed to know was that, no matter what happened, he and Jessica would be together, be there for each other. Then only seconds later, that beautiful vision was rendered impossible.

Toffe's innocent little body was mangled in the accident. So was Jessica's. But she was allowed to go on. No, she was forced to go on. It isn't a privilege; it is a colossal millstone she has had to drag behind her, year in, year out.

Jessica feels a tear roll from her cheek to her chin, drop to the floor. It's as if time has stopped.

The elevator has come to a rest at the sixth floor, and the weak bulb overhead has gone out. Jessica isn't sure how long she's been standing there.

Jessica.

Jessica opens her eyes, not because the voice frightens her, but because she hopes doing so will silence it. The voice is from another world, another time and place, but it's more than just a memory.

Not now. The next tear rolls down Jessica's face, following its predecessor before striking out on its own under the ridge of her cheekbone.

Jessica.

The other reality usually opens up when she's asleep, but occasionally when she's awake, when exhaustion crashes against the lids of her closed eyes.

The yapping of a poodle echoes from the apartment of the crabby old lady who lives on the third floor. Then utter silence falls again.

Jessica can feel her mother's fingers on her shoulders. Their coldness bores through her heavy coat, her shirts, to her skin. Jessica knows the sensation isn't real. There's no way it can be, but like always, she is instantly overwhelmed by doubts that something so concrete, so beautiful and simultaneously ghastly, could be the product of her imagination.

Jessica.

Jessica slowly turns around so she can see the figure gazing at her in the elevator mirror. Mom's face is whole, harmoniously beautiful; the bones aren't misshapen by the ruinous collision. But the quick flashes reveal the truth: they remind Jessica where the gouged brow darkens to a deep red, almost black, with congealed blood. Where the blood drained from the pitted skull, spilling over one eye and toward the jaw. Jessica shuts her eyes, and when she opens them, Mother is herself again. Her beautiful self.

I'm afraid they're coming for me, Mom.

Why would you say that?

I think I saw them today. I think I saw Camilla. . . .

Don't cry, Jessie. You'll be fine, sweetheart.

Her mother sighs tenderly and releases her grip on Jessica's shoulders. There's a finality to the exhalation; it's like the last gasp before eternal cold. Her mother is exiting the elevator.

The truth is always more or less in plain sight, Jessica dear. The truth is contours that must be filled in with colors, and the colors aren't always lying there on the table, waiting for you. Sometimes you have to reach into a difficult place and dig them out.

I don't understand.

Jessica shuts her eyes, and when she opens them, her mother is gone.

Down on the ground floor, the main door opens, and a moment later, the lights come on in the stairwell.

Jessica wipes her tears on her sleeve and opens the gate.

41

JESSICA ENTERS HER apartment and walks over to the bed without taking off her shoes. She sits and shuts her eyes. She hasn't turned on the lights, and with her eyes closed, the darkness feels perfect. The glow from the courtyard cannot penetrate the shades of her eyelids.

Jessica feels an ice-cold pain shoot through her shoulder. She stands and crosses to the door in the opposite wall.

Come home.

I'm coming.

Jessica steps out into the stairwell, key in hand.

The dark stairwell, which a century ago served as the servants' entrance, is like a liminal space separating two worlds, a gateway between two realities. Every night, she comes home from work and is Jessica Niemi for a moment, until she opens the door to the other reality and merges with the name on the mail slot of the street-side residence. *Von Hellens.*

Jessica enters the apartment where Erne spent his final days. The home that, despite its vast size, feels safe, cozy.

She taps in the alarm code, and the lights automatically come on in the generous hallway. She shuts the door behind her and sets the keys down on the credenza.

Jessica makes her way down the hall into the spacious living room, where the enormous windows bask in the bright lights of downtown Helsinki. Somewhere in the vicinity of the Amos Rex museum, a brilliant beam is trained skyward, as if searching for the moon but never finding it.

Jessica enters the kitchen, opens the laptop on the table, and flips on the electric kettle.

For a moment, the stillness is absolute.

The silence reminds Jessica of Erne. She pictures his scraggly beard, his gray foxlike face, its wrinkles lending it playfulness and charisma. Jessica has to envision Erne as he was when he lived, not as he was when he died. Last spring, he was so gaunt the wrinkles were swallowed up by the sunken cheeks. His arms were so atrophied they wouldn't have been able to rescue anyone, pull the young Jessica out of the darkness and into the light.

Jessica shuts her eyes and waits in silence for the water to start burbling in the kettle.

She fishes a bag of rose hip tea from a wooden box and lowers it to the bottom of a mug.

The kettle boils. Jessica turns it off.

The instant the water hits the bottom of the mug, it turns red; it's like blood implacably mingling with the bathwater of someone who decided a razor blade was the best way out. Jessica isn't sure why, but she frequently pictures the visual similarity between the phenomena. There was only one time, long ago, that she considered suicide. When impenetrable black clouds rose over the canals of Murano, cleaving her violated body and soul with sorrow and shame.

Jessica sits down at the table, pulls a memory stick from her pocket, and inserts it into her laptop.

She brings up several image files on the screen: *Lisa Yamamoto. Jason Nervander. Rubber gear in a closet. A gimp hood. The Phantom at the Phoenix. Akifumi2511946. The lighthouse photo. Lisa's sketch of the lighthouse. Olga Belousova.*

"Two blogs," Jessica whispers, and writes down both URLs on a digital note.

www.thelisayamamoto.fi
www.masayoshi.fi

". . . one of which is secret."

At that instant, Jessica's phone rings. The number flashing on her phone is unusually short. Jessica remembers seeing it before.

She raises the phone to her ear and answers: "Detective Niemi."

"You sound tired. Not exactly office hours, I know, but I thought this was supposed to be urgent," a female voice says laconically.

Jessica draws a blank. It takes her a minute to recognize the nasal inflection of the irked, irksome Sissi Sarvilinna; the call is from the medical examiner's office. "Sorry, sure."

Jessica hears frenetic tapping at a keyboard in the background.

"I managed to hurry along the lab and the deceased's hematological analysis. The results are interesting. It would seem something was rubbed into the burn wounds while she was still alive." Sarvilinna's half-grating, half-mumbling tone sounds like her sharp teeth might be gnawing on a pencil eraser.

"What?"

"The substance appears to a peptide cocktail of sorts: primarily dermorphin and deltorphin. They're both opioid receptor agonists; in other words, analgesics like morphine, only much more effective. In addition to other peptides, like dermaseptin and adenoregulin. Those names probably don't say much to a layperson, but the gist is: these peptides, or small proteins, occur in a certain unusual form."

"What?"

"The toxin of a little organism called *Phyllomedusa bicolor*."

"Medusa? A jellyfish?"

"Not even close. A frog that lives in the rain forest."

Jessica takes a big gulp of tea and enters the term in the Google search field: *Phyllomedusa bicolor*.

"Are you there, Niemi?" Sarvilinna barks after losing her audience for all of two seconds.

"Yup. I was just looking at—"

"I assume you've pulled up the Wikipedia article describing how the Marubo tribe uses the toxin to improve their hunting luck. . . ."

"'The shaman burns the hunter's skin with a burning branch and applies the frog toxin to the wound. Vomiting ensues. The shaman tosses the children into the river, from where they soon emerge, healed.'" As she reads out loud from her computer screen, Jessica feels everything click into place. "What the hell?"

"Exactly. What that article doesn't say, Niemi, is that the custom was imported to Western countries as an alternative treatment years ago. I even remember reading about it." Sarvilinna pauses to quietly curse herself: "Darn it, I should have known the second I saw the burn marks on the deceased's skin." Then she continues: "The frog toxin is believed to cleanse body and spirit. The practice is known as kambo."

"What? How . . . I mean . . . can it be fatal?"

"I was just coming to that, Niemi. As a medical professional, I am absolutely opposed to such humbuggery. There is no scientific evidence of any health benefits resulting from kambo. Even if its components produce a euphoric sensation, the substance is a toxin the frog secretes when defending itself against its natural enemies. I wouldn't let that stuff near my circulatory system if you paid me."

Jessica listens to Sarvilinna's words and taps "kambo" into the browser's search bar. The image search brings up dozens of photos of green frogs and red marks burned into skin with a little stick. Some of the marks are burned in a row, others in a circle. The skin surrounding the wounds is raised and reddish, just like the skin on Olga Belousova's arm. There's no doubt about it. The Ukrainian woman took part in this strange ritual.

"But is it possible that—"

"In a hurry to get somewhere, Niemi?"

The question is followed by a few seconds of silence.

"No, but—"

"The short answer is, it's possible to die from kambo. Individual instances of death resulting from kambo treatments have been reported around the world. The *patients* suffered cardiac arrest."

"It sounds like that's exactly what happened to Olga Belousova."

"I'm a big fan of statistics, Niemi. Which is why, despite everything, I don't consider it very likely. But I have a two-part climax in store that might provide some clarification. Part one: traces of other substances were found in the wounds, substances that by no means come from frogs. Or even jellyfish." Jessica hears Sarvilinna chuckle to herself. "The first was codeine, which is of course used as an analgesic. The substance may have been added to the cocktail to relieve the pain resulting from the ritual. As a matter of fact, I conducted a little international Gallup: I called a colleague in London who confirmed my suspicions about kambo and its composition, but said he had never heard of other substances being combined with the toxin. Not even for the purpose of relieving pain. But codeine was smeared into Olga Belousova's wound, and on top of that, relatively large amounts of morphine were found in her blood."

"OK. What else?"

"Right. This is where the story gets interesting." Sarvilinna pauses. "Buprenorphine was also found in her blood."

"Subutex?"

Buprenorphine, the active ingredient in Subutex—or subu, as it's known on the streets—is extremely familiar to Jessica and everyone else on the force. In the early 2000s, local hard-drug users preferred heroin, but the war in Afghanistan put a crimp in opium production. Before long, users found a substitute in a substance originally intended for treatment of opioid addicts: buprenorphine. It generally made its way to Helsinki from France.

"Yes. As you may know, buprenorphine alone cannot cause death, due to the ceiling effect, but together with the frog toxin cocktail and the morphine, it could, I believe, lead to respiratory collapse and cardiac arrest."

Jessica leans back in her chair; she feels her palm start to sweat against the phone.

"So three different opioids were combined in the cocktail?"

"Yes."

"But why?"

"To produce euphoria in the recipient of the *treatment*?"

Jessica shuts her eyes. "Or to get her hooked."

Sarvilinna mumbles something about the addictiveness of honey before the call finally ends.

Jessica lowers the phone to the table.

She opens a new browser tab and types "Lisa Yamamoto" and "kambo" in the search engine. After going through the hits for a while, she finds her way to a web forum where both key words are mentioned several times.

Kambo treatment . . . Social media influencer Lisa Yamamoto . . . Alternative Health & Love Helsinki.

She picks up her phone and rings Yusuf.

"Yo."

"Listen, Yusuf. I think I found something. It seems that Lisa has been promoting a thing called kambo on her Instagram account. People are discussing it on the Internet."

"Kambo? What the hell is that?"

"I'll tell you in a minute. Have you heard of a place called Alternative Health and Love Helsinki? It's a place Lisa has told her followers to check out."

"No."

"Grab your coat and pick me up."

She hangs up, takes her mug in both hands, and studies her reflection in the window, which offers one choice of backdrop: darkness. Black against black.

Outside, the freezing wind swoops up the building and sets the flue of the kitchen hearth wailing, as if it's an enormous flute.

42

THE WHITE WOODEN house, one and a half stories tall, stands in the idyllic north Helsinki neighborhood of Puu-Käpylä, which was developed in the 1920s. There's a little room in the sharply peaked attic where the light burns at the big window every evening. For the past thirty-four years, these cozy fifteen square meters have been the realm of Rasmus Susikoski.

It's dinnertime, and downstairs spoons are clinking against bowls. But Rasmus Susikoski is not staying below to sup with his parents. He climbs the creaking wooden stairs gingerly, so as not to splash the boiling broth of the sausage soup onto his fingers.

Rasmus nudges the door open with his foot and crosses the low space in a hunch. The last time he was able to walk around his room at full height he was twelve years old.

Rasmus sets the steaming bowl down next to his computer and pulls up his super-ergonomic gaming chair. The cat keeping an eye out under the desk dutifully rubs against Rasmus' leg.

This is where Rasmus will eat the dinner his mother cooked, the way he does just about every night. He is surrounded by walls lined with movie posters and shelves groaning with collectibles: a black Atari gaming console, a View-Master with its paper disks, Transformers and Masters of the Universe figurines standing in military formation. Some are unopened, still in their original packaging to retain their value as collectors' items. The board-game shelf boasts classics like Kongman, Ghost Castle, and HeroQuest. Rasmus' room would spark profound nostalgia and admiration among those born in the 1980s. The tragedy is that no one born in the 1980s—except himself—has probably ever set foot in his room.

The only thing that sets the room apart from the ultimate trip through the decades is Rasmus' computer setup, which is anything but retro: two twenty-four-inch HD monitors with G-Sync support, one for surfing and one for gaming. A full-height ATX case with colored lights glowing behind the glass, a delidded Intel Core i9-9900K over-clocked to 5.1 GHz, and modded RTX 2080 Ti graphics cards in SLI mode that are of course kept at safe temperatures by a custom loop, a homemade water-cooling system. The crowning touches on this wonder are a pair of the best gaming headphones on the market, a wireless mouse designed specifically for gaming, a mechanical keyboard, and a Secretlab chair. All in all, Rasmus has sunk a small fortune into the setup, and acquiring it has demanded focused saving. On the other hand, he doesn't pay his parents a penny in rent, and his lodgings come with weekly cleaning and half board. As a matter of fact, the food, litter, and vaccinations required by the house's three feline occupants are the only running expenses Rasmus pays out of his own pocket.

In return for his parents' largesse, trained lawyer Rasmus manages his father's firm's legal affairs, which have dwindled significantly in recent years. The small company's trade is dependent on exports to Great Britain and has stalled badly since the citizens of the island kingdom voted for Brexit. Now and again, Rasmus wonders when his parents will run out of money. Will the day come when they ask him to pay his share of the old house's maintenance? Rasmus would certainly do so; all they have to do is ask. But until then, his funds will go to outfitting this boy cave par excellence.

Rasmus could afford even better gaming equipment on an attorney's salary, but he's unlikely to ever change employers, at least voluntarily. His reasons for working for the police are two. The first is the easygoing, supportive atmosphere, which has deteriorated since Erne's death and Hellu's arrival. Rasmus wouldn't last a second at a job dependent on highlighting one's own excellence or where sharp elbows are mandatory for professional success. Secondly, Rasmus has always been fascinated by mysteries, especially those of the locked-room variety, where an investigator has to find not only the solution but also the elements that support it. As much as Rasmus abhors violence and death, he loves a proper challenge. The sort that tunes his wits to the highest possible frequency.

Normally Rasmus would wolf down his food and then dive into a session of intense game play: Apex Legends, PUBG, Escape from Tarkov, or CoD, depending on the evening and his mood. But he's too distracted now to concentrate on being Everglazer85, the great virtual reality war hero. The present investigation is simply too engrossing.

Rasmus clicks open the email program that just a moment ago delivered a message from Helena Lappi.

The message contains two documents in English: a subpoena and a memo confirming the existence of the preliminary investigation. The message itself is pure Hellu, short and to the point: `Here's the material for Facebook. Hellu`

Rasmus spends five minutes preparing the official request for Facebook. Because this is a murder investigation, chances are good it will be considered urgent in Ireland and the information on the Instagram user known as Akifumi2511946 will be delivered to the investigative team tomorrow morning.

Rasmus double-checks to verify he has filled in the mandatory items on the electronic form and clicks Submit. He stares at the screen for a moment, then starts shoveling soup into his mouth. It has cooled a little and is the perfect temperature for eating.

A siren wails somewhere in the distance, and Rasmus looks out: snowflakes are performing restless rolls and vaults. For the first time this autumn, the world outside the big, drafty window looks wintry.

Rasmus likes winter, the darkness: the fact that he doesn't have to suffer a bad conscience for sitting inside gaming while everyone else is stripping off their shirts. He loves how the cold weather forces him to swathe himself in heavy coats, trousers, and sweaters, how he doesn't have to hide his clumsy, tubby body, like on hot summer days.

Not that winter doesn't have its downsides. When the temperature drops, Rasmus' room is arctic, and he has spent winters since childhood sleeping in heavy full-body pajamas and wool socks. But it isn't cold now. As a matter of fact, it's just the opposite: the warm soup sets his scalp sweating and itching. *I have to remember to apply more lotion.*

Rasmus sets the bowl down on the desk and taps at his computer, and eventually the photo of the young Japanese man appears on the screen. Just this morning, Rasmus was convinced the user who commented on Yamamoto's post could in no way be involved in her disappearance, or Nervander's either. But after coming across the masayoshi.fi website, he's suddenly certain everything is related.

Since morning, Rasmus has been feverishly pondering the significance of the numerical sequence 2511946. At first glance, it appears to be a birth date. But there is one digit too many or one too few. Or it could mean 25 January 1946. Maybe it's a random series of numbers Akifumi wanted to use to ensure the uniqueness of his profile. But if that's the case, he could have gotten by with fewer. Although there are scads of Akifumis, the highest number Rasmus comes across in his search is Akifumi145.

Rasmus leans back in his top-of-the-line gaming chair and sighs. No, 2511946 is not a sequential number, nor is it random. It can't be. If he could only figure out what Lisa Yamamoto's masayoshi.fi site contained before its contents were deleted . . .

Rasmus' phone rings. It's Jessica. Rasmus looks at the name flashing on the screen and reflects how nice and relaxed it was sitting down together at the loud, greasy lunch spot. For a little while, it made him believe that if he just trusted himself enough and forgot his complexes about his appearance and his confidence level, he could be like any other man. Make actual friends, go on dates, have sex. Who knows?

"Hello?"

"Sorry to call so late . . . ," Jessica says.

"No problem. I'm just looking at Akifumi's picture here on my screen."

"Always on the clock, just like the rest of us." Jessica is speaking quickly; she sounds somehow agitated. "Have you ever heard of a ritual called kambo that involves frog poison? Where the toxin is introduced into the body through wounds burned into the skin?"

Rasmus allows Jessica's words to sink in. "Kambo? No . . . Is that what we're looking at here? Those marks on Olga Belousova's body—"

"All the signs point in that direction. In addition, we have reason to believe Lisa Yamamoto has been pushing kambo treatments on social media."

"OK. Sure sounds weird."

"But I've gone through all of her Instagram photos, and there's no mention of kambo."

"What about her stories?"

"I was getting to that. Unfortunately they're only visible for twenty-four hours."

"We'll be able to access them if we get access to Lisa's Instagram account."

"How can it be this hard, Rasmus? Getting Lisa's log-on credentials? I mean, this is a murder investigation."

"There are upsides to it, Jessica. Not allowing the authorities access to everything. There has to be some privacy in the world."

Rasmus scoops a couple of spoonfuls of soup into his mouth while he waits for Jessica's response. He bites into a peppercorn floating in the broth and relishes the warm kick.

"Rasse, you said there's nothing on masayoshi.fi. Now it looks like Lisa deleted everything related to kambo from social media. That means she performed a cleanup operation before she vanished."

"Yes. Or someone with access to her phone did."

"Right now I believe masayoshi.fi had information about kambo on it. If we could find out who performed kambo on Olga Belousova, we might find out who Olga was with on the night she died."

"Kambo," Rasmus says softly as he Googles the term. Frogs and burn marks fill his twenty-four-inch screen.

"I'll start looking into it. At least at first glance there doesn't appear to be anything illicit about kambo; it's being advertised openly online."

"We already have the name of the joint. Alternative Health and Love Helsinki. AHL. We're on our way to talk to the owner."

"Sounds good."

"Thanks, Rasse. It's going to be a long night."

Jessica sighs into the phone and is presumably about to say good night, but Rasmus beats her to the punch. "Jessica . . ."

"Yeah?"

"Thanks for lunch. It was . . . nice."

"Thank you, Rasse. We'll have to do it more often."

43

HELENA LAPPI PULLS up outside the red row house in Konala and activates the hand brake. She looks in through the second-story window and catches a glimpse of a tall blond woman bustling away in the kitchen. On her way to work that morning, Hellu glanced at the refrigerator door, where the pedantic Hanna always posts the menu for the upcoming week: today's dinner will be an Indian dal. Perfectly acceptable, but a little too healthy for Hellu's taste. Plus, Hellu knows she'll wake up hungry in the middle of the night, the way she always does when the evening meal consists of tofu or grains.

She crumples the wrapper of the double cheeseburger into a wad and shoves it in to the glove compartment. Then she cracks her laptop case and fishes out the plastic folder.

The car's engine is still running as she moistens her forefinger on her tongue and flips through the slim sheaf of papers. The basic security check conducted by the Security Police in 2007 is right there on top. It's the routine investigation performed for everyone who applies to the Police College. At the time of her application, twenty-two-year-old Jessica Niemi was deemed to have a spotless background and approved for the application process.

The next document is the confidential report Deputy Chief Oranen recently ordered from the Security Police, which is considerably longer. *Accident . . . Her parents' death.* Hellu can feel her heart hammering. She holds the document up to her eyes so she can read it in the weak overhead light.

Her mother, Theresa von Hellens (260560-1521), father, Axel Koski (040158-113A), and brother, Kristoffer von Hellens (241289-1412) died in car accident on May 4, 1993. According to the Los Angeles County traffic collision report, technical evidence gathered from the scene and statements from the driver and from family members indicate (if not irrefutably prove) that Theresa von Hellens intentionally steered her vehicle into oncoming traffic, with the intent of killing herself and her family.

Hellu jumps when she sees someone flash past in the rearview mirror. A moment later, she sees the receding back of her dog-walking neighbor and returns to the document.

Adopted June 1993. Raimo and Paula Niemi . . . Adoptive parents . . . Father's sister . . . Deceased 2002 (brain tumor) and 2004 (heart attack).

Hellu shakes her head and turns the page. *So much death, Jessica Niemi. Jessica von Hellens. Is that why you became what you are? You lost too much at a young age? Was Erne your third father figure? And now he's gone too.*

Severe damage to the spinal cord. Presumed to cause motor difficulties for the rest of her life . . .

Hellu's phone rings. It's Hanna. She's waving from the window, phone at her ear. "Coming, coming," Hellu murmurs, gestures at the papers in her lap, and turns off the engine.

Hanna is used to Hellu's workdays continuing at home. Hanna's job as a nurse is perhaps even more emotionally draining than Hellu's, but at least she doesn't have to haul patient files home at the end of her shift.

Hellu flips to the last sheet in the stack. It is plainly a photocopy of an older document: a diagnosis from 1998, tapped out on a typewriter and signed by child psychiatrist Olli Vuonamo. A Post-it scrawled by Jens Oranen is fixed to the upper-right corner: *This doesn't appear in any databases! Mikson knew the whole time.* The epicrisis takes up nearly the entire page, and Oranen has picked out phrases here and there in yellow highlighter.

This might well be a presymptomatic stage, characterized by unusual subjective experiences and aspecific symptoms, such as anxiety and depression. . . . Symptoms present include fragmented thinking and behavior, associative dysfunction (dissociation), and delusions with regard to, for instance, her surroundings and other people

"I have you by the balls now, Niemi," Hellu whispers. She shoves the papers back into the folder.

Suddenly dal doesn't sound that bad. Besides, now she's horny; hopefully Hanna's in the mood too.

44

JAMI HARJULA CLENCHES his fingers around the leather steering wheel. At the red light where Meripellontie and Rusthollarintie meet, he shifts into neutral and pumps a few revs, and the engine sings vigorously if a little out of tune. Eastern Helsinki and the November night don't do the engine's timbre justice; it was made to purr on light-filled summer nights at Kaivopuisto. The evenings when Merikatu fills with sports cars from every era, people line up for ice cream, and Jet Skis bob and weave as they race between Liuskaluoto and Sirpalesaari. It's amazing how a city can have two such different faces.

The drive from Harjula's home in Vartiokylä to Aurinkolahti takes only about ten minutes. Harjula parks the car at the corner of Aurinkolahti Square, a hundred meters from the place he parked this morning after being briefed about the body that washed ashore.

Harjula grabs the flashlight from the passenger seat and climbs out of the car. The gusts of offshore wind seem to be enticing him to a dance. The water is a vast plain of blackness; the whitecaps remind the observer that, despite all its suffering, the planet is still very much alive.

Harjula looks around. The white six- and seven-story buildings rising in every direction are built up to the water's edge. Every unit has a glazed balcony. Chichi. He distinctly remembers the face-lift the area underwent at the turn of the millennium. Before that, Aurinkolahti was called Mustalahti, and as part of the transformation, "Black Bay" turned into "Sunny Bay." A relatively brazen but apparently successful rebranding.

Even though it's ten thirty p.m., lights are on in the majority of apartments. More than eight thousand people live in the neighborhood, and not a single one has stepped forward as an eyewitness in the Olga Belousova case. Someone would no doubt remember if she had strolled through the neighborhood dressed like a Japanese cartoon character. That's why the body must have ended up in the water from the sea.

Harjula stops at the water's edge near the marina, which has four long docks and more than a hundred moorings. Only a dozen or so boats are lashed to the walkways, and some look to be in such poor shape that the chance of anyone hauling them out for the winter is minuscule.

Between the marina and the beach runs a stout breakwater three hundred yards long, give or take; its presence precludes the possibility that Olga Belousova's body was heaved overboard from a boat moored at the marina.

Harjula turns in the other direction. Half a kilometer away, at the far end of the beach, there's a smaller marina built into a little harbor more or less sheltered from the breakwater.

Streetlamps illuminate the promenade; Harjula starts crossing the beach so close to the waterline that the waves nip at the soles of his shoes. He climbs a granite slab halfway down the beach and scans the surroundings, as if a rise of a couple of meters would clarify everything.

The spot where Olga Belousova's body was found is about ten meters farther down the beach. Footprints—his and the tech team's—are still visible in the frost-hardened sand.

How the hell did you end up here, Olga?

Harjula eyes the small tree-covered peninsula jutting out between the beach and the second marina, then pulls his phone from his pocket. The peninsula—according to Google Maps, a good hundred meters long and fifty meters wide—has a name: Suorttio.

Expert statements ordered earlier in the day reported that currents make it possible but unlikely for a body lowered into the water outside the bay to drift ashore between the granite slab and Suorttio. The same expert deemed it almost certain that the body was left either where it was found or somewhere nearby, inside Aurinkolahti Bay.

But if that were the case, someone would have had to see something. *Damn it.*

Harjula continues on to the far end of the beach and stops at the brink of the little harbor. Suorttio now stretches seaward to his right, and there are only about ten meters between the peninsula and the outermost dock of the smaller marina.

The wind gusts set the moored boats rocking.

Harjula narrows his eyes. If Olga was lowered into the water from the wooded peninsula, no one would necessarily have seen anything. But first the body would have had to be transported there, either by car or floated from a boat.

Harjula decides to poke around Suorttio. He feels hard rock underfoot and is surprised pines can grow so tall in such stony soil. He dodges the low-hanging branches and advances toward the peninsula's tip. To his right looms the water, and beyond it, at a distance of about a hundred fifty meters, the spot Olga was found. The perfect darkness rolling in from the sea forms a stark contrast with the streetlamps of the promenade. It's like two worlds colliding. Now that he thinks about it, Olga Belousova's body was found where light and darkness mingle.

Suddenly Harjula feels something under the sole of his shoe that's neither moss nor rock.

He lifts his foot. Pressed into the mossy soil is a small book. A notebook, upon closer inspection.

Harjula pulls a pair of plastic gloves from his coat and tugs them over his mitts.

He picks up the notebook and opens it. The bone white pages are wet and ice-cold.

He flips through it from beginning to end. A few pages are torn out toward the front. But the first page that remains bears three names inscribed in a tidy hand.

IT'S FIVE TO eleven, and Jessica is sitting in the back of a police van at the corner of Toinen linja and Castréninkatu. The playground is deserted; the wind is dancing in the branches of leafless trees. Farther off, behind the little park, the City Theatre rises, white against the charcoal sky. The radio in the police van is blasting the number-one hit on the playlists: none other than the title track from Kex Maces' new album, *Kex Maces' Spider's Web*.

The lyrics take Jessica back to her meeting with the vaguely truculent, overly confident rapper at the Sea Horse earlier in the day. She pulls up Instagram and opens Kex Maces' profile. Along with the profile image and the handle @kexmaces, there's a small blue symbol, the stamp of authenticity granted by Instagram. The super-famous have countless fake accounts opened in their names, and the blue dot serves as an indication to followers that a profile is real.

Kex has almost a million followers, and he has posted more than a thousand photos. Pictures from parties, galas, shows, vacations, jogging paths, pleasure yachts, helicopters, home. A spider features in many; a tap reveals this to be Maces' new pet, Escobar. Jessica wonders whether Escobar served as inspiration for the album, or if the eight-legged companion is a PR gimmick to establish the milieu of the new album.

Jessica continues browsing the images, but pauses when she sees Lisa's face. Kex and Lisa are posing cheek to cheek in a black-and-white shot; their smiles gleam. *Finland's hottest blogger. Follow her! @thelisa-yamamoto.* The photograph was taken indoors: the background is a dark gray wall and Jessica sees one corner of a framed work of art. The picture was posted to Instagram a couple of months ago, in September.

"Looks pretty quiet," says the uniformed policeman in the driver's seat. He rolls a pinch of snuff between his thumb and forefinger. Jessica slips her phone back into her coat pocket.

She folds down the sun visor and looks at herself in the mirror. Her black hair is tied back in a ponytail, and she's wearing a dark blue New York Yankees cap. She realizes she looks like one of the hard-boiled female cops from American television.

Diagonally across the street, between a used-car lot and a bar, there's a little storefront with the words "Alternative Health & Love Helsinki" taped across it in ornate lettering. A few of the bar's customers are smoking outside, but other than that the street is dead.

"We done here?"

"Wait a sec."

Jessica takes out her phone and stares at the screen. Yusuf is currently with another patrol, knocking on the door of Jose Rodriguez's apartment only five hundred meters away. When he finally calls, Jessica shuts her eyes.

"It doesn't look like Jose Rodriguez is home," Yusuf says in a tired voice. "We talked to one of the neighbors, who says the last time she saw him was this morning."

Jessica sighs. "OK."

"Hellu didn't authorize a search?"

Jessica looks at her knuckles, which have taken on new shades of red. The justifications for coercive measures like searches have to be watertight these days, which, she supposes, is fine when it comes to privacy and civil rights. But sometimes it leads to pointless waiting, even in rock-solid instances that demand rapid action.

Right now authorization is on hold: surprisingly enough, there are multiple kambo treatment centers in Helsinki, which means there's nothing directly linking AHL to Olga Belousova yet. It all seems so obvious, but it's too flimsy on paper.

"No," Jessica says. "We don't have authorization yet."

"What are you going to do?"

"We're going to take a look through the window. Call me if anything happens," Jessica says, and hangs up.

THE PUNISHING REFRAIN of Rage Against the Machine's "Killing in the Name" pounds her earbuds. Nina Ruska lowers the weights to the rubber mat to catch her breath. Her eyes fix on the large mirror opposite, where she sees a woman in a sleeveless top standing in an ascetic space dominated by white iron, black leather, and colorful weights. Her shoulder and chest muscles are swollen, and the skin protecting them is flushed. She feels her flesh twitch and quiver.

There's no one else working out. The handful of others who lift at night must be in the field or taking a well-deserved day off from the gym. When their duties allow, most of her fellow officers train in the morning. And then there's Yusuf, who shows up whenever, sometimes twice a day. As someone who has lifted rigorously for two decades, Nina cannot fathom the impulsive, haphazard approach of those who discover weight lifting on a whim. Yusuf is a perfect specimen of the type: a plainly athletic guy whose body initially reacts to heavy weights by displaying rapid muscle development and who, delighted by the fast results, loads more weight onto the barbells without a sensible workout plan. When his enthusiasm eventually wears off, his muscles will melt away as quickly as they grew. Even so, Nina has been preoccupied by the nagging sensation that after her week of semi-irresponsible playtime, the only reason she's back at the gym is to run into Yusuf here. Something about his transformation speaks to her. Maybe it has to do with his newly single status; maybe she's subconsciously scavenging for injured prey.

Nina grabs the weights and leans back on the bench, which is set at a forty-five-degree angle. The heavy weights and slow lifts set her chest and shoulders on fire. She maxes out the final reps: *Nine, ten, eleven, twelve . . .*

Nina wants every single muscle fiber in her body to push it to the limit, every cell to give its all and not one iota less. When the hands holding the weights tremble from exhaustion, she sees things more clearly. The exertion empties her head and chases off distractions. It forces her mind to focus on survival.

Thirteen. She sees herself on the floor of the dark basement, helpless and naked, wrapped in a white sheet. Men from the SWAT team are bustling around her.

Her hands rise slowly, and the pang of lovely, searing pain in her breast is so sharp it feels like her heart will burst.

Fourteen.

I looked you in the eye, Micke, and said I loved you. And you said it back. But you didn't know shit about love, you cocksucker.

One more rep. Maybe two. Fuck!

Fifteen!

Jessica Niemi. We never said we were friends. But we were colleagues who were supposed to be able to trust each other. Fuck you, Jessica. Ooh, amazing, all-is-forgiven Jessica, who screwed Micke behind my back and everybody still has a hard-on for.

Nina feels the veins in her forehead bulge.

The betrayal isn't assuaged by the fact that Micke dicked them both over.

Sixteen.

One more. The fists holding the weights strain toward the ceiling; her body is on the verge of giving up. She's almost out of breath, but she has to complete this last rep, damn it, since she said she was going to.

What she needs is a serious ass kicking. My fist, her face, and sayonara, bitch!

Seventeen!

Nina roars like a lioness. The weights drop to the floor and bounce off the rubber mat before rolling away.

Nina shuts her eyes. Her head is spinning. Her arms are completely numb.

She shakes her head, takes her phone from the floor, and snaps a photograph of herself in the mirror.

She looks terrible: her face is beet red and dripping with sweat; her skin is riddled with burst blood vessels. But that's as it should be. *Now, this is what a real workout post looks like.*

```
Instagram. New York filter. #nighttimeworkout #took-
ittothemax #beachbod #beachbod01072020
```

Nina is about to upload the image, but her trembling finger pauses above the screen. It takes her a second to digest what she has just intuited. It's something incredibly simple, something no one has thought to look into yet.

"Holy shit . . . ," Nina whispers, whipping out her earbuds.

47

THE BARFLIES SMOKING on the patio keep close tabs on the police officers crossing the street, two of whom are in uniform. Jessica is leading the way in her civilian clothes, and she pretends not to hear the snide muttering of the two middle-aged men on the terrace. At this particular spot and at this hour of the day, it's foolish to expect anyone to appreciate their efforts on behalf of a safer Finland.

Jessica and the two officers stop at the storefront door. White roller blinds are pulled down in the large display windows framing the entrance.

Jessica tries the door. As she expected, it's locked. The metal handle feels like ice against her bare fingers; she forgot to grab her gloves when she left the apartment.

"Here," the bald, bearded senior officer says, handing her a long-handled flashlight.

Jessica takes the cold battery-packed metal tube and aims the beam through the glass door. She spies a room approximately the size of her studio apartment. Houseplants, a few beanbags, theme-appropriate frog art, a tall counter with a laptop on it. On the floor: rolled-up yoga mats, candles, books, a few buckets. A yellow raincoat hangs on the wall.

And something else that captures Jessica's attention. It's on the floor, partially hidden by one of the beanbags.

"Come have a look," she says. "Is that a phone?"

The closest officer takes the flashlight and squints.

"Could be," he says, forehead to the glass.

"Turn off the flashlight for a sec." Jessica pulls out her cell phone. She brings up the number she gave Yusuf half an hour earlier and calls. A few seconds pass. Then the black shape on the floor starts flashing.

Jessica feels her pulse racing. She knows there's no logical reason for a phone to be on the floor of a kambo spa at eleven o'clock on a Wednesday night. Especially in such a visible place: if its owner had come looking for it, he would have found it immediately.

Jessica knocks insistently on the glass, but no one answers. She waits for a second and knocks again, even more sharply.

No reaction.

The possibility that Jose Rodriguez, seller of kambo treatments, has fallen asleep in his spa at the end of a long day has started to seem unlikely.

"We need to go in," Jessica says. "Get the tools."

The senior officer stares at Jessica. He turns to the barflies monitoring the situation a dozen meters away, then to the lock on the glass door. He holds up the butt of his flashlight.

Jessica looks at him questioningly.

"I'd probably just go in with this," he says.

"OK, I take full responsibility," Jessica says. She steps aside. "Go for it."

The senior officer hesitates no more than a couple seconds before sharply whacking the butt of the flashlight through the glass. The pair watching from the bar's patio starts jeering. *Ha ha! Did someone forget to pay their dog license? Fucking pigs.*

The officer uses the flashlight to peel the sharp shards from the frame, then thrusts his gloved hand through the hole and twists the lock. Unlocking does not trip an alarm; the only sound to break the silence is the crunch of glass beneath their soles.

Jessica reaches for her gun, and the senior officer does the same. The other policeman watches the entrance.

Jessica flicks the switch next to the door and the lights come on. An unsettling stench of incense and burned flesh permeates the place.

Three shelves along the back wall hold clay vessels, glass jars, and other paraphernalia whose purpose Jessica can only guess at. There's nothing in the room they couldn't see through the door.

Jessica picks up Jose Rodriguez's phone from the floor with her free hand and presses the Home button.

12 llamadas perdidas

Twelve missed calls. The phone has been lying on the floor for some time.

Jessica nods toward a black door in the rear wall.

"Jose Rodriguez?" she says loudly, despite how futile it seems. "Police!"

Pistol still in hand, the officer reaches for the door handle.

"Hello. Anyone there?"

There's no response. Jessica nods, and the officer opens the door. It takes a second for the light to penetrate the dark washroom. The eyes of the dreadlocked young man sitting, fully dressed, on the toilet are bright blue. They're still astonished, even though some time has passed since the bullet aimed between his eyes lulled him into eternal sleep and spattered some of the contents of his skull on the light blue tile.

48

RASMUS SUSIKOSKI CHECKS the time at the upper-right corner of his computer screen. It's zero zero twelve hours, and his eyelids are starting to droop. Not that midnight is particularly late in Rasmus' world; even on weeknights, an online game might continue until two or three in the morning. When it comes to physicality, Rasmus has never been much of an athlete or anything even close to it. But he does possess one useful superpower: minimal need for sleep. Whereas many members of the investigative team turn into zombies during intense cases demanding twenty-four-hour attention, Rasmus can go for a week on no more than a few hours of sleep a night and still remain relatively alert and sharp. And he doesn't necessarily need energy drinks to do so, although he generally downs them by the bucketload.

But tonight Rasmus hasn't logged into Apex Legends or Call of Duty. Instead, his screen has cycled through vast amounts of information on and images of frogs, kambo, Jose Rodriguez, and manga clothes.

The smell wafting through his room is a blend of acrid energy drink and sausage soup that has cooled in the bowl.

A faint beep echoes from the earphones connected wirelessly to the computer, and Rasmus brings up the browser window he has open to Facebook Messenger. The message is from Nina.

Rasmus feels his pulse accelerate. He clicks to the chat window.

NINA RUSKA: Awake?
RASMUS SUSIKOSKI: Yes. =)
NR: I noticed you were online.

Did you hear about Rodriguez?
RS: Yup.
Hellu texted.
NR: Same here.

Rasmus leans back and takes a swig of maté-infused soft drink. Discussing work matters on social media is strictly prohibited, even in private messages. But that's what these messages are: private, and no one has the right or even the opportunity to monitor them right now.

NR: I was thinking about Akifumi.
The number.
RS: 2511946?
NR: At first I thought it was a random sequence of numbers added
to the end of the name.
A long one, to make sure the handle is unique.
There are a hell of a lot of Akifumis.
But it feels like there's something there.
Then I just thought of something else. Our workout group has its
own hashtag.
#beachbod010720,
Means we'll all have a beach bod by July 1.
LOL

Rasmus would like to write back and tell Nina that she already has a perfect beach body but decides not to.

RS: And?
NR: And because this whole thing is happening on Instagram, I
decided to check the numerical sequence there.
RS: What did you find?
NR: Hashtags.

#2511946

There are almost twenty.

Rasmus feels a pang. Hashtags? Why didn't he think of that?

He immediately opens another tab, brings up the browser version of Instagram, and taps in the search term "2511946."

There are eighteen photographs marked with the hashtag #2511946.

This is too hot to discuss over chat. Rasmus grabs his phone and brings up Nina's number. A moment later, his fellow investigator answers in a chipper voice.

"I figured you would call," Nina says.

Rasmus scrolls down the page. "Did you look through the pictures?"

"Yup. At first glance they don't have anything in common; they're all taken in different places and posted by different users. But when you spend a little time with them, you realize . . ."

"They're all bars?"

"Yup, and restaurants, hotels, motels. With no people ever appearing in them. But location information is included for every one."

"Are they all—"

"In Sweden," Nina says.

This information deflates Rasmus a bit. He tilts the angle of his gaming chair into a more relaxed position. "Sweden?"

"Yup. Everything from dumps to really classy places. I studied the photos for a pretty long time and tried to figure out why anyone would take a boring picture of a building and its sign, tag the location, and add a bunch of hashtags, including #2511946. It always comes last."

Nina holds a pause.

"Always comes last . . . That clearly indicates some sort of protocol."

"Exactly. The first thing that occurred to me is there's something linking all these places, and that's the reason someone wanted to tag them with this numerical sequence. Think about it, Rasmus. If it's true, an Instagram user could search for a list of locations—"

"As long as they know the right series of numbers." Rasmus takes off his glasses, and the mystery takes on a new, verbal form in his head. "It's a search term."

"Yup. It's a goddamn search term, Rasse!"

Rasmus feels the excitement spread to his neck, then down to his fingertips. The discovery doesn't actually prove anything, and at this point the tagged locations in Sweden don't have any sort of link to the series of crimes they're investigating. Even so, everything appears clear and bright right now. "Maybe a secret search term that would also work as—"

Nina finishes Rasmus' sentence: "A password."

Lovely Nina. Smart, beautiful, clever Nina. Strong Nina. Nina who wants to share her discovery with me and me alone.

"I was thinking, why just Sweden? Eighteen pictures of Swedish companies in the hospitality business. And then I got it: forty-six."

"Forty-six?"

"The last two digits. 2511946. Four. Six. It's Sweden's country code. I switched them out for 358, and guess what."

Rasmus holds his breath and taps 25119358 into the Instagram search field. He presses Enter, and a bunch of photographs appear on the screen: ten, to be precise.

"Otherwise the formula's the same, but these locations are in Finland. And guess which nightclub is one of them," Nina says.

"The Phoenix."

"Bingo."

"Goddamn," Rasmus says under his breath, even though he knows it's not the most credible curse word. "What . . . what about other country codes? Does every country have its own hashtag?"

"I thought exactly the same thing. I tested a few, and it looks like the system works in the Nordic countries, excluding Iceland. There were five tags for Norway and fourteen in Denmark. The same system didn't bring up anything in Germany, France, or Estonia."

"Nordic . . . What? Does this have something to do with kambo?"

"To my knowledge, practicing kambo isn't illegal in any of these countries."

"Drugs?"

"Anything is possible, Rasse," Nina says.

And in this, Nina is absolutely right.

Rasmus thinks about the Tor network, past investigations when it was confirmed you could search for anything online—drugs, ivory, guns, child pornography—using specific search terms known only to members of the ring. That's why the police have a hard time tracking them down.

"Does Jessica know? Or Hellu?" Rasmus asks.

"Not yet. I wanted to talk to you first."

Rasmus feels a warmth in his belly. He's Nina's ICE contact.

In case of emergency.

"OK . . ."

"I wanted to get some idea, even a vague one, about who Akifumi is first. And why he used the country code for Sweden in his Instagram handle." Nina sighs into the phone.

"Maybe he's a whistleblower? Someone who wanted to attract the attention of the police?"

"But why wouldn't he have just gotten a message to the police and told us directly? Why would he have given us such an obscure clue, one we're not even necessarily going to know how to interpret correctly?"

"I don't know. But the good thing is, all we have to do is track down one of the people who posted these images on Instagram, and squeeze them to find out—"

"That's not going to happen, Rasse."

"Why not? We just—"

"The accounts are all fake. And only one image was posted from each account."

Suddenly Rasmus feels incredibly weary. Perhaps hope has kept him awake, but the truth being rubbed in his face instantly extinguishes it. The deeper they sink into the puzzle, the murkier the surrounding view seems to grow.

49

Yusuf leans against the hood of his car and lights a cigarette. A police van is parked outside the kambo spa across the street, and the sidewalk has been cordoned off with blue-and-white police tape. The gray apartment blocks rising on either side of the one-story spa flicker with bright blue light; curious faces peer down from balconies.

Yusuf sucks the nicotine into his lungs, then holds his breath, as if giving the poison a chance to absorb properly into his circulation. Then he releases the smoke in a thin ribbon from the corner of his mouth.

Yusuf has been smoking more than ever lately. He has gradually given up all sports involving aerobic conditioning and focused on lifting. After the breakup last spring, hoisting heavy iron seemed like the only thing that eased his mind. Music playing on his headphones, the clank of weights, chalk puffing up from his palms, the smell of sweat. The lactates flooding his muscles; the burn that washes over the body during the final counts of a long series of negative reps. Muscles bulging and trembling from the strain.

More than anything, this has been about reinventing himself, Yusuf supposes. Enough with the athletic, beautiful dark-skinned boy everybody loves who performs a simple hat trick on the pitch, then hits the showers and rushes home to his fiancée. The time has come to be something else. He wants to experience what it's like being the alpha—and in such killer shape by summer that he'll make panties wet on the Mummotunneli dance floor.

At the same time, Yusuf knows it: the whole thing is *so fucking ridiculous*. In spite of his bluster and the vows he's sworn at the mirror, things have been dead silent on the female front in recent months. Not that he hasn't had plenty of opportunities. But he can't be bothered with sex right now. Generalized irritation has robbed him of his libido.

Yusuf looks up from his shoes to the sight of a double-length semi slowly passing on its way downtown. When it eventually disappears from view, he sees Jessica cross the street and approach him.

"There are a few bottles in the fridge," she says as she walks up. "They'll be taken to the lab for analysis. It's possible all the substances found in Olga's body will turn up, either mixed with the frog toxin or separately."

"I'm sure they will. Unless the shooter grabbed them already."

A tram turns the corner and clanks by lazily, making for Hakaniemi Square and the subway station. A dozen or so students in dark green college coveralls are carousing in the rear.

Jessica sits on the hood at Yusuf's side. "What do you think? About all this?"

He takes a drag, then lifts his face toward the anthracite sky; the heavy cloud layer has made off with the moon. "Olga Belousova came here on Saturday. Maybe alone, maybe with someone. Maybe that someone caught wind today that we found a body at Aurinkolahti. Decided it had to be Olga. That the marks on her arms would lead the police here, that we'd start asking questions." Yusuf scrunches up his nose as if smoke went too far into his nasal cavity. "Whoever it was came here and iced the kambo guy so he wouldn't talk."

"The Phantom?" Jessica murmurs.

Yusuf digs some grime from under the nail of his forefinger. "Has to be."

"The only thing that bothers me . . ." Yusuf turns to Jessica as she speaks. "I did some checking in the car, searched online for information about Jose. He seems to have been some sort of trailblazer in the kambo business. At least in Finland. The guy had a lot of satisfied clients who insist kambo changed their lives for the better."

"And?"

"There's no way he mixed morphine and buprenorphine into the kambo for all his clients. Everyone would have gotten too high. He would have gotten caught. Plus a hit like that is pretty expensive, and I don't think there are that many people willing to pay."

"So you think he created the blend only for certain people?"

"Exactly. That he had two different clienteles."

"Intriguing."

"Think about it, Yusuf. If you want to make someone believe they need to come in regularly for treatment, lacing the toxin with something that not only boosts the high but also causes addiction is the perfect way to do it. But like I said, there's no way Jose could have or would have agreed to do it for everyone."

Yusuf flicks his cigarette butt to the ground. "Keep going, Jessie. You're in the flow."

"There must be more girls like Olga Belousova. They might not know they're addicted, but they are. They don't realize it because they believe in kambo and think certain sensations are part of the ceremony."

"So someone's adding stuff to the frog poison so clients come back for more? Sort of like tobacco companies?"

Jessica eyes the spot where Yusuf just ground out his cigarette. "Exactly."

"OK. So who's behind all this?"

"Someone who brings young women into the country. I'm thinking traffickers are moving past the whole take-the-passport-from-the-girl-and-shoot-her-up-with-drugs thing. You can read despair and fear on the face of a woman forced to sell herself. That's bad for business. Which is why Olga Belousova had her ID on her. These women were captives but didn't know it. Kind of like an open prison where the convicts are free to come and go."

"And the kambo addiction is the invisible cell?"

"At this point we should probably be talking about a kambo-plus addiction, shouldn't we?"

"I guess."

A white tech van pulls in between the two police vans.

"So you think Olga Belousova suffered some sort of complication here?" Yusuf continues as a man and a woman step out of the van and start pulling on their white protective gear.

"Here or somewhere else. Maybe on the boat Harjula was talking about. Wherever it was, no one saw it coming. They tried to resuscitate Olga, but they couldn't take her to a hospital, because the doctors would have been curious to know where a woman who was in the country illegally got pumped full of pharmaceuticals. So she was dumped in the sea on the spur of the moment. And then a passerby found her body a few days later."

"What about Harjula's theory that some sicko wanted an unconscious woman to rape?"

Jessica tugs her coat sleeves down over her fingers. "I don't believe it. I mean, I believe there are people in this sick world who would be interested, but for some reason, I don't think that's what's going on here."

"Good job, Jessie," Yusuf says, and lights another cigarette. "We're going to wrap this case up tomorrow."

They sit there on the hood without speaking. Several hours of light snowfall have laid the asphalt with a sheer white linen. Candelabras and star-shaped ornaments glow in the windows of the high-rise apartment buildings. But right now, with his thoughts consumed by the man sitting on the toilet of his little enterprise, Yusuf has a hard time imagining Christmas is less than a month away.

50

YUSUF PULLS UP outside Jessica's building.

Jessica doesn't immediately reach for the door; she lets her head slump back against the headrest. She and Yusuf have an unspoken tradition of sharing a brief silence before parting ways. It entails the rasp of Yusuf pulling up the hand brake, the thrum of the running motor, the windshield wipers pushing the snow to the side, and the low-volume blast of the Spotify playlist Jessica can't stand. Töölö has never actually been on Yusuf's way, per se, but even so, he has consistently offered to drop Jessica off at her door.

Now and again, Jessica feels bad; she has started taking the rides for granted. Letting Yusuf chauffeur her has folded into the performance meant to telegraph that she's no different from anyone else, depends on little everyday kindnesses: *Can you front me a hundred? You mind taking me home?*

And on rare occasions, maybe only once or twice, Jessica has found herself wondering if Yusuf mightn't want to turn off the engine, leave the car on the street, and come up.

Would Jessica want it herself? Probably not. Yusuf has been a good friend for a long time, and she has no interest in letting sex endanger their relationship. One reason the two of them have always clicked is that there's not an iota of sexual tension between them. Sure, they'd look good together on paper. But Jessica has come to notice she associates Yusuf with Toffe, the little brother she lost so long ago. Besides, up until last spring, Yusuf was with Anna. The high school romance that persisted in blossoming from year to year filled its witnesses with hope that not every relationship comes to an end in discord. And then that castle in the sky came tumbling down too.

"Thanks for the ride," Jessica says. She knows she doesn't say it often enough.

Yusuf gives her a weary smile. "No worries. Back at it tomorrow."

Before she shuts the door, Jessica catches Yusuf yodeling along to the Gasellit as the song builds to its chorus. *S'right. Corny-ass Malaga. I like it here at home.*

51

JESSICA TESTS THE water with her fingertips, then steps over the edge of the tub. The almost scorching bathwater kisses her skin and makes the hairs on the back of her neck stand up. Little by little, she lowers herself in, allows every pore to revel in the tingle of the hot water cocooning her. Soon enough, it will go the way of all pleasures: her body will acclimate, and what was once delicious will become the new normal. Sweet heat dwindles to lukewarm. She wants to relish every sensation when the experience is most acute, live in the here and now.

Easier said than done.

Jessica shuts her eyes, and when she finally reopens them, her eyelids feel less heavy. She lets her gaze meander around the large bathroom. The walls of white tile received a skim of gray microcement not so many years ago. Jessica remembers Erne admiring the simple elegance of the textured matte surface as Jessica helped him bathe. Sometimes he would completely forget the pressure and shame of being a patient and relax, release his need to control. In those moments, he would lower his head against the tub's soft neck rest and shut his eyes as Jessica washed his hair with tar-scented shampoo. Erne liked the smell. He said it reminded him of childhood, of the log outbuildings of Saarenmaa, where the carcasses of just-felled wild boar hung in the cool autumn mornings.

Jessica shuts her eyes again; she can sense Erne's presence and she feels safe, as if he is in the bathroom with her.

"I'M SO HAPPY you have this," Erne says one night in the bath. His eyes are closed; Jessica is rinsing his hair with tepid water. Erne speaks slowly, and his voice is frail but determined. His body may be dying, but his head works the way it always has. For better or for worse.

"What?"

"All this." Erne chuckles and twirls his finger around. After a brief coughing fit, Erne gulps a few times as if to make sure his voice still carries. "But maybe you could . . . maybe you ought to consider opening up your real home to your friends. To good people, people you trust. Yusuf. Or even Rasse . . . I mean, Fubu doesn't even know. . . ."

"Erne . . ." Jessica sighs. "You're making me regret I brought you here."

Erne nods apologetically. "I'm sorry. The older you get, the more advice you want to give. Have you noticed? Or maybe it's not just that you're aging; it's that you're dying. Somehow that convinces you you've grown as wise as humanly possible."

Jessica dries her hands on a towel and stands. It's so quiet they can hear the drops from the tap Jessica just twisted off plop into the bathwater.

"You shouldn't have to be worried they won't like you because of all this . . . or that having money somehow makes you a worse human being. Or any different. Different from whom they've known . . ."

"Maybe it's better not to find out."

"Jessie, I'm just afraid you're alone for no reason. A lot of people are lonely because they don't have a choice. Because they're ugly, crusty, cranky old bastards like me. Decrepit in body and soul after a lifetime of accumulated secrets and mistakes . . . You still have time to open up your life to someone you trust, Jessie."

"Maybe I like being alone here in my fairy castle. Maybe I enjoy hopping between two worlds. Maybe that's freedom."

"Keeping secrets?"

"No, being able to choose who and what you are. Every day."

Erne nods, fatigued; he knows it's no use. Jessica walks over to the sink, pumps moisturizer onto her palms, rubs it in. She looks at herself in the mirror, sees Erne lying in the tub. Jessica knows it's a matter of days now, a couple weeks at most. Right now Erne is relatively chipper, almost his old self, but by the end of the short bath, he will be so exhausted he won't be able to keep his eyes open. Jessica knows time is running out. The doctor said Erne, dulled by the powerful pain medications, will grow increasingly tired toward the end, sleep longer and longer, until one day, he won't wake up. Jessica has already started drafting her speech for the memorial. She absolutely wants Erne to hear it. He can be her dress rehearsal audience.

As Jessica rubs lotion into her forehead, she sees Erne's face twitch in the mirror. She whirls around. "Erne? What's wrong?"

His gaunt face is twisted up in silent, inconsolable weeping. He opens his eyes, looks into Jessica's more deeply than ever before. "Promise me you'll take care of yourself, Jessie. Otherwise I'm going to have to come back and . . . die again." He wipes the tears from the corner of his eye with his soapy hand.

Jessica leans over to dry his face.

I promise, Erne dear.

JESSICA INHALES, RELEASES the air from her lungs, and lets herself sink into the tub, her body slowly sliding to the bottom. She hears the water rush into her ears, sees the bubbles rise from her mouth. Her black hair uncoils toward the surface, like the tentacles of an octopus. Jessica holds her breath. She counts the seconds until her thoughts begin to wander. Then she loses track of time. She has been underwater for a minute. Maybe longer. She can feel the pressure in her lungs, her windpipe. Is this what Erne went through in her guest bed a second before his lungs ceased to function? Was it humane, watching him gradually suffocate like a fish on dry land? Would a real friend have fulfilled Erne's wish: that he die while he was sound of body, be spared the pain and disorientation helplessness brings?

Jessica shuts her eyes and suddenly sees the black-and-white photograph of Tim Taussi and Lisa Yamamoto. There's nothing particularly unusual or suspicious about it, but Jessica can't get it out of her head. She will ask Taussi himself about it first thing in the morning.

52

JESSICA.

The whisper hovers and permeates the room.

The round clock on the living room wall shows a quarter to four. Jessica rose from the couch fifteen minutes ago. At three thirty, at the moment of truth. The streetlamps are swaying on their wires below window level; their beams do not penetrate the old building. Only the tireless glow from the sea of phosphor that is downtown Helsinki gives contours to the furniture and other objects in the room, prevents them from melting into pristine darkness.

Jessica's hand moves fluidly across the paper, forming the meticulous letters the way her mother taught her. But her mother didn't live long enough to see the hand holding the pen grow, to hear the thoughts concealed behind Jessica's beautiful script. The adult Jessica. The Jessica who has something to say, the ability to dress her thoughts in effortless sentences.

Sometimes the girl consciously forgets what he did to her, chooses to remember Venice basking in the June sun. The days before Colombano's powerful fingers wrapped around her throat, before he shed his mask. The moments at his side as his chest rose and fell, at that hour when nocturnal stillness bows to the sounds of the wakening city. Daybreak plays the city: its people and birds are its instruments. Shrieking gulls, a busker's violin. Umbrellas blossoming on patios, unfurling awnings shaking their nightly accretion of dew to the cobblestones. Boats weaving down canals on small motors, the cries of gondoliers, the chatter of tourists. Venice's beauty compares only to her lover's. But when Colombano looks on her with contempt, the clouds seem to choke the sun, and the canals' rancid stench rises to her nostrils. And when he digs his cracked fingertips into her throat, cuts off her breath, and rams his hand where it was once invited, where she once wanted it, the girl feels something inside her die.

Jessica lowers the pen to the table and waits.

Despite the dim lighting, the dark blue ink shows distinctly against the white paper. It takes a moment for her mother to finish reading the sentences Jessica wrote. Or maybe she reads them twice. To understand exactly what her daughter is saying.

Jessie dear . . .

When her mother speaks, a chill washes over Jessica, as if she opened the door and paused there, letting in the icy air. Jessica knots the belt of her bathrobe more tightly around her waist, shields her bare breast.

You're still in his grip, aren't you?

The glossy black fingernails stroke Jessica's handwritten lines. They are surprisingly assured and straight, as if written on ruled paper.

Jessica lifts her gaze from the page and lets it glide up the slender fingers to the white arm, to the black evening gown only partially covering the pointed breasts, to the neckline, and finally to the face. Its shapelessness makes it almost unbearable to look at. It is bathed in blood; the no-man's-land between the battered brow and the crushed cheekbones shows only scattered islands of white skin.

I thought you were stronger, Jessie.

I'm sorry, Mother.

A rattling sigh. Her mother takes the page; her fingers scuttle across it like the feet of a large insect. She folds the sheet in half. For a moment, Jessica thinks her mother will slip it into the purse hanging from the back of the chair. But suddenly the paper crumples into a wad in her mother's trembling fist and is engulfed in the veiny hand, never to appear again. Her mother raises her eyelids, and her eyes seem to widen amid the gore.

Sometimes the way you think hurts me, Jessie. I tried to raise you to be strong.

Her mother's voice is cold, scolding.

I'm sorry, Mother.

Go to bed and forget about that man. Behave as a von Hellens ought.

Jessica lowers her head and slowly stands. The chair doesn't scrape, nor does the old hardwood floor creak the way it does during the daytime. The moment that binds together the night's somber tones selects its own soundscape. Mother's voice. Her own. The faint scratch of the pen against the heavy stationery. The crunch of crumpling paper.

Jessica stops in front of the stairs.

But I killed him.

A sigh from her mother.

He deserved to die, Jessie.

Her mother's voice is contemptuous.

I killed him, Mother.

Jessica shuts her eyes and feels herself float toward another reality, another time and place, with light flooding through the windows, drowning out the endless darkness of winter.

She opens her eyes again. She must play the scene out, utter every one of her lines. Walk up to bed on her own two feet.

Concentrate on the present, Jessie. Focus your energies on things you can still affect.

Jessica watches her mother rise.

Do you remember the card trick your father used to do for you and Toffe? Over and over again?

Jessica nods.

The magician doesn't need to know which card you pick, Jessie. Just the card next to it.

Jessica feels her lips move as they soundlessly repeat the words her mother just spoke.

Good night, Mother.

Good night, Jessie dear.

Jessica looks at the sofa, where she dozed off a few hours earlier. The timer turned off the television. As she starts climbing the stairs to the second story of her apartment, she hears her mother crying. Every tread leads her further from childhood and closer to the present moment. When Jessica casts a final glance at the long table, her mother is no longer there. Just the pen, and the crumpled letter, and the silence that is like a lump in her throat. But Jessica can still clearly smell the scent that roused her: burned wood, like a campfire, and a blooming garden of perfume.

The magician doesn't need to know which card you pick, Jessie. Just the card next to it.

THURSDAY, NOVEMBER 28

53

THE WAIL OF a police siren gradually drowns out her mother's quiet weeping.

Jessica can sense the mingling of the dream with real-life stimuli: feel the people and the sounds around her evaporate as she becomes aware of the weight of her body, of her cheeks, hips, legs, knees, even the soles of her feet, touching the satiny sheet.

It's morning. Finally.

Jessica slowly opens her eyes. She looks at her hand. The room is dim, but she can still see the dried ink on the side of her palm. She feels listless and hungover, despite having only a glass of white wine last night. The nights she spends fully or partially in conversation with her mother deplete her: it's as if they suck out the little charge imparted by nights of chronically poor sleep.

Jessica pays close attention as she moves into a sitting position on the edge of her king-sized bed. The habit dates back to the time when a sudden movement could cause a spike of agony. Mornings were the worst: after a night of sleep, her heels and knees felt as if they were under attack by tiny, furiously spinning pins, like runaway compass needles. The shooting pain in her lower back, shoulders, and wrists was like that of being stabbed with a long sword over and over again by a hand that would never tire.

It would be impossible to explain to anyone what the accident did to her body, how it mangled her spine and nerves. After a difficult operation or blood transfusion, as she lay in the hospital bed, she often wished she were dead. Like her father, her mother, Toffe. Why did she have to be the one who survived the crash? And even if her survival were meant to be, was it too much to ask to suffer less pain? So she could have been in some way grateful for her lot?

Even if Jessica someday learns to appreciate her life, the knowledge of what she did will never fade. She killed a man: stabbed him with a knife and watched the life drain from his eyes. Was the killing purely in self-defense, or was it premeditated murder? Jessica remembers packing the knife along when she left the hotel. She chose fight over flight, as Erne accurately put it. He never spoke of revenge, but Jessica knows that was because of his inherent tact.

You did what had to be done, Jessica.

Jessica clears her throat and straps her watch to her wrist. The time is six forty-five.

She yawns, stands, and rocks between the balls of her feet and her heels, as if to ensure her feet will support her. *It's going to be OK.*

She takes her phone from the nightstand and, still undressed, crosses the black carpet to the bathroom.

She lifts the toilet lid and sits down to pee, phone in hand.

There's a WhatsApp message from Rasmus.

Nina figured out what Akifumi2511946 means. A step, but so far a dead end.

Jessica shuts her eyes. She thinks back to last night. The encounter feels like a dream, but she knows when she goes downstairs, she'll find a pen and a sheet of paper on the big table in the living room. As ever, it was all harrowingly real: the people, the scents, the time, the setting. The next morning, the apartment inevitably feels like an abandoned stage strewn with props the actors have left behind.

Jessica catches a whiff of her mother's perfume.

She flushes the toilet and brings up Rasmus' number.

54

PUBLIC BROADCAST NEWS is blaring from the car radio. Yusuf leans his head against the steering wheel and pretends to snore. The detours resulting from construction work at Helsinki-Vantaa International Airport are causing massive peak-hour backups at Departures. The line of cars advances painfully slowly. The rumble of ascending and landing planes carries into the vehicle. Jessica checks the airline app on her phone; it says the plane Lisa's parents are flying in on from London landed five minutes ago. Right on time, as luck would have it.

An older man and a young woman climb out of the car in front of them. The man takes a suitcase out of the trunk. Maybe a father and daughter, maybe something else. Jessica watches them embrace in farewell; the man's hands rest a moment on the weeping woman's shoulders.

"IT'S GOING TO be OK," Erne says, giving her shoulders a gentle squeeze. Jessica has a lump in her throat; she's having a hard time breathing. They have just stepped out of a cab at Venice Marco Polo Airport. "Did you hear me, Jessica? It's going to be OK." Erne glances around surreptitiously. Two men in poorly fitting uniforms are standing at another entrance farther away. *Polizia.* The sight that made the nineteen-year-old Jessica gasp a moment ago.

"They don't know anything," Erne murmurs. He takes a step backward and lights a cigarette. Jessica smells the pungent smoke, and it calms her. Like everything else about the Estonian standing in front of her.

"That man was . . . He wasn't a man at all, Jessica." Tobacco smoke escapes Erne's nostrils and blends with the fresh early-autumn air of northern Italy.

Jessica pulls her sweater more tightly around her. "I want to go home."

"Good." A tender smile forms on Erne's face. "Let's eat breakfast first."

Jessica shuts her eyes; the whoosh of automatic doors and announcements in Italian carry from somewhere. She can feel Erne's hand on her shoulder.

THEN SHE HEARS Yusuf's voice: *Jessica.*

"Yoo-hoo, Jessica."

"What?"

"Your phone's ringing."

Jessica looks at Yusuf, and then her phone. It's Rasmus.

"Morning, Rasse."

The young woman has made it to the terminal. The man is gone. The line inches ahead.

"You mentioned yesterday that Lisa Yamamoto had maybe deleted the kambo posts from her Instagram."

"Right. Did you find something—"

"Actually, just the opposite. I made some calls and it appears that she deleted other posts too."

"What posts?"

"Don't know. According to some followers, she used to have about a thousand posts on her profile. But now it looks like there're only nine hundred," Rasmus says.

"Can Instagram restore deleted images?"

"Don't think so."

"Shit. OK, thanks for calling."

Jessica ends the call. Then she just sits there, staring straight ahead.

"Well?" Yusuf asks impatiently, pulling into a parking space.

"A hundred pictures were recently deleted from Lisa's account," Jessica says slowly.

"There weren't that many kambo posts, were there?"

Jessica shakes her head.

"So other stuff was deleted too," Yusuf says, letting his forehead drop against the wheel again. "But what?"

"It will be tricky to find out." Jessica gazes at the terminal doors, watches a woman in coveralls pushing a long chain of carts. It's a colossal clanking centipede. "Let's go."

Yusuf raises his head from the wheel. "On to the next adventure."

He slides a cigarette between his lips and opens his door. Jessica opens hers too, and an icy wind impales the vehicle's interior.

They walk side by side toward Arrivals. Yusuf sucks rapid-fire drags of his cigarette and zips up his leather jacket. It's only a matter of time before he'll have to switch it for a less flashy coat, one that's actually warm.

Jessica shoots a glance at the black Škoda in the parking area in front of the terminal. Two men are sitting in the front seat.

"How's the hand?" Jessica asks as she and Yusuf step into the building.

"Don't think I'll be pumping iron for a week or two."

"Good." Jessica dodges a tourist group spread the entire width of the corridor. "You should do some running too."

Yusuf grunts. "I've never felt better."

Jessica doesn't reply. She thinks he's full of shit. But who is she to comment on the way other people spend their time?

As they walk, Jessica ties back her hair and makes sure her striped dress shirt is tucked into her jeans.

They stop outside the sliding doors at the Arrivals hall; an endless stream of passengers flows out. Those recognizable as Finns look rested and a bit downcast. Vacation's over. Just past the sliding doors, the darkness of Nordic winter is waiting to welcome them home with a frigid embrace. There are also a lot of tourists; they're probably expecting to see the snowy landscapes promised by postcards and are sure to feel betrayed by last night's disappointing tissue-thin deposit, which will melt before the sun hits the sky. Those with foresight have arrived in Helsinki only to hop on their next flight, to Levi or Ylläs or one of the other vacation destinations up north where they can actually see a winter wonderland. And Santa Claus. Even Moomins, if they're lucky.

"Jessie," Yusuf says quietly, and nods toward the sliding doors. "There they are."

Jessica turns and sees the couple whose photograph she has saved on her phone. The contrast between the people smiling happily with Lisa in the picture and the pale, visibly fatigued pair in front of her is stark.

She and Yusuf watch them haul their large bags toward the terminal doors. Then Jessica walks up alongside the man and reaches under her coat's zipper to pull out her police ID. Yusuf does the same.

"Excuse me," Jessica says.

For a moment, the man and woman simply stare at them, bewildered. They look exhausted. They have been traveling for a full twenty-four hours, not knowing what has happened to their daughter. Jessica knows what it feels like to gaze out an airplane window knowing you've lost those in the world you love the most. How small you can feel at a height of ten kilometers, how powerless to influence a chain of tragic events.

Lisa's father nods guardedly. He's a broad-shouldered man with a big face and enormous chest. His white dress shirt, sweater, and dark suit probably aren't the most comfortable clothes for a long flight, but he looks like the type who doesn't stint on style, even when traveling.

"Do you know where . . . ?" Lisa's mother—or stepmother—says, letting go of her suitcase handle. Her gaze is uncertain and worried. She is blond, petite, and dressed noticeably more casually than her husband.

Jessica draws her mouth into a firm line and shakes her head. "Not yet. But every hour counts. That's why we'd like to talk to you right away. And separately, as a matter of fact."

Anger flashes in the eyes of the massive Japanese man, but he maintains the imperturbable veneer. "I understand. Where? Here?"

He has an accent, but his articulation is strong and clear. Before hearing him, Jessica had a hard time imagining what Finnish spoken with a Japanese intonation would sound like.

"No, not here. Customs will let us use their premises so we can speak privately," Jessica says. "Please follow us."

55

HELENA LAPPI STARES at her phone, where the health app has drawn a graphic summary of last night's sleep quality and recovery levels. She did all right with sleep, despite waking up around two, after a dream about the case and how Jessica Niemi will react when Hellu informs her about the folder in her possession. In the dream, Niemi totally lost it, drew her weapon, and furiously threatened Hellu. It ended with Hellu giving Jessica a few kung fu kicks, knocking her to the mat, and slipping the cuffs around her slender wrists—by no means a nightmare, just the opposite.

But despite the relatively good sleep, Hellu's body's recovery reading is low due to her HRV, which has collapsed to dismal levels. *Thirteen. What the hell is wrong with me?*

"Hellu?" a voice says impatiently. It's Harjula, sitting across from her.

"Sorry." Hellu focuses her gaze on the notepad Harjula placed on her desk a moment ago. "I didn't sleep well."

"Three names are handwritten in it: Medeya Lazakovich, Miep Loos, and Tamara Jugeli."

Hellu shakes her head to indicate she has no idea what's going on.

"I started looking into it. It didn't take much. I Googled the names, and guess what I learned." Harjula pauses briefly as if waiting for a response from Hellu. When none comes, he continues: "It turns out each one unintentionally crossed the news threshold. They're all prostitutes."

"And crossed the news threshold . . ."

"By dying," Harjula says mechanically.

Hellu drops her phone in her pocket. Suddenly she feels a pang of conscience for delaying the start of the meeting to see how she slept last night. "Dying? What do you mean?"

Harjula licks his fingertip and lays down three printouts on the table. "Lazakovich, twenty-one-year-old Russian citizen. Found dead in St. Petersburg on November 12, 2018." Harjula shifts the first printout aside. "Loos, twenty-eight, found dead in her hometown of Amsterdam on February 4, 2019. And lastly: Jugeli, twenty-seven, Ukrainian prostitute, found on June sixth this year in Lviv, Ukraine. In every case a homicide of exceptional brutality."

"And these women's names were written in that notebook?" Hellu scans the online articles Harjula has printed out; each is accompanied by a photograph of a beautiful, smiling young woman. Then she taps the notebook with her forefinger. "Why wasn't this found yesterday?"

Harjula looks taken aback. "I found it now, Hellu."

Hellu flips through the empty pages of the notebook as if it's yesterday's newspaper. "Either these deaths are somehow linked or Olga knew these women personally."

"Isn't that pretty much the same thing?" Harjula says confidently. "They're all dead now."

"Do these deaths involve manga outfits or kambo treatments?"

"The articles didn't say," Harjula intones solemnly. "Like in Finland, it's not the practice anywhere in Europe to share the details of an investigation with the media unless doing so is absolutely necessary in terms of solving the case."

Hellu isn't sure what to make of her subordinate's behavior. The tone in which he utters the words has a little too much teacher and not enough student.

"Even so, we need to immediately get in touch with the authorities who investigated the murders and find out," Harjula continues.

"Good. I can handle that. The higher the rank, the faster the response." Hellu stands. "Good work, Harjula. Admirable dedication. And if I can make a request . . ."

Harjula has risen and grabbed the door handle to make his exit. "What?"

"Keep this development to yourself for a little while. There are so many moving parts now that I don't want to overwhelm Niemi. I'll see what we learn from abroad, and then we'll inform the team together."

56

JESSICA SETS DOWN two paper cups on the table. She dribbled tea from the machine for herself; Lisa's father asked for water. *Not ice-cold. Room temperature, please. Thank you.*

Jessica and Lisa's father are in a room reserved for customs interrogations. Yusuf is questioning Lisa's mother across the hall.

"Please have a seat," Jessica says. She glances at the passport Lisa's father handed over at her request. Hirokazu Yamamoto.

Yamamoto strokes his knuckles. He seems to be getting more agitated, suspicious, and impetuous by the moment. Even so, Jessica has a hard time believing he would lose it: his polished appearance speaks of a character wholly incompatible with public displays of emotion.

"Lisa." The feet of the aluminum chair scrape the smooth concrete floor as Yamamoto seats himself. He has draped his suit jacket over the back of his chair. "Where's Lisa?"

"We're doing our best to—"

"We've been gone for two weeks," Yamamoto says, hands in his lap.

Jessica folds her hands on the table and studies the man across from her. Yamamoto is truly an intimidating presence, and not only due to his mass. Jessica can't help remembering what Frank Dominis said about Lisa: she's afraid of her father. His eyes are those of a shark: dead, soulless. *Just what sort of man are you, Mr. Yamamoto?*

"I know," Jessica says. "This must be very hard for you."

Yamamoto nods a few times. "It is." He scratches his close-shaven scalp. A long, fine scar is visible at the temple.

"Do you have any ideas what might have happened to Lisa?" Jessica asks. She catches herself tensing slightly in anticipation of Yamamoto's reaction, what he will say next and in what tone. But he doesn't appear provoked by the question; he simply shakes his head lazily.

"Do you or Lisa's mother have any enemies?" she continues.

Yamamoto eyes Jessica, then discreetly tugs down the sleeves of his dress shirt. "Enemies who would have attacked Lisa?"

"It's impossible to say at this stage if anyone has attacked anyone," Jessica replies. "But we need to look into—"

"Do you know a company called SuperServis?"

Jessica nods. She familiarized herself with the information dug up on Yamamoto the night before.

"A self-service laundry," Yamamoto says. "Seven locations. In Helsinki, Tampere, Lahti, Kouvola, Oulu." He counts off the cities with the fingers—the very powerful fingers—of his left hand. "I own Laundromats. Tell me, who hates Laundromat owners?" He spreads his arms, indicating ignorance. "I'll tell you: no one. I don't have any enemies."

Jessica nods. That card has been played now. Time to throw down the ace.

"You moved to Finland in 1998, when Lisa was three years old, correct?"

Yamamoto nods slowly and firmly, in a way Jessica first saw a few minutes ago but will remember for the rest of her life. And then she says: "Kondo."

Something in Yamamoto's eyes dies. They instantly drain of confidence, and the sclera take on a reddish tint. Then he smiles for the first time during their encounter, but his mouth remains closed.

"That's your former surname, isn't it? Lisa's too?"

Yamamoto does not free Jessica from his gaze as he maintains his silence. Pride forbids him from turning aside even when the battle is lost. As Jessica suspected, Hirokazu Yamamoto won't give anyone the satisfaction of admitting defeat.

"Isn't it?" Jessica repeats.

"What does this have to do with Lisa's whereabouts?" Yamamoto finally says. He scratches the wrist beneath the gold watch.

"I don't know," Jessica says evenly. "But we need to eliminate the possibility of a link, no matter how painful that is. So I'd like you to respond to my questions as directly as possible."

Yamamoto blinks as if his eyes have dried during the prolonged staring contest. Then he takes his cup and drains it. There's a crunch, and the paper cup vanishes in the massive fist like a totaled car in a hydraulic press.

"Why did you move to Finland with Lisa? And change your surname? Were you in trouble with the law in Japan?"

Yamamoto doesn't respond. No matter. Jessica knows she won't have to wait for the answer long; they will be receiving Hirokazu Kondo's records from the Japanese police by lunchtime. But right now every minute is critical. Lisa could still be alive, and her father needs to understand that.

As a sign of respect, she addresses him by the surname he chose for himself in Finland. "Mr. Yamamoto. This investigation is aimed solely and exclusively at helping us locate Lisa. What happened twenty years ago in Japan doesn't interest me or my colleagues at all."

Yamamoto doesn't reply. An announcement urging passengers to keep an eye on their belongings penetrates the closed door. Jessica takes a sip of her tea, but it's still too hot to drink.

Cards on the table, Hirokazu Yamamoto.

"You told Lisa not to use social media. Why?"

Yamamoto shakes his head and grunts. "Not true," he says, raising his chin a tad.

"No?" Jessica lowers her eyes to her notes and imbues her voice with a more interrogatory tone. "So, you took your daughter and moved to the other side of the globe. You changed your name. The next thing you did was buy a big house in Järvenpää. All the bells and whistles, but nowhere near the spotlight. You married, opened a Laundromat.

Then another one. Kept your head low, nothing but family and work. Your daughter grew up and moved to Helsinki. Began to support herself as an influencer. Ten, fifty, a hundred, two hundred thousand followers. You started getting worried. Why? I'm thinking you were afraid information technology would destroy everything you had gone to so much trouble to build up. That Lisa's presence on social media would attract attention to you. That someone in Japan would recognize her. Not her face, of course; Lisa was just a child when she left. But maybe put two and two together. A twenty-four-year-old blogger, born in Japan, moved to Finland in 1998. Unlikely? Absolutely, very. Possible? Why not? Which is why you told Lisa to stop. Why take the risk? Wasn't it possible that one of hundreds of thousands of followers was a potential threat—"

Jessica feels the aluminum table abruptly slide out from under her palms, sees it hurtle against the white concrete wall. There's a deafening crash, and red tea splashes to the floor like blood from a gunshot wound. She scrambles backward. The chair topples under her; she stumbles. Her hand fumbles for her gun.

"You don't know what you're talking about!" Yamamoto shouts. He has stepped up and raised a fat forefinger right in Jessica's face. "You don't understand!"

Jessica tries to rise to her feet, but the shadow of the enormous man casts doubt over her and her chances. If Yamamoto struck her now, if he grabbed her throat in his huge hands, he would absolutely have time to strangle her or snap her neck before Yusuf or anyone else could rush to her aid.

The spit sprays as Yamamoto clumsily roars: "You just look for Lisa! Fucking look for Lisa!"

But Yamamoto doesn't hit Jessica. Or strangle her. He brushes invisible dust from his lapel, slowly retreats, and grabs his blazer.

Then, panting like a riled bull, he steps to the door, wrenches it wide, and comes face-to-face with Yusuf, who is just rushing in.

Yusuf looks at Yamamoto, the toppled table, Jessica leaning against the back wall, the tea splattered across the floor. "What's going on in here?"

For a moment, it looks like Yamamoto will bulldoze right through him. The men eye each other like roosters in the chicken run, ready to peck each other to the death.

"We're finished here, Yusuf. Please see Mr. Yamamoto out," Jessica says, letting her breath steady. And then she spots something that escaped her attention before: one of the fat fingers is shorter than the others.

Hirokazu Yamamoto is missing at least half his right pinkie.

57

JESSICA RIGHTS THE table and pushes it back into its place. She's alone in the room, but the explosive mood remains. She can still feel the adrenaline surging through her body. Too much action over too short a time. First she was assaulted on the jogging path, then on the stairs near Lisa's place. Now she was physically threatened by an enraged bull of a man, a father searching for his daughter, whom she managed to provoke with her questions.

Yusuf returns to the room and pulls the door shut behind him. He leans against the wall, arms folded across his chest. He speaks calmly: "What the hell, Jessica? Are you OK? We could have arrested him for that."

"For losing his patience? And then what?"

"What exactly did you say to him?"

"Prompted a little," Jessica says, massaging her temples. "What about the mother?"

Yusuf shakes his head.

"Nothing?" Jessica says as she sits back down.

"No," Yusuf says, stepping closer and wrapping his fingers around the back of the chair opposite him.

Jessica gazes at the framed posters informing passengers of what they are allowed to pack in their bags and the amounts to declare. You could probably say that for anyone sitting in this room, the instructions come too late. The shit has already hit the fan.

"Hirokazu Yamamoto is a former gangster." The words gush out as if Jessica has been holding her breath.

"Did this information come from Japan?"

"No."

Yusuf frowns. "From where, then? Are you telling me he confessed he belonged to the Japanese mafia?"

Jessica holds up her right hand and shows the right pinkie. Pretends to snip off the tip.

"*Yubitsume.* An old tradition among Japanese criminals. If a member of the yakuza, the local mafia, screws up, he has to cut off his pinkie. I guess it's not common anymore, but I'm sure it still was in the late nineties."

"He's missing part of his finger?"

Jessica nods. "Originally I was sure he was running from the police. Or the tax authorities or something. He seemed to have a lot of money when he moved here. But maybe he shortchanged the yakuza."

Yusuf sits down. "Does that mean the Phantom is muscle sent by the yakuza? They want to get back at the old man, so they kidnap Lisa? Maybe they're holding her hostage to flush the father out."

Jessica nods. "Sounds plausible to me."

"Holy shit," Yusuf says. He smiles in satisfaction, then grows serious. "But why did he have to commission the art from Lisa first? And call her multiple times? And what does Jason Nervander have to do with any of this?"

"Or Olga Belousova. Or kambo," Jessica says. She buries her face in her hands, elbows resting on the table.

"In any case, if all this is true, if the Phantom is actually after Lisa's father"—Yusuf hooks his thumb toward the door—"we need to keep an eye on Yamamoto! The muscle might . . ."

Jessica looks up. "We already are."

Yusuf spreads his arms questioningly.

"I ordered a Security Police stakeout of the terminal," Jessica continues. "They'll shadow Yamamoto all day."

Yusuf grunts, impressed. He pulls a little box from his pocket and pops a few mints in his mouth. "How did you know?"

"Know what?"

One of the mints cracks between Yusuf's teeth. "That there was something shady about Lisa's dad."

Jessica hears the question but doesn't respond.

"Huh?" Yusuf continues. "What exactly did Mr. Player tell you yesterday?"

"Dominis said Yamamoto tried to pressure Lisa into quitting social media. It seemed obvious the guy has something to hide. In his eyes, Lisa's work was far too public. And risky."

Jessica stands. She momentarily considers whether to clean up the mess on the floor before she and Yusuf turn the room back over to the Border Guard.

"Dominis said? And Dominis knew this because . . ."

"Lisa confided in him."

Yusuf claps his hands together in jubilation. "So Dominis screwed her."

"Apparently he didn't."

"Come on, Jessie, you can't be that naive."

"Why don't we forget about Dominis' and Lisa's screwings or non-screwings and get back to work?" she says, walking to the door.

Yusuf shakes his head and follows her out into the corridor. "Aw, man. You've gone over to the dark side, Jessie. That dirty dog has you in his clutches!"

Yusuf laughs, but Jessica isn't listening. She has selected Tim Taussi's number and lifted her phone to her ear. A moment later, a man with a tired voice picks up.

"Jessica Niemi here."

"I know." Taussi sounds like he's stretching. "I saved your number. I don't answer calls from numbers I don't recongize."

"Quick question. There's a selfie of you and Lisa on your Instagram. From September."

"Yeah, and . . . ?"

"Where was it taken?"

"Lisa's."

"In Töölö?"

"Yeah, her room. What's this got to do with anything?" Taussi chuckles. "Do I need to lawyer up?"

"I doubt it. At least not yet," Jessica says, then ends the call.

She and Yusuf stride through the terminal, headed toward the doors. Yusuf has to hustle to keep up.

"Who was that?"

"The Nordic Slim Shady."

"Kex Maces? Any developments?"

Jessica stops near the doors and watches men in yellow vests direct the taxi traffic outside. "I found a picture of him and Lisa on his Instagram yesterday. In the picture, they seem somehow . . . a little too intimate. I don't know why it bothered me. I just wanted to ask Kex about it."

"Jessica, those guys pose for a living. You can't draw any conclusions—"

"I know. But Maces just lied to me. He said the picture was taken in Lisa's bedroom, even though the walls in her room are white, not dark."

Jessica shows the picture to Yusuf. He takes a look but doesn't seem convinced. "I don't know. That's pretty weak, Jessie. You saw all that paint at Lisa and Essi's place. She probably just painted since the photo was taken."

Jessica realizes she's irritated, but she's not sure with whom.

"Rasse can perform his meta magic on this too," she says, stepping out through the airport's sliding doors.

58

THE CONFERENCE ROOM is thick with tension; there isn't a drop of the relaxed team spirit that prevailed in Erne's day. Jessica knows Hellu is only partially to blame. After all, screwing your coworker's boyfriend is an unbeatable way of poisoning the atmosphere at the office.

It's clear Jessica going to have to take Nina aside and have a chat one-on-one, but it's hard to find the right moment for what will presumably be an incredibly awkward encounter. Either that, or Jessica has simply been shoving her head into the sand every time one arises. She looks at Nina, who is pulling a spoon and two hard-boiled eggs wrapped in paper towels from her backpack. Kind of a weird snack. Typical Nina.

Jessica smiles almost imperceptibly as she watches Nina lay the eggs down on the table. The judo Nina has practiced since youth and the consistent workouts are evident not only in Nina's wiry arms, but in the way she carries herself, controls her body, and goes about everyday tasks. Although her physique makes her a real killing machine, Nina has ended up in what is probably the least physically demanding assignment in the unit: combing for sources of evidence with a magnifying glass.

"All right, ladies and gentlemen," Hellu says, fiddling with her earlobe. "It's kind of like the Kex Maces song: 'The web is getting tighter.'"

Jessica bites her lip to keep the smirk from showing on her face. She's surprised the industrial gray superintendent has devoted effort to memorizing Maces' lyrics with even this much accuracy.

The rest of the investigative team is in the room too: Rasmus, Yusuf, and Harjula, who is wearing faded jeans and a black turtleneck. At the start of the meeting, Yusuf did his part to create tension by asking Harjula if he was planning on launching a new iPhone during the meeting. Harjula didn't appear to mind the Steve Jobs comparison; he just let his by-now-tiresome Mona Lisa smile play across his lips. *Funny, Yusuf. Good one.*

"Jessica, please. Tell us where we are," Hellu says.

Jessica opens her notebook and reads from her handwritten notes.

"Rasse managed to track down a couple of Lisa's followers who had tried the kambo treatment. They all had a blood test done this morning and we've received the results. None of the drugs detected in their blood samples were a match for those found in Olga Belousova's system."

"*None* of the drugs?"

"One of them had consumed cannabis. But I doubt that's relevant to the investigation."

Judging by the look on Hellu's face, you'd think a serious felony were in question. But she just sighs deeply in response.

Jessica continues. "Which supports the assumption that Rodriguez sold two different treatments at his spa. As of now, what he offered to whom and whether some of his clients ordered the more potent cocktail intentionally remains unknown."

Jessica establishes eye contact with everyone at the table, then returns to her notes.

"Jose Rodriguez, who was murdered yesterday at his spa, has a squeaky-clean record. No drugs were found on the premises, but the place had been ransacked and something was clearly removed from the shelves. In addition, traces of drugs were found on some of the glassware and dishes." Jessica clicks up a photo of the crime scene for everyone to see. "His phone was on the floor, his wallet was in his pocket, and a few hundred euros were in the register. We can shut out the possibility of a robbery-homicide."

"Did you find anything else on the premises?" Hellu asks.

"Not really. A yellow raincoat was hanging on the wall, with a bottle of cleaning spray in the pocket."

Hellu looks Jessica in the eye. "And did that spark any ideas?"

"Actually, yes. Initial impression is the yellow raincoat didn't seem like the victim's style. And then the cleaning spray indicates Rodriguez—if the coat is his—wanted to clean up his tracks. Where and why . . . another mystery."

"There was no rag in the pocket?" Hellu asks.

Jessica shakes her head.

"Anyone see the perpetrator?" Nina asks. She cracks an egg with the side of a teaspoon and begins peeling it. The boiled egg quickly sheds its shell in Nina's powerful fingers.

"No," Jessica says. "No one has come forward as an eyewitness, and there are no cameras at the location. There was an appointment book on the desk, in which Rodriguez noted his upcoming client sessions—"

"Maybe the murderer's name is in the appointment book," Hellu interjects.

Jessica shoots a look at her boss from under her brows and can't help thinking about the chorus from another one of Maces' hits, "Euthanizing Her Softly."

"If that were the case, the shooter would have no doubt taken it when they left the premises," Jessica says as diplomatically as she can.

She fails. Hellu aims a murderous glance at her. If the look could talk, it would say: *Don't you dare humiliate me in front of my unit, Niemi, damn it.*

When Jessica arrived at the station that morning, she was struck by the strange sensation that something had changed. She's certain Hellu's eyes project not only disdain and hatred now, but also jubilation and glee.

"The Phantom is the shooter," Harjula says. No one protests.

But the look on Rasmus' face says the notion troubles him.

"Go ahead, Rasse," Jessica says.

Rasmus looks up in terror. "Me? I wasn't going to say anything."

"No, just say it," Jessica insists. Rasmus is a man of few words, but those few are always worth listening to. Jessica has learned to read the situations where she needs to encourage Rasmus to share his thoughts. They're like ideas that pop into an author's head in the middle of the night: if they're not immediately written down, they may be lost forever.

Rasmus gulps audibly and looks to Nina for support. Either that, or he's staring at the egg, of which Nina just devoured half. An unpleasant smell wafts through the room.

"We actually don't know much about the Phantom," Rasmus begins. "All we know is he was in touch with Lisa and commissioned the painting of the lighthouse and—"

Harjula laughs. "So doesn't that make him the murderer? What more do we need?"

Rasmus doesn't immediately respond; for him, the brief silence serves as a shock absorber. After a moment he says: "Not necessarily. Go back and think about the case from the beginning. If Lisa pushed kambo on social media and we assume the Phantom is responsible for Lisa's disappearance . . . why would he shoot Jose Rodriguez?"

"Maybe the Phantom wanted to put a stop to everything?" Hellu says.

Rasmus looks surprised. "You're saying the Phantom is some sort of charity worker? A man who metes out his justice—"

Yusuf smiles and says: "Dexter. Batman. Tarzan."

"Goddamn it," Nina whispers, and crams the rest of the egg in her mouth.

"The Avengers—"

"Be quiet!" Hellu says sharply, but without raising her voice. "There's no point in speculating about this. We need more evidence. Is there anything else concrete?"

Jessica nods, clears her throat, then says: "Nina and Rasmus made a big discovery yesterday—"

"It was Nina," Rasmus says quietly, to a grunt from Nina.

"Akifumi's identity is still a mystery, but Nina figured out the logic behind the sequence 2511946," Jessica says, bringing up on the screen the file Rasmus sent her last night. "It's being used as a hashtag on Instagram. The last digits in the series of numbers are a country code. For instance 2511946 means Sweden, 2511947 means Norway, and 25119358 means Finland. In every case, the hashtag appears on a photo of a restaurant or a hotel."

Hellu looks entranced.

"Why those locations?" Harjula asks.

"We don't know yet, but it's related to this case somehow. And not just through Akifumi's Instagram profile. One of the ten locations in Finland is the Phoenix. I doubt that's a coincidence."

"Holy hell," Harjula says. "That GM you guys talked to . . ."

"Frank Dominis," Jessica says reluctantly.

Something about the notion of the American with the roguish exterior and questionable reputation being the bad guy of this story is dissatisfying in the extreme. And too obvious. Jessica refuses to swallow it whole.

Either that or she wants to believe in something she by no means should: the innocence of a soul in torment. She did it once before, in her previous life. And why not with Frank too?

"Frank Dominis must know something," Harjula says.

"Jessica and I will go talk to him," Yusuf says.

"What about the Instagram accounts that posted the hashtags? Who are they?" Hellu asks.

"Nina immediately noticed they're all fake profiles," Rasmus says. "I was able to confirm that the accounts were created in a Ukrainian troll factory years ago. Of course I'll try to trace the end user who commissioned their creation, but I'm afraid they've done a pretty good job of erasing their tracks."

"OK. What's the word from Facebook? When can we expect the information on Akifumi's profile?" Jessica asks.

Rasmus shrugs. "I don't know. Soon, I hope. I submitted the request last night. The same goes for the Phantom's mobile phone subscription. I still haven't received a response from the Japanese authorities."

Jessica nods and clicks open the next image. "While you're at it, try to get Instagram to restore any images that have been recently deleted from Lisa's account. Can we do that?"

"If I remember correctly, it's possible within thirty days of deletion." Rasmus starts tapping away at his computer. "I'll submit another request."

"And this is the fourth thing we're waiting for foreign authorities to assist us with," Jessica says. "In this case, Japan."

On the wall appears an image of a broad-shouldered, hawk-nosed man with a face the size of a dinner plate.

"Hirokazu Yamamoto, Lisa's father. Born Hirokazu Kondo. Moved from Japan to Finland with Lisa in 1998. Changed his name. I was informed that Yamamoto ordered his daughter to quit social media. In an emphatic, even threatening tone."

"Where did this information come from?" Hellu says.

Jessica's gulp is barely noticeable. In light of today's information, Frank Dominis might not exactly be the most credible source, but Jessica doesn't understand why he would have made up the story about Lisa's father. Besides, Dominis' statement was supported by the way Yamamoto reacted at the airport. *Get ready to take a licking from the whole team.*

Jessica puts on her bravest face: "Dominis told me."

Jami Harjula bursts out laughing, and Hellu doesn't look particularly convinced either.

Jessica hurries to explain: "Lisa confided in Dominis about the matter. They're buddies."

"Buddies. More like a sugar daddy and a hot young blogger," Harjula says, a generous helping of sarcasm in his tone.

Jessica glances at Yusuf, who she knows is thinking along the same lines. But Yusuf doesn't join in the mockery, not now that things are turning against Jessica. *Thank you, Yusuf.*

"In this instance I believe we can assume Dominis is telling the truth, and that Yamamoto had some reason for telling Lisa to stop using social media. My guess is he's afraid someone will find him. Someone he left Japan to evade. And that this could be the reason Lisa is missing."

"Tell them about the pinkie," Yusuf says before taking a slurp of coffee.

Jessica nods and pauses long enough to pique the others' interest. "Hirokazu is missing part of his pinkie."

"Yakuza," Rasmus says softly.

Everyone seems to know what he's referring to, which is never guaranteed, even on the force: a member of the police administration once confused "yakuza" and "Jacuzzi" at a press conference and is still hearing about it to this day.

"So Yamamoto is a former gangster?" Hellu says. "Maybe he's in witness protection?"

Jessica lets out a sigh of relief. "Exactly. That would explain his displeasure with Lisa's social media activity. That's why I asked the Security Police for help. A couple of plainclothes agents have been shadowing the Yamamotos since they left the airport. They are reporting to me and will intervene if they see anything suspicious."

"Excellent," Hellu says suddenly, then stands. "We're making progress. Good. I have a meeting with the folks upstairs now. Keep me updated, all right?"

No protests. Hellu exits the room.

Jessica stands there; she hears the feet of the chairs around her scraping the floor as the detectives rise to their feet and stretch their limbs. Only Nina remains seated, looking thoughtful. At the beginning of the year, Jessica would have asked her what was on her mind. But it feels tricky to take that sort of initiative now. *Goddamn it. Be the bigger person, Jessica.*

"What's on your mind, Nina?" Jessica says in a thick voice.

Nina trains her gaze on Jessica, and the two of them stare each other down. If looks could kill, Jessica would probably be six feet under by now.

"Something occurred to me," Nina eventually says in a glacial tone. "Nikolas Ponsi, the pastor who reported Jason Nervander missing, said that although to his knowledge Jason has never been violent, his alcohol usage often led to *moral failings*—which is a pretty interesting term for cheating."

It's also plainly a barb aimed at Jessica, but she ignores it. "And?"

"Nikolas Ponsi is—in addition to a vicar—a trained sexologist and sex therapist who counsels young people on issues related to sexuality. I'm wondering why he and Jason grew so close. A middle-aged pastor and an atheist blogger fifteen years younger who either likes whipping people or being whipped."

"It's a little strange, I admit, but—"

"When I met Ponsi, he claimed Jason was active in parish youth work, that that's how they got to know each other. So I made a couple of calls and discovered that, yes, Jason is active in youth work, but not at the parish. At the SWF, the Sexual Well-being Foundation. It's in no way connected to the church. It seems Ponsi didn't get Nervander involved in church youth activities until later."

"So Nikolas Ponsi lied about how they met?"

"Maybe he had to, because he didn't want to reveal they met in a context of sex therapy. What if Jason told Ponsi about his predilections or sexual frustrations? Like the sadomasochism? What if Jason has not only an S and M fetish, but a schoolgirl fetish—and he confessed it to the pastor?"

Yusuf has lingered in the doorway; now he returns to the table, intrigued.

"Based on the contents of Jason's closet, we can say titty mags and even normal Tinder hookups weren't going to cut it for him, right? Maybe that's the whole reason he was at Aurinkolahti that night," Nina says. "Because he paid for a woman. Because he couldn't help himself. But in the middle of everything Olga had a heart attack. Jason tried to revive her. He failed. So then he had to disappear."

"Interesting," Jessica says in an encouraging tone. "But that still doesn't explain why the RIP was posted on his Instagram."

"No, it doesn't. But I think we should have another chat with Niko-las Ponsi. Maybe he didn't feel right going into detail, spiritual shep-herd that he is. I'm positive he knows something about Jason he hasn't told us yet. And I bet it's a lot more scandalous than rubber outfits."

"I'll go to Kallio myself. Thanks, Nina."

Jessica's phone lights up on the table. *Text message from Essi.*

59

JESSICA AND ESSI walk down the short flight of stairs at the small park near police headquarters, then sit on opposite ends of a bench, leaving over a meter of space between them. The surrounding stand of trees and their leafless branches gesture to them reassuringly and provide suitable shelter for the conversation.

Essi's white wool beanie is pulled down to her big mournful eyes. She has more makeup on than she did last time and looks somehow older and more mature than the weepy young woman sitting on her bed, grieving for her missing roommate.

"I guess I could have just called instead," Essi says, glancing around. She is clearly disoriented and afraid. That's the most excruciating thing about missing-person cases: the uncertainty that leaves too much to the imagination. You're consumed by worry about the missing person, but questions also arise about your own safety. If something awful happened to someone close to you, why can't it happen to you too?

"But I was heading past Pasila on the train anyway . . . ," Essi continues. She takes off her right glove and reaches into the pocket of her red parka.

"This is totally fine," Jessica says. Then she leans back and waits patiently for Essi to say what's on her mind.

"This whole thing is really weird," Essi says, pulling something out of her pocket. Jessica sees she's holding a block of black plastic with a long cord attached to it—upon closer inspection, a cell phone charger. An old Nokia one, a model Jessica doesn't remember having seen over the past ten years. Even Erne, who looked askance at technological innovations, got himself a smartphone five years ago.

"I don't really know where to start." Essi presses the charger into Jessica's hand and sighs deeply. "Probably from the sound . . ."

"The sound?"

"I remembered hearing this beep in Lisa's room sometimes . . . like one made by an electronic device, but that seemed out of place in this day and age. I didn't think much of it. I asked Lisa what it was once, but she just said it was probably her email or a push notification from some app. . . ."

Jessica's eyes are glued to the antique charger.

"Lisa had two phones," she murmurs, more to herself than to keep the conversation going. *The Phantom was searching Lisa's room for the second phone. That's why he was snooping around.* Jessica feels her fingertips begin to prickle. She looks up and sees Essi nodding.

"And when that guy was in Lisa's room yesterday . . . ," Essi says, and Jessica sees her shudder. "I know for a fact he was looking for that phone."

"What makes you say that?"

"Because he found it."

Jessica looks at Essi quizzically.

"I went into Lisa's room this morning. It was bothering me. What the hell did he want from there? He'd already abducted Lisa and done whatever . . . and he still came back."

Jessica eyes a dog walker approaching from a distance. Something about the guy reminds her of yesterday morning's assault, the fuggy, boozy breath, her sore knuckles. *Christmas Eve.* Jessica remembers hearing a dog barking as she lay on the frozen ground, the owner calling to it. The police haven't caught the alcoholic madman, at least not yet, but warnings about an assailant in Central Park have been broadcast in the media.

Jessica keeps staring at the dog walker. Something's off about it all. The man at the bus stop. The old woman bumping into her.

"At that point, I wasn't even thinking about any phone. I rummaged through Lisa's stuff for a while; I was a little hysterical and panicked. I thought if I could figure out if anything was missing, I could help Lisa and maybe myself too. . . ."

Jessica turns her eyes back to Essi and inhales. She must keep it together.

"And you found this. . . ."

"It was behind one of the pictures. Most of the art was removed by the police. There are only a couple pieces left, ones Lisa didn't paint herself. One was a tiny bit crooked . . . this Andy Warhol–type picture of a cat, to the right as soon as you walk in the door. I took it off the wall and found this little cubbyhole behind it."

As Essi pulls out a pack of cigarettes Jessica does her best to conceal her frustration and irritation. How could she, Yusuf, and the tech investigators have missed the hidden hiding place? She watches Essi bring out her lighter and hold it to the cigarette planted between her lips. The tip glows a lustrous red, like the embers of a campfire, until Essi stops inhaling and holds her breath. The acrid reek quickly mingles with the fresh air.

Jessica prods Essi when she doesn't appear to be continuing the story on her own initiative: "A hiding place with this charger in it?"

"No, there was nothing in it . . . just this hole cut into the plaster wall. I found the charger behind the next painting over, which got me thinking an old mobile phone would fit perfectly into that little cubbyhole."

"So you think the man who entered your apartment found the phone and took it with him? But not the charger."

"Maybe he forced Lisa to tell him where she hid the phone. He covered his tracks by putting the picture back and didn't think to look for the charger behind the one next to it. And then when he heard us come in and . . . You probably remember the rest," Essi blurts a bit clumsily, although it's doubtful she's trying to be witty.

Jessica drops the charger into her coat pocket. She and Essi watch in silence as the dog walker passes with a big black German shepherd. Jessica sighs.

The critical thing now is to refrain from speculating about the matter with Lisa's roommate. All Jessica needs to do is fish out all the facts, and Essi can be on her way.

"OK," she says, stretching her left arm across the back of the bench. "So apparently Lisa had a Nokia phone from the nineties and she would occasionally receive text messages or calls on it; I suppose that's what you were referring to when you talked about beeps you heard coming from her room."

"Yup," Essi says. The cold weather has put some red in her cheeks. Either that or nervousness.

"And that's everything? You never saw the phone?"

Essi seems distracted; her eyes are following a windblown maple leaf scuttling down the sand path like a huge yellow spider. Then she rouses herself, as if she heard the question at a lag of a few seconds.

"No," Essi says, pulling out her own phone. "But I'm pretty sure Lisa called me from it a month ago."

"How do you know the call came from that phone?"

"She had misplaced her phone. She was a total wreck of course, because her entire career revolves around her phone and social media. Anyway, it finally turned up; she'd left it at a friend's place the night before. But I remember her calling me from some weird number and asking if I wouldn't mind picking up her phone when I got off work, because she was hungover and getting sick or something. When I asked whose phone she was calling from, she said a friend's—even though she was supposed to be sick and hungover at home. It didn't make any sense; I could tell she was lying. But I figured it was some guy's phone and she didn't want to talk about it."

"So you didn't ask any more questions?"

"Not at the time. But it kept bothering me, partially because I'd still hear the ping coming from Lisa's room sometimes. So one day I tried calling the number. I blocked my number first. I heard the ping in Lisa's room. That was when I knew she had another phone and phone number she didn't want anyone to know about for some reason. That she'd been lying to me the whole time."

Suddenly Essi starts to cry.

"What is it?" Jessica says, and when the tears keep coming, she edges closer and lowers a hand to Essi's shoulder. "You have to be strong now; there's every chance—"

"That's not what I'm crying about." Essi dries her eyes on her coat sleeve. The cigarette has been forgotten between her fingers; a stub of ash half a centimeter long dangles from the tip. Essi glances at it, taps the filter with her forefinger, raises the cigarette to her lips, and sucks until the tip glows red again.

"Lisa came to my door and seemed, like, really stern . . . not like herself at all."

Did you just call me?

Huh? No. Why?

Show me your outgoing calls.

"I totally choked. At first I said my phone was out of power. I don't know why it freaked me out so bad . . . the situation, and Lisa too; she was acting so weird. I guess I assumed from the start the phone was shady somehow, that I wasn't even supposed to know about it. And calling it out of curiosity was stupid."

"Then what?"

"Lisa's not dumb. Of course she didn't stomp over and grab the phone from me to check whether it was charged, but she knew it was me who called. She could tell from my reaction; she knows me well enough. She just stood there in the doorway glaring at me. After a second, she came over and sat at the foot of my bed and put her hand on my ankle . . . and said I could never tell anyone about the number. That I had to delete it right away."

"Did you ask why?"

Essi shakes her head. "You don't know how strange Lisa was being. I just nodded and told myself I really didn't want to know any more about it. Then all of a sudden Lisa smiled and said, 'Let's order something to eat.' As if nothing had happened. And the more I thought about it, I figured it hadn't."

Jessica mentally crosses her fingers. "Do you still have the number saved on your phone?" *This could be a big deal.*

"No," Essi says. "But I wrote it down."

Essi opens her wallet and hands Jessica a yellow Post-it with a phone number written down on it.

Jessica discreetly taps out a message to Rasmus. Dig up what you can on this number. No 1 priority!!! Then she locks the screen of her phone.

"Sorry I didn't tell you about this earlier, but I promised Lisa . . . ," Essi stammers.

"It's a good thing you told me," Jessica says. The wind has picked up, prompting her to zip her coat up to her chin. "In this sort of situation, it can be hard to decide which secrets to share to make it easier to find a missing person. But I'm sure Lisa won't be upset if you tell us something that helps us locate her. Or maybe even . . . ," Jessica begins, and instantly regrets giving Essi unfounded hope, ". . . save her life."

"I know." Essi drops her cigarette butt and grinds it into the ground with the toe of her yellow combat boot. Then she slowly lowers her palms, stands up, and smooths out the hem of her pink trench coat. Essi looks like a fashion blogger herself; her super-stylish outfit could be from the cover of *Vogue*'s September issue. Not that Jessica knows anything about fashion; it's been a long time since she tried to keep up with trends. Playing her role has been hard enough without closets overflowing with designer rags.

"I don't think there's anything else to tell," Essi says.

Jessica rises from the bench as well. "I still have a couple of questions for you."

Essi looks at her a little fearfully, as if she didn't expect the conversation to continue.

"Lisa's dad," Jessica continues. "You said you heard Lisa speaking Japanese with her dad."

"Yeah?"

"Have you ever met Lisa's father? Does he visit you?"

"Never. Which is kind of weird, now that I think about it. But they talked on the phone."

"And you know she was talking to her father because . . ."

"That's what she told me."

"So theoretically she could have been talking to someone else."

Essi looks confused. "I guess."

"And did Lisa ever say anything about what her father thought about her profession?"

Essi shakes her head. "No . . . Why? What should he have thought about it?"

Jessica glances over her shoulder. Essi doesn't appear to be aware of the father's threats. Is it truly possible that Lisa confided in Frank Dominis but not her roommate? Just exactly how close are Dominis and Lisa?

"OK, and another question," Jessica says. "Have you ever heard of kambo?"

"Kambo? The frog thing?" For the first time, a thin curve of a smile appears in the corner of Essi's mouth.

"Yes," Jessica says.

"Lisa talked about it. And tried it too."

"Did you try it?"

"No way. It sounded totally crazy."

"What sort of experience was it, according to Lisa?"

"She said it was cool. Cleansing, healing."

"Do you have any idea why Lisa recently deleted all references to kambo from her blog and Instagram?" Jessica asks.

"Maybe." Essi picks some lint from her glove. "I guess she and the guy who owns the kambo place, Jose, had a falling-out."

"Rodriguez?" Jessica says. "Falling-out over what?"

"She said Jose didn't pay her."

"Pay her for what?"

Essi looks at Jessica as if their age difference is much greater than it is and she is being forced to explain things to an imbecilic adult.

"It was a business partnership. Whenever Lisa wrote about something, she was paid in goods or services. Money too. Your basic influencer stuff," Essi says.

"So Jose Rodriguez was Lisa's client, not the other way around?"

"Yeah, theoretically. That's why Lisa sent Jose's invoice to collections and deleted any posts mentioning his company."

"Do you know this much about all of Lisa's customers?" Jessica asks.

Essi laughs joylessly. "Definitely not. But this kambo thing stuck in my head. It was a little too crazy for me."

Jessica turns her face skyward. "Just before she disappeared, Lisa deleted a lot of other pictures too. About a hundred of them. Do you have any idea why? What the deleted photos might have been of?"

Essi shakes her head. No idea.

"Would you do me a favor, Essi? Take some time today to look through Lisa's photos and think if there's anything that stands out through its absence. Is there some person connected with the deleted photos, or maybe some object or place? Something Lisa herself or someone else might have wanted people to forget?"

"I can try. It sounds pretty impossible," Essi says. "Looking for posts . . . that aren't there anymore . . ."

Jessica grunts because she realizes Essi's right. The request is totally absurd. "No stress. Just have a look at Lisa's Instagram." Jessica shivers; the wind is blowing much harder now. "Then one last thing." She hands the phone to Essi. "According to Tim Taussi, this photo was taken at your place. In Lisa's room. But the walls in Lisa's room are white."

"Lisa just painted them. Like, last month," Essi says quickly, then hands the phone back. Jessica looks at Essi and chews the inside of her cheek.

Yusuf was right. There's nothing special about the picture.

As she slides her bare hands out of the biting wind and into her pockets, she eyes Essi, thinking how shocked she would be to learn Jose Rodriguez is lying in the morgue at this very moment.

60

EVEN FROM A distance, Jessica recognizes the man based on Nina's description—although to her eyes, Nikolas Ponsi isn't as short as Nina made him out to be. He's wearing a long pastor's robe and black rubber-soled shoes. He's carrying a black overcoat over his arm.

Ponsi is standing in front of the southern facade of Kallio Church, at the head of a flight of granite stairs that continues into a panoramic view down the street and onto Observatory Hill a kilometer and a half away.

"Detective Jessica Niemi," Jessica says, shaking his hand.

"Of course. I met your colleague last time. Detective Ruska?"

"Thanks for taking the time to meet so extemporaneously."

"My pleasure. Although I do have a mass that's about to begin—"

"This won't take long," Jessica says. "And I need you to answer everything honestly, even if doing so might violate someone's confidentiality."

Ponsi looks uneasy. He glances up at the sky, which is emptying itself of an icy drizzle, and wraps himself in his coat. Then he steps down the stairs, as if hoping to put some distance between himself and the holy building. Maybe this way his discussing Jason's private matters won't carry to the ears of his Lord. "What can I do for you?"

Jessica follows him. "As detectives, we don't rely on rumors, which is why I need to ask you this directly: in what role did you originally meet Jason, as pastor or sex therapist?"

The grave-faced Ponsi chews his lip.

"We know Jason is an atheist," Jessica continues.

"In the role of sex therapist," Ponsi eventually replies. "But under no conditions will I agree to discuss our conversations in greater detail."

"Fine," Jessica says. "And if I happened to require your views as a sexologist—not relating to Nervander specifically, but generally—could I rely on you?"

Ponsi looks hard at Jessica, as if she just laid him a trap.

"I thought you only celebrate mass here on Sundays." Jessica nods in the direction of the church. "You should have come up with a better excuse."

Ponsi looks flustered, then lowers his head. "I'm sorry," he says. "But I feel like I'm doing something wrong by talking to the police about something a young person told me in confidence—"

"I understand. But suppose we discuss the topic at a general level."

Ponsi indicates a nearby park bench, and they both sit. "What topic?"

"Fetishes."

Ponsi doesn't bat an eye.

"Do you know a lot about them?"

Ponsi nods. He turns toward a noise carrying from the street; a homeless man with a long beard is shouting curses in the middle of the intersection. "Fetishes. Funny that you should ask someone who's both a sexologist and a man of the cloth about them. I have a fetish right here under my shirt." Ponsi chuckles when Jessica looks at him in surprise. "The word 'fetish,' you see, originally meant 'a talisman or object related to one's beliefs,' like this here." Ponsi pulls a gold cross out from under his coat.

"Sexual fetishes—to which I assume you were referring—involve interest targeted specifically at an object, although the object of a fetish could be a body part or some other human characteristic. There's a huge range of such fetishes."

"Like types of clothing?"

"For example."

"So fetishes are a pretty normal part of human sexuality?"

Ponsi strokes his beard. "I wouldn't say the matter is quite that simple. We can talk about things generally considered sexually arousing, such things as, for instance, the breasts and legs of women and the abs and biceps of men. But sometimes the targets of fetishism are so unusual the majority considers them strange. That's why the individual with the fetish often keeps it wholly private. One example of a more extraordinary but very common fetish is a diaper fetish, in which an adult person uses a diaper for purposes of sexual pleasure."

Jessica frowns. "That's common?"

"If you only knew."

"So, as a sex therapist, you've encountered a lot of people who have desires that deviate from the mainstream."

Ponsi nods firmly and crosses his legs. "How can I put this . . . ? 'Deviation' isn't the best term. I received my sexology credentials in 1999. As I'm sure you recall, the world was very different then. Sexual minorities continued to live on the margins, and much of my work consisted of simply talking to young people and convincing them there was nothing wrong with them—that they were fine just the way they were. When you consider fetishism was classified as an illness in Finland until 2011, as were sadomasochism and transvestism . . . People were desperately seeking a cure for something that by no means required treatment. That can be tough on one's mental health and self-image."

Jessica looks into Ponsi's eyes for a second, but they're perfectly neutral. He has just mentioned sadomasochism, but nothing in his demeanor indicates he slipped up. Maybe he simply isn't aware of all of Nervander's tendencies. Or maybe they are totally irrelevant in terms of the present investigation.

Jessica reaches into her pocket and pulls out a photograph of Lisa Yamamoto's schoolgirl drawing. "What about this?"

Ponsi takes the photo. For a split second, it seems to Jessica as if he is in thrall to some thought, some memory.

He hands the photo back. "What . . . what about this?"

"Have you ever come across manga fetishes during your career?"

"I believe so."

"Are they common?"

"To my understanding, they're more common in Asia."

"Schoolgirls are a frequent motif in manga art. Does that mean there's a pedophilic aspect to manga fetishes?"

Ponsi looks off into the distance again. The homeless man with the long beard has disappeared from view, but his shouts still carry faintly from somewhere. "Not so much pedophilia. More ephebophilia, or sexual attraction to young people on the cusp of adulthood. The markets for this are massive, when you think about how much pornography is sold and watched using search terms like 'young' and 'teen.' A lot of interesting research has been done on the subject."

"And are the ephebophiles who are fixated on manga art exclusively men?"

Ponsi shakes his head. "The majority, absolutely. But women also have a variety of preferences. By some estimates, as many as every fifth pedophile is a woman."

Jessica digests this information, then slides the photograph back into her pocket. "Thanks for your time. I want to remind you that if you know anything that might save a life if you shared it with us, you are obligated by law to do so."

Ponsi looks at Jessica. He grunts ruefully and nods: "Believe me, I'm well aware."

Then he turns away, which gives Jessica a chance to study his pitted face. The scars on his cheeks are small, but deep. He appears to have suffered from severe acne or a pox at some point. The beard agrees so poorly with his small face that he must have grown it as a mask of sorts, to cover up the scars.

"I have to go now."

"Of course," Jessica says.

Ponsi stands, pulls up his hood, and traipses up the granite stairs. As she watches him go, Jessica notices the leather shoes flashing under the robe. The rubber soles are noticeably thick. Maybe they're intended to give Ponsi's self-confidence a boost.

Jessica pulls her phone out of her pocket. She means to call Rasmus, but he's calling her.

"Hey, I was just about to call you—"

"We have a bead on Lisa's phone."

61

JESSICA LEANS AGAINST Rasmus' desk and taps her nails against its lacquered surface. Two screens stand on it, as do a handful of plastic figurines. Hanging from the cubicle divider is a framed picture of a Victorian gentleman with tentacles sprouting from his collar instead of a head. *What the fuck, Rasse?*

"Did you find anything?" she says impatiently. She notices her peppermint gum has lost its flavor. Normally she can't stand gum, but in her agitation, she took a couple pieces when Yusuf offered her some in the corridor five minutes ago.

"You want the good news or the bad news first?"

"I don't care, Rasse. Spit it out."

"The bad news is Lisa's phone isn't powered on. The telecommunications company can tell us which base station it connected to most recently, but it's going to take a minute."

"The same song and dance! We've been waiting—what?—almost two goddamn days for information from the telecom company and Facebook and . . ." Jessica groans, sweeping aside the hair that has fallen into her eyes.

Rasmus hurriedly continues, as if he's in the presence of an impulsive Cleopatra who has grown tired of excuses and he is desperate to avoid the lions' den: "The good news: the prepaid number gave us the phone's International Mobile Equipment Identity code. Based on the IMEI, it's a 1999 Nokia 3210. I also asked the mobile service provider to send us a list of received and placed calls. We should be getting it at any minute now."

"That is good news." Jessica sighs and watches Rasmus bring up a photo of the old phone model onto the screen. She had one herself back in the day. Didn't the whole country?

"And that's not all," Rasmus says. He taps out something that will carry them to their next destination in the ether. "I was thinking about Lisa's masayoshi.fi site. And how she went to so much trouble to delete the contents. She did such a thorough job that whatever the site contained is impossible to restore. But then . . ."

Jessica pulls over a chair from the neighboring workstation. "What?"

"Argh, the answer is so simple. I was making it way harder than it needed to be. We don't have to restore anything or bring back data from the dead. Solutions for situations like this already exist online," Rasmus says, and smiles. "Time machines of a sort."

"Time machines?" Jessica's knees are bouncing and her heels are drumming the floor. Her body is consumed by suspense: it feels like there's a breakthrough right around the corner.

"Or more like photo albums from the past. A site called archive.org scans websites and gathers data from them at different points in time. Look." Rasmus taps away again, enters archive.org into the address bar, and a moment later the words "Internet Archive Wayback Machine" pop up on the screen in big letters. Rasmus taps www.masayoshi.fi into the Wayback search field.

"So the software captured the site the way it looked at several different points during the year?" Jessica asks.

"Exactly. I can choose this year . . . and June . . . and see what the website looked like then. It doesn't matter what Lisa has deleted since. This is like a photograph of a dead person."

"The Internet never forgets," Jessica murmurs, impressed. Suddenly the warning she has heard so many times becomes completely concrete for her. *Post something online and it's there forever.*

"Look."

The screen fills with photographs of young women.

"What the hell . . . ?" Jessica says softly as Rasmus scrolls down the page. More photos of young women, in suggestive poses, appear. They're all dressed the same way: like manga characters.

"It's a catalog," Rasmus says, pushing up his glasses. "And that one, third from the left there, is Olga Belousova."

62

"RASSE JUST GOT this information from the telecommunications company," Jessica says, then takes a half-turn around the table, where she has just laid printouts teeming with names and phone numbers.

Harjula pulls one of the printouts toward himself. "What are these numbers?"

"Lisa had a secret mobile phone this whole time. These are the calls it received. She also used it to text one number," Jessica answers. "The data shows that more talk time was purchased in October 2018 for a prepaid line acquired in 2010. The account has been in active use ever since—in other words, over a year."

Rasmus jumps in eagerly. "The pattern is always the same: Lisa receives a call from some number. She doesn't answer, but as soon as she receives the call, she sends a text message, invariably to the same number. It looks like Lisa was acting as a switchboard of sorts in the scheme."

"And there's no way of retroactively accessing the contents of the text messages?" Harjula asks.

Yusuf shakes his head. "Unfortunately. There's no way to read the texts now, even if we had a subpoena. Unless we manage to get our hands on that damned phone."

"The phone is presumably in the Phantom's possession now, and he's on the run. He may have already left Finland," Jessica says.

"Just a moment. Let's take a step backward," Hellu says, glancing at her smartwatch. She seems ill-tempered, despite the likelihood of an imminent big breakthrough in the case. "Could you please explain one more time what it is you hope this call data will provide?"

"There are ten phone numbers. And what else are there ten of?" Jessica says. Her answering Hellu's question with a question doesn't appear to improve the superintendent's mood.

"Instagram pictures hashtagged with the numerical sequence ending in 358," Harjula says.

"Exactly."

Rasmus jumps in: "We also found a site maintained by Lisa, www .masayoshi.fi, which still had a catalog of girls on it a couple months ago. We believe it was a site for showcasing prostitutes." He coughs into his fist and continues: "The contents have since been deleted."

"Kind of like Sihteeriopisto?" Nina says. "It's not illegal to sell or buy sex in Finland. Only pimping is." Her explanation is presumably unnecessary; one would assume the detectives sitting in the room are familiar with the pertinent legislation.

"There was no contact information on the site, however." Rasmus projects a view from his laptop onto the white wall. The six investigators see young women in manga clothes flirting with the camera and posing seductively. "Just names. Or role-play names, rather. As you can see, our Ukrainian friend is called Miyamoto."

Hellu frowns. "No contact information?"

"No," Rasmus replies. "As Nina mentioned, selling sex isn't a crime, but that means an escort site like this should have direct numbers or email addresses for the women providing the service. Or, if only one phone number appeared on the site—"

Hellu finishes Rasmus' sentence: "It would imply pandering."

"But this site didn't even have that," Rasmus continues, scrolling up and down the screen. "It's a catalog without any way to buy."

"Which means that communication between the john and the pimp took place through some other channel," Jessica says.

Rasmus is staring at the ceiling, probably gamely doing his best to avoid looking at his laptop or the image projected on the wall more than absolutely necessary.

"Ha!" Harjula says, just loud enough so everyone in the room can hear. He stretches his arms, and now that they're in the air, the limbs resemble those of an orangutan even more than usual.

Jessica shifts her gaze from Harjula's arms to Hellu and catches the superintendent bestowing a satisfied nod upon her pet as she says: "It seems Harjula's theory was accurate. Olga Belousova was a prostitute."

For a moment the room is absolutely silent. Jessica folds her arms across her chest. No one has questioned Olga's profession at any point during the investigation, only why and under what conditions she lost her life.

Eventually Jessica continues: "In any case, forty-five minutes ago, Rasmus and tech started linking the numbers we see on this list with hotels and restaurants. The calls were not made directly from the companies' in-house numbers—an understandable precaution—but we've already found indirect connections in four instances. I'm sure that by tomorrow, we'll have proof of calls placed to Lisa's secret number from all ten establishments hashtagged #25119358. More often from some, only once from others, as shown by the list."

"What was Lisa Yamamoto's role?" Nina asks. She's rubbing her wrists as if they have just been released from an overly tight pair of handcuffs.

"It looks like Instagram was used to direct the customers to the hashtagged locations to request services. A call was placed to Lisa from one of those locations, which she purposely didn't answer. Based on the number that called, Lisa could tell what location the services were required at and texted the pimp," Jessica says.

"And then the escort was sent to the location? To the restaurant or hotel where the john ordered her?" Yusuf says after a long silence. "That doesn't make any damn sense. Why the hell go to so much trouble— why all the secrecy—if the girl is going to pop up at the hotel looking like a manga doll anyway? That's like escaping from your cell and calling out, *I'm going now*, to the guards at the prison gates!"

"But there's no need for all this guesswork, Niemi," Hellu interjects in her nasal voice. "Since we know where the calls to Lisa were placed, let's just ask them."

Jessica nods. *That's the plan, asshole.*

"We're getting a squad together at the station as we speak. We'll start where the vast majority of calls were placed."

"Which is?"

"The Phoenix."

YUSUF LOOKS AT the muscle-bound man sitting across from him. "Smoke?"

Sahib Alem, dressed from head to toe in a red sweatsuit with two side stripes, nods. Yusuf offers him a light, then lights his own.

"Mind if I ask where your roots are?" Yusuf asks, even though he knows the other man has Iranian citizenship in addition to Finnish. This isn't the first time Yusuf has exploited his ethnic background in an attempt to establish camaraderie with someone he's interrogating.

"I was born in Helsinki," Alem says drily, assuming a more relaxed position in his chair.

Yusuf grunts and slides the ashtray closer to the middle of the table. It was just rinsed and drags a wet smear behind it, like snail slime. Smoking isn't technically allowed during interrogations anymore, but it's hard to find anyone who would feel compelled to complain about it. Especially since smoking relaxes the mood and, thus, facilitates faster results.

"Dope. I'm from Söderkulla," Yusuf says, cigarette between his fingers. "In Sipoo."

"I know where Södis is." Alem's tone is deadpan, as if he's welcoming the thousandth guest in a row to the club.

Yusuf chuckles. "My bad. My pops is from Ethiopia."

"Must be a nice place," Alem says flatly, and takes a drag.

The two men eye each other in silence.

"OK, so much for the stimulating and rewarding small talk." Yusuf lowers his gaze to the stack of papers on the table. "If you tell me everything now, maybe you can get off pretty easy. But do me and, above all, yourself, a big favor and don't start making stuff up."

Alem lowers the cigarette to an indentation in the ashtray and folds his arms across his chest. It's a high-stakes poker game: there's enough evidence to link the prepaid number to Alem, but only indirectly. The phone used with the subscription is not in Sahib's name; it's in his sister's husband's. The connection is too obvious to be coincidental, but too circumstantial to support arrest.

"I want to know why and under what circumstances you made calls to this number." Yusuf pushes a printout across the table. The calls presumably made by Alem are highlighted in yellow; the other numbers are redacted with black marker. "There are over a dozen calls. They were all placed during opening hours at the Phoenix when you were working the door. We checked."

Alem glances at the papers. Yusuf isn't sure what he's reading in the bouncer's eyes. They're a little rueful, maybe. Even bitter.

"If you don't know anything about these calls, Sahib, we're going to have to bring in your brother-in-law. Or maybe it was someone else from his household—"

"Stop." Sahib looks Yusuf dead in the eye. "Don't get my sister involved in this."

Yusuf leans back and conjures a look of surprise on his face. Alem can't get the impression he was just successfully bluffed.

"Then talk to me, Sahib." Yusuf watches Alem reach for his cigarette again. It has gone out, and Yusuf offers him a light. The physically intimidating Alem is clearly no Sunday school boy, but there's warmth in his eyes. Yusuf is sure that at heart he's not a bad guy; then again, few people are. But the worst mistake you can make during an interrogation is to come up with your own interpretations based on kitchen-sink psychology. The truth is, Yusuf doesn't know anything about Sahib Alem except what Alem decides to reveal about himself today.

Yusuf takes a drag of his cigarette. "The prisoner's dilemma."

Judging by the look on his face, Alem gets the reference.

"There are quite a few of you, and you can bet someone's going to talk. If and when that happens, keeping your mouth shut is only going to hurt you," Yusuf continues. "Seriously, if you think of this as a game, you have a better shot at winning if you come clean now."

Alem looks at Yusuf from under his brows, takes one last drag, then rolls the cigarette against the bottom of the ashtray until it's snuffed out.

"Söderkulla, huh?"

"Yup," Yusuf answers, and he feels a glow in the pit of his stomach. *Round one to Yusuf.*

Alem sighs deeply. "Tehran. The folks, I mean. I'm from here. Pisses me off how people don't get it."

Yusuf can almost hear the ice cracking. He pours himself a glass of water from the pitcher. "I feel you on that."

There's no longer any rush.

"OK," Alem eventually says. The muscles in his face seem to relax; he has dropped his guard. "I don't really have much to tell. I don't know shit. I got instructions, and I followed them. Got a little extra cash for doing it."

"What sort of instructions?"

"I was given a SIM card. I was supposed to use an old phone model, and it couldn't be registered to me. I was given a number I was supposed to call. Listen to it ring three times and hang up. That's it."

"Call when?"

"When someone came to the door and asked if James was around."

"Who's James?"

"The guy who proposed the whole thing to me. At first I didn't understand what his game was, but then I saw him pick up one of the people who came by asking for him. Black Benz SUV. He was the driver."

Yusuf glances at the recorder to make sure the red light is still burning. "So this James would pick up the person who came to the Phoenix looking for him?"

Alem nods calmly.

"And you don't know where the person who asked for James was driven?"

"No. That's the truth. I got a couple hundred per gig."

"So all you had to do was call that number, and a little while later, James showed up in his SUV?"

Alem nods and wipes his forehead.

"How was your cut delivered to you?"

"James would come by and see me at the downstairs door. A couple of times a month. Slip me a wad of cash."

Yusuf slides his chair a hair closer to the table. "Were there a lot of girls who worked the Phoenix?"

Alem looks surprised. "It's not like anyone encouraged hustling there, if that's what you mean. If you're appropriately dressed, you get in. When you're working the door, it's pretty hard to start guessing who's a whore and who isn't."

Yusuf knows Alem is full of it. It's a small city, and the bouncers are plenty familiar with the girls who crawl the nightclubs looking for customers. But the matter isn't relevant in terms of the present investigation. "Did you see any women with James?"

"Never. James was always alone. All he did was pick up the john."

"The john? So you do know where—"

Alem bristles. "So fucking what? I said 'john.' They were johns, all right? I was pretty sure James wasn't taking them down to the local bakery to buy a loaf of bread. But I have no idea what was waiting for them at the other end: a mountain of crystal, a cockfight, an underground poker game, or a whorehouse. It's none of my business, OK?"

Yusuf doesn't want to ease up, keeps the questions coming. *The guy's warming up. Keep throwing on the wood.* "Did you ever see the same customer on multiple occasions?"

"I got to know a few of their faces."

"Men?"

"Yup."

Alem shoots a questioning look at the pack of smokes. Yusuf nods, and Alem pulls out another for himself. Footfalls echo from the corridor as Yusuf leans in to light the cigarette.

"What did James look like?"

"Dark hair. Big dude. I figured he was Russian."

"Would we see him on any of the cameras outside the Phoenix?" Yusuf asks.

"You can try. He came by the downstairs door last Saturday. Brought me an envelope."

"Saturday? The day of the record launch?"

Alem watches the smoke disappear toward the air-conditioning vent. "Yup. Early, between noon and one. I was helping set up."

Yusuf pushes out his lower lip and eyes Alem, his red sweatsuit and massive biceps. For a moment he can't help wondering whether having the exterior of a bodybuilder is worth it after all. Especially if its purpose is to serve as armor, and the soul imprisoned within is condemned to as much insecurity as anyone else's. Sahib Alem looks like a man who created his intimidating appearance first, then started living up to it, not the other way around.

"Sahib, I'm going to ask two more things, and you need to keep going with the hundred percent real answers," Yusuf says.

Alem appears to weigh the matter for a few seconds, then nods.

"I'm sure you guessed what the phone and James' arrival implied. But did you *know* anything about it, other than what you just told me?"

"No," Alem says convincingly and without hesitation.

"And did anyone else at the Phoenix know about this? Or anywhere else?"

Alem shakes his head and glances at his enormous watch as if he can claim to be in a hurry and stroll out of the station. But he no longer has that freedom.

"Only me and James. I just wanted to earn a little on the side. That's it."

64

RASMUS HUMS THE melody of a childhood TV show as he browses through Jason Nervander's Instagram. The guy has posted more than a thousand pictures to his profile, and Rasmus has already gone through them multiple times. But he still might have missed something. An hour earlier, he submitted a follow-up request to Instagram to restore the images deleted from Lisa Yamamoto's account.

Rasmus glances around, then pulls two golf balls out of his pocket and slips them under his feet. He needs to follow the instructions he was given religiously if he wants to open up the locks in his body.

Wait a second.

Something on the screen has captured Rasmus' attention. He caught only a glimpse of the photograph, and now he scrolls back up to it. Taken in the summery sunshine of this past July, the picture shows the strong-jawed, handsome Jason sitting in shorts and no shoes on a white surface that, upon closer inspection, appears to be the deck of a boat. *What the heck?* Rasmus remembers seeing the photo earlier, but he didn't pay particular attention to it due to the tight cropping. It's impossible to say anything about the boat, if indeed it is one.

Jason doesn't own a boat. We already checked.

Rasmus clicks open the comments. There are dozens, and they're littered with hearts and smiley emojis. Generic messages presumably written by people who don't know Jason personally or at least aren't particularly close to him.

But one comment stands out from the others in its personal tone.

Awesome day! Let's do it again.

Rasmus clicks the profile of the person who posted the comment and discovers to his relief that it isn't private. It belongs to a young man who, judging by the number of images, spends a lot of time on social media. Rasmus scrolls down the photo roll until he finds the images posted in July.

Please be there, please be there. . . .

Rasmus chews his thumbnail, rolls the golf balls harder and harder against the arches of his feet, and then spots it: a photograph taken at the Katajanokka marina in central Helsinki. A large motorboat with a group of young men on deck.

"Harjula!" Rasmus calls out.

The tall man raises his head out of the bowels of his cubicle only a few meters away. "What?"

"Take a look at this. You know about cars and boats . . . ," Rasmus says as Harjula walks up behind him, arms folded. "What kind of boat is that?"

Harjula looks at Rasmus' computer monitor. "Is that the only shot?"

"For now."

A momentary silence follows. Rasmus can feel disappointment spread through his innards. The photo simply isn't detailed enough. "I understand if the angle doesn't—"

"Nine-meter Aquador 28C. I'd say a 2006." Harjula squeezes Rasmus' shoulders. "Sweet little watercraft."

65

JESSICA DRIBBLES ICE-COLD water from the cooler into the plastic mug, raises the mug to her lips, and feels the iciness bore into her temples. Brain freeze. She sees Yusuf walk up between the cubicles.

"How does it look?" Jessica asks.

"Alem admitted to calling the number anytime anyone asked for James. He was paid to make the calls and denies knowing anything else about the scheme."

"Fucking bullshit," Harjula says, stepping out of the men's room. "We should arrest the club's entire staff for running a prostitution ring."

"I believe Alem," Yusuf says. Jessica shoots him a pointed look. "These organizations work best this way. The henchmen and soldiers don't know diddly about the operation, just what they need to. Anything else is too risky."

"What about anyone else from the Phoenix?" Jessica asks, and is unnerved by the note in her voice—both hopeful and fearful.

"Alem claims no one else knew anything," Yusuf replies.

Relief washes over Jessica. Not just because she would have looked stupid if it turned out Frank Dominis, whose credibility as a source she has defended, is part of the scheme, but because she liked Dominis the instant she met him. She hopes her intuition won't betray her this time as it has in the past.

"And you believe him?" Jessica asks, eyes glued to her computer screen in feigned indifference.

Yusuf pulls up a chair next to her. "I do. This James guy only needed one contact at the Phoenix. Someone who's always on the clock. Getting the GM involved would have been too much of a risk. Worst case, he might have put a stop to it."

Frank gets a clean bill of health.

Jessica looks up at Harjula, who looks anything but convinced.

"Alem is being moved downstairs to await further questioning," Yusuf says. "Rasse and Co. are tracing the other numbers. Apparently two more have been confirmed."

"Six out of ten," Jessica murmurs.

"And folks are being hauled into the station as fast as we find them. But somehow I get the feeling none of them knows any more than Alem does."

"I am getting the same sense," Jessica says with a look at Yusuf.

"Was this bouncer able to provide a description of James?" Harjula asks.

"Apparently looked like Wladimir Klitschko. Maybe Russian."

Harjula smiles annoyingly. "Klitschko is Ukrainian."

"Who fucking cares?" Yusuf retorts angrily. "You think that's going to make or break the investigation?"

"Knock it off, guys," Jessica says sharply. She stands. "Does James appear in any camera footage, since it sounds like he visited the Phoenix?"

Yusuf nods forcefully. "Apparently he was there about six hours before Kex Maces' record launch. I propose I go through the recordings. I think I already have the whole day from the Phoenix on my computer."

"Good." Jessica undoes her bun and lets her hair cascade over the shoulders of her dress shirt. "And I'd like for everyone to be thinking about the following as they go about their work: what should we make of all this? The web of connections, I mean." Before answering her own question, she draws a breath. "It all started from Akifumi. Some creep in a mask tipped us off to both the Instagram hashtag used to identify the locations and the masayoshi website."

"So, what is it you want us to be thinking about?" Harjula asks.

"I want you to be thinking about who the hell Akifumi is and why we were fed this information in the form of that comment on the post!"

At that moment, the young woman assigned to help Rasmus process data appears from behind a divider. She looks tentative, as any inexperienced assistant forced to interrupt a meeting of more senior colleagues would. It must be something extremely important.

"What is it, Riikka?" Jessica asks.

"I just got a call from the Security Police. They've been trying to reach you."

Jessica feels a pang in her breast: her phone is on silent. *Damn it.* The men who have been shadowing Lisa's father have been trying to contact her.

"Is it Hirokazu Yamamoto?" Jessica says.

The investigative assistant nods. "In Järvenpää . . . It sounds like he tried to kill himself."

66

JESSICA IS THROWING on her coat and rushing toward the elevator on Yusuf's heels when she hears Rasmus' voice behind her.

"Jessica."

"Not now, Rasse. We have a situation here."

"But this is important," Rasmus says urgently. "Jason had a boat at his disposal. A big one."

Jessica and Yusuf pause and look at Rasmus questioningly.

"I called Traficom. It's the only Aquador 28C registered in Helsinki. And it's owned by a foundation Jason is actively involved with."

"What foundation?"

"The one Nina was talking about earlier: SWF, the Sexual Wellbeing Foundation. They help people who are struggling with their sexuality—"

"And they have a boat for foundation activities?" Yusuf asks incredulously.

"The boat was donated by the founder over ten years ago. In any case, I called the foundation and they told me Jason Nervander is the one who looks after the boat: he handles maintenance, winter storage, and other necessary arrangements."

"Is it being stored at Aurinkolahti?" Jessica asks. "At the marina?"

Rasmus shakes his head. "At Lauttasaari. But the foundation also has a mooring at Aurinkolahti. Think about it. Jason is the only one who really knows who's been using the boat and for what purposes."

"It's pretty goddamn strange no one figured this out earlier," Jessica says.

"The foundation chair told me over the phone that she lost her temper with Nervander the morning of the day he went missing. The boat had been promised to them for a donor activity, but Nervander didn't know where it was. Said he had lent it to someone. . . . Said he would look into it."

"We really need to get out to Järvenpää. Rasse, find out everything you can on the boat. Including where the hell it is now."

67

JESSICA CLIMBS FROM the car and takes in the large property spreading before her, the vegetable garden in the middle, the big pale yellow house beyond. A grilling area, a greenhouse, and a hot tub. It is all blanketed by a modest layer of snow, which is more impressive than the paper-thin skim in the city.

There are two faint slams as she and Yusuf shut the car doors in nearly perfect unison.

"Looks like the laundry business is cleaning up." Faithful to his vice, Yusuf lights a cigarette. "This is when the hard work pays off."

Jessica steps aside to avoid the cigarette smoke. "Until you put a rifle in your mouth?"

The air inland is drier and colder and smells cleaner than the air in Helsinki. The tinkle of a wind chime carries from the house, and there's a Christmas-card prettiness to the view. But the reason for their visit oppresses the mood.

"You guys didn't waste any time getting here," a voice says behind them. A figure has climbed out of the police van parked across the street.

Jessica sees the Security Police car a little farther away. It's ironic the men sitting in it were oblivious to what happened until the emergency vehicles arrived on the scene.

"Officer Kajo, Teppo Kajo." The slightly hunched, mustached man in civilian clothes extends a hand. A Järvenpää Police ID hangs around his neck. "The wife's inside," he continues, and honks his nose into a blue handkerchief. He seems to have a cold, but even so has decided it's OK to shake hands with Jessica and Yusuf. Jessica discreetly wipes her hand against the bottom of her coat. The skin under Kajo's nose is dry and cracked from too much blowing.

"Is he alive?"

Kajo frowns, further crinkling his furrowed brow. "Yes. But he's in critical condition."

JESSICA AND YUSUF enter the large living room, where gargantuan windows overlook the yard and the cars parked on the road beyond. The log walls are packed with woolen hangings, decorative objects, animal skins, and mounted animal heads. Paula Yamamoto is sitting on the sofa, the head of a menacing wolf above her. The sight seems imbued with uncanny symbolism.

"Hirokazu is alive," Yusuf says reassuringly as he takes a step closer.

"I should be there," Paula replies in a trembling voice. Her eyes are firmly fixed on her blue fingernails.

Yusuf shakes his head and slowly approaches her. He's the one who questioned her at the airport; she's familiar with his soft voice. "There's nothing you can do for him right now."

Jessica sees Paula raise her sad, bewildered face from the floor. The eyes shoot Yusuf an unconvinced look, but no protest emerges from her lips.

"I'm sorry." Jessica speaks loudly enough to ensure Paula hears. "I'm going to have a look at the room where . . ." *Your husband shot himself in the head,* she silently continues, hoping she won't have to put the thought into words.

Lisa's stepmother nods and indicates a door next to the kitchen. As she passes the kitchen, Jessica catches a whiff of the sea. She sees a gutted fish on a cutting board, its preparation evidently interrupted by the shot that rang out from the study. Art adorns the log walls, but contrary to what one might expect, Lisa's paintings are conspicuously absent.

There's an open door at the end of the hall.

Jessica takes a pair of blue plastic protectors from her pocket, slips them over her shoes, and steps into the study. The blood spilled across the shag rug almost looks like it belongs there, as if it is part of the rug's ornamental pattern. On the floor to the right of the desk lies a hunting rifle, at first glance a Sako Custom or Prestige. Perhaps the most remarkable thing about the scene is that Yamamoto, who as a former gangster must be familiar with weapons, put the rifle into his mouth, pulled the trigger, and survived.

Jessica sticks to the bare floor, skirting the rug to avoid stepping on the blood that drained from Hirokazu Yamamoto's head. The medics were not as mindful, but that's no reason for Jessica to be sloppy. *You can never afford to be careless, Jessica.* Erne always used to say that.

A fat stack of mail sits on the stout oak desk. *A two-week trip to Brazil.* Opened envelopes and piles of invoices. In the middle of them, on top, is a sheet of writing paper and a black envelope that has been unsealed.

Jessica takes the paper and unfolds it.

私たちは彼女を見つけました。
私たちは彼女を使いました。
私たちは彼女を殺した。
（そして彼女のボーイフレンド）

Jessica immediately takes a picture of the letter and sends it to Rasmus. *Translate immediately, please!*

She waits for confirmation that Rasmus has seen the message, then slides her phone back into her pocket. She studies the characters that, based on the circumstances, she assumes are Japanese. The dark blue symbols are a little smeared in places, as if they have come in contact with water. Then Jessica realizes: it was tears that made the ink smudge. Yamamoto's suffering brought the text to life.

68

HELLU CLENCHES THE receiver; the spiral cord is pulled taut against her chest. The gadget is from a totally different time and place, and the sensation of the solid plastic at her ear puts Hellu in mind of her childhood. Long calls with friends; Dad's perpetual orders to get off the phone so others could use it.

"Hello?" a female voice says in English.

"Yes?"

"I apologize for making you wait. We follow a very strict protocol when it comes to sharing information. Last month, a reporter from a major newspaper managed to fish out the details of an investigation by pretending to be an assistant at the prosecutor's office here in Amsterdam . . . which of course caused a huge shitstorm. Pardon my French. People were fired right and left—"

"I understand," Hellu says, tapping her pen impatiently against her mouse pad. This is the third and final call. Over the course of the conversations, her suspense has made way for a vague dread.

"But to get down to the point: the answer to your question is yes," the voice says. "Dienst Landelijke Operationele Samenwerking confirms that, upon discovery, Miep Loos was wearing clothing that matches your description."

Hellu swallows to moisten her dry throat. "Could I ask you to send photographs from the scene? We'll be happy to reciprocate."

"Certainly."

"And I suggest you contact the police at the homicide units in both Lviv and St. Petersburg. I'll send you an encrypted message containing the information once we're off the phone. But we suspect Miep Loos was not the killer's first victim or his last."

When the line goes silent, Hellu looks out the window and sighs deeply. If the walls could talk, and maybe take notes, one day they'd be able to recount how a very anxious superintendent sat in this office one November afternoon.

69

JESSICA WALKS BACK into the living room with the letter in her pocket. The fishy smell from the kitchen seems to have intensified over the intervening minutes; Jessica's senses are tuned to the extreme. Paula Yamamoto is speaking softly, and Yusuf is taking notes.

"I'm sorry," Jessica says. "We'll be on our way soon. I understand you have someone coming to be with you."

"A friend." Paula wipes a tear from her cheek. "First Lisa disappeared, and now this. . . . I don't want to be alone."

Jessica calmly makes her way to the sofa and notices a fire burning in the hearth. Yusuf must have built it to bring a little warmth into the room. Only a country boy from Söderkulla could coax firewood into a full blaze so fast.

Jessica feels the weight of the letter in her back pocket. She isn't sure whether Paula noticed it when she found her husband on his study floor. Or if she did, whether she read it or understood it. As long as its contents remain a mystery, there's no time to probe.

Yusuf stands. "I have everything we need for now."

"Do you understand Japanese?" Jessica asks Paula.

A quizzical look forms on Yusuf's face, and Paula Yamamoto shifts her startled gaze to Jessica. "How do you mean?"

Jessica doesn't repeat the question or offer clarification. There's a brief silence.

Eventually Paula answers tremulously: "No. I don't speak Japanese. Hiro always speaks Finnish. . . . More English at the beginning, of course . . . but never Japanese. He doesn't like speaking it. It's part of a past he doesn't want to remember."

"What sort of relationship do Hirokazu and Lisa have?" Jessica asks.

For a moment Paula Yamamoto gapes at Jessica as if she doesn't understand the question. She lowers her gaze to her hands, which are still shaking from shock. Then there's a shift in her demeanor, as if she has suddenly changed her mind. "Not a very good one. They barely speak. They had disagreements I never understood."

Jessica pulls the letter from her pocket. "You said you don't speak Japanese."

Paula Yamamoto looks in apparent confusion at the kanji characters drawn on the sheet of white paper. "I don't. What is this?"

"I found this on your husband's desk. According to the postmark, it was mailed the day before yesterday. Your husband must have read it after you came home."

"What does it say?" Paula asks quietly. Her distraught voice grows concerned; then her hands begin to shake more violently. "Please tell me. What does it say?"

"We don't know yet," Jessica says. "But I'm afraid it's somehow related to your husband's suicide attempt. . . ."

At that same moment, she feels her phone ping in her coat. As Jessica reaches into her pocket, she watches Mrs. Yamamoto sob on the sofa. A second ago, Paula silently performed a calculation with an unfortunate if obvious outcome. *Hirokazu received bad news.* So bad that he wanted to end his days in the darkening Järvenpää afternoon.

Jessica opens the message. It's from Rasmus.

And although Jessica has known for many minutes, it's only now, as she watches Paula Yamamoto's mounting agony, that it becomes concrete.

We found the girl.
We used the girl.
We killed the girl.
(And her boyfriend.)

70

"THE CASE IS much more complex than we ever could have predicted. Much, much more complex." It's Hellu, and her voice is coming over the car's speaker. But instead of sounding keyed up, the superintendent's voice is preternaturally calm. "Harjula found a notebook yesterday at the location where Belousova's body was discovered. The names of three women were handwritten in it. I made some calls, and it turns out the women were prostitutes who had been brutally murdered in Russia, Ukraine, and the Netherlands over the past two years. Like Belousova, they were all dressed in manga clothing when they were found. Apparently we're dealing with a serial killer or some strange cult. . . . No links were drawn between the earlier cases because the authorities of the jurisdictions in question weren't communicating with one another as they should have been."

Jessica and Yusuf exchange glances.

"In regard to our turf, I just spoke with Deputy Chief Oranen. The case is starting to take shape. It's clear we are dealing with an international human-trafficking ring, one that uses Instagram codes to spread its tentacles across the Nordic countries as well as, as far as we understand at this juncture, Russia, Ukraine, and the Netherlands. And what happened in Järvenpää—the letter and Lisa's father's suicide attempt—confirms your suspicions were correct, Niemi. The former gangster was trying to worm his way out of his past that caught up with him."

Jessica tries to get a word in: "But that doesn't—"

Hellu clears her throat to rebuff the attempt. "I know a lot still needs to be resolved. However, at this stage, it appears clear Lisa Yamamoto was forced to cooperate with the trafficking ring and that the criminals wanted to exploit her status as an influencer."

"I think too many open questions remain for us to—"

Hellu cuts Jessica off again, this time with a heavy sigh that crackles from the phone's mic into the car's speakers. During the two seconds of silence that follow, Jessica guesses what Hellu means to say next. Even so, the words pierce her heart like a nasty insult spit in her face in a grade-school hallway.

"The case is being transferred to the National Bureau of Investigation."

"What the fuck?" Yusuf says from the wheel. Jessica buries her face in her hands.

"They're coming in to meet with us tomorrow," Hellu continues. "The case has taken on dimensions beyond the capacity of the Helsinki Police Violent Crimes Unit to manage. We shouldn't even try."

"So you're admitting it?" Jessica hisses. "That you can't manage the case?"

Hellu doesn't reply; she seems to bypass the remark without exacting any sort of penalty, which infuriates Jessica even more. The asshole is turning over the case now that the top-notch groundwork has been done. Which is fine for Hellu, obviously. Why would she fight to keep the case? As the superintendent answering for the investigation, she has everything to lose from this point on if the team, despite its endeavors, comes up empty-handed. Hellu is aware of this; at heart she's a calculating politician executing her five-year plan. She doesn't need to catch the Phantom or find out where Lisa and Jason are buried. All she cares about is Jens Oranen extending a big, hairy hand and congratulating her for laying such a solid foundation for the investigation.

"I know this is a disappointment for you. But Europol has already been in touch with the NBI. It's perfectly possible they'll bring us in on—"

Jessica blurts: "Bring us in?"

"Skim the cream off the top," Yusuf mutters.

Meanwhile, Hellu continues her monologue in the background: "I've already spoken with everyone on the team. The plan is to keep plugging away until tomorrow morning, then see what sort of role is assigned us moving forward."

"Hellu! It doesn't matter how many bodies there are in Russia or the Netherlands! We have four homicides right here in Helsinki. It makes no difference, and it wouldn't even if some secret space program or JFK's assassination were tangled up in this."

"As I said, I understand your frustration. But the decision is final," Hellu says coldly. And just as Jessica is turning her gaze out at the gray fields flashing past, just when she thinks things can't get any worse, Hellu continues in an even more mechanical and colorless voice:

"And, Niemi, I'd like to see you in my office as soon as you get back to the station."

71

JESSICA SHUTS THE door behind her. Hellu's tiny office is grayer and more oppressive than ever today. Maybe because the bitch whose fifteen-square-meter territory Jessica just entered looks suspiciously self-confident. Her behavior has changed: it lacks the insecurity-fed aggression that Jessica has found incredibly irritating yet somehow reassuring. But now every pore on Hellu's serene face is screaming something Jessica can't make out: the brown eyes gleam in jubilation, and for the first time, the lips are painted red. Hellu has gussied up for this awards gala.

"You asked me to come see you," Jessica says, taking a seat across from Hellu.

Hellu is not intently shuffling through her papers, nor does she make Jessica wait. She is sitting comfortably in her chair, hands folded on the table, and she looks Jessica dead in the eye.

"We have a problem," Hellu begins in a neutral voice. Unlike her demeanor, her tone does not project malice or glee.

Jessica consciously sits up straighter. "What sort of problem?"

"In the aftermath of last spring's events, old issues rose to the surface. First and foremost, the NBI and Security Police combed through Mikael Kaariniemi's background to figure out how an investigator from the Violent Crimes Unit could secretly belong to a sick, murderous cult. At the same time, they wanted to ensure Mikael Kaariniemi was the only one of his ilk and discover if anyone else might have been aware of his proclivities . . . and mental health issues."

Hellu twists the yellow cap off a bottle of mineral water, and Jessica now notices two glasses have been set out on the table. But it's only when Hellu offers some water to Jessica that she realizes something is seriously awry. The lemon-flavored sparkling water is not a sign of solidarity. It is the last steak dinner or cigar of a death-row prisoner. Hellu no doubt means to strap her to the electric chair.

"No, thanks," Jessica says quietly.

"And lastly, the grand finale: the Security Police wanted to find out why the witch cult set their sights on you specifically, Niemi." The way Hellu says Jessica's last name sounds as if she's using air quotes. Jessica's heart skips a beat.

"There has to be a reason, doesn't there? Even though, by your own statement, you have no idea," Hellu continues.

Jessica stares down her boss. The woman she didn't want as her boss, the woman she would have never picked for the job. She does her best to see the human behind that beady stare, one who has her own pressures and her own asshole boss to deal with. The human she has spent the past few weeks comparing to Erne, unfairly at times. And yet despite the hatred smoldering inside her, Jessica understands this is not coming from Hellu; it must be coming from higher up. Hellu is the one relaying the baton, but Jessica would be screwed regardless of whose office she was sitting in right now.

The two women look each other in the eye, long and hard. Hellu knows Jessica knows she knows. There's no escape. There is only profound shame.

Hellu licks her finger and opens a folder resting on the desk. She takes out a sheaf of papers and slides them toward Jessica. Jessica lowers her gaze to the documents, notes the date, the title in bold, and the lines picked out in yellow highlighter. She feels the stifling suspense turn to physical nausea. She exerts every iota of willpower she can muster; she wants to stay strong, be her own brusque self, the Jessica who will look up indifferently from the pages and say: *So what?* But she can't. The hole that Hellu—or life, actually—has dug is too deep, and she has already signed her confession with her silence.

Hellu raises her glass to her lips, moistens her throat, and gives Jessica time.

This makes the situation almost unbearable, Hellu approaching the matter with a revolting delicacy. Hellu does not mean to kick her while she's down.

"What would you do in my position, Niemi?" Hellu eventually asks.

Jessica's voice has grown hoarse: "Who has seen this?"

Hellu shakes her head. "Almost no one. Nor does anyone else have to."

Then she rises to her feet and takes a couple of steps toward the window, as if to imbue the moment with more drama.

"This isn't personal," she says, and Jessica knows this is half true. "But it's rare to have an opportunity to reach a potential resolution as favorable to all parties as we have here. And I'm hoping we can take that opportunity together."

72

JESSICA WAITS FOR the elevator doors to close.

She has to get away. To the parking garage.

At the third floor, two men from administration step in, and the fresh scent of shower gel wafts in. One is carrying a black gym bag. His hair is wet.

Jessica's phone rings in her pocket.

The decision to resign is yours to make. And if you do resign, these documents were never found. They don't exist.

Jessica maintains her poker face.

The men exit on the first floor. The smell of soap lingers in the car, as does the moisture given off by shower-fresh skin.

The elevator descends to the parking garage. The doors open.

Jessica crosses the small lobby, pushes open the glass door, and strides between the cars toward the exit ramp.

She can feel her pulse in her ears. Her brow beads up in a cold sweat.

Don't run, Jessica. Don't run away.

What is she if not a police officer? What will she do if not this work?

You're just a rich, spoiled brat who's screwed up in the head.

Her phone rings.

Breathe.

She's about to lose her whole world: suddenly she can smell the cardamom rolls in the conference room, the freshly brewed coffee and the fruity rose hip tea, Yusuf's deodorant, the hoodies Nina wears that smell of tanning salon, Erne's cigarettes, the shooting-range reek of sweet gunpowder and still-warm shells ingrained in palms, Rasmus' sweat, the air freshener from the women's bathroom. Blood spilled across a floor, death that has rotted in a woodshed for months, desiccated urine and feces.

Jessica sees the garage door and the light peering beneath it.

She waits for the pain to come. She is sure that it will come, that it will pummel her body from head to toe and force her to the floor, make her writhe in agony like a wounded deer anticipating the sight of the hunter's muzzle to release her, usher her into the white light and ultimate peace.

She expects to hear her mother's voice.

But the pain doesn't arrive, nor does her mother appear behind her. No one takes her by the shoulder.

There's no white light. No peace.

She notices she is utterly numb.

She realizes she is completely alone.

She weeps, but no tears well up in her eyes.

Now Jessica hears a voice. It isn't her mother's; it's her own. And it's saying that Jessica has just lost everything, that she would rather have taken the pain, so at least she'd feel like she's still alive.

73

YUSUF STALKS DOWN the seemingly endless hallway, his sleet-soaked rubber-soled sneakers squeaking with every footfall. A few moments later, he pulls up behind Rasmus' workstation. Rasmus has his headphones on and doesn't register Yusuf's arrival; he appears to be kicking around a golf ball in his stocking feet. When he notices Yusuf, he jumps and punts the ball under the desk. *Weird dude.*

"Where's Jessica?" Yusuf asks, out of breath. "She's not answering her phone."

The flustered Rasmus shrugs and pulls his shoe back on. "I thought you guys just—"

Yusuf lowers a buttock to the corner of Rasmus' desk. "Yeah, she went to talk to Hellu and now I can't find her anywhere."

"What's wrong?"

"I just got a phone call while I was out having a smoke." Yusuf runs a hand over his mouth. "We have an eyewitness for Rodriguez's murder, someone who lives in the neighboring building. She was watching TV and stepped out onto her balcony for a smoke when the ads came on. She noticed a flare of light in the spa's windows, like a camera flash going off."

"The muzzle flash from a gun?" Rasmus mutters.

"The possibility didn't occur to her at the time, of course, but she says a man dressed in black stepped out and pulled the handle to make sure the door was locked. He was carrying a couple of bags. They must have contained the substances and supplies we were looking for."

Rasmus looks gobsmacked.

"She didn't get a good look at the guy, but she could tell he wasn't very big. Maybe even short. Her balcony is on the sixth floor, it was dark, and the guy was wearing a black coat with a hood."

"Short . . . So could the shooter have been a woman?" Rasmus says.

Yusuf stands. "I asked the same thing. But she thinks it was a man."

Bursts of laughter sound from the end of the hall. The tetchy old bastard who has investigated insurance fraud for twenty-five years is celebrating his last day, and the attendant cake and coffee, bouquets, and hugs are being doled out.

Now Rasmus speaks: "I have a couple of things too. They have to do with that letter. I got a call from the expert in Japanese and kanji to whom I sent the contents for translation. He said when he took a closer look at the characters, he noticed they were pretty good technically, but they show a clear lack of familiarity. Kanji characters are typically drawn in a specific order, one stroke at a time. The handwriting is analyzed by ascertaining where the pen lingered the longest, leaving a darker, broader mark on the paper. A lot of the strokes in this letter were drawn in an atypical order, as if whoever made them used a template."

"Are you saying that whoever sent the letter didn't really know how to write Japanese?" Yusuf asks.

"The expert was pretty sure that was the case."

"What the hell . . . ?"

"And another thing, Yusuf," Rasmus says. "Look."

Yusuf crouches down next to Rasmus and looks at the monitor, where a CCTV recording is ready for viewing.

"The letter to Lisa's father was written on a light blue two hundred and twenty gram specialty paper I've never seen before. There's a Paper Poetry watermark at the bottom-right corner. Black envelopes are relatively rare too."

"Are you saying the stationery can be traced?"

Rasmus nods. "Both the paper and the envelope were presumably bought with cash from an arts-and-crafts store at Itäkeskus Mall on Tuesday morning."

"Can we work out who bought them?"

"No," Rasmus says, to a frown from Yusuf. "But there's a mailbox right next to the stationery store. We know the letter was postmarked that same day, and we can easily check the CCTV footage from the camera right overhead. See if the perp went somewhere to draft the letter, then slipped it into the nearest mailbox. The box is emptied at two p.m. on weekdays, so the letter must have been mailed before then."

"Rasmus, even if it is the right mailbox, you don't know who to look for. How many people dropped mail in that mailbox on Tuesday morning? A hundred?"

Rasmus' face beams with hope. "The black envelope."

Yusuf grunts. "True. Is the color of the envelope visible from this angle?"

Rasmus points at an old woman sliding a white envelope through the slot. "Yup."

Yusuf takes Rasmus by the shoulders and gives him a gentle squeeze. "Way to go, Rasse. Let's hope you're right. I'll try to find Jessica."

74

JESSICA WALKS UP to the door, key in hand. She has passed through it for years, stepped into the narrow corridor and the tiny, cramped elevator that carries her to her studio apartment on the sixth floor. The studio has served as a facade, and the side-street entrance was the gate to the world she wanted everyone to believe in. If anyone had ever followed her, or happened to see her enter through the other door, would it have shattered the illusion?

Is she the magician her mother was talking about? Are the doors to the stairwells two cards, one of which is meant to serve as a distraction?

Jessica fiddles with her key ring and twists out a different key. Like the first one, it has a black head, but it's marked with a yellow plastic ring instead of a blue one. She turns, steps down from the stone doorstep, then walks to the corner and around to the right-hand side of the triangular block.

The key sinks into the lock, and a moment later, it opens to her: the spacious lobby she hasn't seen in years but whose museum-like smell she still remembers.

The door shuts with a thunk, and Jessica steps in tentatively, as if entering a medieval church where some invisible force seems to monitor every footstep.

No one in this stairwell would recognize her, even though she owns the largest flat in the building as well as the attached studio. She is the mysterious Jessica von Hellens, who for years has been represented at building association meetings by an attorney.

No more skulking in through the side entrance. No more studio apartment.

Jessica opens the gate to the old-fashioned elevator.

Her phone rings again. Yusuf has called her four times already. She has to answer; he has to hear it from her.

"Hey, Yusuf." Speaking seems to intensify the sensation of having a lump in her throat.

She hears Yusuf exhaling cigarette smoke against the mic. "Where'd you go?"

"Home. I came home, Yusuf, because—"

"I got a call an hour ago from an eyewitness who says she saw someone dressed in black, not too tall, leave Jose Rodriguez's kambo spa around the time we believe the murder took place—"

As she hears Yusuf's eager words, Jessica stares at the pattern in the lobby's marble wall: it's as if a few drops of black ink have been dribbled into clear water. She shuts her eyes. "Yusuf—"

"Listen, Jessie, goddamn it! Rasse just spotted someone in a CCTV recording dropping a black envelope in a mailbox at the Itäkeskus metro station on Tuesday at twelve fifteen p.m. A hooded black parka, cargo pants, and combat boots—"

"Yusuf—"

"The face isn't visible, but the height is a match for Rodriguez's killer. Maybe one hundred and sixty five centimeters. Slight build—"

"Yusuf!" Jessica snaps. Her voice ricochets around the elevator— this lift accommodates more than one passenger at a time.

Yusuf finally falls silent. Jessica can picture his surprised face at the other end of the line. She listens to his breathing for a second, then says: "I left the station because I'm not on the case anymore."

"What are you talking about, Jessie?"

"I'll tell you later."

"What do you mean, you're not on the case? Did Hellu assign you to something else?"

Jessica's voice is trembling: "It doesn't look like I'm a police officer anymore, Yusuf." She takes a deep breath, holds it, then presses the elevator button. She has to pull herself together.

"What do you mean, you're not—"

"Don't tell anyone yet. I want to tell the team myself tomorrow," she says, and ends the call.

Jessica wipes her eyes. Yusuf deserved a better explanation. He deserved to hear the whole truth. Maybe she'll tell it to him after she sleeps on it.

As the elevator comes to a halt at the sixth floor, Jessica grasps that, as much as it hurts, she is finally free. No one can tell her what to do anymore. Control her actions. She is free, but she's more alone than ever.

Nor is there any way she can sleep in her real apartment, because it reminds her too much of Erne right now, of the huge hole his death left in her heart. The elevator lurches downward.

Jessica browses through her received calls and selects the name of the one person who can ease her mind tonight.

75

"DON'T YOU LOOK dapper today?" Jessica says as Frank Dominis walks up to the table, coat over his arm. He's wearing a blue dress shirt and a dark suit with a tie. Jessica's heart beats in a way she doesn't remember having felt in ages.

Dominis responds with exaggerated surprise as he takes off his suit jacket. "This is how I dress whenever the club is open. It's my work uniform."

"Right . . . even though you said it was your first night off . . . in what? Two years?"

Dominis smiles. "I just came from meeting the Phoenix's owners. They're planning on opening two new restaurants, in Helsinki and Turku. They want me to head up both projects." He takes out his cuff links and rolls up his sleeves. "It looks like I know what I'm doing."

"Congratulations, Frank," Jessica says, gesturing the waiter over. "Another reason to celebrate."

"Another?"

Jessica shoots him a look as if she let something slip. "Let's just say I'm wrapping things up at work."

"What does that mean? Did you solve the case? Is Lisa—"

"Frank. It doesn't look like I'll be part of the investigative team anymore."

Dominis nods and folds his hands on the table. The hiked-up sleeves reveal dark-haired wrists covered in tattoos.

Jessica orders a dry white wine; Dominis a Coke. Nelly's "My Place" is being broadcast from the restaurant's speakers. Yusuf once pronounced it *one of his boot knockers,* poisoning it forever.

Dominis says: "Then let's not talk about it. Let's hope whoever's investigating finds Lisa."

"I had a couple of hours to process things today. Two things took me by surprise."

"What were they?"

"In the first place, I had this bizarre urge to call you. To meet up and chat."

Dominis smiles tenderly. "I'm flattered, Detective."

"The other thing—it involves the word you just used, actually."

"That I'm flattered?"

Jessica rolls her eyes. *"Detective."*

She can tell by the way Dominis looks at her that he grasps the implications.

"Jesus Christ. You mean . . . I'm sorry . . . I guess."

"It's all right. I'm not sure I want to be an investigator anymore. Or a police officer at all, for that matter."

Dominis looks intrigued. The server brings their drinks to the table. As she lights the candle, Jessica surveys the room and sees the candles at the nearby tables burning. The act doesn't indicate, then, that she has made any inferences about the nature of Jessica and Frank's relationship.

"Why don't you want to be a police officer?"

"I lost a friend last spring. He was a mentor of sorts. To cancer."

"My condolences," Dominis says. He slowly pours his cola over the ice in his glass without taking his eyes off Jessica.

"He was a police officer too, an anchor for me in this world. Now that he's gone, I'm not sure I ever had a calling for this work. Or if it was just a way of keeping family close. And by family, I mean my colleagues, because"—Jessica checks herself, to keep from sounding like a total idiot as a bottomless wave of self-pity washes over her—"they're the only family I have left."

"Think positively," Dominis says. "It's fantastic you have a relationship with your colleagues."

"*Had.* Past tense. That's exactly what I'm talking about, Frank. And why it's time to go, I guess."

High-pitched laughter carries from the bar. *Can we get some UFOs? No? Fernet, then. We're living it up tonight.*

Dominis grunts: he registers the racket but doesn't pay it any mind. In his universe, drunken commotion is background noise that indicates everything is as it should be. Deep silence is what makes him wonder if something's wrong.

"OK, so you're not a cop anymore." Dominis smiles behind his glass. "That's why you had the guts to call me."

"What do you mean?"

"If you were still investigating a case and really felt you owed something to your employer, you never would have asked me out for a drink. You would have thought it was inappropriate."

"Don't flatter yourself, Frank. You were only questioned as a potential witness."

Dominis bursts out laughing. "Even so. Do your colleagues—your former colleagues, I guess—know you're sitting here with me?"

Jessica doesn't say anything. She looks at Dominis. His eyes project sensitivity and perceptiveness. Maybe Frank Dominis is the one who ended up in the wrong profession. Jessica can picture him, palette in hand, at a canvas, wearing a snow-white dress shirt daubed with its share of splatters from the universe forming there.

"No," she eventually answers, and rewards Frank with a smile.

"So I'm right."

"Are you saying I subconsciously recused myself? Just so I could watch you sip a soda on a Thursday night?"

"The human brain is a curious contraption." Dominis wipes the corners of his mouth with his dark red napkin. "I'm sure you're an excellent police officer. But I also believe you'd be excellent at just about anything you put your mind to, Jessica."

Jessica has seen and experienced too much to let herself be dazzled by flattery, but something about Frank's words feels genuine, honest. Last night as well, Jessica had the overwhelming sensation that Frank has no interest in playing games: he may have once crowed over his conquests, but those days have passed.

"Wow, Frank." She puts on a bored look, an attempt to pump the brakes. "I think that was the first time you said my name."

Dominis loosens his tie and folds his arms across his chest. An ambulance speeds past the bar, sirens blaring. As she listens to the dwindling wail, Jessica can't help but think she's hearing her former life fade into the unknown.

"So long, Detective."

Jessica takes in the lips pronouncing the thick American English, the coarse stubble, the thick black hair that's going gray at the temples. There's an undeniable similarity to Erne: charismatic, rough around the edges, more or less the same age. And although there was never the tiniest hint of romantic tension between Erne and Jessica, she catches a glimpse of something inside her that could develop into genuine attachment to Frank over time. As she did with Erne, Jessica feels like she met Frank ages ago, that they've known each other forever.

She lowers her finger to the rim of her glass. "I think I'd better get another one of these."

JESSICA OPENS THE door to her studio and takes off her shoes, leaves them under the coatrack.

"Cozy," Frank Dominis says. He stands at the threshold of the flat's lone room and looks around without taking off his shoes.

"You think so? I've seen cozier." Jessica walks over to the refrigerator. "I have a couple beers here. . . ." She catches herself and raises a hand to her forehead. "Sorry. I forgot. . . ."

Dominis laughs warmly and waves dismissively. "No worries, Jessica. You have no idea how many times I've ordered a double Scotch over the years only to be reminded of reality and offer it to someone else."

"Mineral water?"

"Please." Frank slips off his brown leather shoes and leaves them next to Jessica's.

Jessica pulls two glasses from the cupboard and pours mineral water into both. She raises her own and drains it. *OK, I need something stronger.*

"You mind if I have a drink?" she says.

Frank smiles and shakes his head. He has walked over and accepted the glass of mineral water from her. He takes a swig and indicates the window. "Nice view. I like the courtyard."

Jessica grunts guardedly; this sort of small talk isn't helpful to either of them. Over the course of the twenty years Dominis has played host to the city's elite, he has surely visited the most exclusive VIP venues in Helsinki, from the penthouses of Eiranranta to the villas of Kulosaari. He has probably flown on private jets with celebrities and partied on yachts in Monaco, even if he has done it sober, as he claims.

Nothing about this modest studio could possibly impress him. *Cozy. I like the courtyard.* Bullshit. Part of Jessica wants to grab Frank by the wrist and drag him out the back door, into the stairwell, and across to the luxurious home worth an estimated four million euros. Show him police officers know how to live it up too: lead him into the huge living room and past the expensive art to the staircase, steer him through the upstairs lounge into the black-carpeted bedroom, then screw his brains out in the king-sized bed. She would love to see the shock on the face of the king of the Helsinki demimonde as he took it all in—the opulence no one would believe belongs to her.

Why shouldn't she? Now that her career in law enforcement is over, what's keeping her from revealing her truth? What does she need the facade for anymore?

But deep down, Jessica knows she can't. She has played her role for so long that it's going to take more than an impulsive whim to burn the set. She will have to dismantle it with class and extreme deliberation, as carefully as she constructed and maintained the lie for so many years.

Jessica is roused from her thoughts when Dominis sets his glass down on the windowsill and lowers a hand to her shoulder. His other hand tentatively scratches at his coarse stubble.

"Jessica, I'm not sure . . . I don't want you to think—"

"What do you mean?" she blurts. The words echo in the room more brusquely than she intended.

Dominis raises an eyebrow. "What—"

"OK." Jessica's face remains stern, but her voice is steadier. "Why are you talking about nice courtyards and what you want or don't want? What don't you want me to think?"

Frank reveals his straight teeth as he laughs incredulously. "Wow."

"I'm not some fucking twenty-year-old bimbo you scraped up from the bar."

"Jessica—"

"Jessica what? I thought you'd spare me all the greasy horseshit."

Frank releases Jessica's shoulder and takes a step backward. "Sorry. I was just thinking—"

"Sorry, sorry. Sorry! Where the hell is Mr. Frank Dominis, the city's most notorious fuck boy? The one who screws nine out of ten?"

Dominis stands there, his hands on his hips, staring at Jessica. Then he snorts and steps toward the entryway. "You want me to go?"

"You're not going anywhere." Jessica grabs Frank by the collar of his shirt. "You're going to screw me in this sweaty studio apartment right now. You're going to screw a lonely future ex-cop who doesn't want to be by herself at nine o'clock, who wants to be one of the nine."

The sentence ends in a wet whisper, and Dominis looks alarmed. It's as if his reputation as a Casanova has no basis in fact, is merely a rumor that turned into a self-perpetuating story.

"You're a wild one, Jessica."

Frank wraps his arm around her. He has recovered from his confusion in a split second, and his eyes once more burn with relaxed self-confidence.

Suddenly Jessica can't help smiling. She presses herself against Dominis, brings her face to his face, opens her mouth, slips her tongue between the straight teeth.

And Dominis finally begins to show some promise. Jessica senses sure fingers at the back of her neck; a moment later, they're unbuttoning her top buttons and helping her tug her shirt over her head.

Jessica's skin flushes with goose bumps. She feels Dominis' tongue wander across the skin at her throat, and she roars out in lust. The bra unsnaps smoothly and drops to the floor; then Dominis sweeps her up and tosses her onto the bed.

Dominis strips off his shirt, revealing a heavily tattooed torso and a large scar across his abdomen. The tightness of youth vanished from the musculature long ago, but like his face, Dominis' physique oozes experience, the sort of safety exuded only by a body that has seen it all, a body that has taken its share of the world's blows and survived. Frank is like an otherworldly embodiment of scents, sounds, and sensations who has chosen Jessica as his own here and now. Nothing else matters. Everything else comes tomorrow.

Jessica feels his head glide down her stomach. Her panties vanish, making way for his mouth. The soft, wet tongue swirls whispered words against Jessica's clitoris, accompanied by callused but gentle fingers that plunge deep inside again and again. Jessica can tell her body is primed to climax faster than it has in a long time.

"Holy shit," she whispers as Frank's fingers move faster and faster. "I'm going to come. . . ."

"No, you're not. Not yet." He stops licking. "Not without me."

Agile as a panther, Frank pounces on top of Jessica; his dark black curls have fallen in his eyes. Jessica feels him sink into her, take her knees, spread her legs, and launch into a series of rhythmic thrusts, no two alike. Frank tests his boundaries, switches up the tempo, and the whole time his thumb continues where his tongue just left off.

"Don't ever stop," Jessica murmurs as she feels the approaching orgasm. And then it strikes, searing, from deep in her spine, and washes over her body like an unbearable pain.

The only difference is, she wants what she's feeling now to last forever.

77

YUSUF GAZES AT the framed black-and-white photograph hanging above the drinking fountain. The man from rural Estonia, the smiling superintendent in his dress uniform, is watching over his former subordinates—and why not others too? That's what Jessica said when she hung Erne's photo there toward summer's end.

Yusuf and Rasmus are sitting at Rasmus' computer. Yusuf scrunches up his nose: Rasmus' deodorant has let him down again, and his pores are broadcasting a pungent sweat.

Yusuf leans back, while Rasmus is so severely hunched over the screen it looks as if his spine might snap at any moment. The CCTV video files from the Phoenix are playing on the screen.

"Wasn't Alem able to give you a more precise time frame? Morning?" Rasmus says.

"Apparently between noon and one. At the downstairs door."

Suddenly Yusuf lets his torso drop to the desk and buries his face in his arms, as if he has totally lost his grip. "Goddamn it, Rasse," he groans. He can hear his voice being muffled by his shirt.

Rasmus clicks open a new video file and narrows the search by time of day. "What's wrong?"

"Why are we sitting here this late? It doesn't make any sense. The assholes from the NBI will be here tomorrow morning and blow it all up anyway." Yusuf unburies his head and rests his cheek on the back of his hand. He watches the ever-changing footage on the screen. Crates of drinks and other supplies are being carried in for the album drop.

"I know what you mean." Rasmus folds his arms across his chest. "It's a tough situation. . . . But aren't you interested in finding out the truth? When it comes down to it, isn't that the whole reason we do this?"

"It's definitely not the pay," Yusuf replies. "It just would have been nice to get at the truth ourselves, instead of looking over our big brother's shoulder."

"We don't know how roles will be delegated in the morning. Maybe they'll let us keep working on the case."

But Yusuf's attention is fixed on the monitor now. He feels his breath catch. "Look."

The screen is divided into four identical squares, each pane displaying video footage from the day of Kex Maces' record launch. The digital clock at the upper-right corner reads six past twelve. Yusuf has pressed his finger to the pane showing the downstairs entrance to the nightclub, off Narinkkatori Square. When he pulls it away, a man in a long black coat is revealed. Yusuf glances at Rasmus, who looks like he has seen a ghost.

"Is it—"

"The Phantom," Yusuf says quietly. He takes the mouse from Rasmus' hand and pauses the video.

The two men study the Asian man. He approaches the entrance to the Phoenix but stops a few meters away. He stands there waiting patiently, just like he does later that night at the actual party. Minutes pass; nothing happens. Then he lifts his chin and looks around. Eventually his gaze falls on the camera, and for a moment it's as if he is staring Rasmus and Yusuf in the eye.

"What the fuck is he doing?" Yusuf mutters.

"It's like he wants to be seen," Rasmus says.

Two more minutes pass. And then a figure in a hooded jacket emerges from the door. He shakes hands with the Japanese man, and the two of them step to the side. The face of the man in the jacket isn't visible in the shot, but judging by his build and clothing, it's a middle-aged man.

Rasmus zooms in; the resolution grows grainier. The Phantom seems to hand the other man something, but it's impossible to say what.

"Who the hell is that?" Yusuf says in a low voice.

"Too scrawny to be Alem."

The two men in the footage appear to converse. A minute passes. Another. Then the Phantom looks abruptly to the left, toward the door to the Phoenix and the parked cars. He plainly sees something, because he turns his face away and hurries off camera.

Now Yusuf is excited. "He jetted. What freaked him out? Bring up the camera from outside the club."

Rasmus clicks open another camera angle. At first there's nothing in the image but the nightclub's white van, which has been there for a while. But then a black Mercedes SUV pulls up alongside it.

"Look," Yusuf says.

Out climbs a muscular man in a dark suit and black overcoat. He has a massive jaw and a striking nose. *He really does look like Klitschko.*

"I bet the next person we see enter the shot is going to be Sahib Alem. . . . Goddamn, what a congregation," Yusuf continues.

"The Phantom didn't want James to see him."

Yusuf pulls a pack of gum from his pocket. His jaw works restlessly in anticipation. "Go back to the first camera."

Rasmus brings up the previous angle. The man who was talking to the Phantom is still standing there, hands on his hips, watching the Phantom go.

"Turn around so we can see you, asshole." Yusuf tosses a few pieces of chewing gum into his mouth. *Come on, turn around. . . .*

And then the man turns and starts walking back to the entrance. The hood of the coat casts a shadow over the face, but even so, profound emotional turmoil can be read on it.

"Goddamn it . . . ," Yusuf says eagerly as the man steps back into the nightclub. "Call Jessica right now!"

78

It takes Jessica a second to register that the sound is coming from her phone. It's still in her jeans, which are on the floor next to the bed.

"Yusuf . . . I told you—"

Yusuf's voice is agitated. "Are you asleep?"

Jessica cracks her eyes and checks her watch; she can barely make out its face in the darkness.

"Yeah, why?"

"Dominis!"

The name crackles loudly from the phone, and Jessica quickly lowers the volume. "Umm . . . hold on."

She gingerly climbs out of bed. Frank Dominis raises his head from his pillow.

"Work call," Jessica whispers, phone pressed to her chest. She tiptoes into the bathroom and shuts the door.

Dominis knows she is no longer a police officer.

Jessica looks at herself in the mirror, brings the phone to her ear. Her heart is pounding strangely, wildly, in her breast.

"What did you say?" she says, uncertain if Yusuf actually uttered the name Dominis into the phone just a moment earlier. Jessica hopes with all her heart that she misheard. Or that Yusuf called just to tease her.

"Frank fucking Dominis, Jessie," Yusuf says again.

Jessica's fingers clasp her phone more tightly. "What . . . what about him?"

"He met the Phantom," Yusuf says. "I knew he was mixed up in this shit . . . and he supposedly didn't recognize the Phantom when we showed him the photo. He knew we were turning the city upside down looking for him!"

Jessica feels like she's falling. Every cell in her body is on high alert. *This can't be happening. The lies.* For a moment, Jessica is irritated with Yusuf, because he's the one who woke her up at the end of a perfect evening to slander the man who cannot be involved in Lisa's disappearance in any way. *We already checked.*

"Did you hear me, Jessie? They met. Last Saturday, the day of Kex Maces' record launch, at twelve oh six p.m. outside the Phoenix. I figured you ought to know, even though—"

"Wait." Jessica turns on the tap. She hopes the sound of the running water will drown out her voice, block it from carrying into the next room.

Her tired brain is processing what Yusuf just told her. But it seems so absurd; there's no way it can be true.

"What are you talking about, Yusuf? What do you—"

"Rasmus and I are looking at the CCTV footage right now. The Phantom and Dominis together outside the club. There's no doubt. That bastard has been screwing us over this whole time. He knows exactly who the Phantom is and why he got into Kex Maces' party."

Jessica's heart skips a beat.

Yusuf continues: "So does Sahib Alem. We didn't find the Phantom on the guest list because he wasn't on it! Dominis told Alem to let him in without asking any questions. Rasse and I rechecked the footage, played the moment the Phantom arrives at the coat check: Alem only pretends to cross a name off the list. He clicks out the tip of the pen when the next guest shows up. I didn't catch it earlier."

"Goddamn it." Jessica's voice is quavering, and she can feel the tiny bathroom start reeling like a carousel.

"You want me to send out a patrol to pick up Dominis from his house—"

Jessica brings her hand to her forehead and speaks softly. "Yusuf."

The truth is simultaneously chilling and embarrassing, but Jessica's fear outweighs her shame.

"What?"

"He's here." Jessica slides her right hand under the tap, and the warm water sends shivers across her goose-pimpled skin.

Yusuf doesn't reply. It sounds like he's holding his breath. "What?"

"He's here. At my place, in Töölö," Jessica whispers as she locks the door.

"What the hell, Jessica . . . ?"

Jessica can hear the blood rushing in her ears. She pictures the man in her bed, the man she just shared a moment of intimate pleasure with.

Jessica pictures the tattooed knuckles, the thick hair, the lips that taste of a life lived to its fullest. It's happening all over again. Colombano is once more in her bed. *Voglio fare l'amore con te, Zesika.*

Suddenly the decision to meet Frank seems incomprehensible. She can't even really remember the moment she decided to sleep with him. It's as if she erased it from her memory. Total blackout.

"Come here, Yusuf. Please. Now."

"OK, Jessie."

Jessica turns off the tap, leans against the edge of the sink, and studies her reflection. Her agitation makes it happen at lightning speed, as if her heart is beating the time for the metamorphosis taking place within her: her mascara drips down her cheeks; the black streaks form whorls against her smooth skin. Her complexion grows even paler, and her irises wholly disappear. A moment later, her eyes are completely white. And at that point Jessica understands the liquid draining from her eyes isn't tear-diluted mascara, but something much thicker. And as so many times before, she tastes the iron flavor of blood on her tongue.

I told you, Jessica, but you didn't want to listen.

What did you tell me?

The magician needs to know only the card next to your card.

Her mother is standing right behind her now, doing what Jessica used to love so much as a child: lowering her fingers to Jessica's bare shoulders. Energy, warmth, and love would transfer from skin to skin.

Jessica hears the hardwood floor creak on the other side of the door. Frank has climbed out of bed, is walking across the room. The kitchen cupboard thunks shut.

The question is: who summoned the magician, and why?

What damn magician, Mother? What are you talking about?

The magician is the one who gets you to look elsewhere when you should be looking at him. At his hands and fingers, what he's doing with the cards.

Jessica shuts her eyes.

When she opens them, her mother has drawn the shower curtain closed. All she can see at its edge are gaunt, bony fingers, ragged black nails.

She looks at her trembling hands for a moment, then raises her eyes back to the mirror. Now she sees the Jessica who climbed out of bed a moment ago looking back at her. Her mascara has streaked a little, and her eyes are red.

Jessica bites her lip and collects her thoughts: she could stay in the bathroom. Turn on the shower and wait. But something inside her prevents her from hiding. *It can't be true.* If she had enough courage to trust, she must have the courage to face the *full* truth, no matter how painful.

Jessica sighs deeply. She unlocks the door and turns the handle, then emerges from the bathroom warily, holding her breath.

Electricity seems to have charged the air in her tiny studio during the few minutes she spent in the bathroom. She thinks she hears a low buzz, like an enormous fly or the sound of the television turning on. *It's all in your head, Jessica.*

Frank Dominis isn't lying in bed anymore. He's sitting at the small table next to the window, wearing nothing but his boxers. The yellow light falling through the window gives his furrowed face an almost painterly aspect in the otherwise dark room.

His expression is anything but serene.

Jessica sees his hand rise to his face, his head drop backward, and the tall glass hit the table with a faint thud. Dominis takes the bottle and pours himself another shot. The bottle is already half empty. Jessica got the whisky from Fubu last year for Christmas and left it in the kitchen cupboard, unopened.

"Frank . . . ," Jessica says softly.

And then she notices her holster on the table and the gun in Frank's left hand.

79

"Last night when you asked . . . ," Dominis says, swirling a splash of whisky in his glass. "Yes, I was."

"You were what?"

"A soldier. In Alaska. A long time ago." Dominis lowers the gun to the table, tosses back the alcohol.

He stares at the empty glass in his hand for a moment and smiles euphorically, as if meeting a long-lost friend. Which is, by all signs, what is happening. The generous pour of tawny-colored poison was apparently sufficient to bring his body to a state of weightlessness. Jessica eyes the door: if she's fast, she might be able to make it to the stairwell and escape before he aims and fires. Or he might have time to fire, but miss.

"Fourth Brigade Combat Team, Twenty-fifth Infantry Division, ma'am," Frank says, mimicking a Midwestern accent.

She edges slightly, almost imperceptibly, toward the door. Dominis grabs the gun, clipping the wings of any silly ideas.

"Don't go, Jessica." The words sound more like a plea than an order.

Jessica draws a breath. Her eyes are acclimating to the gloom, and now she can see Frank's face and bare, tattooed torso more clearly in the dim light falling through the window.

"What exactly have you done, Frank?" Jessica says. "You were involved in—"

"I figured it was just a matter of time before the whole thing blew up in my face, like a live grenade mistaken for a dud." Dominis fills the glass on the table, this time almost to the rim. The gun remains firmly in his left hand.

"Come sit down, Jessica," he says. When Jessica doesn't immediately react, he repeats the plea a degree more emphatically, but ends it with a calm "please."

Jessica glances at the door and realizes how hopeless the situation is. And in that instant, she also realizes she put Yusuf's life in danger during the phone call. If Dominis shoots her, he will no doubt do the same to Yusuf when Yusuf tries to enter.

"They're coming, aren't they?" Dominis makes a face; he just downed a third of the glass.

Jessica nods and slowly approaches the table. "It doesn't have to come to this. I can help you."

Dominis laughs incredulously and studies the pistol in his hand. "A Walther P99. A gun that puts quite a bit of trust in the hand that wields it: no external safety." He raises the mouth of the barrel toward the ceiling. Then he nods at the seat across from him, signaling for Jessica to sit.

"Did you hear me, Frank?" Jessica says, taking a seat at the table. Despite the pressure, her movements are slow and controlled. "Tell me everything. I can help you—"

"Look at me, Jessica." Dominis raises his glass. "Eight years, five months, and three days. Will I live long enough to be able to say that again? Would I even be free yet . . . in 2028?"

"The only thing you have to do now is—"

"What? Give you the gun? Wake up tomorrow morning in a holding cell with the worst hangover of my life, knowing it will be years before I see daylight again?" Dominis empties the glass in one swig. His face screws up in a grimace that speaks of sense-numbing pleasure. "Do you remember when I told you I came to Helsinki looking for darkness, the same darkness I grew up with in Anchorage? Well, I definitely got what I was looking for. I've seen night in the truest sense of the word. Sold my soul to the devil, or whatever the articulate way to put it would be. Got mixed up in things I never wanted to get mixed up in. And why? For money and money alone. And damn it, Jessica, if anything is darkness, that is."

"Tell me," she whispers, lowering her shaking hands to the table.

Frank stares into Jessica's tearstained eyes. He has done something bad, but he is not bad to the core. Jessica is still sure of it. Frank isn't like Colombano or the dozens of cold-blooded sociopaths she has put behind bars over the course of her career. Frank's face tells thousands of stories. It reminds her more and more of Erne's. Erne, who was like a treasure trove of secrets. Erne, the one who taught Jessica that a black-and-white worldview is a privilege not granted to all, a luxury only those who are offered everything on a platter can afford. Not even them, necessarily.

Jessica cautiously takes Frank's glass, pours herself a drop, and tosses it back. She hasn't tasted whisky in ages; she gasps at the smoky, peaty flavor.

Dominis grunts, presumably because he interprets this as a sign of solidarity. *All right, let's drink together, then.*

"When I met that Japanese guy . . . I knew things were about to go to hell, that my house of cards was about to come tumbling down."

Dominis licks his lips. He lowers the gun back to the table but doesn't let go of it.

"Help me understand," Jessica says. "And I promise I'll help you."

"I guess I probably wasn't ever meant to get off scot-free . . . and I guess there's something poetic about this too. In my coming—excuse me—our coming here to your place, making love . . . Maybe I subconsciously wanted to turn myself in tonight. Who knows?"

Dominis steadies himself against the table and slowly hauls himself to his feet.

"Tell me, Frank," Jessica says.

Dominis steps over to Jessica and strokes her cheek with the back of his hand. A tender smile, simultaneously seductive and paternal, flashes across his face.

"You're not nine out of ten, Jessica. You're one in a million," Frank says in a low voice. He grabs the bottle and walks toward the door, Jessica's Walther P99 in his other hand. His gait is steady; the liquid poison hasn't had time to produce the desired effect despite his prodigious consumption.

Jessica feels a huge lump in her throat. She feverishly considers her options. "Frank."

Frank's gun hand grips the door handle. She has to do something.

Frank takes a long swig and steps out into the dark stairwell in his underwear. The familiar clank echoes as the heavy cables lurch into motion. A moment later, the elevator appears in view, like the sun rising behind a mountain.

Jessica stands and starts walking toward Frank. "Frank, what are you . . . ?"

The elevator stops and Dominis opens the door to it.

Jessica steps into the stairwell, but Frank pulls the iron gate shut and stands there, looking at her through the grille.

Jessica no longer feels any fear, just an inexplicable yearning. "Frank . . ."

"I've been really damn happy for days now. Because at the beginning of the week, I made the decision to leave this world. I've been floating every day since. And this"—Dominis aims the gun first at himself, then Jessica—"this was real."

Then he raises the bottle to his lips and presses the button for the first floor. The elevator begins its slow descent, and a moment later Frank's intense, woeful gaze disappears from view.

"Frank! Wait!" Jessica shouts. She grabs a coat from the rack to wrap herself in and takes off after him.

Her bare feet slap against the stairs, faster and faster; she feels the cold marble underfoot and hears the old elevator pop and clatter as it descends to the first floor.

"Frank!"

Her cries echo keenly in the stairwell. On the fourth floor, one of the neighbors opens their door as Jessica runs past. *What on earth is going on out here . . . ?*

Jessica hears the bottle thud to the elevator floor. Now she flies down the stairs.

When she reaches the third floor, she catches a glimpse of the interior of the elevator car; she has almost caught up with it.

Then she hears a gunshot echo deafeningly in the grim stairwell. Startled dogs start yapping insistently behind doors. As she descends the last two flights, Jessica's mind goes blank. Her footsteps slow; suddenly she is no longer in a hurry.

At long last she arrives at the ground floor, feels the coarse red runner beneath her feet. She opens the elevator door, then the gate, and sees the half-naked man lying lifeless on the mat. He's slumped against the wall, with a ragged hole at his temple. The elevator mirror is smeared with blood.

And Jessica is standing there in the center of it, her face a mask of despair.

She feels a hand on her shoulder. The fingers are bony, cold.

Look in the mirror, Jessica.

Someone turns on the stairwell lights, and the hand on her shoulder disappears. The sound of sirens carries in from outside. Yusuf has alerted the cavalry.

At that instant, the pain strikes. The tiny needles start their march along her neural tracts, setting out from the tip of her spine, transfixing her organs, continuing on to her hands and feet, straining to burst through her fingers and toes. A moment later, she feels the floor against her cheek and meets Frank's serene gaze, which seems to be begging for forgiveness.

80

HALF AN HOUR has passed since Frank Dominis pulled the trigger, but in Jessica's world, time seems to have stopped; she can still hear the shot echoing, still smell the heavy scent of gunpowder.

Jessica is looking out the window, holding a glass with a splash of whisky at the bottom. She can see Frank's face in the window: the bright, mournful eyes meld with the darkness. The blue lights of the emergency vehicles parked on the street penetrate the portico, flicker against the windows of the courtyard's lower stories.

Yusuf is sitting on the bed, hands in his lap. Minutes have passed since either spoke.

The door to the apartment is closed, but indistinct sounds carry from the stairwell: Dominis' body is being moved from the elevator to the vehicle that will transport it into Sissi Sarvilinna's care.

It's as if an enormous rock is weighing on Jessica's chest. She feels like she just finished a long run; it's hard to breathe. She isn't grieving for the man she barely knew. She's grieving for herself, grieving the fact that once again she stepped on the same land mine, fell for a monster, despite having promised Erne she never would again. There's something wrong with her. She is bad, and that's why she seeks out badness. It's the badness inside Jessica that made her mother kill her family. The fact that Jessica killed Colombano, plunged a dagger into his neck, proves it's true. Jessica is a venomous spider who tangles others in her webs. Just like in the Kex Maces song.

Nothing but death, Jessica.

Jessica doesn't react. She refuses to listen to her mother's reprimands, but her mother moves her mouth closer so the cold air flows into Jessica's ear.

You're the one who asks for it, Jessica. . . .

"Be quiet!" Jessica shouts.

She hurls the empty whisky glass against the wall. Shards shower to the floor. Yusuf springs from the bed like a spooked horse.

"What the fuck, Jessica?" His hands are at his ears, but he must realize how ridiculous he looks, because he drops them to his waist. "I didn't say anything!"

Jessica feels a cold sweat form on her skin. Her heart is beating wildly; she can hear herself hyperventilating.

I'm crazy, Yusuf. I'm really screwed up in the head.

"Sorry. I don't . . . ," Jessica says, but she knows explaining everything to Yusuf is impossible. There might be a time and a place, but it's not now.

"Jessica, what's going on?"

Yusuf takes a few steps closer, and glass crunches under his shoe. Jessica is still barefoot; her black wool coat is the only thing shielding her naked body.

"Everyone at the station knows now, Yusuf," Jessica says softly. "My reputation is shot to hell."

Yusuf stops and shakes his head, but is in no hurry to answer. Jessica feels her stomach lurch; she has the urge to vomit. Yusuf squats and picks up two large shards from the floor.

"Right?" Jessica insists. She isn't sure which would make her feel better: Yusuf denying her words or not commenting, confirming what she already knows.

Yusuf sighs and stands. "No one thinks that, Jessie. Of course not." He sets the pieces of broken glass down on the counter, then walks over to the window and takes a seat at the table. In the chair where Frank opened the whisky bottle not more than an hour ago. His final draft of venom before carrying out his self-imposed sentence.

"I know you warned me—," Jessica says quietly.

"Who gives a shit what I said, Jessie? What the hell do I know . . . ? I don't have any right to go around giving people relationship advice. I haven't been with a woman in months. Besides, what I said applied only to Dominis' reputation as a ladies' man. I never thought he was . . . part of this sick setup. . . ."

"I should have known," Jessica says. She looks at Yusuf.

"You're extremely capable, Jessie. But you're no oracle. Or Nostradamus."

Jessica looks at the bed. A few hours ago, she writhed in pleasure under those sheets. She fell asleep under them, with a man at her side. And she crept out from under them and into the bathroom, with her phone in her hand. *Dominis*. That was the first thing Yusuf said. It must have been the only thing Frank heard in the silent room. Roused by the sound of his name, he climbed from bed, considered whether to pull on his trousers and flee into the night or if now would be the perfect time to execute his suicide plan. Maybe he spotted Jessica's pistol and needed courage to be able to use it. Or maybe he stumbled across the bottle first. The chain of events is a mystery; all they can do now is guess.

Jessica listens to the sounds from the stairwell. She can't make out what they are, but in her head, she hears the clicks of the photographers' flashes, the crime scene investigators' conversation, the mobile phones' rings. Jessica imagines Frank's skin turning blue—Frank, whose warm body she felt against her own just moments ago.

Jessica glances at her phone. Oddly enough, Hellu hasn't called. Maybe that's only logical, considering she basically booted Jessica out of the unit yesterday. On the other hand, if the cow doesn't call, she'll miss out on her last chance to humiliate Jessica.

At that instant, her phone bursts out ringing on the table. But it's not Hellu calling; it's Rasmus. Jessica stares at the tirelessly flashing device.

"Aren't you going to answer?" Yusuf asks.

Yusuf probably has no idea what a superb question he just asked. Jessica really doesn't have any good reason to pick up. But she hasn't told the team she's leaving yet. She had better see things through the right way.

"Hello?" Jessica says tiredly.

"Are you OK, Jessica? I heard—"

"Yes, Rasse. Is that why you called?"

"What? No, not . . . The thing is . . . we found Lisa Yamamoto's second phone. We don't have it, but we were able to track it. . . ."

Jessica feels her head clear. Despite having accepted her fate earlier that night and acknowledging she is no longer involved, she's suddenly at the heart of the case again.

"Well? Where is it?"

"That's what's so weird." Jessica hears a door shut at the other end of the line. Then Rasmus continues: "The mobile service provider gave me a link so I can monitor its location live. In other words, I can see where the phone is at any given time with an accuracy of about twenty meters. Right now it's in Konala . . ."

"Yeah?"

". . . at Helena Lappi's home address."

81

HELLU SELECTS THE basic cycle and shuts the dishwasher. She hears the water run through the pipes, the appliance suck it in. And the machine launches into the mechanical hum that will last the next hour and a half. That will give Hellu enough time to clean the kitchen—not as thoroughly as she would like, perhaps, but certainly sufficiently for a little face-lift.

Hellu wets the rag, sprays cleaner into the sink, and wipes it one last time. She thinks about Jessica and how tomorrow she will have to take a new approach to asserting control over her subordinates. Divide and conquer. The timing is perfect for a tactical move: Jessica doesn't have many friends in the unit right now, loyal followers who will be sad to see her go and start asking dumb questions, suspect a conspiracy. No, it will be plain to one and all that Jessica Niemi decided to step aside of her own volition. And yes, Unit Superintendent Helena Lappi finds the decision surprising, but in the same breath, she notes Finland is a free country and no one can force Jessica to continue working for the police if she doesn't want to. This is how it will appear outwardly, and this is how it is supposed to appear. And when Hellu passes Deputy Chief Jens Oranen in the corridor, he will give her a pleased look, call her into his office, and shake her hand. *Good work, Lappi,* he will say, and her career will shoot off into an even more stratospheric climb.

Hellu jumps when she feels something on her hip.

"I'm going," Hanna says in her ear. She has wrapped her arms around Hellu's waist.

It takes a moment for Hellu to grasp Hanna's meaning. "Today? The night shift?" she says in surprise, turning to look Hanna in the eye.

Hanna looks amused. "Are you a little stressed out? It's not like you to forget my shift schedule. You usually know it by heart." She presses her lips to Hellu's, and Hellu feels her cheeks flush.

Hanna is beautiful, much more beautiful than Hellu. And she is most beautiful up close, when they kiss. When they touch. When Hanna's playful eyes laugh as she bites her bottom lip, touches Hellu, gives her pleasure.

"I guess I'll see you in the morning," Hellu says.

Hanna's fingers are still caressing Hellu's neck. "Maybe one day we'll have an evening off together. Or morning."

At that moment, the doorbell rings.

"Were you expecting someone?" the still-smiling Hanna asks. "Did you tell your lover to come by an hour too early?"

Hellu chuckles and flings the dishrag into the sink. "Your logic is flawless. I didn't even remember you were working tonight."

"I'll let her in on my way out." Hanna has her coat on but not her shoes. She hoists a light blue canvas bag over her shoulder. "See you." Hanna winks, disappears into the living room, and descends the stairs to the front door.

Hellu leans against the kitchen counter, dries her hands, and freezes so she can listen. The front door opens, and Hellu hears faint speech. *In English.*

She creeps to the top of the stairs, sees Hanna's lower back as she pulls on her shoes without sitting. Hellu sees a pair of brown leather shoes and a strip of dark trousers outside the door.

"Hellu, there's someone here to see you," Hanna calls.

And then Hellu smells the strong saccharine aftershave.

82

YUSUF SWERVES INTO the bus lane to pass the dump truck, then hurtles back into the left lane so sharply the car almost grazes the taillights of the bus in front of them.

The flashing blue light fixed to the dash lets other drivers on the road know this is not your average Volkswagen Golf; it's an unmarked police car racing toward danger in the line of duty.

"Isn't she answering?" Yusuf asks. He slams the gas in a low gear, sending the revs into red.

Jessica lowers her phone. No, Hellu isn't answering, but there could be several reasons for that. "Give me your phone," she says.

Yusuf pulls his phone from his pocket and hands it to Jessica. She brings up Hellu's number, brings the phone to her ear, and a moment later achieves the same result: no answer. *What the hell is going on?*

Jessica sets both phones down on the console. "Goddamn it."

Yusuf speeds through a yellow light. "Why would Hellu want to hide the fact that she has Lisa's mobile phone in her possession? We've been busting our butts trying to find it."

Jessica gets why Hellu wouldn't have informed *her*. But it's only logical that someone on the team ought to know about it because it's highly relevant to an ongoing investigation. The information should have reached Yusuf, or at least Rasmus, who probably represents some sort of neutral ground.

The chassis bounces on the shocks as the tires hit a patch of frost-buckled road head-on. Jessica grabs the door handle. She shouldn't be here sitting in a car in the middle of the night, headed to the home of the homicide unit's director so they can ring her doorbell and—

Yes, what then? Ask for the phone? Conduct a search for the damn thing?

And yet she feels like she's in exactly the right place, barreling toward a new mystery with Yusuf at her side. Suddenly she notices the debilitating pain that struck in the stairwell has evaporated.

Just now, as Yusuf steers the car through a busy intersection and on to Vihdintie, she is glad she answered Rasmus' call. She isn't sure what would have happened if she had decided to stay at home alone.

"Jessica," says Yusuf, leaning his left arm against the window, "do you think Hellu is mixed up in this case somehow?"

Jessica looks out at the dry snowflakes hurtling past the windshield, watches the urban landscape instantly give way to leafless woods, as if magic is at work. "I don't know, Yusuf. Maybe she found Lisa's phone. Or else she found Lisa. Or the Phantom paid Hellu a visit."

83

Yusuf pulls over at the side of the road. He turned off the lights a moment earlier. Ten meters ahead starts an asphalted drive that runs between two red row houses. A gray Toyota Prius is plugged into a charging station at the end unit, where a light burns on the second floor.

"That's Hellu's hybrid," Yusuf says, and pops a piece of gum into his mouth.

Jessica looks around, then glances at her watch. It's twelve thirty a.m. "Why the hell isn't she answering?" she mutters, checking her phone again.

Yusuf kills the engine. "This thing is really starting to smell rotten, Jessie."

They sit there, staring at the yard and the drive bathed in the dim glow of the streetlamps. There's not a soul in sight, but a light is on in one of the other units on the block. The moon peers shyly from behind the clouds. Leafless shrubs quiver in the wind like shivering hedgehogs.

It's an idyllic spot, ideal for families with children. Kids' toys and athletic gear dot every other doorstep. Big Wheels, shovels, ice hockey sticks, plastic goals. Flexible Flyers, snow saucers, and sleds—for which there has been little use so far this winter.

"Should we ring the doorbell?" Yusuf asks.

"And say what? 'Hey, Hellu, sorry to show up at your door at one o'clock in the morning, especially since you pulled me off the case, but is Lisa Yamamoto's secret cell phone here by any chance, and if so, why didn't you tell anyone?'"

"It's here, damn it! Rasse just said it was!" Yusuf insists, beating the steering wheel with his fingers.

Jessica massages her forehead. "Even if it is, we can't exactly call Hellu to account for herself."

At that moment, she sees movement at the upstairs window. "Look." And even though Jessica's not sure whether the person she saw was Hellu or someone else, she says: "There she is."

As Yusuf trains his eyes on the window, a light comes on downstairs.

A moment later, the front door opens.

Jessica holds her breath.

"Someone's coming out. Is it Hellu?"

"No," Jessica says.

It's a figure wearing a black parka and a hat of some sort.

The figure passes the gray Prius and heads toward the road—and the car Jessica and Yusuf are sitting in.

Yusuf's gum-chewing jaws stop. He whispers: "Who the hell is it?"

"It's a man."

The man walks slowly but purposefully, hands in his coat pockets, gaze on the ground. His face shaded by the brim of his hat. *It can't be . . .*

"Get down," Jessica says, and she and Yusuf slide down in their seats until they're out of sight.

The wind catches on the man's hat, and he has to grab to keep it from flying off.

"What the hell . . . ?"

Then he looks up and glances around. Like a gazelle tuned to the presence of predators on the savanna, he seems to sense something is wrong. His footsteps drag, then stop completely.

He lets go of the brim of his hat and raises his chin in order to see better.

Yusuf places his fingers on the ignition. "He's going to notice us."

Jessica hears Yusuf's words but is too consumed by her own realization to respond. She now has a clearer view of the face illuminated by yard lights and realizes she has seen it before. Many times. The pale, angular cheekbones, the mouth drawn into a cruel line.

Cold pierces Jessica's body, as if her mother has lowered a hand to Jessica's bare skin. Jessica fumbles for her gun, then remembers a man just committed suicide with it, and it's been taken in for technical analysis.

All is perfectly still; she can't even hear Yusuf breathe.

"The Phantom; it's the Phantom," Jessica whispers.

And in that instant, the man spots them, sees that they see him, takes a step backward, and turns on his heels. The hem of the long black coat obscures his feet, and the figure glides over the white yard like a ghost.

Yusuf and Jessica lunge out of the car. Yusuf aims his gun at the receding back. "Stop!" he roars in English.

But the Phantom doesn't turn around; he walks faster, then runs.

"Stop!" Jessica shouts. She darts after the man, right on Yusuf's heels. Standing still won't do any good, no matter how naked she feels without her gun. There is no way he's getting away this time.

Thoughts fly through Jessica's head. They're pursuing the man who has been at the heart of the case the whole time. The Phantom knows what happened to Lisa. And to Jason. He may have also shot Jose Rodriguez.

"Stop!" Yusuf shouts even more insistently.

A yard adjacent to dozens of row houses is the last place to fire a weapon, whether a warning shot or a bullet intended to prevent flight. Yusuf is a boss at the shooting range, but he's also aware enough of realities not to do anything foolish.

The Phantom's coat is flapping in the wind; he runs toward Hellu's door, then abruptly changes course and hurdles a low fence, heading toward the middle of the yard and the rug-beating rack there.

"Stop!" Jessica shouts.

A light comes on in the neighboring building.

What the hell was the Phantom doing at Hellu's? Did he kill her? And why?

Jessica bursts into a sprint. She pulled on her sneakers when she left the house, and her choice of footwear has proven lucky.

The frozen sandy ground crunches underfoot. Jessica spies the gleam of frozen puddles, warning of their treachery. One step on their slick surface could mean the end of the pursuit.

Jessica sees Yusuf raise his gun skyward, presumably to fire a warning shot.

But suddenly the man they're chasing vanishes. It's as if the earth swallowed him up.

Yusuf slows to a walk, his pistol still aimed at the sky. "What the hell?"

They hear a moan in the darkness, but it's immediately enveloped by the wail of the wind.

Jessica says: "Where did he—"

At that instant, the man appears behind a sand bin. He tries to stand but collapses to the ground, holding his ankle.

"Careful, Yusuf," Jessica says.

Maybe it's a trap. This guy is armed, guaranteed.

"Freeze!" Yusuf says with gusto, as if he has been waiting his entire life to give the order in English.

Now Jessica catches sight of the laundry line next to the rug-beating rack: a lethal rig and nearly invisible in the darkness. Jessica wouldn't be the least bit surprised if the fun-hating Hellu had set it up as a booby trap for children making too much noise in the yard.

"Wait," the Phantom says as Yusuf approaches him. "I can explain."

Jessica looks around. The light is still on upstairs at Hellu's place. She and Yusuf know from experience that the man clasping his ankle is extremely dangerous. He threw Yusuf through a glass table and knocked the wind out of Jessica with a punch to her diaphragm. And ran. And kept running. And now he's finally in their clutches.

"You see this, asshole?" Yusuf asks in English, holding up his bandaged hand. "You have some explaining to do." He takes the handcuffs from his belt and tosses them to Jessica.

"Let me explain. . . . Your boss . . ." The Phantom winces in pain. He must have thrown quite the somersault when he collided with the laundry line, then dropped down on his leg full weight.

"What about our boss?" Yusuf asks.

Jessica steps past him and prepares to cuff the man. Her heart is pounding furiously in her chest. She grabs his wrist.

"Careful, Jessie," Yusuf says.

And then they hear a familiar voice behind them. The tone is guarded but unsparing: "Wait."

Hellu's front door is open, and she's walking toward them. Yusuf glances at her but doesn't lower his gun. For a split second, it looks as if he means to aim it at her. "What the hell, Hellu?"

"I understand this looks peculiar." Hellu glances around uneasily. "Let's go inside and you can hear the whole story."

Jessica scoots to one side. What the hell is Hellu mixed up in?

Lights are coming on in more and more windows.

Hellu steps between Yusuf and the Phantom. Yusuf shifts to the side so he won't lose his bead on the Phantom.

"Put that gun away before someone calls the police," Hellu hisses.

Yusuf grunts and keeps his gun trained on the Phantom. "Before someone calls the police? There are already three of us here."

Hellu sighs.

"No, there are four. Stand down. That is an order."

85

JESSICA AND YUSUF are on the brown sofa in Hellu's second-story living room, staring suspiciously across the round coffee table at the man with an ice pack on his swollen ankle. A thin red abrasion runs the breadth of the man's forehead.

Jessica can't believe this. The Phantom's image has been front and center on the flip chart in the unit's conference room since yesterday. They were sure this man was behind the disappearances of Lisa Yamamoto and Jason Nervander and presumably also mixed up in running the prostitution ring.

"So you traced Lisa's second phone," Hellu says, setting on the coffee table a tray of hexagonal glasses and a plastic bottle of mineral water. The Phantom's sweet aftershave, which Jessica and Yusuf would recognize in their sleep, permeates the room.

"Rasmus traced it," Yusuf says unenthusiastically. "Could you please tell us who the hell this guy is now?"

Hellu seats herself and sighs. "It would probably be polite to continue in a language we all speak," she says in English with a nod at the Phantom.

The Phantom draws a breath, and when he finally speaks, his voice is utterly unlike what they expected: slightly hoarse, thick, and, to their surprise, the accent is British.

"My name is Nathan Reddick. I work for Europol, investigating human trafficking at the international level." Reddick moistens his lips. "The reason for my secretive behavior is simple: I'm here on an undercover assignment."

Jessica and Yusuf exchange skeptical glances.

Hellu pours water into the glasses and firmly says: "It's true. I confirmed with the Hague today."

Reddick folds his hands. His stony face twists up in a smile of appeasement.

"So you're investigating the manga girls?" Yusuf asks.

"Yes. That's why I've had to watch my back, behave like a criminal. Resort to the use of force." Reddick indicates Jessica and Yusuf in turn. "I apologize for the pain and inconvenience I've caused, but for the purposes of solving this case, it was of the utmost importance I not be exposed."

"You could have explained," Jessica says. "You didn't need to sock the wind out of me in the middle of the street. Or knock Yusuf—"

"Ah, but could I have? Explained? Would you have listened to me a moment ago if your boss hadn't happened to live a stone's throw away? If nothing else, explaining would have squandered precious time." Reddick's amiable expression evaporates and makes way for a sterner, more arrogant one. "As I said, I apologize. . . . I don't know if you've ever done undercover work, but a different set of rules applies. If you want to credibly play a criminal, you have to think like a criminal. Behave like a criminal, up to a certain point. Even when there's a risk of taking a bullet to the head."

"OK." Jessica crosses her legs and leans back on the sofa. "So tell us what you've figured out."

Reddick leans in and looks enigmatically at Jessica.

"Earlier today, Europol informed the Helsinki Police Department about the operation. Credit for solving the case goes above all to your team, Detective Niemi."

Jessica raises a tired eyebrow. "Fascinating."

Reddick laughs drily and turns to Hellu for support, but she offers no more than a shrug. *That's Niemi for you. A real asshole.*

Reddick reaches over and takes a glass, then fills it with water from the bottle.

"It's a long story; I'll try to be as brief as possible. Sinija Skarpijony, a Belarusian criminal league, is behind everything. Unlike many Eastern European mafias, up until now they have focused on prostitution and prostitution alone. Now the league is backed by some extremely influential and intelligent people. The entire criminal ring is built using social media and the latest technology, and they keep the target segment tightly defined." Reddick swirls the glass in his hand. "High-income men in the Nordic countries who have hebephilic or ephebophilic tendencies, manga fantasies, and a fascination with sadism."

"Wait, so . . . pedophiles?" Yusuf asks.

"Not exactly. Pedophilia refers to sexual desire for prepubescent children. Hebephiles are interested in children who have just reached puberty, and ephebophiles are primarily interested in older adolescents, seventeen- to nineteen-year-olds."

As Jessica listens to Reddick's words, she remembers what it was like being nineteen: how she felt like an adult, although in truth she was nothing more than a naive child raped by a smooth-tongued psychopath in a moldy canal-side apartment in Venice.

"Based on what I've told you, what's the first thing to come to mind?" Reddick asks.

Jessica and Yusuf exchange glances.

"It's a pretty narrowly defined clientele," Jessica says.

For the first time, Reddick smiles enough to reveal his teeth. "Exactly, Detective Niemi. And what makes it possible to define the clientele so precisely?"

Jessica considers.

Reddick continues: "How are most companies with an online presence able to offer you exactly what you happen to want?"

"The Internet gathers information about me."

"Exactly. Sinija Skarpijony is a well-funded organization operating against a backdrop of perfectly legal operations: brick-and-mortar retail, app developers, even a start-up incubator. It employs an army of hackers and developers who create platforms not just for legal businesses, but for illegal ones too. Which is how Europol first sniffed out this very cleverly and carefully crafted prostitution ring. A crew that actually stays only so long at a certain location and then moves to another, thus avoiding getting caught so easily."

"Can you elaborate?"

"Our cyber monitors, good hackers, happened to notice a range of malware had been installed on nearly all the servers hosting major pornography websites. They were fishing search terms and information on the type of pornography being watched at specific IP addresses. Imagine a site user, even an unregistered one, watches dozens of hours of pornography a year using search terms like "manga," "young," "teen," "choking," "punishing," "beating," "petite"—these are the most common, if I recall—and conducts online searches for related material. The Sinija Skarpijony hackers created online triggers that retrieve the IP address as soon as certain conditions are met. And because high-income men are the only desired target audience, their affluence is confirmed by monitoring other online purchases, membership fees, and social media. The rest is child's play. The league identified thousands of such men and contacted them, warily, probingly, without revealing too much. And got hundreds of interested customers."

Reddick tosses back the remaining water in his glass. Jessica looks at Hellu, who is tapping her nails against the armrests of her chair.

"Of course, we didn't know how it worked at first. All we knew was someone in Belarus was fishing information about people's pornography preferences."

"How did you start making headway?" Jessica asks.

"The undercover operation began the second I rented a flat in Helsinki and—"

"Started watching porn?" A smile flashes across Yusuf's face. "I can think of worse gigs."

"Officially I arrived in Helsinki from Tokyo via the Hague to consult on the merger of two e-commerce companies. In reality, I used my time to conduct searches for pornography using the terms in question. A lot of searches, and fast. I also performed dozens and dozens of searches implying a high salary: I searched for time-shares, downloaded PDF price lists for luxury vehicles, opened an account for stock-market speculation. I created an Instagram account and followed expensive brands. The only limit was the imagination." Reddick looks at his bandaged ankle. "Two other Europol detectives did the same thing, one in Stockholm and one in Gothenburg."

"But your bait is the one they took," Jessica says.

Reddick nods. "A mere eight days after I arrived, I received a DM via Instagram, the kind you can view only once before it disappears. I did, however, take a screenshot."

Reddick taps at his phone for a moment, then passes it to Jessica.

Jessica turns the screen toward herself. "We've been busting our butts trying to track this phone's movements."

"Now you know why you couldn't."

Jessica holds the phone so Yusuf can see the screen too.

```
I know what you want, big boy.
masayoshi.fi
#25119358
Show up looking classy and ask if James is around.
```

Jessica hands the phone back. "Who sent you the DM?"

"As you can presumably guess, a beautiful young woman wearing manga clothes. Her handle was Aluna25119358." Reddick looks out the tall living room windows, then adjusts his injured leg with both hands. "And as you know, when you enter that numerical hashtag on Instagram, ten images appear. A couple hotels, a few bars and restaurants. The Phoenix."

Jessica nods. "What happened next?"

"I threw on a suit and tie and marched up to the little hotel at the top of the list. I asked if James was around. The desk clerk clearly didn't know what I was referring to, but he asked me to wait in the hotel bar. Half an hour passed. Then a big Mercedes SUV pulled up outside the door. The male driver came inside to retrieve me. He spoke English with an Eastern European accent and introduced himself as James. Once we were inside the car, he asked for my Instagram profile handle, as if to verify they had reached out to me—that they had found me, not vice versa. Then he told me I could pick a girl from the catalog, which was identical to the contents of masayoshi.fi."

"And the catalog was in the car?" Jessica says.

"Yes. Leather bound, the works. They were aiming at a truly high-end concept, luxury for the privileged few. All the girls in the pictures were dressed almost identically. A few were Asian; most were European. The names were next to the photos. At first I picked a girl called Kasumi, but I was informed she was no longer available. I ultimately decided on Miyamoto . . . and she is who you found on the beach at Aurinkolahti."

"Olga Belousova . . . ," Yusuf says. "What happened to her?"

Reddick raises a finger, insisting on patience.

"James gave me the prices. The basic rate was a thousand euros. That would get me an hour with the girl. But for twenty thousand, I could have the girl and a room for five days. On the fifth day, I could do whatever I wanted with her. And they would clean up after me." Now Reddick looks heated, as if he's listening to the story instead of telling it.

"What did the driver mean by that? That they would clean up after you?" Jessica murmurs. "Do you mean . . . ?"

Reddick looks out the window. "Yes, that I could beat her. Strangle her. Slash her throat. Kill her."

A profound silence settles over the room.

86

JESSICA SPLASHES COLD water on her face. Nathan Reddick's story has made her nauseous.

The bathroom is sparkling white. Every surface gleams spotlessly, which is no surprise to Jessica, knowing Hellu. Jessica dries her face and hands and wonders if Hellu's wife is the same, a pedantic control freak. Or totally different? Why would anyone want to be with a back-stabbing asshole like Helena Lappi anyway?

Jessica opens the door and makes her way back to the living room. Colorful serigraphs hang on the walls, presumably for the purpose of softening the home's military starkness. But the art has been hung in a meticulous, calculated manner, indicating that it wasn't acquired because the buyer liked it, but because it's what you're supposed to put on walls.

Jessica takes her seat at Yusuf's side. "Sorry. Let's continue."

"I know this is hard to hear," Reddick says.

Jessica stares at the Europol agent. *I've heard, seen, and experienced plenty of hard things, asswipe.* "Please go on," she says neutrally.

"As soon as I got into the car, I saw an antenna-equipped antipositioning device, the sort that blocks GPS signals, plugged into the dash. I realized I wasn't supposed to know where we were going. I told James I wanted two hours, that I would think about more time later. James accepted my decision without complaint. He explained the rules: I had to turn off my phone and turn it over to him for the duration of the drive. Then he handed me a pair of big wraparound sunglasses. It was impossible to see anything with them on."

Reddick takes off his cuff links and rolls up his sleeves to his elbows.

"The drive lasted half an hour. At the beginning, we stopped constantly. Then we drove a longer stretch at a slightly higher speed, and I figured we were leaving the city center. Eventually, James turned off the ignition and told me I could remove the sunglasses. We were in a windowless subterranean parking garage. It wasn't very large, maybe two to three hundred square meters. I could hear the thunder of a powerful engine and the rumble of large tires outside the door. James let me out of the car and escorted me into a freight elevator. Once we were inside, he asked me to submit to a pat-down. I did. We exited at the next floor, then walked down a short corridor to a black door. James knocked, and the door was opened by a man—judging by his appearance and accent, a Finn. He said his name was Sam. Sam showed me around. It was a large suite, maybe sixty square meters, and well-appointed: a top-of-the-line kitchen, a bathroom, a liquor cabinet, a television, and a large bed. But there were no windows behind the curtains. Sam said twenty-four-seven room service was available; I would find the menu next to the television. When I was ready to leave, I simply had to press the button next to the door. And if I wanted to call anyone, I could use the landline. My mobile phone would be returned to me once I left."

"What happened next?" Yusuf asks.

"Sam looked me in the eye and asked me if I agreed to follow the house rules. I nodded. Then he said: *'Enjoy your visit, Mr. Watanabe.'* I caught the threat implicit in the ostensibly courteous remark: *We know your name. We choose our clientele. We know everything about you.*"

"Watanabe?" Jessica says.

"It's my undercover name, which Europol painstakingly crafted a background for." Reddick toys with his left ring finger, where he perhaps wears a ring under normal circumstances. "These people would never accept someone they didn't have enough information on as a client. They want name, address, photograph, workplace, children's names, day care . . . That's how they make sure no one talks to the police."

"Even though the clients are left with no evidence of the scheme," Jessica says.

"Exactly. Even though." Reddick sits up straighter in the armchair. For a moment he looks like he would stand up and walk around if he could.

"You met Miyamoto. I mean, Olga," Jessica says. Yusuf pulls more gum out of the pack.

Reddick nods. "I did." He looks Jessica in the eye. For the first time, he seems somehow vulnerable. He plainly understands what Jessica is driving at. "There are no clear guidelines for situations like this. Contingencies, various scenarios, are reviewed prior to the assignment: how we must do what's right while keeping in mind the big picture, the success of the assignment—and what will happen to the women if we have to pull up stakes and the assignment fails."

Jessica lets out an involuntary grunt and shakes her head. "You had sex with Olga."

A brief silence follows. Reddick studies each of them in turn. Hellu doesn't look surprised; she has already heard the story.

"I had just gotten my foot in the door. I had to come back, Detective Niemi. Otherwise they would have guessed I was a police officer—"

"Would Olga have told her traffickers you didn't want sex?" Jessica interjects.

Reddick raises both forefingers and points around the room at random. "Think about it! They built that whole place for that specific purpose. Do you really think those bastards weren't recording every move I made with cameras and mics? Because as it turns out, the league's true business model—as I later discovered—centers on surveillance."

"What do you mean?"

"They wanted twenty thousand euros for the pleasure of beating the woman if I wanted to. Or, in the worst case, killing her. Twenty thousand isn't so much, when you consider how much money and trouble goes into finding a prostitute and bringing her to Finland. Not to mention the loss in profits that would result from the prostitute's death. Wouldn't it be smarter to stick to the thousand-euro hourly rate and forget the rest? If the setup truly was what it seemed?"

Jessica feels her heart skip a beat. "Unless . . . ," she says softly.

"Their primary business isn't prostitution but extortion."

87

"So it's a honey trap used to lure in rich psychopaths. An hourly rate of a thousand euros is enough to scare off the clients who aren't bloodthirsty enough to take it any further. Before long, opportunity outweighs any moral compunctions. The pressure grows too great. Some sadistic asshole who has paid through the nose has the chance to live out his sickest fantasies without ever getting caught. All the secrecy, turning over your phone, being transported to the site . . . it's not only a precaution, but creates the illusion for clients that what happens in that room stays in that room."

"Even though the truth is just the opposite," Jessica says.

Reddick sighs. "Exactly."

Jessica glances at Yusuf, who is lost in thought. The Phantom, aka Europol agent Nathan Reddick, has offered them a lot of information. But even so, the biggest questions remain unanswered.

"Yes, I had sex with Olga Belousova," Reddick says. "I'm not proud of it, but I had to keep the big picture in mind. I had to leave the back door open so I could return."

"Somehow you had to figure out where they drove you, right?" Yusuf says.

"I considered various alternatives. I thought about contacting the Helsinki Police and asking for backup. Your crew could have shadowed the car James used to drive me to the site, for instance."

"Doesn't sound like a bad idea. Why didn't you?"

"The more I thought about it, I came to the conclusion that the league would have surely taken the possibility into account. And that a failed operation would endanger the women's lives. So I decided to try another approach on my own: I rented a car and staked out the hotel, waited for James' black Mercedes to show up. A few days passed. I was on the verge of giving up. Then one afternoon, I saw James pull up outside the hotel."

"James went inside to pick up a client?" Jessica asks.

"I was too far away, so I couldn't make out the client. But there was no doubt where they were headed."

"Continue," Jessica says.

"When I pulled into traffic, a gargantuan SUV drove past, a last-decade Chevrolet Suburban. I was sure it was the vehicle whose engine I heard thundering outside the parking garage. I gathered there were two vehicles, and the function of the second one was to look out for and shake off anyone trying to follow them."

"So you gave up?"

"I would have gotten caught, and that would have been it for the operation."

"What about the license plate numbers? Did you get them?" Yusuf asks.

"Both vehicles are registered in Finland but owned by a Ukrainian company. Europol looked into it and came up empty-handed. There was nothing solid to follow up on there."

"But you continued your investigation anyway?" Jessica asks.

Reddick nods. "I went back to the hotel. Used the same phrase. Waited half an hour. James came to pick me up. But this time, something had changed."

"What?"

"We climbed into the car. I told James I wanted an hour. He reminded me of my options. That I could only take it to *the next level* if I bought the girl for five days."

Hellu hasn't spoken for ages, but at this point she looks sternly at Jessica and Yusuf and jumps in: "Do you understand the implications? The driver actively pushed the twenty-thousand-euro package on the clients. Everything else was a taster, bait to get them in the door."

"I pretended to be interested, but I stuck to my guns. *'Maybe next time,'* I said. And a few minutes later, I was back in the room with Olga."

"What was your plan?"

"Get information. The kind of information that wouldn't arouse suspicion, if and when we were eavesdropped on."

"Such as?" Jessica says impatiently. She still has difficulty trusting the Phantom, especially since he seems to have returned to the scene of the crime with a thousand-euro note but no real plan.

"I knew if I didn't come away with anything useful, it wouldn't be long before I . . ."

"Had to pay for the whores out of your own pocket?" Jessica interjects. She takes a swig of water. Reddick looks flustered. Hellu looks like she could lunge at Jessica at any moment.

". . . would have to inform the Hague that I wasn't making any progress. That the best of several bad options would be to shadow James and bring him in for questioning. And that probably wouldn't work. You see, I noticed James always said something into his phone when the car set out and when we arrived at the parking garage. Any deviation from the routine would have been noticed immediately." Reddick licks his lips, then continues more earnestly. "But I also noticed something I hadn't the first time. I'm assuming because they weren't there yet. . . ."

"The burn marks on Olga's arm?" Yusuf says.

Reddick nods. "I asked what they were, but Olga said she didn't want to tell me. Considering the context and the league's business model, I initially assumed they had been made by some sadistic client. But after thinking a little, I realized that didn't make sense in terms of the scheme. You could only abuse the girls if you bought them for yourself. So at that point, the matter remained a complete mystery to me."

"Where did you take the investigation from there?"

"I knew I had to dig out the number the desk clerk called to contact

James. That was the only thread I had to start unraveling the web, but there was no way for me to get at it. Stealing the desk clerk's phone would have alerted the league and made them pause operations. I was at a dead end," Reddick says. "Have you heard of the box Leonardo da Vinci designed that is locked with a numerical code and contains a valuable parchment inside? You can force the lock, but then a vial of vinegar stashed in the box will shatter and destroy the parchment. This was a comparable situation. Getting to the heart of the case demanded extreme delicacy."

"But you found Lisa. How?" Jessica asks.

"Masayoshi.fi. The site administrator had been cleverly masked using a Tor network, but it didn't take our IT experts long to discover the site's Analytics ID had been used with another URL—"

"www.thelisayamamoto.fi."

Reddick nods and leans forward. "It was a perplexing discovery. It was a strong indication one of Finland's most popular bloggers was somehow mixed up in the case."

"So you approached her?"

"I saw on social media that she was not only a blogger, but a talented artist as well. I contacted her and proposed doing business together. I pretended to represent a Japanese art gallery, told her we paid handsomely, and that I wanted to get a feel for her work. I figured the fact we both had Japanese roots couldn't hurt. The Hague threw up a credible website with a background story in under twenty-four hours, just in case my approaching her raised suspicions. I contacted her through Instagram."

"And Lisa took the bait and invited you to her home?" Jessica says.

The parts were falling into place, maybe even too neatly.

"Exactly. I met with Lisa at her place on November twentieth, a little after five in the afternoon. We agreed that she would paint a piece for me. I would pay five thousand euros for it. And that we could keep working together in the future too."

"The lighthouse with the schoolgirl standing in front of it?" Yusuf says.

Reddick nods. "Lisa suggested it herself."

"But what was your actual plan?" Jessica asks suspiciously.

"I planted a bug under Lisa's desk." Reddick spreads his arms. "Fine. I admit my methods don't exactly stand up in the light of day."

"The story is just beginning and you've already had sex twice with a human-trafficking victim and installed a surveillance device in Lisa Yamamoto's apartment without a warrant from the courts. Furthermore, you don't officially have the authority to run an operation in Helsinki," Jessica says. "But go on, please! I want to hear how this ends. Did Lisa jerk you off in the toilets at the Phoenix? Was that also relevant in terms of the investigation?"

For the first time, Reddick seems to lose his patience. "What the bloody hell is your problem? We're on the same side. Without me, you'd have a lot less—"

"Cool it!" Hellu barks so sharply Reddick seems startled. His eyes have grown somehow soulless, the way Jessica remembers seeing them on the CCTV footage.

"So, I staked out the hotel and hoped I would hear the phone ring in Lisa's room."

"And did you?"

"I did. It wasn't Lisa's iPhone; it was an older model. At first I thought it was a text message, because I didn't hear Lisa answer."

"Three rings," Yusuf says.

Reddick nods.

"And then you waited for James to appear outside the hotel," Jessica says.

"It didn't happen, which of course doesn't mean I was wrong. There were ten potential meeting places. But on the evening of the second night of the stakeout, James pulled up at the hotel only twenty minutes after I heard the phone ring in Lisa's room. It was a remarkable moment. The entire scheme was so far-fetched from the outset that it felt incredible to have the pieces click into place. I remember shouting in delight. Lisa Yamamoto was up to her ears in trafficking these women."

"But why Lisa specifically?"

"I started from the assumption that Lisa either wasn't initially aware what she was mixed up in or that the league used blackmail to force her cooperation. I believe the league wanted to bring in a young influencer whose presence on social media they could exploit in some way or other."

88

Jessica looks up at the recessed spots that form two parallel lines across the ceiling. If even one of the bulbs were to go out, Hellu would no doubt replace it in a heartbeat.

"The evening it was confirmed that the hotel was, indeed, calling Lisa, I contacted her. That was Friday," Reddick says. "I mentioned the art project and asked to meet again. My intention was to reveal my cards and get her to talk."

"And did you meet?" Jessica says.

Reddick sighs. "At a café at Töölöntori Square. We were the only ones there. I showed her my badge and told her I knew about masayoshi.fi and that she was mixed up in it. That a lot of human lives were at stake, and she had nothing to worry about if she just came clean about everything she knew."

"How did she react?"

"Played dumb. She got up from the table and started walking away. . . . At the time, I was sure I had stepped on a land mine and made a terrible mistake. That I absolutely should have requested help from the local police and acquired a warrant for Lisa Yamamoto's arrest. That she would immediately call James and tell the league the police were onto them and . . . then it would be over. They would kill every single one of the women."

Reddick sighs deeply and looks Jessica in the eye. Suddenly he looks tired.

"I ran after her, caught up to her at the door, and told her she didn't want all those lives on her conscience. That she should call me when she came to her senses. She told me I was crazy and walked out."

"Your bold strategy backfired," Yusuf says.

"I was sure Lisa was being blackmailed. But I had no idea what they were using to do it. Until Superintendent Lappi informed me tonight that Lisa's father is a former gangster. Suddenly it all makes sense. They told Lisa they'd kill her father if she didn't play ball."

"But you didn't give up at that point," Jessica says. "You wheedled your way into Kex Maces' record launch."

"I kept listening in on Lisa. I heard her mention the record launch multiple times in English over the next few days. It turns out, she was talking with the general manager of the Phoenix."

Jessica feels a pang in her gut. "You met with him yourself."

"On Saturday morning. I had concluded that only certain workers knew about James. Anything else would have been unnecessarily risky. I started from the assumption that the manager wasn't in on the scheme; this was supported by the fact that Lisa didn't say a word to the manager about my approaching her. If he had been part of the league, I'm sure they wouldn't have chatted casually on the phone."

Jessica is overcome with relief, as if an enormous burden has lifted from her shoulders. At the same time, she can't help but wonder why Frank resorted to such drastic measures tonight if he played no part in the scheme.

"You mean Frank Dominis wasn't involved in the league's activities?" As he asks the question, Yusuf turns to look at Jessica.

Reddick calmly shakes his head. "I don't believe he was."

"Then why did you meet him on Saturday morning?"

"I needed a ticket to the party. I needed one more chance to talk to Lisa. She wasn't answering my calls anymore, and I figured she was about to pull a disappearing act."

"Which is exactly what happened," Jessica says.

Reddick nods. "I was in touch with Frank Dominis and arranged to meet him on Saturday morning. Before that, I asked the Hague to look into Dominis' background. It turns out he was a former infantry sergeant from Alaska. An investigation into an international MDMA smuggling and distribution ring led straight to the doorstep of the Phoenix. It was clear the boss was involved. When I met Dominis, I told him he needed to get me into Kex Maces' record launch, no more and no less. Otherwise he would face immediate arrest."

Jessica looks at Reddick with glazed eyes. She has the urge to hurl her glass at his face. She clenches the armrest in her trembling fingers. *Frank wasn't the monster you momentarily mistook him for, Jessica.*

But he was a criminal who knew he would be going to prison for a very long time.

89

"JUST AS I was concluding my business with Frank Dominis, James pulled up outside the nightclub. I knew he would recognize me, so I immediately left. But I lingered around the corner to monitor the situation and saw James hand the bouncer something. That's when I realized the contact at the Phoenix was Alem."

Jessica turns to look out the window. She has listened to the recordings of Sahib Alem's interrogation, and the stories support each other in every respect.

"And that evening you went to the party?" Yusuf says.

Reddick nods. "I was the first one there."

"Why didn't you just go ring Lisa's doorbell?"

"Don't you understand? I was trying to recruit her into acting as an informant. I wanted not only to pressure Lisa to talk, but to have people see us together. I wanted Lisa to know that our little chat was being recorded by the security cameras. And that whoever was running the league wouldn't look too kindly on that."

"So it was your way of threatening Lisa?"

Reddick calls up the cold, analytical look Jessica and Yusuf recognize from the CCTV tapes. "Yes."

"But it didn't work," Yusuf says.

"I told Lisa I would wait for her call the next morning. And I'm quite convinced she seriously considered it."

"But then she disappeared," Jessica says.

The mood in the room has grown tense. Everyone present seems to be thinking the same thing.

"Your gamble backfired, Reddick," Jessica says.

"We can't be certain of that."

Jessica chuckles. "What do you mean? You wanted Lisa to be seen in public with you. You believed it would convince her to open her mouth. But things went just as you threatened. They realized you're a police officer, Reddick. And they killed Lisa."

"That's merely a guess—"

"The fuck it is!" Jessica stands. "What the hell did you think would happen? You hang out at a party attended by the coolest kids in Helsinki, where gossip travels as fast as people give air kisses! What were you thinking?"

"Niemi . . . ," Hellu says quietly.

"Don't you 'Niemi' me, goddamn it," Jessica says in Finnish. "Can you imagine a more egregious case of misconduct than what our friend here is guilty of? And when you add the fact he returned to Lisa's room, removed evidence, and assaulted two police officers, why the hell are you standing up for this asshole?"

Hellu looks annoyed. She rises slowly from the sofa and walks to the window. A dozen little houseplants stand on the dark brown windowsill, each one in a white pot.

"I agree with Sergeant Niemi," Hellu eventually says in English, hands on her hips. "You've behaved recklessly, which in all likelihood cost both Lisa Yamamoto and Jason Nervander their lives. The league cut town, and on the way they murdered Jose Rodriguez to cover their tracks."

"Hindsight is always twenty-twenty," Reddick says.

"And there's one critical question you haven't answered," Hellu continues. Jessica feels an unexpected satisfaction that, for the first time, Hellu is on her side. "If Lisa disappeared early Sunday morning and you have no idea where she is . . . how did you get your hands on the keys you used to open her apartment door yesterday? Her roommate had locked the dead bolt."

Utter silence falls over the room, and Jessica wonders why this hasn't occurred to her.

"I took them from her purse at the Phoenix," Reddick says.

"What?" Yusuf says. "Now you're lying."

"I have nimble fingers. Lisa turned around for a second to talk to someone, and I slipped my hand into her purse. I believe you'll be able to confirm it on the camera footage if you look closely enough."

"You didn't think Lisa would realize they were missing by the time she got home?"

"Of course."

"Why did you wait until Wednesday?"

"I didn't. I tried to go to Lisa's straight from the Phoenix. But when I cracked the door, I heard someone humming in the shower. That's when I realized two women lived there."

"What time would that have been?" Jessica says.

"I don't know. Maybe ten."

"Essi said she heard something that night," Jessica says to Yusuf.

"I quietly shut the door and returned to my car, which I had parked a little way down the street just to be sure. I checked social media to see what Lisa's housemate looked like and found pictures of this Essi. I waited in the car for Essi to leave the apartment. After all, it was Saturday, and the night was still young."

"But Essi stayed home."

"Correct. No one came out the front door all night. At some point I think I even dozed off. When I came to, a woman with black hair was standing at the door. By then it must have been after three."

"Was it Lisa?"

"At first I wasn't sure, but when I saw her rummaging through her purse, I concluded she was probably looking for her keys. I knew the buzzer was broken, but I thought she would call her roommate, have her come down and open the door."

"What happened?"

"Lisa glanced at her phone but didn't even try to call. I was already climbing out of the car—I couldn't let Lisa freeze to death in her little dress in the icy wind—but she started walking toward the stairs at the side of the building—"

"Where you socked me in the diaphragm," Jessica says.

"I hurried out of the car and after her. She had a head start of about a hundred meters but didn't seem to be in any hurry. But when I walked down the stairs to the neighboring street, she was gone."

"Gone?"

"Gone. A car was driving away, and I assumed she had climbed in."

"Did you see the license plate or—"

Reddick shakes his head. "For the next few days, I staked out the building. My chance didn't come until Wednesday, when the roommate finally left the apartment."

"The day we first met." Jessica leans in; she and Hellu exchange discreet glances. "Do you know what happened to your girl, Olga Belousova?"

"No," Reddick replies quickly.

"Where were you between Saturday night and early Sunday morning?" Yusuf continues as if he has read Jessica's mind.

Reddick looks gobsmacked. "You don't—"

"Answer the question, please," Hellu says.

"As I said . . . I was in my car, staking out Lisa's building. I dozed off and waited for the roommate to leave for so much as a moment—"

"Can anyone confirm your story?"

Reddick lashes out: "Check my phone's base station data."

"Rest assured, we will," Jessica says as a bright light pierces the dim room. Jessica looks out to see a police van pull up outside Hellu's home.

FRIDAY, NOVEMBER 29

90

IT'S EIGHT A.M. Yusuf ends the call and lowers the phone to his desk. Jessica sits down next to him and stares ahead expressionlessly.

"That was the building manager. There's an entrance to the bike storage from Topeliuksenkatu. It also leads to the laundry room after a few twists and turns," Yusuf says. "The laundry room that, according to the sign-up sheet, no one used last week except for the residents of unit A23."

"And A23 is Lisa's apartment?"

"Yup. Maybe they have a lot of laundry."

Jessica closes her eyes and sighs deeply. "So from the bike storage you can get to the laundry room, and from there to the stairwell?"

"Yup. There's a long hallway in between, a couple of heavy doors."

"So Lisa didn't get into a car that night on Topeliuksenkatu; she got into her building through the bike storage." Jessica shakes her head in disbelief. "Reddick lost Lisa, and she was right inside the building."

"The building manager said you need a separate key to get into the bike storage. Lisa must not have kept it on her key chain."

"But if she accessed the stairwell through the basement, why didn't she ever ring the doorbell? Essi was at home asleep and would have opened the door for her."

"Maybe someone was waiting for her in the bike storage," Yusuf says.

Both of them sit in silence, gathering their thoughts.

"You know what, Yusuf?" Jessica eventually says. "I'm sorry."

"About what?" Yusuf says.

A nearly imperceptible tear rolls down Jessica's cheek. "You'll be solving this case without me."

"But—"

"After this meeting, I'll be off the investigation."

Jessica rises from her chair and starts walking toward the conference room.

91

JESSICA LOOKS AT the investigative team waiting in front of her.

"So it's clear that Europol's and Reddick's rogue activities prompted the league to pack things up and end operations. All we have is one face recorded on video, one Mercedes SUV registered to a foreign holding company, a few relevant phone numbers tech is tracing as we speak, and ten henchmen who, based on preliminary questioning, have no idea of the operation's true nature. One of them is Sahib Alem from the Phoenix."

Jessica looks everyone in the eye, one at a time. Rasmus is the only one sitting at the table; Yusuf, Nina, Harjula, and Hellu are leaning against the back wall, arms folded across their chests. Next to them stands the National Bureau of Investigation agent who will assume responsibility for the investigation by lunchtime; Jessica didn't catch her name. Deputy Chief Jens Oranen stands at the open door, decked out in his dress blues today.

"Based on the evidence we have gathered as well as the statements of witnesses, we have reason to believe Lisa Yamamoto was forced to cooperate with the league. It's likely Jason Nervander was also somehow pressured to work with them. Although their bodies have not been found, both bloggers are presumed to have been killed by this so-called manga league. As influencers, they served as lures and persuaders young women found it easy to identify with. Kambo was promoted as a miracle cure, and we assumed from the beginning, when laced, it kept them from escaping. According to Sarvilinna, a single dose of such a cocktail would have been shockingly addictive."

"So the women were able to move freely around the city?"

"We assume so. They presumably all lived in the same place, from where they were transported to the suite where they met the clients."

"Do we have any idea where the suite is located?" Nina asks.

"Reddick never determined that, unfortunately. Tech is looking into whether the holding company that owns the vehicle has signed any rental agreements for properties in the Helsinki area."

Harjula speaks up: "So these women were brought to Helsinki to be slaughtered?"

"What about Akifumi?" Nina asks. "Without Akifumi we wouldn't have anything. Have we really not figured out who the hell is behind the handle yet?"

"As Nina notes, Akifumi's comment led us to a lot of useful information. Whoever he is, he must have wanted the league to get caught. Based on the statements of Nathan Reddick, we presume Lisa was standing outside her building around three a.m. on Sunday. Reddick lost her on Topeliuksenkatu. She either climbed into a vehicle there or entered the building through the bike storage. The building manager went by this morning and found no signs of a struggle. The roommate is sure no one rang the doorbell or pounded on the door in the middle of the night."

Jessica lowers her notes to the table and steps back.

When no one has more to add or ask, Hellu pushes herself off the wall and walks to the head of the table. "Questioning of Nathan Reddick continues today. His superior and the individual responsible for the undercover operation will be on the next flight to Helsinki to conduct an investigation postmortem. And as you all know, prior to that the NBI has scheduled a joint meeting where roles will be assigned to those who will continue on the investigative team. If you have any complaints or questions, please see me."

An expectant silence spreads through the room. Then Hellu takes a seat at the table, as if giving a previously agreed signal, and Jessica coughs into her fist and clears her throat.

"You all heard what happened yesterday. Frank Dominis . . ." Jessica feels a pain in her shoulder. "The reason for Dominis' presence at my home is personal."

"Wait a minute. What are you talking about?" Nina says. "We questioned him!"

Jessica looks at her coworkers. Their curious gazes cling to her like burrs. Jens Oranen reveals his role in the scheme by pulling out his phone and vanishing through the door. Yusuf also knows what's about to come; he looks incredibly sad. Jessica feels the lump in her throat swell.

"Last night I informed Superintendent Lappi that I am turning in my resignation. The sole reason for my being here today is to share this information with you."

"What?" Rasmus exclaims in shock. Harjula and Nina look stunned; the glee Jessica expected to see on their faces does not materialize on either one.

"My reasons are personal," Jessica says, closing her laptop.

The room is dead silent.

Nina turns to Yusuf: "Did you know about this?" He responds by lowering his eyes to his shoes.

"But, Jessica . . . the case is still open," Rasmus stammers.

"You guys will do great." Jessica wipes a tear from her cheek. "Sorry. I thought this would be easier."

And then she walks out.

THURSDAY, DECEMBER 5

92

FOR THE FIRST time in weeks, the sky is clear. Töölönlahti Bay opens up to the black vastness of space; the yellow half-moon is projected against it. Jessica is sitting on a rock right at the waterline, letting her gaze rest on the inky liquid lapping at her feet. Majestic nineteenth-century villas rise on the opposite shore, sighing with the romance of centuries past. Curt gusts of wind carry from the sea, greetings from the darkness that accompanies the year's shortest days. For several nights now, Jessica has been coming down to sit by the water, drink dry white wine from a thermos, and reflect on the past year and the people who played a role in its events. Lisa Yamamoto. Olga Belousova. Yusuf, Erne, Rasmus, Nina, sometimes even Hellu. And of course Frank.

Frank has been assigned his own niche among the memories, because unlike with the others, Jessica finds it impossible to place him in any one continuum. Or even time or place. Frank existed for her for a mere moment in November, in Helsinki. But to Jessica it feels as if he has been there forever, at least in some form. For her.

I've seen night in the truest sense of the word.

Jessica sees Frank's worn face, feels his coarse, hairy chest against her own.

This was real.

She shuts her eyes.

Her thoughts unfurl and ramble, but they always lead to her last investigation as a police officer.

It's over, Jessica.

Jessica now knows Akifumi's Instagram profile was created in Helsinki last summer. That was confirmed on Friday, just as Rasmus predicted. Yusuf called right away to tell Jessica the news, presumably out of habit and because he wanted to process the development with her. But she wasn't interested. She told Yusuf to stop calling. A few days later, he emailed her a zip file containing the images deleted from Lisa's Instagram account. He wrote by way of explanation that the majority were selfies and photos of Lisa's manga art.

Jessica tries to push the case from her mind. She knows the NBI took the reins, that the reckless Nathan Reddick flew back to the Netherlands, chastised by his superiors. That's all she needs to know about it. She is no longer an officer of the law. She could be just about anything in the future, but not that. The world is her oyster, yet the walls of the cage feel like they're closing in more than ever.

Now and again Jessica loses her sense of time at the water's edge. Dusk turns to darkness; the joggers running down the waterfront path morph into menacing, aimlessly roaming figures. Jessica hears a whistle, catcalls, the drunken laughter of young men. But she's not afraid. She knows she's safe here, one with the snowless terrain that, like her, conceals myriad secrets within.

The cold wind sweeps the smell of reeds up the bank; Jessica inhales it through her nostrils. The tips of the stalks dance freely above the water, but soon the ice will form, followed by the snow, trapping them for months. The bay has yet to freeze this winter.

93

IT'S LATE. JESSICA is sitting in front of the television, watching the previously recorded press conference. It's one of the day's top stories. Sitting at a row of microphones caught in photographers' flashes are Helena Lappi, Jens Oranen, and some bald big shot from the National Bureau of Investigation. Each repeats the same phrases in turn: 'international league,' 'manga,' 'murders,' 'series of homicides,' 'prostitution ring,' and 'Europol.'

Jessica hears but she isn't listening. She sees the manga drawings projected on the screen and shuts her eyes. The police have shown their cards, and now the magician knows what they know, even though no one can say what the trick was.

Wake up, darling.

Jessica opens her eyes and feels a weight on her chest. It's as if a small person is sitting on her breast.

I want to show you something, Jessica. . . .

The bony hand gestures for Jessica to rise from the sofa. Her mother hooks her white fingers over the back of the chair like a bird locking its sharp claws around a rail.

Jessica rises to sitting and feels the child's weight in her arms.

Curly brown hair presses against her cheek. The boy has wrapped his hands around her neck; his chin rests on her shoulder. Jessica cannot see his face, but she knows without a doubt that she loves the child in her arms with all her heart.

Come here.

The choking sensation forms in her throat with paralyzing rapidity. Jessica wants to cry. She feels the soft five-year-old body against her own. She hears the boy's wheezing breath, inhales the scent of clean hair. *I've missed you, Toffe.*

Beautiful Toffe. Whose little body was mangled under the driver's seat while his mother was at the wheel.

All right, children. Come here.

The voice is a man's. Is it their father's? What does their father's voice even sound like?

Jessica can't see Toffe's face. But as she glances down at the sofa, she notices something crawling under it. A figure with a black void where the face should be. *Akifumi . . .*

Jessica hears Toffe snoring. *I'll take care of you, Toffe.*

Look at them, Jessica.

Her mother steps aside, and now Jessica sees every seat at the table is occupied. Every face is shielded by a mask of the Japanese politician. Behind the masks, voices whisper. To Jessica's ears, it sounds as if the tiny feet of insects are scuttling across the floor, inside the wall, against the insulation overhead.

The living room has changed. The art is missing from the walls. The white walls are dark blue.

It's not me, a figure says, removing his mask. Frank's face is white, and his left temple displays the bullet's exit hole.

No, it wasn't you.

I was looking at the wrong card the whole time, a woman says. She strips her mask. At first Jessica doesn't recognize her, the bruised shoulders and swollen face coupled with a black-and-blue throat and snapped neck.

Sleight of hand, another woman says.

Wait. Who are . . .

And then Jessica understands why they are sitting at her dining table in the middle of the night, why her mother has invited them here. Jessica shifts her gaze to the tall figure at the table whose white hair hangs to her shoulders under the mask. And now she removes her plastic mask too.

I'm not Akifumi. I was fooled, just like the rest of you.

Hunks of hair have been ripped from her scalp. Her face has been beaten with a blunt object. A fist, perhaps.

Don't you see, Jessica? her mother says, and the flesh and bone visible under the broken skin squelch in time with the words.

The magician isn't the magician. It was an illusion.

Think where Akifumi wants you to look. And then look in the opposite direction.

Jessica hears the scrabbling under the sofa again. And suddenly she feels the child in her arms lose his roundness, the reassuring weight go light as death, the soft, warm arms turn to bone.

Toffe!

Jessica tries to scream, but her voice catches in her throat.

Then she hears the insistent ringing that drags her out of that nocturnal living room and into the light—and perfect loneliness. In the light, she has no one.

94

"WHAT TIME IS it there?" Sissi Sarvilinna asks. Jessica hears laughter and some sort of pseudo-upbeat elevator music in the background. She yawns and looks at the clock.

"Four in the morning." Jessica is staring at the white walls of her living room, head to the pillow and phone to her ear. The art is hanging in its place again. Her sweaty T-shirt is glued to her back. She can still hear the beetles' scuttling inside her head.

"You don't say." Sarvilinna takes a bite of something. "We're already eating breakfast here. I have to say, when you're traveling solo like this, a competent staff is worth its weight in gold. I just had the loveliest conversation with the waiter about the local honey—"

"Four a.m., Sarvilinna," Jessica says flatly, covering her eyes with her elbow.

"Of course. Oh my, it must be dark there. Ha ha. Well, in any event, Niemi, I told you before I left this Aurinkolahti case intrigued me deeply. Which is why I asked my backup to send me any and all information related to the death of Olga Belousova. I've been doing a lot of research here on kambo and its effects on health and I don't—"

Jessica massages her forehead. "Sarvilinna, I guess no one told you I'm not—"

"Hold your horses now, Niemi. You're already awake, so you may as well listen to what I have to say. Remember that day at my office when I mentioned I found something on Belousova's fingers as well as under her nails? Well, apparently there has been some sort of communication breakdown here, but I left for vacation while things were still in process and evidently no one has been able to reach you—"

"The reason no one has been able to reach me is because I'm not—"

"In any case, that substance has been analyzed. It's cellular poly-urethane foam."

Jessica is on the verge of repeating herself, informing Sarvilinna she is no longer involved in the investigation, but she decides not to complicate things. The medical examiner's phone call has sparked her curiosity.

"Polyurethane?"

"A cellular polyurethane foam. When you consider the discolor-ation on the fingers and palms and the fact that polyurethane appears under the nails, my guess would be the victim was tightly gripping the wheel of some motorized vehicle. Not a brand-new one."

Jessica sits up. "A steering wheel?"

"Of a boat, I'd say."

Jessica shuts her eyes.

When she opens them a moment later, she suddenly sees it all clearly. She thinks back to the dream she just had.

What did my father's voice even sound like?

She flings off the blanket and runs to the kitchen.

HOURS HAVE PASSED since he turned off the television, but the man continues to be haunted by the evening news. He sets down the glass, which gives off a smoky aroma even when drained.

He presses his eyes shut and sees their terror-stricken faces against his retinas: the young women in schoolgirl uniforms, axes jutting from their breastbones, their arms and legs severed. Nails hammered through their heads, tongues torn from their mouths. Their torsos hanging from ceilings. An ocean of blood.

How could I have . . . ?

He buries his face in his hands.

Then he stands. He wraps his coat round himself and pulls on his rubber-soled shoes. And as he opens the door, he casts a final glance at the sculpture of a bearded man hanging from a cross, a crown of thorns on his head.

JESSICA OPENS HER laptop. She clicks on the email Yusuf sent her earlier in the week and downloads the photo files Instagram restored. She opens them one at a time. They truly are all selfies taken by Lisa. Not quite the original resolution, but the quality is high enough.

Jessica chews her thumbnail and thinks back to her dream. In it, the color of her living room walls had changed: they were dark blue, not white. She brings up the selfie Kex Maces took at Lisa's place. In the photo, the wall is dark blue, and there is no sign of the manga drawings that filled the walls when Jessica and Yusuf visited.

She opens a bunch of the posts, as well as other material that shouldn't actually be in her possession anymore: Lisa Yamamoto's manga-themed drawings, the crime-scene photographs of the murdered prostitutes—the same women who stripped off their masks in the dream she just had.

```
Medeya Lazakovich . . . born 1998, body found in
the Vasileostrovsky District of St. Petersburg on
November 12, 2018 . . . wearing a Japanese schoolgirl
uniform.
Miep Loos . . . 1992 . . . Amsterdam February
2019 . . .
Tamara Jugeli . . . Lviv, Ukraine, June 6, 2019.
```

She has seen the gorgeous blond Tamara somewhere before. Jessica brings up Instagram on her phone and starts looking through Lisa Yamamoto's posts. She has gone through the photos before, but she isn't sure if she remembers correctly. Shoes, nails, bags, restaurants, sunsets, selfies. Endless selfies: from the gym, jogging, the couch, nightclubs, elevators, the street, movie theaters, airplanes—

And then suddenly it's there. A group of young women posing in a Central European square with an ornate old building in the background. Location stamp: the National Opera and Ballet in Lviv. Date: June 6, 2019. Jenny's bachelorette party. #Oceans13 #bridetobe

Jessica slowly shifts her eyes from her phone to the file displaying Tamara Jugeli's image and information.

June sixth . . . What the hell, Lisa?

The dates match, but none of the women in the photo is Tamara Jugeli.

Jessica continues browsing. Manicured, filter-enhanced shots race past her eyes.

And then: February 5, 2019. Anne Frank House, Amsterdam. #neverforget #holocaust

Two out of three.

Jessica feels a lump in her throat.

No, it can't be true. . . .

In the photo, Lisa is posing with five young women. Jason Nervander stands to the left in the shot.

Jessica swipes and the images dash off again.

Eventually, after skipping back a few more months, Jessica sees the post. . . .

Strelka Vasil'yevskogo Ostrova, St. Petersburg. November 10, 2018.

Three murders, Lisa. That just happened to take place in cities where you were traveling.

And then Jessica realizes where she has seen Tamara Jugeli before.

97

IT'S TWELVE THIRTY a.m. Jessica has called Yusuf three times, and now that he finally answers, the words spew from Jessica's mouth like water from a just-breached dam.

"What's wrong . . . ?" says a woman's voice in the background. Yusuf is finally moving on with his life and has found himself some company.

"Sorry to bother you—"

"It's kind of a bad time, Jessie. Besides, my phone is about to die—"

"Yusuf, listen. Things are really screwed up. Firstly: you told me yourself—the woman smoking on the balcony said she saw someone short wearing a hoodie leave Jose Rodriguez's spa around the time he was murdered. Secondly: the CCTV tapes clearly show a figure dressed in a beanie and a hoodie—who, based on the build, could be Lisa—dropping a letter into a mailbox on Tuesday, November 26. And although the face isn't visible, the coat and the black cargo pants are Lisa's. She's wearing the exact same outfit in a relatively recent Instagram post. I just saw it when I went through her photos again."

A momentary silence, then Jessica hears Yusuf shut the door. "Are you saying Lisa murdered Rodriguez and sent the letter to her father—"

"Exactly! Think about it: Lisa and Essi were roommates for a year and a half, and according to Lisa's stepmother, she wasn't talking to her father during that period. Plus, Lisa's stepmother said her father refused to speak Japanese, remember? When Essi heard Lisa talking Japanese on the phone, Lisa claimed to be speaking to her father."

"Yakuza?" Yusuf says.

"I don't think the Japanese mafia has anything to do with this. Fake news! That was Lisa's way of making it look like she was forced into cooperating if the police stumbled across the league's activities." Jessica hears her voice growing agitated; it has been weeks since she last felt so alive.

"But Akifumi—"

"You're not understanding, Yusuf. Lisa Yamamoto is Akifumi."

Dead silence on the line.

"So Lisa wrote and mailed the yakuza letter to her father to stage her own death?"

"Exactly, Yusuf! Lisa wasn't just part of the organization; she was an active consumer of sexual services. Think about all those paintings on the walls: Lisa Yamamoto had a powerful manga fetish she was able to live out through the ring. Nikolas Ponsi reacted strangely when I asked him about manga. He must have heard about Lisa's tendencies from Jason. Jason was confused and concerned about Lisa's behavior."

"That would definitely explain—"

"And listen: the painting at Lisa's place I couldn't stop staring at that Wednesday . . . The model for that painting was a woman named Tamara Jugeli. Jugeli was a prostitute. She was found strangled to death in Lviv, Ukraine, on June 6. She was wearing manga clothes when she was discovered."

"What the hell?"

"And if you browse back to Lisa's Instagram photos from June, you'll see she was in Lviv at her friend's bachelorette party at the time Jugeli was murdered. Do you believe in coincidences, Yusuf?"

"Jesus . . . ," Yusuf whispers.

"I think every single one of the manga pieces Lisa painted has a living model—or a dead one, actually. I'm betting Lisa painted all the prostitutes she killed. At least Belousova, Lazakovich, Loos, and Jugeli have had the honor of being immortalized on canvas. You can go admire their portraits in the evidence room at HQ."

There's a sound at the other end of the line as if Yusuf is scratching his head furiously. Or brushing his teeth.

"This doesn't make any sense. Lisa's a—"

"A young woman? Ponsi said twenty percent of pedophiles are women. Why couldn't a young woman like Lisa be a sadist who gets off on dominating and abusing women? It's an expensive habit. Maybe Lisa worked for the ring for the perks alone."

"I don't know, Jessie. It all seems too crazy to be true."

"Think about it, Yusuf. We were primed to believe the only reason Lisa was involved in criminal activity was because she was being blackmailed, because she didn't have a choice. That kind of assumption always comes back to bite you in the butt." Jessica pulls on her coat. "I'm also pretty sure that, one way or another, Jason smelled a rat a year ago. Lisa had to make sure Jason wouldn't have any credibility among their crowd. So she made up the story about him beating her and told everybody. So there would be no chance of anyone believing him."

Yusuf sighs into the phone. "OK, Jessica. Let's say you're right. So Lisa created Akifumi's profile to expose the whole scheme? The hashtag and the masayoshi site?"

"Right. Akifumi's masayoshi comment was a subtle clue for us. It was meant to help us figure out what happened to Lisa without any key figures in the league—including James—getting caught. Even if they were, they wouldn't know to pin it on Lisa. She wanted to disappear without making any more enemies. That's why she suggested to Reddick that she could paint him a lighthouse with a girl standing in front of it. Lisa knew Reddick was law enforcement, and the painting, together with the almost identical Instagram post, would reinforce the notion that maybe she and Jason were tossed overboard at Söderskär."

Yusuf doesn't answer. Jessica hears the woman laugh and Yusuf mumble in the background. *Wait. I have to finish this call.*

"Yusuf?"

"Yeah, sorry." It sounds as if Yusuf turns on a tap. "So you think Lisa is alive and fled the country."

"Yup. From the Söderskär lighthouse. She was taken there on the boat owned by the foundation, which was also used to transport women between Helsinki and Söderskär. Jason loaned Lisa the boat whenever she needed it. He didn't dare ask any questions. That's how strong of a hold she had over him. Olga brought the members of the league and the other women to the island in the middle of the night, and someone picked them up and took them to Russia or Estonia. Meanwhile, Lisa stayed in Helsinki, murdered Jason first, and then Rodriguez."

"Wait a sec. . . . Why would Lisa murder Rodriguez?"

"I believe Olga Belousova was piloting that boat Saturday night. She was wearing her manga outfit because she thought she was going to work. But then she ended up being shanghaied into something totally different. Sarvilinna just called. A polyurethane used in, among other things, boat steering wheels—the Aquador's, for instance—was found under Belousova's fingernails. Olga's Facebook page has a lot of pictures of her boating on the Black Sea, off Odessa. Lisa knew all the trafficked girls; she knew Olga had enough experience as a sailor to ferry the entire crew to Söderskär. Harjula said the seas were rough that night, so Olga had to work hard and grip the hell out of the wheel to make it first to Söderskär, then back to Aurinkolahti. Almost an hour each way. When she eventually made it back to the marina, she ended up in the water somehow. Three days later, she was found dead a hundred meters away, on the beach."

"Who tried to resuscitate Olga, then? That's the one thing I don't get."

"It must have been whoever moved the boat from Aurinkolahti, because there wasn't a single boat like that there Wednesday morning."

"Maybe there was someone else in the boat? Someone who wanted Olga alive . . ."

"Exactly," Jessica says. "Now we come to your question about why Lisa killed Rodriguez. I was thinking about that when we found the raincoat and cleaning spray at his spa. Rodriguez was on the boat with Olga, maybe keeping an eye on her. Olga had an attack of some sort and Rodriguez tried to resuscitate her. She died anyway, and Rodriguez threw her overboard. Then he piloted the boat back downtown and wiped his fingerprints from the cabin."

"But Jason was also at Aurinkolahti that night," Yusuf says.

Jessica presses her middle finger and thumb to her temples. "Or maybe he wasn't. Maybe it was just his phone, which Lisa . . ."

Jessica shuts her eyes so she can concentrate. She can't see the conclusion forming in her head yet, but the separate threads seem to be coming together, entwining more tightly. Her thoughts are like empty sheets of paper being tossed around by an ever-stronger wind.

Bike storage, laundry room . . . Decorative brick. Plaster.

"Yusuf . . ."

"What?"

"Do you remember how loud the washing machine was in Lisa's apartment the first time we went to talk to Essi?"

"Yeah . . ."

"If they have a functioning washing machine, why the hell was Lisa using the laundry room?"

Yusuf doesn't answer.

"Think about it, Yusuf. Jason wanted to see Lisa. But Lisa waited for the right moment; she wanted Jason to disappear at the same time she did. They met early Sunday morning in the bike storage, where Lisa killed him. Now, what could you do with a body in downtown Helsinki, especially if you're handy with tools—" Jessica stops when she realizes she doesn't hear the sound of water at the other end anymore. "Hello?"

She hears three short buzzes. Yusuf's phone is dead.

Jessica lowers her phone to the table.

Lisa is handy. Bricks stripped from the apartment. Plaster. Visits to the laundry room. The noise the neighbor heard in the middle of the night. Lisa prepared everything so Jason could disappear without a trace. Somewhere no one would think to look for him . . . And then she disappeared. . . .

Jessica stands up. She can't just sit there waiting for Yusuf's call. She has to take action. Now.

THE SHORT, SLOUCHED figure passes the recessed, graffiti-scrawled metal door, then climbs the flight of stairs leading from Topeliuksenkatu to the pale green apartment building on the corner. The granite blocks forming the side of the staircase have been bombed with the word "CHUCK," whatever that means. An icy drizzle whips the hood the man has pulled down over his sparse hair.

He takes a moment to scan the deserted street. The wet asphalt glistens like a dolphin's back, and gusts toss the widely spaced streetlamps on their taut wires.

He walks to the door of the building, sees his reflection in the glass. The heavy beard and pitiless pockmarks. And a pair of blinding headlights approaching from downtown, cleaving the street that was deserted a moment ago. He waits for the car to pass.

But it doesn't.

In the reflection, he sees it's a taxi that has pulled up about ten meters away. When he glances over his shoulder, he recognizes the dark-haired woman emerging from it. Goddamn it. Now he's going to need wits and courage of the sort Witold Pilecki possessed.

He turns away and pulls his cigarettes from his coat pocket.

99

JESSICA JUMPS OUT of the taxi. Messeniuksenkatu is empty except for some hooded guy near the door smoking a cigarette and, as she can hear, talking on the phone.

A loud crackle belches from the bowels of the buzzer, and Jessica yanks the door open. She walks toward the elevator and comes face-to-face with Essi in the corridor. Essi descends the marble stairs in her robe, hauling the sledgehammer Lisa used to demolish the wall between the kitchen and the living room.

Essi greets her doubtfully: "I brought this like you asked, but . . ."

Jessica knows she had no right to wake the woman up in the middle of the night and order her to open the laundry room door; Jessica isn't a police officer anymore. But Essi doesn't know that right now. And maybe she doesn't need to.

100

A RAT SCURRIES over to a hamburger wrapper dropped in the gutter.

The man raises the phone to his ear and pretends to talk to someone. He hears the sound of the buzzer and of the front door opening. Jessica Niemi steps into the stairwell, and the man takes a few swift strides after her, slips his foot in the door just before it closes. Then he hunches down so he's impossible to see from inside the building.

He hears voices in the corridor. The man peers through the glass and sees Niemi holding a huge sledgehammer. A young blond woman is standing across from her. *What the hell?* Then the two women start walking down the stairs, toward the basement.

The man takes a deep breath and cracks the door just enough to slip into the dark stairwell.

Essi slides her hand into the pocket of her robe and looks uncertainly at Jessica. Her voice is a little raspy: "What is going on?"

"There's nothing to worry about. But I need to take a quick look around the laundry room. Could you let me in?"

Jessica gestures toward the stairs that wind down behind the elevator shaft.

Essi hands Jessica the sledgehammer, which is surprisingly heavy, and looks groggily at Jessica. The keys slip from her sleepy fingers, and the tinkling crash echoes through the stairwell. Essi picks up the keys and continues down the short flight of stairs. When she reaches the bottom, she fits the key into the lock.

Jessica follows Essi to the stout metal door. At the doorway, Essi lets Jessica pass. They walk single file down the long, low hallway to the laundry room at the far end. They hear the heavy door clunk shut. Fluorescent lights are sandwiched at regular intervals between the air ducts and bundled cables running along the ceiling, bathing the corridor in their pallid glow.

Jessica opens the door to the laundry room, aims the light from her phone at the brick wall, and quickly spots the light switch.

The space doesn't smell like fresh paint, but there's a square-shaped area on the rear wall where the white paint is a little brighter than on the surrounding walls. This is where Lisa was renovating.

"Don't come any farther, Essi," Jessica says, and walks toward the stretch of white wall, sledgehammer in tow.

JESSICA SWINGS THE sledgehammer. It sinks into the wall like a knife into melted butter. Clouds of gray plaster form as bricks rain to the floor.

"Stay back!" Jessica shouts, gesturing for Essi to step away.

When the dust settles, Jessica sees some of the bricks have been knocked inside the hollow wall. But they haven't fallen to the floor; they've come to a rest on something at a height of about a meter. And then it floods the room, the smell Jessica would recognize in her sleep: death.

It's Jason.

Jessica grabs the wooden handle with both hands and raises the sledgehammer again. This time she's more careful so the massive head won't strike what she assumes is a body. She taps at the edges of the hole until it's bigger.

She swats the heavy dust out of her face and sees a black plastic bag inside. A fine layer of powdered brick and plaster has settled onto it. Jessica drops the sledgehammer to the floor.

She draws her hand across the plastic, feels the dust against her fingertips, senses the alternating soft and hard beneath.

She covers her mouth and trains her phone's flashlight on the bag. There's a zipper running up the middle. The longer she looks at it, the surer she is that when she draws it back, she'll be looking at a dead man's face. Scalp, forehead, nose, cheeks. She takes a deep breath and examines the hole in the wall. Black body bags are a rarity these days, replaced by the white ones that make it easier for investigating authorities to spot. When it comes to concealment, black has no rival.

This body was not wrapped by the authorities. This body was not meant for closer inspection.

"Don't come in here," Jessica repeats to Essi, who is still at the door.

She coughs, picks up the sledgehammer again, and raises it into the air one last time. Now it strikes lower, smashing the wall at a height of half a meter. There's a hollow thud; crumbs of brick patter to the floor.

Jessica grabs the corner of the bag with both hands and tries to drag it out of the wall. She struggles and strains and eventually the heavy load follows, plopping to the floor. Jessica sits there next to it, catching her breath, then wipes the sweat from her forehead and reaches for the zipper.

The moment of truth.

She is looking upon the dark blue face of a young man. His eyes and mouth are agape; it looks as if he might have been frightened to death.

I'm sorry, Jason. I'm sorry we couldn't do anything for you.

The body of Jason Nervander has languished for two weeks in the sealed bag and, despite its chilly tomb, begun to decompose. The stench is revolting. According to some studies, the smell of a corpse consists of more than four hundred elements. It is pungent and rank, and once you've smelled it, it's impossible to forget or confuse with anything else. Jessica gags into the crook of her arm and turns her watery eyes to Essi, who is still standing in the doorway with a confused look on her face. Jessica should never have brought her here. "Go back to the stairwell, Essi! Call the police."

But Essi doesn't budge. She must be in shock. Jessica continues: "You don't have to see this. . . ."

Jessica zips up the bag and stands. She needs to call Hellu or Yusuf right away.

But then she sees something strange inside the wall. . . . *What the hell . . . ?*

Jessica takes a step toward the hole she made in the wall, and now she notices there's something else under the bricks. She lifts her phone and crouches down to peer in.

Another body bag.

Jessica kicks at the loose brick so she can reach the second bag. She's going to have to knock down the lower part of the wall to retrieve it, but before she does, she could try to ID the body.

Holding the flashlight, Jessica focuses on the zipper and grips the tab with the fingers of her other hand. Dust has jammed the mechanism and the zipper won't open. Jessica tugs at it for a moment, and it comes loose.

A face emerges from the blackness of the second bag, one that bears little resemblance to those hundreds of photographs Jessica has seen of it. But there's no doubt it's her.

Jessica suddenly understands she made a terrible mistake. It's the face she never expected to find there. And it belongs to Lisa Yamamoto.

103

Rasmus knocks on the door of Helena Lappi's office. When there's no reply, he tries the handle, and the door opens. Rasmus sees Hellu sitting at her desk, facing the window, hands folded in her lap. She shows no indication that she is aware of his presence.

"Am I disturbing you?" Rasmus asks tentatively.

Hellu sighs and shuts her eyes.

"Hellu?"

"No, you're not disturbing me," Hellu eventually says, still gazing out into the darkness. "What are you still doing here at this hour, Susikoski? Go home."

Rasmus steps in and shuts the door behind him. "The Bureau reorganized the teams. I just wanted to let you know I'm not on the manga league case anymore . . . but you probably already knew."

Hellu seems to frown. She shakes her head and lowers her eyes to her smartwatch. Her voice is quiet, downcast: "They don't tell me anything."

"But as superintendent who answers for the investigation, you're—"

"Did you hear me, Susikoski? They're keeping me in the dark. Everything went to hell the second those vultures landed here. . . ."

Rasmus has never seen Hellu in such a state. Three empty coffee cups and yesterday's pastry plate are on the desk, which is extremely out of character for the generally tidy superintendent.

"Anyway, I came across something that requires urgent attention." Rasmus approaches Hellu's desk. "And I'm not sure whom to inform. Especially with it being as late as it is—"

Hellu reluctantly turns her head and torso toward Rasmus. "Inform about what?"

"Do you remember about a week ago, when I checked the metadata on Lisa Yamamoto's lighthouse photo?"

"Yes, I remember." Hellu massages her forehead. "iPhone 7 or whatever—"

"iPhone 8. And I said all we could determine was the device's technical information, but not its owner. . . ."

"Yes. Which made the whole meta-analysis pretty pointless . . ."

". . . unless we somehow miraculously managed to locate the phone by some other method and compared its metadata to metadata we already had."

Suddenly Hellu looks intrigued. Rasmus can feel his palms sweating. He doesn't know what to make of the development or if there's any way it is even possible. That's how crazy it is.

"In Finnish, Susikoski," Hellu says. But her tone isn't nasty.

"I performed a meta-analysis on Lisa Yamamoto's photographs. The majority of the photos were taken with her phone, but some were taken with a different one. I guess it's natural enough for other people to take pictures for a blogger, then send them to her to be edited and posted."

"And?"

"I decided to focus on the photographs taken in St. Petersburg, Amsterdam, and Lviv. Yamamoto made tons of Instagram posts from every trip. And from those trips, all the photos Lisa appears in—except the selfies, of course—were taken with the same iPhone 8 as the most recent image posted to Lisa's Instagram account. The lighthouse photo."

"Wait a minute," Hellu says. "Are you saying whoever took the photograph of the lighthouse was on those trips with Lisa? Snapped vacation shots of Lisa and others?"

"Yes. For instance, this group photo taken in Lviv, at a bachelorette party—it was taken with the phone in question. There are a total of twelve women in the picture, including Lisa. But the hashtag #Oceans13 indicates there were thirteen people on the trip."

"One person is missing from the photo," Hellu says softly. "Because she's the one who took it."

"Exactly. I checked with the airline that took the group's reservation—"

"Well? Who is it?"

"That's the craziest thing about this, Hellu. . . . It's someone we for some reason completely overlooked."

104

JESSICA STUDIES LISA Yamamoto's waxen face. The black hair has fallen across her open eyes, and her mouth is agape. Lisa looks like she's trying to shout herself awake from an eternal nightmare. The mingling of beauty and death is nothing new to Jessica; her past won't let her forget how they look together. The combination follows her to the mirror every day, and every night it follows her into her dreams.

Jessica feels an icy breeze blow through her, and she knows her mother is in the room with her now.

I tried to warn you, Jessica.

Jessica feels her heart beating wildly.

The magician doesn't need to know which card you choose, Jessie. He only needs to know the card next to your card.

And then it all falls into place.

Sleight of hand.

"They were supposed to disappear forever," Essi says.

Jessica hears her phone ring as she turns toward the other woman. Her voice is hoarse: "What?"

The confusion on Essi's face has morphed into determination. Jessica feels the chill climb from her knees to her back, her neck, and set her head pounding. "Essi . . . ," she murmurs, then coughs into her fist.

"Lisa and Jason. No one was supposed to find them."

Now Jessica sees Essi has taken the sledgehammer from the floor, has it in both hands. It takes Jessica half a second to remember she didn't come here in a law enforcement capacity. She doesn't have her gun.

"How did you think to look for them here?" Essi says softly, stepping closer.

The fluorescent lamps at the ceiling hum more and more loudly with every passing moment.

Jessica slowly rises to her feet. "Lisa wasn't Akifumi. . . ."

Essi shakes her head. "Lisa was an airhead"—her mouth now twists up in a shy smile—"who did whatever I told her to. Do you think she was even interested in manga? No. That was me. I'm the artist."

"But why—"

"I always knew there was something wrong with me, Jessica. Of course there is. It's so easy for these things to get out of hand. One thing leads to another. It's like a drug. . . . You need to up the dose to keep getting the high. Suddenly you realize drawing something, or even humiliating your partner, isn't enough. You look down at the whore tied to the bed and realize you don't want to let go of her throat. . . . Just the opposite: you want to squeeze harder, watch the life in her eyes go out."

Essi takes another step toward Jessica and the body. Her grip on the sledgehammer tightens; her knuckles go white. It's as if she's channeling the rage surging through her into the weapon. Its steel head sways ominously in the air.

"It was you the whole time? Akifumi—"

"You have no idea how critical anonymity is in this business."

"Jose Rodriguez, the letter to Lisa's father . . . the masayoshi.fi website. The manga league's telephone exchange—"

"Of course. There's no way Lisa would have known how to use a Tor network. I helped Lisa with everything involving computers. I helped her monitor the number of followers she had on her blog. Which made it simple for me to add masayoshi.fi to the same Analytics ID."

"So you did that on purpose?"

Essi nods. "Isn't it obvious by now? I think it was a pretty slick way of getting the police to suspect Lisa. You guys thought Lisa came up with this little scheme behind the league's back. That she went rogue, wanted out. No, the way the league's operations are structured, the evidence gathered by the police won't be enough for a single arrest. Over the last six months, we've gotten a bunch of rich clients whose violent fantasies have been recorded on hard drive, making them the perfect targets for extortion." Essi studies Jessica's reaction, which apparently doesn't indicate surprise.

Then she smirks. "Wait. Wow, Jessica. So you figured that part out. Congratulations. I'm impressed. I never would have believed it. But it won't change anything. Anyway, the league always moves from locale to locale, leaving nothing but a scapegoat behind. So in this case if the police were to discover anything, it was all pinned on Lisa . . . who disappeared."

The phone in Jessica's pocket starts ringing again.

"So Lisa was—"

"Lisa was the lightning rod. It was all supposed to look exactly the way it does. And it has to stay that way, which is why you can't answer that call, Jessica."

Essi takes a step closer; barely a meter remains between the two women. Jessica feverishly ponders her next move. The sledgehammer looks menacing in Essi's hands—especially since she's a murderous sadist who has already taken the lives of two of her friends.

Jessica gulps. She has to buy time. But how much can she get? A minute? Two? What then? No one knows she's here. Yusuf and Erne won't be rushing into the room this time; a SWAT team won't be storming the place.

"But what about the phone? The guy from Europol found it in Lisa's room—"

Essi smiles. "Because it wasn't Lisa's room. It was mine. I actually didn't come up with the hiding place until the morning you came to interrogate me. I dug a hole in the wall. I was a little pressed for time; I expected you guys to find it right away."

Now Jessica remembers the words of the old man they saw at the front door: *You here because of the noise? Someone was really pounding on the walls again.*

Kex Maces wasn't lying about the photo, Jessica sees now. He really was sitting in Lisa's room. And Reddick didn't know which room was Lisa's; he made his assumption based on the art and the painting supplies.

"A few months back, Lisa and I agreed she would present my art as her own, because her fame might make it possible to sell some. I suggested that if anyone bought anything, we split the money fifty-fifty. Lisa was cool with that. Of course I just wanted the police to focus on investigating Lisa's manga fascination. So instead of hauling all that stuff back and forth between the rooms after Lisa died, I decided Lisa's room would be mine and vice versa. I obviously moved her personal stuff—her makeup, her photos—into my room and changed the sheets. I figured a little trick like that would be hard to catch. Why on earth would a roommate lie about whose room is whose?"

"Which is why you deleted all the photos of Lisa taken in her own room."

"Yup."

Jessica sees Essi's fingers wrapped around the handle of the sledgehammer. She feels an icy touch on her shoulder and her mother's cold breath in her ear.

Play for time, Jessica dear. Delay your death moment by moment. It's not over until it's finally over.

Jessica tries to remain calm. "You murdered those women on trips you and Lisa took together?"

Essi smiles; it's as if she's caught hold of some heartwarming memory.

"Yes. Even before. That's how I originally came across the league. I convinced them there was a business model here that would allow them to charge their customers twice. And the second bill would be ten times the amount of the first one. If we could just create the conditions that would allow the customer to relax. Be himself."

Challenge her a little. Not too much, just enough.

Make her explain. Make her tell.

"Didn't it ever occur to you—"

Essi's face contorts in fury. All trace of humanity vanishes from the big eyes. Jessica can now see that everything else has been a facade, that Essi truly is a psychopath, her eyes inhabited by a soulless darkness. "If you think I don't know what it feels like to be on the receiving end—to be raped, humiliated—you're fucking mistaken, Jessica. Trust me, I know. I've been through it. It's been done to me a hell of a lot."

Essi is a victim too, Jessica.

The phone is again vibrating in Jessica's pocket, and she discreetly slides her hand into it. "Essi, you have to—"

"I don't have to do anything anymore!"

Essi takes a couple of brisk steps toward Jessica and holds the sledgehammer out to the side. She aims it at Jessica's head and swings with all her strength.

Jessica doesn't have time to dodge the blow. She bellows in terror, throwing up her left hand to shield her skull. The sledgehammer's steel head makes contact with the back of her hand, crushes it. She staggers to the floor; her phone tumbles to the wall. The pain explodes, surges to Jessica's shoulder. She roars in agony, holding her wrist.

"Stay still, Jessica." Essi lowers the sledgehammer, lets it dangle.

Jessica looks at her hand. The skin is flushed crimson; the fingers hang limp and mangled. It's as if her hand has been replaced with an empty glove.

"Let's not makes this any more difficult than it needs to be."

"Stop, Essi!" Jessica shouts, using her healthy hand to drag herself away. "Help!"

"There's no point in shouting. This was a band practice room up until a couple of years ago. This basement has been soundproofed to within an inch of its life. By morning that wall will be bricked up again," Essi hisses. "And those little fucking lovebirds will be joined by the lady cop who disturbed their rest."

She prepares to swing the sledgehammer again, this time over her shoulder, so Jessica won't have the tiniest chance of protecting her head from its lethal force.

Those little fucking lovebirds . . .

"Wait!" Jessica shouts.

Essi imitates Jessica's panicked voice: "What?"

"Were you . . . you and Jason?"

Essi stops the sledgehammer midswing. For a moment, she looks almost sad.

"Jason wasn't supposed to be there that night. . . ."

105

LARGE SWELLS BUFFET *the prow of the Aquador 28C. Essi feels her stomach lurch. The trip from Söderskär back to Aurinkolahti has already lasted an hour and a half. Olga has vomited over the side of the boat four times, forcing Essi to take the wheel. Olga's nausea is not, however, due to the rough seas, but to the kambo treatment she had earlier in the day. How fucking stupid do you have to be to let someone put frog poison in your veins? But they're lucky to have Jose Rodriguez, who came up with the idea of lacing the kambo with opiates and making the dolls dependent on the treatment—and them.*

Essi looks at the screen of the navigator. A black mass has now appeared at the right edge; they're approaching land.

Essi eases up on the throttle. She has never skippered a boat before, but she has seen Olga do it a few times, during trips to Söderskär to pick up fresh shipments of dolls. As the speed drops, the prow dips and the boat rocks violently in the crossing waves.

Essi knows she'll never see them again: Sami, James, and the five dolls who are still breathing. She and Olga just ferried them to Söderskär. They will be picked up from there at daybreak and taken to Sosnovyi Bori, west of St. Petersburg.

Sometimes Essi wonders how none of the dolls smell a rat, how they actually believe some of the girls have gone home. Maybe they know the truth deep down but don't want to admit it.

The rumble of the boat's engine has died. Over the wind, Essi hears the bile spew from Olga's guts again and again. Increasingly violently. She sees Olga's convulsive movements as she leans over the railing.

Something's wrong.

Jose warned them a few months ago that the frog poison could cause serious complications if combined with opiates. But it wasn't likely. Besides, vomiting after a kambo treatment is totally normal. It's just not supposed to go on this long.

"Everything OK?" Essi asks without turning to look. Olga is the only one of the girls who speaks almost perfect English.

But Olga doesn't reply; she just keeps heaving, even though it's been a while since it sounded like there was anything left to vomit up.

"You need to steer us into dock," Essi says.

She releases the wheel, and the boat slides across the water toward the lights of Aurinkolahti. The city looks like an oasis emerging from the darkness.

"Did you hear me? You need to steer this boat into the fucking dock, Olga!"

Olga turns to Essi. Her face is as white as a sheet, and her eyes are bulging out of her head. She says: "I don't feel very good." Then she wipes her forehead: it might be sweat, or maybe spray from the waves that mists her face. It doesn't matter.

"You'll do as you're told," Essi says. She steps back from the wheel to make room for the whore wearing the schoolgirl's uniform.

106

TEN MINUTES LATER, *the boat is rocking in place, and Olga is lashing the line to the pier.*

Essi steps from the prow to the dock and looks around. The marina is deserted, as it usually is this time of night. All that's left for them to do is get the rest of the stuff from the suite and stow it on board. Then Olga will motor back to Söderskär, sink the boat, and wait to be picked up from the lighthouse. What happens to her afterward makes no difference to Essi.

"Akifumi," Olga says, steadying herself on the prow's aluminum railing. Her eyelids are drooping.

"Come on," Essi says impatiently. The plastic mask is glued to her cheeks; it feels sweaty.

"Essi?"

It's not Olga's voice; it's a man's.

Essi feels her heart drop. Only league members know her real name. To the dolls she is Akifumi, who always wears a mask. The mask has traveled with her for a long time now; she has seen numerous lives extinguished through its eyeholes.

Essi turns around and sees a man at the head of the dock.

It's Jason.

"Essi? What the hell—"

"Wait," Essi calls to him.

"You promised to bring the boat back this morning. . . . What the hell . . . ?"

Olga has appeared on the dock. Her eyes wander from Essi to Jason. Then she drops, unconscious.

Now Jason is running toward them.

Essi looks at the woman sprawled on the dock. Her gaping eyes are staring up at the starless sky.

Essi turns her face to the sea and slips off her beanie and her mask.

"Essi, what the hell . . . ?" Jason has reached the end of the dock. He stares at Essi. Then he squats next to Olga, who is lying on the dock, limp. His voice is panicked: "Who is she . . . ? She just collapsed." He flips Olga onto her back and starts applying pressure to her chest.

"Jason—"

"She's not breathing! Call an ambulance—"

"Did you come alone, Jason?" Essi says, crouching down at his side.

Jason doesn't answer; he just shoots her an incredulous look and keeps rhythmically pressing Olga's chest the way he must have learned from some fucking first aid manual. He keeps at it; he's panting heavily. A moment later, Olga's chest crunches revoltingly. Jason flinches and pulls back. He looks at the body in a panic, then whips his phone from his pocket.

"Jason," Essi says quietly as he brings up the emergency number, "put the phone away."

"Why?"

"I'll explain what's going on."

"We need to call—"

Essi swats the phone from Jason's hand. It arcs toward the sea and vanishes into the dark water's depths.

Jason shouts: "What the hell, Essi?"

Essi looks around and makes sure she doesn't see any other pairs of eyes in the darkness.

"Listen, Jason. Just listen for a second, goddamn it. I'll explain everything to you. Then if you still want to, you can call the police," Essi says. "But right now that can wait. She's clearly dead and we can't do anything for her."

Jason sobs. "Who is she?"

"I'll also explain that in a second. But first I need your help." Essi wipes the tear from Jason's cheek. "The body can't be found here by the boat. If it is, you'll go to prison too."

107

ESSI STANDS THERE *with her hands on her hips, looking down at the lifeless body of Olga Belousova lying on the shore of the little peninsula of Suorttio. Someone will be sure to find it there, but not until morning. Maybe not for a few days. The fucking little whore went and died just when everything was going well.*

Essi lowers her hand to Jason's shoulder. He's sobbing on the ground.

She opens Olga's backpack. There's a blister pack of Subutex at the bottom. Now Essi realizes what killed the whore: the drug interaction Jose warned them about.

There's also a notebook. Essi rips out the few pages where Olga scrawled something in Ukrainian and writes down a few names the police will immediately take an interest in. An improvised addition to the plan. It can't hurt, at least, now that Olga has gone and died. Every step Essi takes must bring her toward a single goal: making Lisa look like the culprit. She drops the notebook where someone is sure to find it.

Then she asks: "Jason, are you OK?"

Jason sobs. "This is murder."

Essi shakes her head. "No, it's not. Olga had a heart attack."

"But we should have helped her. . . . I think I broke her sternum or something—"

"So there's no point in thinking about calling an ambulance, right?" Essi sits next to Jason. "What are you doing here? Why did you come out to the boat?"

"I was supposed to return it today. . . . Lisa promised to get it to me yesterday. I didn't know she had loaned it to you. . . ."

"Just relax."

"And I wanted to talk to Lisa." Jason falls silent. "I want her back."

Essi looks up and out at the sea and feels her diaphragm quiver in revulsion. Jason is weak. Weak in every way. He was weak when she screwed him behind Lisa's back a few months ago. For Essi, the whole thing was a psychological test. A true classic. Could she get her roommate's boyfriend to come inside her? As a matter of fact, Jason is the last person Essi screwed without the mask. As Essi, not Akifumi. Even so, she never considered hurting Jason. It was never part of the plan. But the circumstances have changed.

She lowers her hands to Jason's shoulders. "I know where Lisa is."

Jason looks up. "What?"

Essi flashes her specialty, her sympathetic smile. It almost hurts, doing that to her face. "Let's go. I have a friend who can move the boat to Lauttasaari; I'll drop the keys off on the way. We'll go back to my place, and you can talk to Lisa. Work things out." She gives Jason a pat on the cheek.

"OK," Jason says hopefully. His face grows dark again when he sees the body lying in the shallows.

Lisa was always supposed to go missing today, but Jason sealed his own fate by stepping onto the dock on this dark November night.

LISA YAMAMOTO FEELS *her head spinning. The man who showed up at the party threw her off her game, and it took a few rounds of shots and a couple lines of coke to restore her celebratory mood. She looks around. Things are getting wild: sport coats and bow ties have been flung aside; girls are dancing barefoot on the tables. Lisa sees Kex climb up on a table too, cradling a vodka bottle the size of a fire extinguisher like a baby. The shouts grow louder, and the spirits spill into the open mouths of those besieging the table.*

Lisa glances at her phone. A text message from Essi.

Lisa, you're in danger.

Turn off your phone right now.

Take a taxi and meet me in the bike storage.

Make sure no one follows you.

Essi

ESSI CRACKS THE *heavy metal door to let Lisa in.*

"What's wrong?" Lisa is slurring. "I want to go to bed—"

"Come in and I'll tell you." Essi scans the deserted street from end to end.

Lisa steps into the bike storage. The laces of her white Superstars dangle untied. She has walked all the way home from the Phoenix. At first she thought she would grab a cab from the Kamppi taxi stand, but she couldn't find her card case anywhere. On the way home, she realized it was in her coat pocket. But her key chain is still missing, so she couldn't get in the front door.

"I guess I went a little overboard," Lisa mumbles. She exhales heavily. "I think I'm gonna puke. . . ."

Essi stalks down the gray corridor, Lisa stumbling at her heels. When they reach the last door, the one leading to the laundry room, Lisa says, "What the hell is going on?"

"Did you do exactly what I told you to, Lisa? Turn off your phone and—"

"Yes," Lisa says wearily. "Is this about that Japanese guy? Did he come—"

"Maybe. The main thing is he didn't see you come home."

Lisa laughs. "Is that why we're meeting in the bike storage? You think he's out there watching the building?" A muffled belch escapes her lips. She is heavily inebriated, but for some reason, she senses something about Essi is off. For a second, she regrets coming home; she'd rather be surrounded by people at Kex Maces' after-party.

Essi opens the door to the laundry room and urges Lisa to cross the threshold.

And then Lisa sees Jason sitting on top of a dryer, looking sad. She turns to Essi. "What—"

"Lisa, please—," Jason sobs.

"Both of you just shut up for a second," Essi snaps, startling Lisa.

And then Essi reaches into the pocket of her black overcoat and pulls out a little pistol with a silencer screwed to the barrel. Lisa feels her heart skip a beat. "Essi—"

"I want you both to know that all the problems you had . . . all those rumors and lies that got back to you. That was me."

"What are you—"

"I never thought I'd care about anything like that. But I guess I was a little jealous of what you guys had. Besides, it all fit in with the big picture."

"What fucking picture? What are you talking about, Essi? What is that?"

Lisa falls silent as Essi raises the gun. She feels a lump in her throat. When she looks at Jason, she can tell he's just as lost as she is—that they both stepped into this room wholly ignorant of what the subsequent moments would bring. Her voice cracks: "Essi?"

For a second, Lisa thinks she spies warmth in Essi's big eyes, a glimmer of humanity. But then she realizes the gleam isn't generated by fluorescent light bouncing off tear ducts.

What Lisa sees in Essi's eyes is arousal.

110

JESSICA FEELS THE shock fade and the pain escalate in her mangled hand. It is burning hot, as if it is soaking in boiling water up to the wrist.

"I guess I could have killed Jason whenever and wherever. Even that night at Aurinkolahti. But Lisa I absolutely wanted to bury here. There was something beautiful about the thought. I found the idea of the whole country looking for her while she was bricked up in a wall less than ten meters from her home funny. In any case, my decision to brick both of them inside this wall . . . there was something poetic about it. Now the lovebirds can spend some quality time together," Essi says.

And just as Jessica is to about reply, the sledgehammer swings again. The head grazes Jessica's thigh and smashes into the floor, gouging the concrete. Jessica wails and slips her healthy hand into her pocket.

These days she always carries it with her.

Essi drops the sledgehammer and slides her hand into her robe. In the two seconds it takes Essi to draw the pistol, Jessica twists herself to her knees and squirts the pepper spray in Essi's face. The gun goes off; the shot rings out deafeningly in the small, grim room, but the bullet flies past.

The pepper spray didn't land in Essi's eyes; she swats the air in front of her and raises her hand to shield her face. "You fucking whore . . . what the hell did you just do?"

Jessica aims the spray at Essi again, and releases a long squirt from the canister, but it is deflected by Essi's raised hand. Jessica drops the spray and roars out in pain—she can feel the bones in her crushed hand crumble as she heaves herself to her knees and throws herself at Essi. *The final assault.*

Essi hasn't fired again; apparently some of the spray reached its target after all. She's wiping her eyes on the sleeve of her robe when Jessica knocks her to the floor and lands on top of her.

Essi shouts: "You fucking whore, I'm going to kill you!" The look on Essi's face is one Jessica saw before, long ago. It is void of human feeling.

Jessica rolls onto Essi's gun hand with all her weight. She grabs Essi's hair and bashes her head against the concrete as hard as she can. As the arm beneath her writhes, Jessica continues bashing the head, again and again, into the concrete. Just when she thinks Essi's head can't take any more blows, she hears a gunshot, and her shoulder feels like it has exploded.

It's over.

In the seconds following the shot, Jessica feels fatigue spread throughout her body, the concrete floor against the back of her skull. She watches the disheveled figure before her rise slowly to its feet. The white robe is covered in blood, and more spills from her battered brow. Jessica has time to reflect that the mauled, bloody face is like something straight out of her dreams. That this is precisely how her loved ones manifest to her. And that this is how everything is supposed to end.

"Nice try, cop," Essi says. She spits blood in Jessica's face. Then she aims the gun. Jessica looks deep into the pistol's barrel and bids the world a silent goodbye.

But instead of the shot, there's a soft thud as the sledgehammer swinging through the air connects with Essi's torso. Essi crumples at Jessica's side like a bag of sand; a faint rattle escapes her mouth.

Then Jessica sees Nikolas Ponsi kneel at her side.

"I called an ambulance. Help is on the way!" he says, tearing a strip from his coat and bandaging Jessica's wound.

FRIDAY, DECEMBER 13

111

Nikolas Ponsi's hands are folded on the table and his head is lowered. Nina can't help but think he's uttering a silent prayer.

"How is she?" Ponsi says quietly. "I didn't mean to hurt her badly but—"

"You did what you had to do. You saved a police officer's life. And probably many others."

Ponsi takes a swig of coffee and scratches his face. Judging by the bags under his eyes, he hasn't slept a wink.

"Shall we continue?" Nina asks.

Ponsi nods, and Nina's fingers reach toward the recorder, turn it on. "Tell me everything again, in your own words."

Ponsi shifts his gaze to the white wall, perhaps imagining he is looking at the photo of Witold Pilecki. "Four years ago, Jason asked me to meet with his old friend Essi, who he'd been worried about for a while. Apparently she was suffering from some sort of existential crisis, depression. . . . We met for coffee, and I immediately realized that while she was socially gifted, this young lady exuded an apathy of an unusual variety."

"Could you be more specific?" Nina says.

"The impression I got was that Essi acknowledged her problems but wasn't genuinely interested in doing anything about them. In other words, what her friend Jason had interpreted as depression or some sort of crisis was purely frustration."

"Frustration about what?"

"After that initial meeting, I met with Essi once a week in a therapeutic context. I really wanted to help her, but I had a hard time getting at the core of the problem. Before long, I suggested she see a psychiatrist. But she and Jason were convinced that, as someone who had worked a lot with young people, I was a safer option. Jason trusted me, and I guess that's why Essi felt safe with me too. I gradually came to understand her frustrations were sexual in nature. That, like many people who conceal their sexual orientation, she was frustrated because she was not able to freely live out her urges. It was as if she were living in a pressure cooker."

"And the true nature of Essi's urges began to become clear to you?"

"Yes. One time she showed me her drawings." Ponsi shakes his head. "Essi really knew how to draw and paint. So talented. But at that point I understood she might be sick."

Nina opens a folder resting on the table and flips it around so Ponsi can see the contents. "I am showing the witness, Nikolas Ponsi, photographs of drawings found in the suspect's home," she says into the recorder, then turns to Ponsi. "Are these the sort of drawings you're referring to?"

Ponsi raises his hand to his mouth as he looks at the photographs, then nods.

Nina has no interest in seeing the images; she already did once. But as she closes the folder, she catches a glimpse of blood-soaked schoolgirl uniforms, sawn-off limbs and severed heads, nails hammered where eyes should be.

"You didn't believe Essi would truly live out her fantasies?"

A tear spills down Ponsi's cheek and slaloms between the pockmarks, disappearing beneath the chin.

"Young people. They come to me. Anxious, afraid, confused. Building trust is a long, vulnerable process. I picked up the phone to call the police, but I couldn't help thinking Essi's drawings were nothing more than that: drawings, stream of consciousness, a way of channeling her pain. . . . And that if I was wrong, there would be a high price to pay."

"What happened next?"

"Two years ago, Essi stopped coming to see me. Jason said she was doing better. There was no way Jason could have known how things truly stood, and of course I couldn't talk to him about it. But I asked him to keep an eye on Essi and let me know if things deteriorated."

"And Jason never mentioned the topic again."

"Never. I occasionally asked how Essi was doing, but apparently they weren't in much contact anymore. And then . . . a few weeks ago, Jason disappeared."

"Please go on."

"Last night when I was watching the news, I saw the photographs the police released of the manga clothing. At that point, I understood Lisa Yamamoto's disappearance and her roommate's obsessive, violent fantasies could not be unrelated. I had a look at Lisa Yamamoto's Instagram for the first time and saw the manga drawings. Of course the images are nothing like the ones Essi drew years before, but there was no doubt. The paintings and drawings weren't done by Lisa. They were done by Essi. . . ."

"So you went to see Essi?"

"I was in shock. I didn't have a plan, but I had to see Essi before . . ."

"Why didn't you call the police?"

Nikolas Ponsi indignantly drops his gaze from the ceiling to Nina's face. "How could I? I didn't call the police two years ago. Nor would I have now until I heard the words out of her mouth. I wanted to hear her say it . . . that I wasn't the one who violated our trust. She was. I thought I was doing the right thing. That I was being brave. But when I stepped onto those basement stairs and heard Essi confess everything to Detective Niemi . . . I froze and wept in silence. I realized then that I had made a huge mistake. And then . . . then I finally called the police."

MONDAY, DECEMBER 16

112

JESSICA'S FORMER BOSS is brimming with a new sort of energy; with her hopeful eyes and fitted jacket, it's as if she's reborn. It takes Jessica a second to note that Hellu has, in addition to everything else, dyed her hair; the brown calls to mind a hare that has decided to shed its camouflage for the snowless winter. The other major change is the disappearance of the massive smartwatch from her wrist. Maybe the pain of knowing too much proved unbearable.

"The information Essi provided held up," Hellu says, picking at the desktop with her finger. "A bedroom suite renovated into an underground storage space. Near the Vuosaari golf course—as a matter of fact, partially beneath it. Nathan Reddick has confirmed based on photographs that it's the same place."

"Did they find anyone there?" Jessica asks.

Hellu shakes her head. "But now we know the name of the company that rented it, as well as those of some subcontractors who participated in its renovation. I don't know if it will be enough for anything when it comes down to it, but it's no longer in our hands or even those of the Bureau."

"What about Essi . . . ?"

"She's undergoing a battery of psychological tests. But it's clear that, in laypersons' terms, she's a lunatic." Hellu looks up from the desk and into Jessica's eyes. *Speaking of lunatics . . . ,* she seems to be thinking, but she doesn't say it.

"Things are shifting here at HQ, Niemi. Jens Oranen is leaving. Some upper-management position in the private sector. That changes things."

"Are you saying you're going to become the new deputy chief of police?"

Hellu lets out a joyless snort and vehemently shakes her head. "Everyone and their mother is interested in the position. Besides, I just started in the unit." She leans across the desk. "But Oranen's departure affords me a lot of leeway in some matters."

"Such as?"

Hellu answers Jessica's question with prolonged pointed eye contact.

Jessica rolls her eyes in disbelief. "Are you serious?"

Hellu curls her lower lip, momentarily resembling a sketch character from some comedy show. "Listen, Niemi."

"At least call me Jessica, *damn it.*"

Hellu shakes her head. "It took me a little while to realize you're the captain of this team."

"And you're . . ."

"The coach, I suppose. And Oranen is the manager who's on his way out."

"OK," Jessica says expectantly, arms folded across her chest.

Hellu pulls a folder from her desk drawer, the contents of which Jessica has seen once before. "I'd like to know how all this . . . this here, in this folder . . . How does it manifest?" she says cryptically, as if she's not even sure what she's trying to ask.

Jessica looks the superintendent in the eye and, as the moments pass, grows convinced this is not one of Hellu's idiosyncratic jokes, tests, or traps. As strange as it may seem, apparently the superintendent is extending her an olive branch.

Jessica can't help herself: "What are you playing at, Hellu?"

But the superintendent's conciliatory demeanor doesn't fade.

"Nikolas Ponsi will regret not reporting his suspicions about Essi to the police for the rest of his life. If I'm going to take a risk that's even remotely comparable . . . Goddamn it, Niemi. I just want to understand, that's all. I think I have a right."

Jessica looks the other woman in the eye.

Maybe now would be the time to start being honest and see how far it takes her. After all, she isn't even sure she wants to be a police officer anymore.

The silence is broken by the drone of helicopter blades churning nearby.

After taking a moment to choose her words, Jessica says: "Sometimes I see things other people don't."

Hellu seems to take this information in stride. She flips lazily through the report she has presumably read dozens of times.

"Do you have a hard time telling them apart? What's real and—"

"No," Jessica says quickly, her eyes on the sling hanging over her left shoulder, the plaster cast carried in it. She shakes her head, then continues more slowly, as if wanting to correct a statement made in haste. "But that day may come. When it becomes hard to tell them apart."

"Do you promise to let me know when that happens?"

Jessica chuckles softly. "Do you think I'll know when it happens?"

Hellu looks at Jessica for a moment as if she means to order her to stop being a smart aleck. Then she lets out peals of rollicking laughter, the sort Jessica never would have anticipated in her wildest dreams.

"Touché, Niemi."

"Call me Jessica."

"Niemi."

113

JESSICA GLANCES AT the window of the Sea Horse, and her eyes strike on a laminated lunch menu.

Pea soup and pancakes.

A powerful engine growls to life down the adjoining driveway. Jessica takes a few steps toward the arched portico leading to the courtyard of the hundred-year-old building. She hears the steady thunder of the approaching engine. A second later, the nose of a dark blue Mercedes-Benz G500 appears in the narrow passage.

Jessica waits for the front door to fully emerge, then pulls it open and jumps into the passenger seat.

"What the fuck?" Tim Taussi exclaims, stopping before the car reaches the cobblestone street.

Jessica shuts the door, and the alarm echoing in the beige leather interior dies. "The doors don't automatically lock until you're going about twenty, right?"

The rapper is leaning against the door of his luxury vehicle, putting as much space as possible between himself and Jessica.

Then the surprise on his face abruptly turns into something else. He has recognized her.

"You're a hard man to get ahold of, Tim," Jessica says, running her fingertips across the flawlessly contoured dash. The car smells of new leather and aftershave.

"How are you gonna just jump—"

"Into your fancy car? It's pretty sweet, I must admit. What does a ride like this cost . . . three hundred g's?"

"With these specs, about, yeah."

"You buy it new?"

"'Course."

Jessica grunts joylessly. "Maybe I'll get myself one too."

Taussi bursts out laughing. "Word. Good idea."

"You don't think it's possible for a police officer to have a little money stashed away?"

"Man, what do you want? I'm in a hurry."

Jessica shrugs. In reality she could buy a hundred of these and watch Kex Maces' jaw drop. Now, that would be something. "I'd like to know why two hundred grand was recently transferred to a Ukrainian holding company from your account."

Taussi's face goes white, but he tries to hide his panic with a feigned smirk. "What?"

"You heard me." Jessica pulls out her police ID to remind Taussi who's asking the questions.

"It was an investment."

"Great. So now you're a rapper and an angel investor. A real Dr. Dre. In what?"

"In what *what*?"

"What did you invest two hundred grand in?"

"I'm not about to start explaining—"

"What field? Was it a start-up? A brewery? A next-generation Chernobyl?"

Taussi drums the wheel with his fingers and looks around. "I gotta jet."

"So go ahead and jet. But if you suddenly get the feeling it wasn't such a hot investment after all, you're probably right. You see, we know you and a lot of other people were blackmailed. Every single one of you decided to hand over that exact amount without a peep. We've been wondering over at the station: what could be worth two hundred grand?" Jessica opens the door. "It must be a real deep secret. The kind that, if it came out, would take everything from you. Your career. Your reputation. Even your freedom."

"Man, get the fuck out of here," Taussi says, lowering his oversized sunglasses from his forehead to his eyes.

"Sure. It's your ride. For now."

Jessica raises her right foot out, but she then turns back. "How does it feel, sitting in the driver's seat for a change? Rumor has it you prefer the backseat. At least when it comes to Benz SUVs." Then she steps down and shuts the door.

The SUV lurches into traffic and races up the hill. As it disappears from view, Jessica whispers: "You're in deep shit, you sadistic asshole."

She glances at her watch. Lunchtime. Pea soup and pancakes don't sound half bad.

114

"Yusuf," Jessica says, sweeping a strand of hair out of her eyes.

"What?"

"I want to show you something." She lowers her empty beer can to the table and gestures at Yusuf, who is sitting on the sofa, to follow. They step through the door in the kitchenette and into the stairwell.

Jessica makes sure the door to the studio is properly shut. Then she pulls a key ring from her jeans pocket and fits one of the keys into the lock of the neighboring door.

"Where are we . . . ?" Yusuf whispers, looking around. There's no elevator in the stairwell; the carved stone steps lead down to the fifth floor and up to the attic.

Jessica doesn't answer. She opens the heavy wooden door and taps a sequence of numbers into the alarm. The console emits a brief whistle, and the lights come on automatically.

Yusuf squints in the brilliance of the entry hall's dozens of recessed ceiling lights. The contrast to the dimness of the studio apartment is immense.

"Jessica . . . ," he mumbles in confusion.

Jessica has seen expressions on Yusuf's face showing dozens of emotional states, but nothing like this. It is, perhaps, a mix of awe and amusement. A dash of fear? It seems to be asking: who the hell are you, Jessica Niemi?

"Take off your shoes," Jessica says. It's not only a request to keep the place clean; it's a comprehensive answer to the question Yusuf has left unspoken. *Yes, this belongs to me.*

Jessica sets the keys down on the credenza and follows the lost-looking Yusuf into the living room, where the row of bay windows in a semicircular configuration gives onto a panoramic view over Töölön-lahti Bay, the Parliament House, and downtown Helsinki beyond.

Jessica glances at Yusuf, who turns to examine the art hanging on the wall. "Edelfelt . . . Is this genuine?"

"Yes," Jessica says calmly. She pauses at the foot of the white spiral staircase twisting next to the wall.

"Wait. There's a second floor?"

"Yup. Another hundred and fifty square meters up there."

"Whose . . . I mean . . . You're saying this is your place?"

"My home. This is my home, Yusuf. My real home." Jessica notices regret creeping into her mind. This whole thing, bringing Yusuf here after all these years, may well be the dumbest thing she has done in a long time. It's like jumping from an airplane without a parachute, hurling herself into a free fall, and hoping she'll survive. But crashing into the ground no longer frightens her. Which is why she decided to bring Yusuf into her secret world.

They climb the stairs. Jessica opens one door at a time, and Yusuf peers in through each of them. He slides his fingers across walls and doorjambs, smells the scents of sawn wood and fresh paint that permeate the uninhabited rooms, as if he is a potential buyer who has shown up for a private tour.

They tour all the rooms without saying a word, and Jessica feels a warmth flare up inside her: years of secrecy will come to an end in one fell swoop only if she comes completely clean. Yusuf appears unsure what to make of what he's seeing, but he's clearly impressed by it. The truth is, Jessica can only guess what he's thinking.

They pause for a moment at Jessica's bedroom door, then continue on to the next bedroom, almost as large, with a view of the little park next to the National Museum. Jessica doesn't need to say anything. Now Yusuf understands Erne was the only one who knew. He was allowed to die in this room under Jessica's care.

After a prolonged silence, Yusuf says: "Why didn't you say anything?"

His voice is a little hoarse. And as usual, Yusuf's questions feel justified and intelligent. Even when they're this simple.

"What do you think?" Jessica says.

"But if Erne—"

Jessica touches Yusuf's fingers with her own.

She hears the trembling exhalation, senses the long-stifled pain escape, sending a tear rolling down Yusuf's cheek. "Sorry." He wipes the tear away. "I miss Erne, Jessie."

And at this moment, Jessica realizes nothing Yusuf has seen over the past ten minutes makes any difference. For good or for bad. Seeing Erne's deathbed is the only thing that touched him. At the end of it all, the thing Jessica has spent years shielding from other people's eyes is utterly meaningless.

"Me too," Jessica says. "A hell of a lot."

Yusuf turns away to hide the emotions welling up inside him. Jessica doesn't rush over to comfort him; she lets him pull himself together. "It's been a rough year. I miss Anna.... I don't know...." Yusuf dries his eyes on his shirtsleeve. "Sorry. I don't know what came over me."

"It's OK, Yusuf."

"And this ...," Yusuf says, indicating the surroundings. He pauses to weigh his next words.

He looks around the room and trains his red eyes on Jessica. It's impossible to say where the moment will lead. Maybe Yusuf is somehow shocked by the luxury he's witnessing, how far it is from the world of bloody stab wounds, gunpowder-perfumed crime scenes, decomposing bodies, and boozy excuses they deal with every day. Or maybe he's just disappointed Jessica didn't trust him enough to tell him sooner.

"I assume this apartment isn't the whole story ...," he finally says.

"No. There's more. A lot more."

"So you're a real mogul."

"Yup," Jessica says softly. "I always have been. I inherited all of it when I was a minor."

Yusuf shakes his head. "OK."

"Everything all right? Are you pissed off?"

"Yeah, I'm pissed off. We've been drinking in that crappy little studio of yours when we could have been having toga parties over here," Yusuf says, smiling his beautiful smile.

TUESDAY, DECEMBER 24TH

HELENA LAPPI PULLS on her coat and looks at her mechanical wristwatch. No more smartwatch, no more pointless data. The less information, the less stress. She sighs, walks over to her desk, and takes one last look at the photograph of the burned, blackened body found in Central Park. Small stones are arranged in a tidy circle around it. The victim, who was so badly burned that he is unidentifiable, is missing two front teeth. Huge amount of alcohol in his veins. That's all that's known about the deceased at this point. Harjula can brief his team first thing in the morning.

Wake up, Jessica.

Jessica opens her eyes and realizes she can't breathe. All she sees is blackness. She feels as if she is trying to inhale through a big soft pillow being held firmly against her face.

She tries to cry for help, but the sound rising from her throat echoes faintly in her ears.

It feels as if ice-cold shackles have been fastened around her wrists and ankles, holding her limbs in place.

You're awake, sweetheart.

Then something is pulled away from her face, and the pitch darkness turns into the dusk of a summer night.

Jessica sees her mother's cold hands unclench from her wrists.

Bloody, dripping hair hangs in her mother's face like black scum scraped from an overfertilized pond. The crushed angular cheekbones make it look as if her mother's mouth is twisted up in a sick grin. A red pulp where one eye should be, a gory crater in place of the nose.

The cold, wet breath floating across Jessica's face seems to freeze against her sweaty skin. Jessica suddenly feels like she's shivering.

Sit up.

Jessica doesn't tense her stomach muscles, nor does she notice herself rising. But suddenly she is sitting on the edge of the couch. The clock on the cable box reads three thirty.

Without Jessica noticing, her mother has risen from the sofa and is sitting at the long table, her back to Jessica. She is brushing her hair; her hands' movements are clipped, mechanical.

Something hisses in Jessica's ear.

She feels something squeezing her bare ankles. She leans forward to look over the lip of the couch and sees a figure beneath it gripping them. The figure has no face. Just blackness.

Why did you do it, Jessica?

I wanted someone to know. Because Erne isn't here anymore.

Jessica sees Erne's face flash by at the kitchen door. Maybe Erne has been watching them this whole time, but now all she sees is an old man's back disappearing into the kitchen.

I want to help you, Jessica. We're here for you.

Jessica stares at the figure under the couch. The fingers wrapped around her ankles are long and bony, like a vulture's talons.

Let me go.

Jessica feels panic surge into every cell of her body, like a tidal wave flooding a labyrinth.

I've always wanted to protect you. You and Toffe. And now you're spoiling it all.

Her mother has risen from her chair. She slinks toward the kitchen in her black dress.

Say you're sorry.

I'm sorry.

They all rise to their feet at the same time. Figure after figure emerges from the gloom, like tall plants thrusting through the soil and toward the sky.

Her mother stops at the door and turns her gaze toward Jessica.

The day you fear the most.

So they are here, aren't they?

Her mother nods.

Look out the window.

Jessica steps slowly toward the window, presses her forehead to the glass. It feels cool.

She sees the streetlamps sway in the wind, their beams of light lapping at the black asphalt. A group of figures marches down the middle of the otherwise deserted street, looking up at the sixth-story window. Jessica sees the gray faces of the animals, the forking horns sprouting from their heads.

Suddenly her mother is smiling tenderly at her side.

Jessica feels her breath catch, her mother's naked bones against her skin.

Christmas Eve.

THANKS TO

Pauliina, William, Lionel, my parents, and my whole family. My friends, who mean more and more to me with each passing year. Particular thanks to Joonas "Mad Dog" Pajunen, who read and commented on the manuscript.

My editor, Petra Maisonen, and the folks at Tammi, my Finnish publisher.

Michelle Vega and the amazing team at Berkley. Thank you for the confidence and this unique opportunity. It's a dream come true.

Jon Elek, Mark Smith, and everyone else at Welbeck Publishing. So grateful.

Tomi Tuominen, for bouncing around details of digital technology with me. Any mistakes or unrealistic elements that have slipped into the story are mine and mine alone.

Antti Sajantila, professor of forensics at the University of Helsinki, who reviewed the details of cause-of-death analysis with me. The previous statement applies here too.

Mikko Ponsi, Pasi Ojapalo, and Jari Vuorenpää, who shed a sensitive light on the everyday aspects of police work.

Niko Lindholm and Saku Vesslin, who helped build Rasmus Susikoski as realistic a man cave / gaming den as possible.

Upon its publication, The Ice Coven had already been sold in twenty-four countries. This achievement was made possible not only by first-class sales material, but by the superb Elina Ahlback Literary Agency and those who work there: Elina, Julia, Nicole, and Toomas. I am also very grateful to Rhea Lyons from HG Literary, who has had a huge role in bringing Jessica's adventures to the USA and UK.

And last but certainly not least I'd like to thank the translator, Kristian London.

THE
ICE
COVEN

MAX SEECK

QUESTIONS FOR DISCUSSION

1. Jessica has several challenges to navigate at the start of *The Ice Coven*. She's dealing with a new boss, a new case, and the ghosts of her past. How do each of these things affect her at the beginning of the novel? How does she approach each issue?

2. As partners, Jessica and Yusuf have a strong bond. How is that bond challenged throughout *The Ice Coven*? How is it made stronger?

3. Hellu and Jessica have a difficult relationship. How does it evolve over the course of the book? Do you feel that Hellu treats Jessica fairly? What colors Hellu's perception of Jessica, and vice versa?

4. Medical examiner Sissi Sarvilinna is an intriguing character. How do her insights contribute to the investigation? How does her work influence her personality and the various idiosyncrasies she's developed?

5. In *The Ice Coven*, we learn more about Rasmus Susikoski. How has Rasse's upbringing affected his life? Does his personality ever hinder him? If so, how? How does he use his quirks to help the investigation?

6. Jessica mourns the loss of Erne, her mentor. In what ways did Erne change Jessica's life? How does Erne's death impact the investigative unit?

7. Nina has very strong feelings about Jessica. Do you think these feelings are justified? How do you think Jessica has handled her issues with Nina?

8. Jessica experiences visions of her dead mother, Theresa von Hellens. Are these visions a comfort or a help to Jessica, or just terrifying episodes she is forced to endure? Do they bring us any closer to the true nature of Jessica's relationship with her mother? If so, how?

9. Along with the visions of her mother, Jessica sees other frightening things throughout the course of the book and has a few scary encounters. Do you think these instances are only in Jessica's mind or do they have a basis in reality? Please explain.

10. How does the setting of Helsinki play a role in the investigation and in the lives of the investigators? In what ways does where you're from shape who you are?

11. Jessica meets Frank Dominis in *The Ice Coven*. Why do you think she's drawn to him? How does Frank's past influence his decisions?

12. Social media plays a large role in both the execution of the crimes and in how the case is investigated. Discuss how technology and social media are used throughout the book. How have these things changed your life and the way you view the world around you?

Photo by Marek Sabogal

International and *New York Times* bestselling author **Max Seeck** writes novels and screenplays full-time. His accolades include the Finnish Whodunnit Society's Debut Thriller of the Year Award 2016 and the Storytel audio book award for Best Crime Novel for *The Witch Hunter*, known internationally as *The Faithful Reader*. An avid reader of Nordic noir for personal pleasure, he listens to film scores as he writes. Max lives with his wife and children near Helsinki.

CONNECT ONLINE

MaxSeeck.com/books

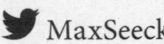 MaxSeeck

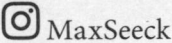 MaxSeeck

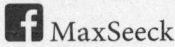 MaxSeeck